LEE TULLOCH

TEXT PUBLISHING

MELBOURNE AUSTRALIA

The Text Publishing Company
171 La Trobe Street
Melbourne Victoria 3000
Australia

Printed and bound by Griffin Press
Designed by Anthony Vandenberg
Typeset in 12.5/15.5 Baskerville MT by Midland Typesetters

National Library of Australia
Cataloguing-in-Publication data:

Tulloch, Lee.
Wraith.
ISBN 1 876485 15 9.
I. Title.
A823.3

This project has been assisted by the Commonwealth Government through the Australia Council, its arts funding and advisory body.

Thanks to Christina Zimpel and Patric Shaw for the title design, Frankie Foye for hair and Susan Houser for make-up.

FOR MY PARENTS
BETTY AND JACK TULLOCH

WRAITH

am not alone in my miserable little cell.

Berenger hovers on the edge of the hard mattress but making no dent in it, her chalky fingers picking at a binding she can't feel, her small teeth gnawing at a lip that isn't really there.

'I was, like, cursed,' she says.

'Oh, come on,' I scoff. 'That is utterly ridiculous. I was there, remember? I saw how much you suffered. Trunks of couture gowns and Concorde everywhere and Spanish playboys following you in packs.'

'You don't understand.' Her jaw, which is no more than a pale line drawn in air, tilts upwards, the same stubborn set to it she had in life. She raises her arm and scrutinises it, as if she were seeing it for the first time. It looks like a jagged arrangement of chicken bones wrapped in translucent egg noodle. And then she turns those white china eyes on me. 'If I wasn't cursed, then what is *this*?'

You can't ever argue with a ghost.

The name on my passport is Jane Ann Kirk.

It's a very ordinary name but it has caused some consternation in the New York Police Department and at the British consulate. Some of the things Jane has done they are blaming on Nile. Some of the things Nile has done they are blaming on Jane. It's one or the other, in the paperwork. Jane or Nile. I told them that we are both innocent. But they don't seem happy about that. They keep coming and asking me questions.

I have been Nile as long as I can remember. I invented it. I didn't like being called Plain Jane by my Nana Jean. She thought Plain Jane would keep me in line, keep me from straying down the path of my mother Claire. But she shouldn't have bothered: I went part of that way, anyway.

She *is* plain, that's all I can say for Jane. I look like the kind of person you can trust, dull, reliable, patient. My face is too round, my eyes too small, my lips too thin and turned down bitterly, my hair neither dark nor fair, my body two sizes too big to be called 'slender' or 'fashionable'. But who decides these things? I have spent a year with people who are preoccupied with weight and height and skin tone and still I don't know.

I often ask myself, where did 'Nile' come from? Perhaps a book about Cleopatra I read as a child? I never saw myself *on* the Nile, floating down it on a barge. I saw myself *as* it, going somewhere wonderful, fringed by palm trees.

What I like most about Nile, now that I am grown, is the flatness of the word. Nile. Like nihilism. I couldn't have been thinking of that as a child, but it was the right name then. Once I was nothing.

My lawyer says I shouldn't fret. He is appealing the decision to deny me bail. I won't have to stay in this pink-painted prison on Riker's Island to await my trial, trapped behind bars with those howling child-murderers. He'll get me out. But he doesn't understand that it's not the women's prison I fear. It's stinking London. I won't go back to that foul place, that city of shopkeepers and stockbrokers, those suburban-minded philistines, the council flats, the single bar heaters in the middle of winter, the Mars bars, the boys with crooked teeth reeking of aniseed balls, hockey sticks, buttered crumpets, corgis, Wedgwood, Crabtree & Evelyn, Fortnum & Mason, Marks & Spencer, Gilbert & Sullivan, the whole cringing quaintness of it all.

Please don't let them send me back to London, I implore. My lawyer thinks this is touching, my attachment to America, like I'm some singing and dancing Puerto Rican fresh from a stint in *West Side Story*. Everyone free in America: that is his belief. He pats me on the head like a child who needs comforting. The grand jury will see that I'm a nice girl, he says, very refined.

I know that what is refined about me is that I have an English accent and that an important man like Aaron Karsner is paying my bills. That is all you need to be refined over here. But Sidney van Doren is the best lawyer money can buy and, bless his soul, he doesn't know a thing about fashion or rock music. And when he met me he didn't try to tell me I had nice eyes. So he's all right by me.

I have been in this prison for two days now. They put me before a woman judge who didn't like the look of me and then sent me to this place in a patriotic red, white and blue bus, locked in a cage as if I were some kind of violent offender. I can't do much except sit on my cot and flip through an old dog-eared novel Sister Forsythia has brought me. It's Dickens, unbelievably.

3

I suppose she thinks it will be a great comfort, a book about my homeland. But she might have considered the title more carefully. *Bleak House*. I've lived in enough of those. And this little cell doesn't look any better.

The one thing I am is desperately hungry. The food they give you here turns my stomach. A thing called a Sloppy Joe, which is minced meat in a congealing sauce, no attempt made to keep it hot. Corned beef hash, which looks the same but tastes saltier. A white bread sandwich filled with orange-coloured cheese, shiny as plastic. It almost makes you long for English cooking. Almost.

For entertainment, I try to pee in the stainless steel bowl in the corner without actually sitting on the seat. You never know who's been there before you, my Nana used to say. If she was still alive she would be ashamed of me, more ashamed than at any other time, and she was ashamed of me often. She would have sat there in that harvest gold vinyl rocker-recliner of hers in that little maisonette in Morden and steadfastly refused to talk to the press, the only woman in England to remain unimpressed by a microphone in her face. Don't make a display of yourself, was her motto. Well, I made a display of myself all right. And the thought that it might have mortified her pleases me no end.

It's impossible to sleep here. There are comings and goings all day and night, clankings and shoutings and bellowings. Americans love to hear their own voices even—maybe especially— when no-one is listening. The woman in the cell next door is calling for her mother. Her mama. She shouldn't waste her breath. Mothers don't come when you need them most, in my experience.

Listen to me. I've only been in jail forty-eight hours and already I sound like a hardened criminal.

The one thing I'm curious about is the blue mat, like the kind they use for gymnastics, which is pushed under my cot. I wonder if I might be getting a cell-mate, if she'll be noisy too, if she's the kind of prisoner who lies on the floor and sobs, or paces the cell, or comes to you in the dark with intrusive fingers. I imagine her

4

sitting impassively on her mat, watching me with guarded eyes when I pee.

But, so far, no sulking detainee has appeared to invade my space.

Except, of course, for Berenger, whom no bars can hold.

I suppose everyone knows the sodding story by now. Or think they know it. Stop anyone on Times Square and ask about me and they'll say, 'Oh, yeah, the Killer P.A.'

But that's not the story and that's not who I am. It sounds so cold-blooded, the word 'killer'. I prefer 'avenger'. Like the television series, the re-runs of which I was not allowed to watch as a child, in case they gave me 'ideas'.

As if anyone could stop me getting ideas.

I didn't mean to kill anyone. Look at me, I want to shout, I'm just an ordinary girl. A shrinking violet. A mouse. I would never take a person's life. I would never take the life of a person who did not deserve it. But I am allowed to read the newspapers for a few minutes each day and I can see that no-one will believe me. I have become not a girl, but a headline. Berenger is now and forever 'Dead Supermodel' and I am 'Killer P.A.'.

Where do I begin? A neat little biography of her life? Ha. That would take all of one sentence. 'She lived fast, died young and had a beautiful corpse.'

But that wouldn't be right. 'She lived young, died fast and had a beautiful corpse.'

No. There's something wrong in that too. The corpse wasn't beautiful.

I woke up the morning of Berenger's death with the strangest presentiment: *Don't wish for something too hard, you might get it.*

My room in the building at 89 Wooster Street was more of a cell than the one I have now. In *Architectural Digest* they called it the 'maid's room'. Or rather, '*a* maid's room' which suggested a nameless drudge was grudgingly accommodated there.

Which, in fact, was true.

There was nothing small or cheap about the room by most people's standards. The floors were honey-waxed herringbone parquetry and the walls were lacquered in seven layers of burnished ivory glaze. The vast closet, with its panelled doors, was lined in a pink cedar that smelled like pencil-shavings, too grand for my pathetic collection of clothes. (Berenger kept on giving me clothes that had been given to her but they never fitted, which she knew they wouldn't and which was the point.) The sheets on the bed were Egyptian cotton and the bedside tables were inlaid with shagreen. The shower had complicated stainless steel dials that only fashion people, who travel to Europe often, could work. I took baths.

But it felt like a hospital. A hospital where the inmates wander around in muslin smocks, tearing at their hair.

I woke up that morning staring at the pressed-tin ceiling which, even though it was fourteen feet above my head, always made me feel as if I were lying in some kind of medical receptacle, like a wasted syringe.

I was lying on top of the sheets, my arms rigid beside my body, my feet slightly splayed—and, I was to discover, fully dressed, as if someone had deposited me there and arranged me like a doll. It took a few minutes for me to realise I could move my limbs, that I wasn't trussed and ensnared. It seemed I was my own prisoner. But hasn't that always been the case?

I blinked several times to rid myself of a dull pressure behind my eyes. No luck. There was a blur of red back there and some kind of vital knowledge that, at this moment, felt as if it were buried under a soggy mass of chewed white bread. I sat up straight and looked at my feet, legs and lap as if none of these belonged to me. The black dress: for a moment I didn't recognise it. My high-heeled shoes were like old acquaintances who smile at you in the street but you can't-for-the-life-of-you put a name to. It was only when I looked at the black-painted fingernails that I recognised the outfit as my laughable attempt at gothic style.

I fumbled for my alarm clock. It was 8.35 a.m. I groaned as I heaved myself off the bed. I hid behind the riveted canvas shower curtain, gave the shower contraption a sneer and soaked myself in a punishingly hot bath for ten minutes. Like an automaton I dressed, picked up the keys and wrestled with the freight elevator until it delivered me to the first floor. I headed to my office down the hall to the left, opposite a 3000-square-foot space that contained the industrial kitchen which, despite the vegetarian menu that was unfailingly prepared there, always seemed to me to be as frigid as a meat locker.

I turned the key in the lock and went into the office, which was decently large with two arched windows facing the street. I checked the e-mail and quickly ran through the voice-mail in case there was something urgent. It was the usual guff. The Fat Booker had called from Bridgehampton at midnight, sounding drunk and tearful, imploring Berenger to take a job in Arizona she'd refused. Darien Apps, Berenger's current best friend, had called at 5.27 a.m., stoned and tearful, babbling on about how Berenger had ignored her all night—I pushed the fast-forward button and kept it there until I heard the gravelly voice of a famous fashion photographer—female—calling her from a shoot in Afghanistan. Berenger's trainer, Ruby, called at 6 a.m. to tell Berenger she couldn't make it tomorrow—she was 'too out of it, babe, after last night'. A few more stoned, tipsy or tearful people of unknown identity mumbled their troubles into the machine and I stopped before the end and turned it off. I had never planned to be a nanny again, but it seemed as if I was surrounded by children.

I checked the diary and noted that Ronny was supposed to bring the limousine around at ten. The desk clock said it was

9.20. Remarkably, Berenger usually got herself up by eight to work out at the gym attached to her bedroom. Her silence was unusual. She should be hollering by now for *something*. (A piece of toast that didn't scrape her gums perhaps? A cotton puff that didn't scratch her sensitive eyes?)

How appropriate it would be to report that the housekeeper was a creeping Mrs Danvers type, lurking in the shadows and snarling at you whenever you creaked a floorboard. But there were no shadows to creep in, no curtains on any of the windows to create them and abundant internal light to thwart anything that might be called 'mood'. Besides, the floorboards in our happy little home were supposed to creak because that was a sign that they were authentic warehouse, circa 1893, despite the $3.1 million renovation that made the whole place look like a sparkling space-age laboratory.

The housekeeper, Alison Bow, did not fit the matronly, lantern-jawed stereotype, either. She was petite and Anglo-Asian, of indeterminable age, and wore crisp navy linen Chinese pants and jacket, which her brother shipped to her from Hong Kong. She was as sharp as her clothes, as if her whole attitude to life had been starched and knife-pleated at birth. She said very little and gave great but painful shiatsu massages, which I was allowed, once, on my birthday.

I slunk into the kitchen and interrupted Alison's prayers. She had built a small shrine in one corner of the kitchen and I suppose her only confidant was the little brass Buddha, to whom she offered copious amounts of hot food at every meal when she gave everyone else a few slivers of sliced fennel and a peeled beetroot. Today, she had plates of cold vegetables and steamed buns in front of her idol. I shuffled around and coughed to attract her attention, but she didn't look up. In status, I was lower than the woven red mat she knelt on. Eventually she unfolded and dusted herself down. She turned and looked at me with curious zircon eyes. 'Yes?' she asked politely.

'Has Berenger been down yet, I haven't heard her and you

know the car is coming at ten?' I blathered, as I always do in the face of unnerving stoicism.

'Not this morning,' was all Alison said, and turned to the stainless steel counter and picked up a chopping knife.

'Oh, all right, thank you,' I said, as if there were something to thank her for. And then I followed it with a 'sorry', from force of habit: we British always feel we have something to apologise for. In this case, perhaps I did.

It must have been 9.30 or 9.35. I took the elevator to the fourth floor and went into the gym, which was accessible both from the elevator and from Berenger's bedroom. The gym was uninhabited, unless you counted the perky face of a newscaster soundlessly relaying some vital information about snowman-making in Pennsylvania, or wherever, on the tiny screen attached to the handlebars of one of Berenger's lifecycles. This evidence suggested that Berenger was already up, had exercised and was perhaps in the shower. She hated being interrupted in the shower—all that lathering and exfoliating meant physical co-ordination which took massive concentration—so I crept to the door that adjoined the bedroom, pushed it gently open, and listened for the hiss of water. No sound.

Absence. That's why I hesitated. With Berenger there was always *presence*. She was never silent. Even when she sulked, she galumphed and hurrumphed around the place. If she was in her room, the television was always on, casting blue light over the walls and she'd be perpetually on the phone, deep in whispers that might have started two or three hours before. When she was asleep, even when her mind was shut down by drugs, her body was still kinetic. She turned, she groaned, she hissed, she snuffled. And if Aaron was there with her—yes, editors of Page Six, I believe he had made it to her bed once or twice—his breathing was a loud rustle, like the pages of old librettos he had written being shuffled.

I hesitated because I expected to hear water running or snatches of telephone conversations or the television or clothes and shoes being thrown all over the room or the unmistakable sounds of purging from the toilet. From the door I could hear right through the room, through the triple-glazed windows to the cobbled street outside and the tinkle of bottles being unloaded.

I pushed the door. On more than one occasion, its merest creaking has set off Berenger's migraine, which lurks in the swollen recesses of her brain waiting for those moments when the day's commitments—say a studio full of art directors, hair-dressers, make-up artists, caterers, studio managers, publicists, photographers and their assistants and their assistants' assistants standing around in anticipation that Berenger was about to show up for a single photo for the advertising campaign for her lingerie line—are too overwhelming. I was sure, however, that this day was not likely to be a Migraine Day as Berenger tolerated Marrakech—'enjoyed' is too strong a word, but she was veering towards that concept —and the Fat Booker had managed to arrange a two-day vacation at the end of the shoot where it was supposed that Berenger would stroll the North African beaches looking for seashells.

She usually took me with her. I was indispensable as a tipper and demander of ice buckets. But why should I go to Morocco, especially when there was a chance of vacation at the end? I'd be the first one to be sent on that creaky old bus to Bratislava, all right, but send me where it's warm and the air is perfumed with spice? There would be ebony men and delicious African food. I might have a chance to see some sun instead of the inside of studios and hotel rooms and the lounges at airports. Goodness knows, I might even be distracted by a dusky busboy or a photographer's assistant in his cut-off shorts (my social equals). No, she would have to spend too much time working out trivial and frustrating things for me to do in a desert paradise. Whereas in Eastern Europe I'm usually already more than occupied enough just figuring out who to bribe. Therefore no Marrakech for me: I had to save up all my energy for next month's trip to Calcutta.

I hesitated at the door because Morocco did not spell

Migraine Day to me. Or Food Poisoning Day. Or I Feel Bloated Day. Or, as she became more famous, I Can't Be Bothered Day.

As it turned out, she had a better excuse for not being at the airport than any she had managed to dredge up before.

She was lying on her bed, face down. I can't say, when I first saw her from the doorway, I felt anything but relief. She was home from the party, that was enough: I didn't have to trawl the Filofax looking for her.

I called her name, tentatively, half expecting a shoe or hair-brush to come hurling my way, furious little missiles I was adept at dodging in the mornings. When she didn't stir, I came closer. And then it was all wrong.

When she was asleep in that big bed, with its tall posts carved into elongated Balinese dancers, the pinnacles pointed like the spiny tops of their golden crowns, she always sprawled, with her arms spread wide, the little fingers pinching the sheets, as if the bed were likely to take off at any minute, flip over and dump her on the floorboards. She usually lay with her face and hips turned left, and then she would moan and turn herself in the other direction, face and hips facing right. That, of course, was her worst angle, but sleep always betrayed her. She might do this fifty times in one night, even with enough Rohypnol in her to kill a rhinoceros. She would snore, croak, kick one foot repeatedly. She would mumble, snort, drool on the mattress. She would never cover herself with a sheet, even when the night's activities had left sticky snail's trails down her thighs.

'Berenger?'

She didn't answer me, but she didn't look dead. This is the irony of it. She looked like she'd been gently laid down, a porce-lain doll resting in cotton wool. Her arms were by her side, palms up. Her right foot crossed her left ankle, as if she were scratching an itch. She still had on those beautiful delicate shoes with the ugly name. Blah-nik. The bugle-beaded hemline of her mini-dress barely covered her buttocks. But there was something funny about her head. I could see the back of it, long strands of dark hair splaying across her shoulders. She had big ears—creamy white, strange Dumbo ears. It was only when I reached the edge of the bed I could see that these weren't ears, but soft down pillows. She was face down, quite precisely face down, her neck wasn't twisted or turned in any way, and the weight of her skull had made such a deep indentation in the pillows that they had puffed up around at the sides, almost swallowing her whole head. She looked like as if she had been held in a marshmallow vice, actually. I couldn't suppress a laugh.

I crouched on the bed and grabbed one of her arms, fully expecting her to shrug it out of my grip. She wasn't cold, not really. She was still loose. I've heard that bodies seize up, starting with the toes and fingers. But it was hot in there. It was stuffy. And I didn't know she was a dead body. She was just a perverse one.

I grabbed her by an upper arm and tugged at her shoulder. If her neck seemed tight I didn't notice. She might have been resisting me, like that game she sometimes played when she pretended to be in a coma to avoid getting up. Her face stayed in the pillow, so I tried tickling her. In the end, I straddled her hips and heaved her over. I was irritated, not afraid.

She was purple and I still thought she was alive. There was a smear of blood at the corners of her mouth and congealing under her nose and I still thought she was alive. Her face was covered by a spiderweb of speckled vomit and I still thought she was alive. I thought she was alive because to think she would give up the ghost so soon was unimaginable.

She would have hated it.

Her nose, where it had pressed against the bed, was white, but dark purple blood had collected in the capillaries of her chin and cheekbones and around her eyes. But her cheeks were dry, and when I pressed a finger gently into the crevice beside her nose the imprint stayed there, a kind of jaundiced colour like thick spit. It was all very curious. Her eyes were closed, but the veins bulged over them and up towards the temples as if sinister electrodes had been placed on them by some mad scientist. The blue glittery cream shadow a make-up artist had smudged over her lids when she was alive didn't help. But she wasn't to know then that the effect would be Bride of Frankenstein. In any other circumstance and without flinching she would have fired the art director who'd cooked up this scenario.

I remember what Darien used to say about making love, one of her many handy hints to the sexually deprived (me): *Never* be the one on top—the flesh on your face falls forward and looks like a lump of pizza dough to the person underneath. I always thought she was joking. But, even when I turned Berenger on her back, the baby fat on her cheeks stayed pressed forward as if her adorable little face was being squeezed and shaken affectionately between the veiny hands of an overenthusiastic great aunt. Her face defied gravity, something her breasts had done all along.

Her lips had frozen in their customary state—a pout—but they were crusted with dried spittle, of a colour you'd never see on the beauty pages of Italian *Vogue*, even when they'd been doing peculiar make-up a season ago. Between her lips was a glob of something which I fished out with a bent finger, leaving the tips of her teeth gleaming with congealed spew and streaks of crimson. It was a huge, mushed-up ball of bubble gum and I flung it off the bed. The police weren't very happy about that. But I didn't think about police. I didn't think about smell, or erupting body fluids, or the fact that her lower torso was damp with piss. I only thought about getting her cleaned up and on the road to Morocco.

But I didn't in the end, did I? I must have sat with her for a few minutes, doing nothing. That's when I thought about the hatpin. You see, all along I thought she was punishing me, that it was a joke. I thought if I hurt her she would have to cry out. But she didn't. And then I went blank. The police estimated I was there twenty to thirty minutes when they talked to the others. I can't remember half of it.

Was she there with me when I was sitting with her? Was she still trapped in that stiffening body? Was she still trapped in it when the Medical Examiner shoved that thermometer up her rectum to estimate the time of death? When he swabbed all her orifices for semen, saliva, blood? Was she there when the turnip-shaped cop shone a torch into her eyes and called her, with a grunt of satisfaction, 'nice and fresh'? When the paramedics wound her carefully in her sheet and dumped her in a garbage bag? When they did whatever they did to her on the autopsy table? Uncovered her pretty chest, slashed it with a blade and broke the breastbone? Took out her kidneys and weighed them on a scale? Rolled down her face like a turtleneck and sawed the skull open? Did she stay attached to herself when they shipped her off to the embalmers and drained her of all her blood? Filled her cavities with embalming powder and wired her jaw shut? Was she there in that gleaming coffin when it bumped its clumsy way down the conveyor belt to the furnace? Was she inside when her outsides melted, carbonated and collapsed?

I need to know, Berenger, where you were, for any of this to make sense.

When did the room become full of sweaty men, moving around the 'crime scene' (was there a crime? I was surprised by that) like dogs circling an upended trash can? Who summoned them? And why were they being mean to me?

One of the sweaty men, in a uniform, escorted me roughly from the bed, wrote my name in a book and sent Alison, who was hovering silently, downstairs to get me a cup of sweet tea. I kept my head down but I could hear low chatter like the buzzing of electric powerlines. I registered a series of flashes from a camera. Someone moved me against a wall and took pictures of me too, of my face, my hands, my shoes. I felt ashamed, but why I could not say.

When Alison brought me the tea, she barely nodded at me and kept her eyes on the bed. I followed the direction of her narrow stare. Berenger had been turned over and her hands and feet were bagged in plastic. She still didn't look dead to me: it might have been yet another fashion shoot where the stylist had gotten excited about aping 'real life', except this time Berenger was lying there patiently instead of complaining of a headache and the police photographer had not, as far as I know, had his work published in *Harper's Bazaar*. There were probably eight other people in that room now, uniforms, paramedics, a man with rolled-up shirt sleeves looking intently at the gas heater—

heavy men moving about like shadows, bagging, combing, making absurdly delicate brushstrokes on the cable box.

Ask her, I wanted to scream out, she's the one who knows. She can tell you. The invaders weren't, in fact, exclusively male. There was one woman present, who might have been a detective, who might have been the police-issue cleaning lady waiting to take the sheets off and scrub them clean of sick and blood for all I knew about this kind of thing. She was a lumpy thing in dark jeans and a padded grey bomber jacket, standing by the bed, staring down at Berenger with a look of pure hatred, but whether it was hatred for having to look at dead bodies all day or for Berenger herself I couldn't tell.

It turned out she was the bad cop. And her partner, a fiftyish man in a tan suit, who appeared later and made an almighty fuss about the body being moved before he could view it properly, was the bad cop too. Wasn't one of them supposed to be soft and reassuring? Obviously I had been exposed to too many of those dismal television programs Berenger watched in hotel rooms.

They took me into the gym when they'd finished with Berenger. They sat me on a bench while they both stood. He was much taller than her and wider at the girth but she had a way of standing with her legs apart, dusty black vinyl sneakers planted on the floor, that made her seem more threatening, as if she were a tree sending out roots that were going to take hold of you until you told the truth. She had dishwater blonde hair cut away from her head so it stood out like a short wig, and bloodless cracked lips, and she kept biting at the dead skin with her bottom teeth. She would have made a better corpse than Berenger, except that her eyes were penetrating blue and Berenger's were now milky white and as unfocused as jelly. Her name, it appeared, was Detective Ostrowsky. She didn't say, but I bet her name was Carol. She looked like a Carol to me.

The other detective, Detective Breen (Joe?), started in on me first. I say this, because there weren't any niceties, like I supposed they'd usually give to the bereaved. Maybe they didn't think I was bereaved: I was just the P.A. All he did to announce himself was hoist his sagging pants up over his belly and tighten the belt a notch. It was such a John Wayne thing to do, I let out a snort.

'Funny business this, to you?' he grunted, still fixing his belt.

'No sir,' I said, waiting for him to look up and connect. I couldn't look at the woman.

He straightened his tie, took a crumpled spiral-bound notebook out of his inside jacket pocket, flipped the page and patted his hip pocket for a pencil. He cleared his throat and read. 'We have here the body'—I flinched, it was the saying of the word that hurt—'of Be-ring-er Karsnan—'

'Karsner,' I corrected him.

He raised his eyebrows. 'Oh, yeah? How's that?'

'K-A-R-S-N-E-R.' I spelt it out. 'But she doesn't go by that name. She has only one name. Legally. B-E-R-E-N-G-E-R.'

'One name,' the cop repeated stupidly.

I felt a compulsion to explain this. 'It's a thing they do, you know, models. They only *need* one name.'

'Yeah, well, they'd have difficulty remembering anything more than that,' deadpanned Ostrowsky. I looked at her to see any spark of humour, but she had made her eyes go flat. A cynic after my own heart.

'Anyway, it's not confusing,' I went on. 'There's only one Berenger.'

'Was,' said Breen.

'Was what?'

'*Was* only one Berenger.'

He, too, had adopted a poker face. I was supposed to take offence at that, I knew it. They were like two ancient tennis pros lobbing the same tired ball over a net. They had probably seen everything they would ever see, and that included many semi-naked nineteen-year-old millionairesses who died suddenly in their sleep and many, many twenty-seven-year-old psychopaths who had been discovered with the bodies of their employers after strangling, bludgeoning, incinerating, decapitating or detonating them in a murderous rage. The butler always did it and, failing to find any convenient manservant, they honed in on me. And Alison. I was sure Alison, being one of the serving classes (although try telling her that) and inscrutably Asian to boot, would soon be subjected to the same interrogation that I was currently enduring.

Detective Ostrowsky was still coming to grips with the nomenclature. 'Birth certificate?' she demanded.

'Mine or hers?' I asked nervously.

'Let's stick to the deceased for the moment. What does her name say on her birth certificate?'

'I don't know. Truly. She was adopted when she was three months old.'

'Oh, yeah?' asked Detective Breen. I gave him the details of Berenger's adoptive mother, Chantal, who owned some kind of farm in Peachland, British Columbia. I'd never met her and knew very little about her, except the few things Berenger had told me, and they were all negative. The way Berenger described her, she was a sluggish and bovine anachronism, wading through the pig-muck in her wellies, intolerant of a teenage girl with the need for nailpolish and Nirvana.

Breen grunted in amusement at the name Peachland and then looked at me suspiciously, as if I were making it up.

'Really,' I assured him.

'So the deceased was a Canadian?'

'She came to New York, when she was fourteen. Her mother kicked her out.'

'The kid was trouble?' asked Breen.

'I don't know the whole story.' And I didn't. All I knew was that Berenger played the incident to the hilt in interviews. The teenage rebel, misunderstood.

While I was talking, Breen scribbled something into his notebook. He tore a sheet out, folded it, and went out of the room.

Ostrowsky just eyed me until he came back a moment later. A glance passed between them.

'OK.' Breen leaned against the railing of the Stairmaster and sighed as if he were a principal about to tackle a recalcitrant student. He paused and it seemed interminable. I wanted to scratch my ankle but I was worried it might look like a gesture of nervousness. Of guilt. Finally he asked, 'So, tell us how it is that you're sitting on a bed with a corpse at—' he checked his notes— '9.35 in the morning and you don't even call the cops?'

'I didn't?'

He shook his head.

'Shock?' I asked, as if this was a quiz and I was running through the multiple-choice answers.

'You tell us.'

'Well,' I answered, struggling with my thoughts. I *was* confused. How could efficient little old me have failed to call the cops? 'I didn't think she was dead,' I lied. 'She was still there.'

'But she wasn't breathing?' asked Ostrowsky.

'I don't think—'

'So you could have at least called the doctor?' Was that an accusing tone in her voice? If I was a suspect, shouldn't they have been reading me something, my rights?

'She was dead.'

'But you just said you didn't think she was dead.'

'I didn't say that. What I meant was…she looked dead—physically. But I thought her soul was still there.'

'Soul!' snorted Ostrowsky.

'The M.E. tells us the corpse's fingertips were badly muti-lated,' said Breen. 'You were found with a sharp implement in your hand.'

'Was I?'

'A hatpin covered with blood.'

'I tried to wake her up.'

'With a *pin*? By stabbing her? That suggests to us some kind of…complicated emotion.' Ostrowsky looked smug.

'My Nana said they used to do it.'

'What's that?'

'My grandmother said they used to do it in Scotland. Put a pin under their nails to make sure they were dead.'

'Wasn't once enough? It looks to us like you did it about fifty times.'

'I suppose I wanted to make sure.'

'How did you feel about that?'

'When you were sure she was dead?'

'I don't know,' I answered.

'You weren't very surprised, then?'

'Am I a suspect?'

'A suspect in *what*?' Ostrowsky demanded.

'Her...death?' I offered lamely.

'All we are trying to establish now is how you came to be with the body. These are only preliminary inquiries. There is no suggestion of foul play at this point, although,' Ostrowsky lowered her voice ominously, 'the Medical Examiner might lean that way. At this point we are investigating a possible suicide and drug overdose. Anything you can tell us will greatly assist our inquiries and hopefully bring an early closure to the situation.'

The situation. It was A Situation.

'Do *you* have reason to suspect foul play?' I could feel Breen's bleary eyes hard on me too.

'No, no. She...died. She was only nineteen.'

'Any reason to think she suicided, then?'

That shook me up. 'Why would she do that? She was rich.'

'She was rich,' repeated Ostrowsky, writing it into her notebook. 'Rich people have been known to kill themselves.'

'Well, beautiful, too...'

'She didn't look that beautiful to me,' said Ostrowsky flatly. 'What else?'

'She was about to go to Morocco.' I know that sounded pathetic.

'You didn't mention the husband,' Breen chipped in. 'Any reason for that?'

Aaron! My God! Where was he?

I jumped up and started for the door, but Ostrowsky put an arm out to stop me. I pushed against her as if he were a turnstile. She said, firmly, like I was a child being soothed out of a nightmare, 'The husband looks OK. They found him upstairs. At the piano.'

'Oh,' I said weakly and dropped back onto the bench.

'He do that often?' Breen.

'What?'

'Snooze at the piano?'

'Sometimes,' I said. 'He *is* eighty-two.'

'Imagine that.' Breen clicked his tongue. 'An old geezer like that with such a young piece of—'

'What Detective Breen meant to say,' interrupted Ostrowsky, giving him a poisonous look 'is that it's a most unorthodox... arrangement.'

'Marriage,' I insisted. 'The word is marriage.'

'So there was no trouble between them? No other men in her life?'

'Why should there be?'

'Just answer the question.'

'Why don't you ask him?'

'The old guy's a bit shaken right now. His doctor's been called.' Breen didn't take his eyes off me. 'We're being sensitive—'

'The sooner you tell us what you know, the sooner you can go find out exactly how he is,' interrupted Ostrowsky. She said it like a threat.

I took a deep breath. 'All right. Go ahead.'

'Let's start at the beginning, when you first found Miss— *Berenger*—on the bed.'

I told them the time I entered the bedroom, how the room looked, why I thought Berenger was just sleeping. Alison, it seemed, had already filled them in on the earlier part of the morning, my stopping by the kitchen.

'Was there any chance at all she was still breathing when you first saw her? Did she make any noise?'

'She didn't look…alive when I turned her over.'

'Exactly why *did* you turn her over?'

'To wake her up. I shook her a bit.' I looked at their frowning faces. 'Are you mad at me for that too?'

Ostrowsky said slowly, 'It might have complicated the investigation.'

'Her lips were blue,' I explained. 'She was limp.'

'Did you notice anything strange about the body?'

'Everything was strange about *her* body! She wasn't in it!' (But now I'm not so sure.)

'Did you notice any unusual marks on the arms, perhaps, or elsewhere on the body?'

'Nothing.'

Breen: 'Was there anything different about the room?'

I thought for a while. 'It was hot.'

'Heater?'

'No, no, it's just she hated having the heating on too high. It was always cool in there. But this morning it was hot.'

Breen wrote that down.

'Any drug paraphernalia? Powders? Pills?'

'No. Nothing.'

'You sure?'

'I didn't see any.'

'What was with the costume?' Ostrowsky asked.

'She gave a costume party at a nightclub last night. With Darien Apps. That's her best friend.'

I gave them Darien's number and the club's address.

Breen asked, 'You go to the party?'

'I was there all afternoon, supervising the decorations. She wanted buckets of paint thrown over all the walls, like blood. And "PIGS" written in blood over the mirrors…Sorry,' I quickly said, thinking they might have taken offence at this. 'It was a Charles Manson party,' I added as if this would explain it.

'Tasteful,' said Ostrowsky.

'It seemed funny at the time.'

'You left the club when?'

'I came back here to get dressed about eight-thirty. I returned to the club at midnight. With Berenger.'

'It was her party and she didn't get there until *midnight?*'

'Well, the invitation said eight, which means ten. No-one much came before eleven. Berenger always wanted to make an entrance.'

'What was her state of mind before the party?'

'The usual. She hated her costume. She had changed her mind about the stomach. She was threatening not to come.'

'So she was in low spirits?'

'No, not at all. That was her *good* mood. If she was in low spirits she wouldn't have turned up at all and I would have been out on the streets looking for her.'

'The streets?'

'It would have been difficult to find her. She would have gone somewhere…unexpected.'

'Like where?'

'She didn't go anywhere, all right? She was at the party, from about midnight on. I don't know how long she stayed. I left about two. Two—oh—six to be precise, Detective. I looked at my watch.'

'A bit early wasn't it?' I could sense the sarcasm in Ostrowsky's voice but I didn't know where it was coming from. 'She didn't expect me to stay. I'd done my job. Besides…'

'Yes?'

'Well…she was…busy.'

'That's not what you meant.'

'I suppose she was a bit…out of it.'

'Drugs?'

'No, just champagne. We'd ordered in fifty crates of Krug. She liked to mix it with Stoli.'

Breen: 'She pay for that? Must have cost a bit.'

'No—well, yes, sort of. You see, we get it at discount.'

'Still—must have cost, what, twenty bucks a bottle?'

'Actually, more like forty.'

'Jeez.' Breen scratched his head. 'A kid like this can afford that?'

'The old man's rich,' Ostrowsky told him.

'It's not his money,' I said.

'Oh?' They both looked at me.

'One of the contracts she's got pays a million dollars, or thereabouts, for five days work.'

'A week?'

'What?'

'She's got some job that pays a million for five days work a week?'

'A *year*. Five days work a year.'

They both started scribbling. 'So,' Ostrowsky said casually. 'Where was the husband during this shindig?'

'At home, working. He's writing his autobiography.'

'Much money in that?'

'A bit. He gets royalties, too, from his songs. He's not poor, in case you're thinking that.'

'Why would we be thinking that?'

'Well, in case you thought he was…involved.'

'You're saying the husband was *involved* in her death in some way?'

'No, no. He was home working in the study.'

'But we haven't established when she got home and whether he was awake then. They sleep in separate beds?'

'Look,' I said with as much conviction as I could muster. 'They were happily married. He is a great man, a legend. They've named a theatre after him, for Christ's sake!'

'Saw him on television once,' said Breen. 'Channel surfing, boring night, seventy-eight channels and not one of them any good. Those songs—they're nice old things. Danced to some of them at my wedding.'

'They're *standards*,' I informed him.

Fortunately, Ostrowsky didn't seem too interested in Aaron. You could tell she was the kind of person who had sex and drugs on the brain. But not sex and drugs that involved a man of eighty-two. She cut in with 'Let's get back to the party. How many people were there?'

'We invited about two hundred—it was a close friends kind of thing, supposed to be small—but I would say it was more like double that.'

'Gatecrashers?'

'God, no, the security was *intense*. People bring friends, you know. Sometimes someone's been to another party and they bring the whole room with them.'

'Fifty crates of champagne for four hundred guests,' Breen was calculating. 'Must have been a few drunks.'

'They don't always *drink* the champagne,' I felt the need to explain. 'They shake it up and pour it over each other.'

'You said there weren't any drugs,' Ostrowsky said blandly.

'I didn't say that.'

'So there *were* drugs. Did the deceased take any?'

'I didn't see her.' All I did see was Berenger go into the bathroom and not come out for fifteen minutes.

'But that doesn't mean she didn't take any,' piped in Breen. 'Did she act peculiar?'

'Not at all.' I answered this confidently: Berenger acting peculiarly would be Berenger sitting quietly in a corner having a cup of tea.

'Did you have any reason to believe Berenger was taking drugs last night?' Ostrowsky rephrased Breen's question.

'I didn't see her,' I said stubbornly.

'To your knowledge has she ever taken drugs before?'

'Look,' I said. 'They *all* take drugs, OK? They smoke, they drink. They're not virgins. They need that stuff. Imagine what it's like running from casting to casting all day, or standing for hours on a piece of seamless paper—'

'Or having to work five days a year,' interrupted Ostrowsky.

'Going to parties all night,' added Breen.

'Poor things,' sneered Ostrowsky.

'The parties are work too,' I argued. 'They meet photographers and clients.' I knew how feeble that sounded, but it was true nevertheless.

'Come down to the precinct any midnight,' said Breen, 'and I'll show you some other girls who meet their clients after dark.'

'And they're never skinny enough. Drugs help. It's a professional thing.'

'What drugs are we talking about?' asked Ostrowsky.

'Coke, crystal meth, special k...sometimes smack.'

'They shoot up? What about track marks on that lovely expensive skin?'

'I suppose they snort it. Or shoot it between the toes. Into the mouth.'

'You know a lot.'

'Everyone knows that.'

'You a user?'

'No!'

'So Berenger used.'

'Sometimes. But it wasn't a problem.'

'And when exactly does it become a problem? When they waste so much money on poison that the villa in Monte Carlo's got to be repossessed?'

'Serious junkies never get work. Clients won't book them. Agencies won't take them on. No-one wants to take the risk.'

'The risk of what?'

'Of them not turning up for a job, of course.'

'What about the risk of having a damaged young girl on their conscience?'

'That too.'

'Nice bunch of people. So drugs are bad for business and Berenger wasn't a junkie?'

'No.'

'And she was happily married?'

'Yes.'

'And she wasn't depressed?'

'No.'

'Financial trouble?'

'No.'

'Not likely on—what is it? Let's see—$200,000 a day?'

'She worked other days, for less. She did some editorial for *nothing.*'

'That's very generous of her. As far as you know, nothing happened at this party or in the days before it to precipitate any crisis?'

I tossed around in my brain what the police would consider a crisis. 'No,' I shook my head.

'So she was beautiful, young, rich, sweet, happy and generous. A regular fairytale princess.' Ostrowsky closed her notebook.

'She was only nineteen,' was all I could think to say.

'Where do you fit into this picture?' Breen asked.

'I don't know what you mean.'

'Your accent—where you from?'

'Britain,' I said as casually as I could.

'Oh, yeah? Like London?'

'Like London, yes.'

'You been here long?'

'A few years.'

'How long have you been working for the deceased?'

'A year. But I was originally hired to work with Aaron...before he married her. I still do, in a way. I'm helping him with his memoirs.'

'You ever work for a model before?'

'No.'

'So what did you do?'

I didn't like this question. I didn't want the police to dig too deeply. I'd been illegal then, before Aaron had sorted it out. He'd used his influence to get me a three-year visa. I was a special talent, he had claimed. The first time anyone had said that about me.

'I was a nanny.' It was vague enough.

Breen nodded his head. 'Yeah, my sister's got one of those, for her kids. A girl from Ireland. I told her, Pammy, these British nannies, you've got to check them out. You never can be too careful.'

'No,' I replied. 'You never can be too careful.'

Ostrowsky sighed impatiently. 'Could you give Detective Breen a list of all the deceased's close friends, business partners, anyone relevant?' She handed me her card. 'If you suddenly think of anything that might have disturbed this bucolic picture of blissful happiness, give me a call at the number here.' She'd underlined one of three numbers in red. I watched her walk out briskly and then glanced at the card again.

Her name was not Carol, it was Grace. Grace Ostrowsky.

Detective Breen took down the names of any of Berenger's friends I could think of right there. I knew I was missing some vital connection, but my brain had shorted itself on a Berenger–Sharon Tate–Berenger circuit.

We had finished, but Breen seemed tense about something. I watched him fish around inside his jacket and come out with a battered wallet that was so thick with dog-eared papers it could barely be snapped closed. He coughed once or twice, flipped through the wallet and handed me a small passport photo of a toothy girl of about thirteen.

'Very pretty,' I said to be polite, not sure what he was getting at.

'You think so? That's my youngest, Mia. She's eleven.'

'She looks older.'

'She's a tall one. Five foot three already.'

'Nice,' I said, wanting to be out of there.

'She's mad about fashion, see. The carry-on each morning before she goes to school! Will I wear the pink dress? Will I wear the blue one? And she's always got her head in some magazine. Pictures all over the walls. Of models and TV stars. Probably got one of Berenger up there, I bet. Won't she be excited when I get home and tell her what Daddy did today?' He cleared his throat. 'But anyway, I wanted to ask you, knowing how interested she is in all that stuff, and being pretty and all, as you can see…'

'Yes?'

'I was wondering…do you think she could be a model?'

He was *sick*. They're all sick. See the chance for an easy buck and they'd all sell their daughters' souls without blinking. Parents. Girls would do better without them.

I know it's not wise to be rude to a police officer but I turned on my heels and left him standing there.

A uniformed cop escorted me back through the bedroom, attempting as he did to block my view of the body, as if some secret ritual of the burial chamber was being carried out by men with their shirtsleeves rolled up. I could see the sheets, the ice-blue linen ones embroidered with serpentine Bs she'd stripped from her suite in a Berlin hotel, cascading like cold water to the floor at the foot of the bed. I caught a glimpse of the body, a dead, pale fish washed up in the spill, the shimmer of scales—no, sequins—the skin a slash of plastic like the morning's catch being unwrapped on a fish-monger's counter. I thought, ridiculously, of a fish-and-chip shop, the leaden fillets waiting on a shelf for their coat of batter, the wire basket of splintered potatoes being lowered into the fat. If Berenger were the fish, then it was me descending into that spitting oil.

Burial...funeral...wake. Part of me folded in on itself in dread. These were things to which I would have to attend. There would be no-one else.

In the corridor I barely hesitated before taking the elevator to Aaron's study. It was me he would need, not some police department bodyguard or locum with a syringe of horse sedative. If he had survived the shock, maybe the scandal would kill him. I knew enough of Berenger's life to understand what her death would bring. Reporters and cameras and the ruination of any life lived outside this sterile fortress. I didn't think Aaron could cope with the loss—not of Berenger, he'd get over *her*, but of the last embers of pleasure in his life, the theatre, the ceremonies that honoured him, the vigorous morning walks.

The alarm in the elevator started honking and I realised my finger was on the 'close doors' button. I was leaning into it, hard, while my mind rambled over the rocky places where Aaron and Berenger had been. I was suddenly losing my nerve. I did not want to see Aaron crushed. Death is like a great stone dropped into a pool...it was the ripples I couldn't stand. I was bad with the aftermath. I was a novice at condolences. I had always escaped these things before.

I must have released my finger from the button because the elevator doors shot open and the space was filled by a uniformed cop with his hand on his gun.

'May I help you, Ma'am?'

'Aaron. Mr Karsner,' I explained and I could hear the agitation in my voice. 'I've got to see him. I'm his assistant. The funeral...' My voice trailed off.

I expected him to ask me for identification. I must have looked dishevelled, desperate. But he nodded and stood aside.

My appearance always did inspire confidence. Nobody who looks this mundane could ever do any harm.

I knocked on the door. I could hear no sound from inside. The hallway was quiet as a sepulchre, except for the cop's belt, creaking with hardware. I knocked again and then, after some hesitation, grasped the doorknob and turned it.

My heart sank—although why I could not say—when Alison Bow turned from where she was seated on the edge of the day bed, her face showing as much surprise as the flat features would allow. I suppose she had expected me to be arrested, carted off with my ankles in chains and my hands locked behind my back. She would have liked that, I was sure. Two subservients in one house was one too many in her scheme of things.

What unnerved me was that Alison was not loading or

31

unloading a tray—there was no hot sweet tea, no plate of comforting seaweed in sight—but sitting at Aaron's side, holding his hands between hers. No thought of impropriety crossed my mind, not that: it was simply that I had not before observed any kind of empathy between servant and master. I didn't think Alison was capable of it; nor did I imagine that Aaron thought she was any more than the shadowy figure Berenger had employed to wreak havoc on his taste buds. Was I redundant in this scenario? Were there always to be three of us, even now that the most demanding one had gone?

'I'm sorry…' I stammered, as if I'd disturbed them at something intimate.

Aaron was leaning back against pillows, but he was dressed formally, in one of the dark suits he saved for going to the theatre. He had a paisley cravat tucked into his pink shirt and mono-grammed leather slippers on his feet. It surprised me how unruffled he looked—his trouser legs still held a sharp crease where an iron had pressed them, his shirt cuffs were snapped neatly an inch below his jacket sleeve. He had not fallen asleep at the piano in this outfit. Had he been composed enough to dress himself or had Alison helped?

I had expected him to be ashen, grey. But, as always, he looked younger than his eighty-two years. Berenger's death seemed to have had no immediate effect on him. His skin seemed soft, a healthy pink, and stretched over some inner light…as if he had been preserved from within. His hair had gone white, without a trace of the dirty grey that usually comes with age and it was cut quite fashionably close to his head which made his watery blue eyes jump out from under brows that had stayed black and thick. His soft lower lip betrayed the droop of his years and the liver spots on his hands and cheeks were prominent, but his fingers were very beautiful, his eyes fierce, his movements elegant.

How did I ever miss it?

At the sound of my voice, he shook his hands free of Alison's grasp and pushed back into the pillows with them as if to sit up straighter. 'Nile,' he said. I thought he said it nervously.

'They're finished with you?' Alison asked, getting up.

'Surprised?' I countered.

'That's not what I meant, Nile,' she responded calmly, shifting into holier-than-thou gear.

'Thank you, dear,' said Aaron to Alison. He fixed his red-rimmed eyes on me. 'Do you think I'm ready for the police now?'

'You don't have to see them,' I told him. 'I can always say you've been sedated.'

'I've never been sedated in my life, my dear, and I'm not starting now. Take those wretched things away, will you?' He nodded in the direction of a vial of pills sitting on a stack of music manuscripts by the day bed. Alison scooped them up and put them into a deep side pocket in her tunic.

'Would you like anything from the kitchen, Mr Karsner? Can I contact anyone for you?'

'No, thank you, Alison, Nile can do that later. You can tell the police I will be available in five minutes.'

'You are sure?'

'Absolutely.'

Alison nodded at Aaron and then me, and closed the door behind her.

'I'm sorry, Aaron.' The words came out in a tangle. 'I really am. I mean…I don't know what happened. I wasn't…You don't think I?'

'Is it over?' he interrupted. 'Just tell me that.'

'I don't think so,' I answered honestly. 'I don't think the press will give us any peace for a long time.'

'I don't give a damn about the press,' he said sharply. 'Where's Berenger?'

Was this a metaphysical question?

'Where is she *now*?' he added impatiently at my hesitation.

'I think they're…taking her away.'

'Where to?'

I didn't want to say 'morgue'.

'Where *to*?'

'The police…The coroner…Where they go…'

'To hack her to pieces, you mean?'

'No! Well…'

'Never mind. What is she wearing?'

'A dress.'

'Is it short? Long?'

'Short.'

'Does she look decent, Nile?'

No, I screamed inside. She's the most indecent thing I've ever seen. I nodded instead.

'Don't lie to an old man, Nile. She never looked decent for one moment when we were married. Short skirts, little bits of fabric tied here or there, blouses you could see through, bare feet. I don't want them to see her like that.'

What does it matter, I wanted to shriek. They'll soon see everything there is to see.

'Will you find a nice dress for the funeral, Nile? Something pretty…young? She was very young.' His voice wavered on the last word and I could see what an extraordinary effort he was making to form cohesive sentences. 'We must have a small funeral. You must take charge of that. I'm depending on you. None of those hangers-on, none of those *fashion people*.' He spat the two words out and I was surprised at the vehemence. 'Do it quickly.'

'Don't worry,' I reassured him. 'You won't have to think about it.'

'Thank you,' he sighed and closed his eyes again. 'I'm not very good at funerals. At my age they are affronts. I always expect to be next. But I never am.'

'I'm glad of it,' I said. I was still standing away from the bed but I too felt the urge to sit beside him and hold his hand.

Sensing that, I think, he said, 'Come here.'

I moved closer, tentatively. He patted the bed. I sat.

'I was up here all night, you know.' He looked sombrely into my eyes.

I nodded. Yes.

'I assume she was out late.'

'Yes.'

He took one of my hands. His was light and dry as tissue.

'It was a party? You were together?'

'For some of the night,' I said carefully. 'I came home earlier...'

'Was she with anyone?' He watched me unflinchingly.

'No, not that,' I shook my head. It was the first time he raised that...spectre. Did he know?

'I was up here all night. I fell asleep at the piano. She didn't come up to wake me. If I had gone down it might have been different.'

'You don't know that.' I squeezed his hand.

'Don't I? I should have gone down more often.'

I didn't understand what he meant.

'I was up here writing her a song, Nile.'

'You were?' A song! I didn't know why I should be so surprised. Isn't that what songwriters do? Write songs for their lovers? But Aaron hadn't written a song for years. It seemed ironic that he would have written one now. In the pit of me I knew I was jealous. Here I was, surrounded by songwriters, and no-one had written a song for me.

'I wrote it for our wedding anniversary.'

'Oh.' I felt strange. 'The anniversary.' There had been elaborate plans in the works for that.

'It was going to be a beautiful song. But I won't finish it now.'

'But why not, Aaron? She would have liked it, I'm sure.'

Aaron frowned. I knew how phoney I sounded. But before he could say anything, there was sharp knock on the door.

'Yes?' I called out.

'Detective Breen!'

'Just one moment!' I stood and smiled at Aaron. 'Breen's all right,' I tried to reassure him. 'A bit—' I pointed an imaginary gun at my temple.

Aaron smiled wanly.

'Do you want me to stay?' I asked.

'No.' Aaron sat up straighter. 'This shouldn't affect your young life, too.'

'But it has. You can't help that.'

Aaron made a signal for me to hurry along. As I moved toward the door he said, 'Oh, one more thing, Nile.'

'Yes?' I turned back.

He held my eyes. His were puffy, ringed with red, but bright and clear in the centre. 'The song for Berenger...I don't mind if people know about it.'

'All right.'

'And Nile,' he added, settling back into his pillows. 'Will you make sure the press have it? Then there can be no doubt.'

At the time I thought he meant that there would be no doubt that he loved her. But I was wrong about that too.

I didn't know what to do next. I did not know the protocol. Should I go with the body, as Aaron's proxy? Should I rally together some of his friends? Should I cancel Berenger's appointments? Should I throw myself on my bed and grieve? Or laugh? Should I just walk out of there and leave them all to it? I knew I was very close to hysteria, but of the sad or funny kind I couldn't tell.

I felt detached, but agitated at the same time, as if there were an uninvolved me and an inextricable me. The ghastly corpse was one thing...the feeling I couldn't help shake off, of *responsibility* for it, was another. I had been her minder after all. Had I minded enough? The expression *to mind* and all its devious connotations were bitter on my tongue.

But Aaron's composure disturbed me most. I expected shock,

revulsion, sorrow, disintegration. I had not expected…control. And something else I could not put my finger on. Curiosity? And yet death must have held no surprises for him. He had outlived three—now four—wives and countless colleagues and friends. Perhaps it was a matter of pride for him, something he could do, control his suffering and negate it.

I heard later that he broke down while being questioned by Breen. That he simply turned towards the wall and refused to go on. That his sentences became fractured and meaningless and eventually little more than grunts. He had stood there, ramrod-straight, facing a wall of photographs from his life, shut down in a kind of autism which Breen and Ostrowsky, and later his doctor, could not reach. It was pronounced a shock-related nervous breakdown but at the time I thought it was Aaron's silent 'Enough!'

It was just another kind of control, I told myself. He was of a generation that believed you had to hold out against unhappiness, hide its occurrence from others at all cost. The only acceptable way to express it publicly was through art.

And so, he retreated to write about it, to a place no-one else could go.

But where was I going to go? I didn't have anywhere to hide. Before Berenger died, I had intended to walk out of there and make a new life. But now, my strength and determination fell away. I couldn't leave like this. I had to get Aaron through the next few days, no matter how I felt. I wanted to go to my bed, pull the blanket over my head, and draw the darkness around me. But even that relief was denied me. I was the personal assistant. I had responsibilities.

In the end, I went down to my office, the only place where I could have peace. I had to think. Not just about death, but about life. My life. And other lives too. Lives that hinged on me.

There was a cop hanging out by the kitchen, probably hoping

Alison would do the housekeeperly thing and whip him up a nice strong coffee. I nodded at him as I went past. No hope in hell, lad. Not in that kitchen. I almost tripped over Berenger's hairless cat which came scampering out of the sitting room and across my path. I picked it up and took it into the office.

The answering machine was flashing a backwards digital 3, which is what it always did when the tape was exhausted. So the word was already out. I reached over to pull the machine and phone out of the wall but, as I did so, something caught my eye out the window.

I had a claustrophobic view of one of the three loft buildings across the street. Unless I went right up to the window, I couldn't see any sky, just veiled windows, the occasional fizz of a computer screen, a crate of wine left out on the fire escape to chill or someone's dismal attempt at Christmas lights. In summer, one of the residents would oil himself into a slick and come out on to the fire escape with a plastic chair and sit with his feet up on the railing as if he were in the Hamptons. By now, in the middle of winter, the fire escapes were usually deserted, even though the frigid sky blazed alpine blue.

But today, some of the usually anonymous neighbours had their heads out the windows, staring down at the street below. Some had actually climbed out on to the fire escape to get a better view. One woman was in a bathrobe, despite the cold. Another was leaning over the railing smoking a cigarette. A man in a dark coat was talking into a cell phone, his breath condensing in the air. A boy on the fourth floor of one building was calling down to a boy on the third floor of another, who was clutching a poodle. The film star who lived on the top floor of the building opposite had come out to watch the commotion in her exercise gear, with a fur coat thrown over her shoulders.

I could see across the street, where a crowd had gathered on the pavement outside the huge clothing emporium that filled a space once occupied by a gallery. Two of the shop assistants were standing in the doorway with their arms folded. The crowd was about four people deep, pushed back on the sidewalk by a couple of cops who were allowing the occasional car to go through.

I couldn't see what was happening on our side of the street and so I pushed up the window and climbed out on to our fire escape. It was probably not the most sensible thing I could do: I was only wearing a light cardigan and skirt. The wind blew my straggly hair about but I was too numb to feel the cold. The Living Christmas Tree in a pot that Berenger's agency had given me and which I had put outside to breathe was now thoroughly dead. Another living thing I'd killed.

Through the iron slats underfoot I could see the flashing light of a police car. A helicopter hovered deafeningly overhead. I went to the railing and leaned over. I felt woozy and pulled back a bit. The police had put up blue barricades and strung yellow tape around a section of the pavement outside our building. It looked almost festive, like the street fairs they hold in Little Italy in summer. I could feel excitement emanating from the dense crowd below. Outside the barricades a man with a trenchcoat flung over his shoulders was swamped by a barrage of video cameras, bouncing booms and aggressive microphones. I could hear journalists yelling questions but I couldn't distinguish what they were asking. I could imagine, though.

'Have you identified the body yet?'

'Is it male or female?'

'Is it true this is the home of Berenger Karsner?'

'So is it foul play, guys?'

'Any drugs involved?'

'Dangerous sex?'

'Do you have a suspect?'

That's what they always asked. And what was a suspect anyway? The poor person who got left with the corpse or all those people whose manipulations and insults over the years had led the body to find itself there in the first place?

I am so used to being invisible that it took me a few moments to realise that I was attracting attention by my presence on the fire escape. One of the boys opposite was waving at me. 'Hey you! What's happening? Someone get murdered?' he called out through cupped hands.

I shrunk back against the brickwork, but not before another person in the crowd below noticed me and pointed. I could see faces turn up and people step back into the street to get a better view of me lurking on the landing. I could tell by their startled expressions they imagined me to be a thief or murderer making a daring escape. A cop leaning on the hood of his squad car looked up from his messy hamburger in my direction and put his hand on his gun. I edged back quickly and slipped through the open window.

I pulled down the wooden blinds and collapsed at my desk, frightened now. I don't know how long I cringed in the darkness. I felt like a piece of carrion being circled by vultures. The crowds outside, the answering machine clicking on and off, the police officer lurking in the hallway. I had navigated my way through the interview with Breen and Ostrowsky without any apparent slips, I was sure, but why had they warned me not to go anywhere without informing them? What could they imagine I had done? Murder her?

Suddenly I started to shake, so badly I had to steady my leg against the desk. This was not the way things were supposed to work out. Berenger, the moron, had brought the police to our door. She hadn't died from an overdose of alcohol and cocaine or whatever was inside her sour little stomach. She'd died from an overdose of perversity.

How many times had I wished her dead? But she was never going to be dead while there was still speculation about her life. She might have lived to a nasty old age and just faded away. But now she would live on, for months, or years, in the supermarket tabloids and television news magazines. The press and the public loved a tragic beauty. And even if that beauty wasn't particularly tragic to start with, she'd be that way by the time they finished with her. Joan of Arc was nineteen when they burned her at the stake and she'd had a dream run since then. By the time they finished with Berenger she'd be a statue in Central Park and a charity. I'd never be rid of her.

Even then, I could feel her reaching to me from the grave.

Eventually, I forced myself to make some phone calls. There were things to be done. Berenger's manager, Erik Sklar, was on his way over, although I tried to get his assistant to stop him. What would Erik do here? Embrace Aaron? I couldn't imagine it.

'Too, late, darl, he's switched his mobile off,' the assistant said.

'I think we should close the office, don't you?' worried Berenger's booker, the adipose Shelley. 'I mean, it's like an asylum in here. We've all been crying our eyes out since we heard. The friggin' press has got the place staked out. None of the other girls wants to work. There's like a million cancellations. Her clients are freaking. You should hear 'em, running around like someone's set their butts on fire. "But what about the campaign? What about the campaign?" Like, hey, there's not a nineteen-year-old girl dead around here. Do you think the cops'll come and talk to *me*?'

'Has anyone been arrested?' asked the PR agent crisply. I could hear her tapping into her laptop. 'I s'pose I've got to run the press release by the old man. You think he'll want her cremated? I'd strongly recommend burial. I don't mean to sound crude, but a body in a coffin and a romantic graveside always make a better photo call.'

'Ohmygod, Nile, what happened?' Carla Fracas, the designer of $2000 silk slips, sobbed into her cell phone on the way back from a truncated visit with her yoga master in Southampton. 'It wasn't anything sinister was it? We've just done a whole happy campaign with her. God knows how it's going to play in the malls now. But that's not what I should be thinking about, it's wrong of me. I should be focusing on what a wonderful person she was. A true friend, a free spirit. She was like a daughter to me. I suppose I could make a donation in her name to a charity. Do you think breast cancer's visible enough? Or too visible? What about the ovarian thing? It doesn't sound too nasty does it? Too *terminal*? I always think that about AIDS: what's the use? Do you think they'll have the service next Monday? Because I simply couldn't go. I'm hosting a ball in Los Angeles. Sarah Ferguson's coming. I'm needed there. You'll have to make sure they don't have it Monday. Oh, or Tuesday, either, because I'll be *en route*.'

'What is her mother's address? We will, of course, be sending flowers,' said the assistant to the editor-in-chief. 'I'm dialling Robert Isabell as we speak.'

'Jesus bloody heck,' said photographer Nick Standard from his home in London. 'The poor little love. I can't believe she's not gonna be standin' on the old white seamless again throwing one of her fuckin' tantrums. Who'da believed it, eh?'

I spent a good part of the morning involved in conversations like this. Eventually, I had to stop. I couldn't stand it anymore. Everyone made noises about how shocked they were but I knew they all thought it exciting, inevitable. What kind of people were these, who thought that the death of a nineteen-year-old was inevitable? But in their accelerated world, where twelve-year-olds had perfect skin and fourteen-year-olds perfect bodies, nineteen was not so young. In the middle ages they might have had several babies by nineteen and become tired and haggard with the effort—in Berenger's world, it was airline schedules and vodka for breakfast and hours in front of a mirror having their hair backcombed, not babies, that did it.

I did try to place one other call—to Berenger's mother, Chantal, in Peachland. The telephone was constantly engaged. She must have taken it off the hook.

Many of Aaron's friends were in contact, but I put them off, promising to call back when Aaron was ready to speak. Not one of them asked after Berenger. She had ceased to exist: for Aaron's friends, this was a relief.

One person who refused to be fobbed off was Aaron's friend Lilian Gessman, a Hungarian-born theatre director who was in her early sixties and had been a close friend of Aaron's since he'd written her a note admiring her work on a production of Samuel Beckett's *Endgame* back in the 1960s. Lilian was squat and jowly with unruly curly grey hair pinned in fingerwaves. She wore men's suits and looked you straight in the eye and I found her prickly whenever I had cause to deal with her over Aaron's memoirs. Aaron and she would disagree all the time, over names and dates and the assessment of minor characters in their lives. They squabbled like brother and sister although, at a stretch, she could have been his child. I never really knew why he bothered with her. She reminded me of a gnarly old witch from a fairytale, the kind who stole children's dreams.

Lilian had heard the news from another source before I could call her and was furious with me. 'What is it you have done with him?' she spat over the phone. 'Drugged him to the eyeballs?'

She hung up on me before I could protest and was in my office fifteen minutes later, waving her silver-tipped cane, which she carried as an affectation, and demanding that I contact this and that person on her behalf as if I, too, were her slave. When she finally left, I could hear her giving the police officer in the corridor a tongue-lashing about the crowd outside.

Once Lilian got her hands on Aaron, I knew I wouldn't hear from him. I could hear movement in the corridor from time to time, but I lay low. Occasionally a police officer would come in and ask me for a phone number or directions to the nearest deli. I stared at Berenger's appointment book for the longest time, trying to find some clue in my familiar neat handwriting. Almost every entry was crossed out three or four times, reflecting her habit of changing her mind. The next few pages were blissfully blank except for one or two reminders. These were to be the days I would spend with Aaron, while Berenger shopped in a Moroccan souk.

I flipped through the remainder of the agenda—I had made entries up until next Christmas, blocking out whole weeks at a time for the seasonal fashion shows in London, Milan, Paris and New York. In May, Berenger was due to make an appearance at the fashion collections in Sydney. I had written this in pencil because I knew she would cancel at the last minute—she hated long flights—leaving the organisers in an uproar that I would have to smooth over with lies and much ego-stroking. In July it was the couture in Paris. In April and October she was booked out for a week for a Calvin Klein campaign. In February it was South Africa, followed by a meeting with some dignitary in Moscow. There were birthday reminders scattered through the pages—for colleagues and hairdressers and even the occasional celebrity pet. Every now and again I could see where I had made the annotation 'Addam—Seattle' or 'Addam—London' and then erased it.

'Addam—Mexico City.' 'Addam—Montreal.' Addam. Addam. Addam. If you stare at a familiar word long enough it ceases to make any sense. It is just a jumble of letters. Addam becomes Ddama, becomes Madda, becomes Addma, not the person I was too cowardly to call.

I was interrupted from my reverie by Erik Sklar's sudden appearance in the doorway. Under his suntan, he looked ashen. He gave me a stiff, awkward embrace. It was as phoney as his set of perfect white teeth. We had never even shaken hands before.

'It's terrible,' he said in his curious American accent, with its edge of Scandinavian. There was a tremor in his voice he was fighting to disguise. This touch of humanity was a new experience for me: Erik had always seemed as if he had been booted-up rather than born. 'I've dragged girls out of beds and out of jail and I've even put my fingers down their throats when they've been choking on their own vomit, but none of them has died on me. I must be slipping.' He brushed

44

a lock of black hair out of his left eye with a tense hand.

I wondered: would Erik put his fingers down my throat if I were choking? I looked at his impeccable suit and his fine, manicured hands. Probably not.

He was one of those gay men who was always outrageously flattering to beautiful women and treated the rest of us like Kleenex, to be sneezed on and discarded. He was tanned and finely muscled and wore open white shirts under his dark blade-sharp suits. More than one beautiful society matron imagined he was smitten with her. I don't think he worked very hard to dissuade the illusion.

'She used to call me ten times a day. Should I go here, Erik? Should I wear this? Should I speak to this person? But she didn't call me last night, when it counted. I feel—*dumped*. It's a peculiar feeling, I must say.'

It was peculiar to me, too, the sudden absence of a person making demands on me day and night. Once, when she was in Havana without me, she called me here in New York to ask me to phone room service for her and order a Diet Coke.

'What could have been going on in her mind?'

'We don't know that anything was going on,' I said.

'No,' he said. 'I can't accept that.'

'Erik, what would you have said if she had called? If she had been in trouble?'

'I would have told her not to be such a fucking cry baby. To grow up. Tough love always works best with these girls.'

These girls. Not that one.

'Well, she didn't want to grow up, did she?' And, I felt like adding, it hadn't suited you until now to let her.

'So you think it's suicide?'

'I don't know what I think.'

'But why would she do it deliberately? We'd just made her a citizen of the world to minimise her tax. She had another cover of *Vogue*, the most covers any girl has had in a single year. We were negotiating with Matt Damon's people about a movie. And she was going to meet Nelson Mandela next month and get some kind of medal. What more could she fucking well want? It couldn't have been drugs. She was straight, relatively speaking.'

Relatively speaking, meaning disappearing during shoots for a quick toot in the bathroom, dragging on joints in the dark corners backstage or cadging pills from acquaintances to wash down with splits of Krug at after-show parties.

I was thinking of the last bathroom I dragged her out of when I could feel Erik examining me with those steel-blue eyes. 'What do you know that you're not telling me?'

'Nothing.'

'You were with her last night.'

'I came home before she did.'

'It was that creep, wasn't it? What did he do to her?'

'What creep?' I tried to say lightly but I could hear my voice dragging like a lead balloon.

He ignored me. His brain was clicking over what he knew of Berenger's life like a calculating machine. Calculating the loss to his business of his most valuable asset. I didn't think for a moment he was upset about losing her. But he was furious with himself that he had let her slip away, as if she were a stock option he had failed to exercise at the right time.

'I didn't care about the others, but he fucked with her mind. I should have stopped it. God knows, I tried to separate them, send her off to Vanuatu when he was touring Romania or whatever, but somehow they always seemed to run across each other in some transit lounge somewhere in between.' He raised an eyebrow. 'You don't happen to know anything about that, do you?'

'Ask Shelley,' I said. 'She did all the travel arrangements.'

'She *planned* all the travel arrangements. But you know Berenger, changing everything at the last moment. She couldn't have done it herself. She didn't know how to use an ATM machine, let alone dial an airline.'

'I don't know what you're talking about,' I said.

He sighed. I could hear disgust in that exhalation of air. 'What was in it for you, Nile? You get your kicks out of that sort of thing? Fucking up everyone's lives?'

'What do you mean?' It was not a question, but a protest.

'You know what I mean. It's called living vicariously.'

'I only did what she wanted.'

'She didn't fucking well know what she wanted!' He smacked the edge of the desk with the palm of his hand. I was startled by his intensity. 'She was a halfwit!'

'Let's not speak ill of the dead.' I was trying to be calm.

'And now it's up to me to clean up the mess. Dying like this—halfway through all those contracts, the tax thing still pending. Christ, it's a financial nightmare.'

'I wouldn't worry myself too much about it if I were you, Erik. There must be something in it for you.'

He looked at me with such dark hatred, I actually flinched.

'How did it really feel, Nile? To be the one who…engineered their relationship? To be in the next room and hear them together? Was that fun for you? I bet you had your ear to the wall every night, listening. Was it hot, their fucking? Did you get off on that?'

I wanted to say I wasn't there. I was never there to listen. But it was true. I did the meddling. And despised myself. 'It wasn't like that at all,' I said weakly.

'It wasn't? Don't you think Berenger had a good laugh about it? She told me you were like a dog panting for someone to throw it a scrap from the table. What made you think there would be any scraps? You couldn't have him so you arranged it for her? I only wish I had stopped it in time. She would be alive right now.'

'Alive to keep you in Gucci suits and that ocean-front "shack" at Montauk?'

'You think too much of her. There are always other girls.' He picked up Berenger's agenda before I could stop him and started flipping through it. 'I want you to send over every document you

47

have, every file, every diary entry. We need it all for the fucking IRS.'

'Too late,' I said, snatching the agenda back. 'The cops have already asked for it all.' It wasn't true, so far, but I resented Erik's interference. 'Anyway, this is all Aaron's property now. I can't just give it out to *anyone*.'

'I don't think we have to worry about Aaron.' Erik's parting shot was delivered with a hand nonchalantly smoothing back his hair. 'I don't think he'll make it to dinner.'

I stood staring at the door long after Erik had gone.

Was it hot, their fucking? Did you get off on that? You couldn't have him so you arranged it for her.

I could feel the anger surging inside me. Who did they think they were, Erik and Berenger and all the others? Did they think that because I was plain no-one had had his hand up my skirt before? That no-one had kissed this neck or stroked these breasts or licked these plump thighs with his tongue? That because I looked like this I couldn't be aroused or stirred or…loved?

It was my fault, of course. They knew nothing about me. I'd made certain of that. Not my real name or exactly where I'd come from or even how my voice really sounded. It had been easy, this subterfuge. They weren't interested in me, they didn't look closely. I was just a conduit to Berenger, a path they tramped back and forth on, not knowing whether it was stone or tar. Not once did anybody, Berenger included, ask me anything about my past. Not a thing. Not even, for politeness sake, the first question they ask you in England: what school did you go to? I had prepared stories to dampen unwanted curiosity but they remained untold. A shame, really. They were little masterpieces of dullness.

I was set on *uninventing* myself, bleaching myself of every shred of personality and will, so that no-one who met me would ever dream of speculating 'Isn't she?' or 'Wasn't she?' or even 'Didn't she?'

It had worked. *A dog panting for scraps at the table*, Erik had said. How dare he.

Well, my friends, I thought, as I started dialling Addam's number, every dog must have her day.

And it was time this dog had hers.

ddam Karsner is Aaron Karsner's twenty-eight-year-old grandson. With a name like that he might have been a dentist or an editor at a literary magazine. But he is not. He is a rock star, the lead singer of a band called Detox. Describing him this way conjures up provocative images of hotel rooms trashed, motorbikes crashed, speedballs mainlined, girlfriends bashed. Which is, in fact, a lyric from one of Addam's songs. And which is, in fact, not Addam's story at all.

He should have been merely a decorative footnote to this drama, the character who delivered Berenger to us and then bowed out. He should have been gone before the end of the first act, perhaps in a blaze of rock-star glory—an overdose, a fatal brawl in a nightclub, a drive-by shooting, a fall from the stage. This would have been his story in a perfect tabloid world. But, instead of a dead rock star, we have a dead supermodel. Not an entirely novel occurence, either.

Addam's phone rang stubbornly for a while and then a strange, terse, voice answered flatly, 'Yeah.'

I knew it was a cop. My stomach churned. I shouldn't have procrastinated, I should have been the one to tell him.

If he hadn't known already.

There it went again, this doubt. I hadn't gone to him because I feared what he would tell me. I was a coward and I had failed him.

Hearing the cop's weary voice, I was shaken out of my stupidity. I didn't want Addam to be surrounded by strangers.

I could see him sitting on that mattress on the floor, hugging himself, with the cops circling. He was a celebrity and open to all the misinterpretation that could bring. The police wouldn't be sympathetic. They'd want to hurt him. And then they'd ask for his autograph.

There was no way out of our building except through the front door. Berenger had once hired a security expert to evaluate the building and he'd suggested an elaborate plan to build a secret passage into a back lane. She had applauded the idea with child-like glee and then dropped it like a hot lump of coal. The passage was never built and she left by the front door like everyone else. She pretended to be indifferent to her fans, but the truth was she loved being recognised. She would scowl and pout at anyone who pointed at her in the street but, as she turned away, I could see her smile go all the way down to her toes.

'Back doors are fine for servants,' she said to me pointedly one day. 'But I don't intend to go, like, sneaking out of my own home.'

I pulled a cap over my head and turned my coat collar up but I think I only succeeded in looking more intriguing. The late afternoon sky was darkening and it had started to rain lightly. I tried to scuttle sideways between the struts of some scaffolding attached to the building next door. There were fewer people outside now and the yellow police tape had broken and was flapping in the wind, but still my shadowy appearance caused an uproar.

'There's someone!'

'Catch her!'

'Wait!'

'Miss!'

I was still 'Miss' then, not a person to whom they could attach a name. They didn't pursue me very far down the street as

I scurried away. I turned into Broome Street and found a taxi.

The traffic resembled a pack of cards that had been scattered from the sky. Drivers queued over intersections, rode up on gutters, butted across lanes impatient to gain another inch on the person in the car beside them. There was a tanker accident on the approach to the Manhattan Bridge so I paid the driver and walked the last few blocks. The sky spat tiny shards of ice in a light rain, tapping me on the face like sharp reprimands.

A crowd had gathered outside Addam's loft building on East Broadway, its attention drawn by the two squad cars parked on the kerb. My stomach twisted in a knot when I saw the TV crews but I tried to calm myself down. They only want a sound bite from him, I told myself. Nothing at all is wrong.

Four uniformed cops kept the crowd at bay. There were about thirty people milling around, a carbon copy of the crowd that had lingered outside Berenger's place that morning, except that here and there a few Chinese faces looked expectantly towards Addam's front door. I could swear that the same little girls I'd seen on Wooster Street were here on East Broadway, holding out their autograph books eagerly. A group of teenagers was crouched in the gutter, smoking. How did they know Addam lived here and how did they know their idol was in trouble? I was stunned for a moment and then the realisation dawned: the internet. Bulletin boards all over the country were probably lighting up that very minute with speculation about his role in Berenger's death. The fans probably knew before the police did that he kept his stash in a cigar box on top of the keyboard. They probably knew before I did.

I watched Addam's illuminated fifth-floor windows for a while, hoping he would come into view. But all I saw was the back of a man in a tan suit, the jacket riding up over his hip, revealing the black lump of a holster. It was Breen. What a busy day he must have been having. I wondered who had pointed them at Addam. Erik, of course.

Two of the cops on the street were arguing with a girl in a

black coat. I didn't pay much attention as I came closer until I heard her protest, 'But I'm Addam's girlfriend!'

'Yeah?' said one of the cops, his mouth twisted cynically. 'Prove it.'

She gave a frustrated shrug. 'How can you prove something like that?'

How *could* you prove something like that?

I looked closely at her. A fan, trying it on. She didn't argue any further with the cops but stepped back and lit a cigarette, obviously accustomed to being turned down.

'Miss?'

'Officer, I have to see Addam.' I realised I was sounding too agitated.

'Reason?' It was the cynical cop.

'I work for'—I was going to say Berenger, but I hesitated—'for Addam's grandfather.'

'Grandfather? That's a new one.'

'You don't understand—'

'Course we do. You love him, right? Well, line up with the rest of 'em.'

'I'm not like the rest of them,' I argued, feeling the shudder of someone walking across my grave. Was it Berenger, even then? 'I've got a message for him...'

'Why don't you just move back like everyone else? You'll get your chance to see him if they bring him out.'

I didn't like the sound of that. 'Why would they bring him out?'

'Look, just move back, all right?' He took my elbow.

I wished I had thought to bring Berenger's key and pretend I was a tenant. 'Officer,' I tried again, trying to shake him off. 'Why don't you ask—' I was going to say, Detectives Breen and Ostrowsky, but they cut me off.

'Be a good girl and stand over there with the other fans.' He gripped me firmly, dragged me to the gutter and turned his back.

'Breen and Ostrowsky!' I finally managed to spit out, but he didn't hear.

'Fuckers,' came a throaty voice from beside me.

I looked down. It was a small girl in cut-off shorts over thick striped tights, chewing on a cigarette. She didn't look older than ten. She held her cigarette between her thumb and first finger, like some old alcoholic down at the local pub, and looked me up and down. 'In case you have other ideas,' she muttered. 'He's mine.'

'Oh?' I asked.

'Now that bitch is dead, he's mine.'

I had no place in this. I took a taxi back to SoHo and asked the driver to drop me a few blocks from the loft, lest he, too, started asking questions.

'Nile!' someone called out as I was stopped by one of the officers outside and showed him my key. In the half an hour I'd been away, they'd found out my name.

The police found a ziplock bag of marijuana and a few tabs of ketamine, a horse anaesthetic, in Addam's loft. I suppose the mayor needed another high-profile drug arrest to boost his credentials, because they made quite a show of rough-handling Addam into a squad car. I watched this on television that night with the rest of the world. I couldn't catch his face in any of the footage. His head was always down and twisted away from the cameras, but the television channels all intercut their coverage with clips from Detox's latest video and the same ancient photograph of Addam with his arm around a zonked-out sixteen-year-old Berenger.

The police booked him on a minor drug possession charge. His hearing was rushed forward, he got a fine, and then left for a five-week tour of Europe as scheduled. This I know from the gossip columns. His phone was disconnected and his assistant, Trini, didn't bother to return my calls. If he ever spoke to his grandfather, Aaron, I didn't know about it. He was out of the country for Berenger's funeral and he didn't send flowers. I don't know what the police read into that.

He had been spirited away. And I was left in that lifeless SoHo asylum with a sullen Aaron, a stony Alison and a growing awareness that we had not, by a long shot, rid ourselves of Berenger yet.

So we disposed of the body in haste. Decent haste. We had to wait a week: the Medical Examiner wanted for some reason to hold on to that putrefying skeleton for as long as possible. I entertained wicked thoughts of him going to her at night, sliding her tray from its cold steel drawer, and tenderly ministering her to autopsy wounds for hours, like the embalmer, Dr Pedro Ara, who would not give up Eva Peron's corpse. In the end, Aaron's lawyers got the body released and the funeral was held on the eighth day.

It was eight days of agony for me.

I was the one to approve all the funeral arrangements, including the mortician's attempt at a make-over of our ravaged cadaver. I had not wanted ever to look at her pinched little face again and reluctantly stood over the coffin with my eyes shut, breathing deeply, before daring to open them a sliver. The corpse certainly looked dead to me, but I had to be reassured it was indeed Berenger, the face unfamiliarly puffy and misshapen, the skin yellow from its cosmetic varnish, the eyebrows sketched a shaggy black they had never known in life.

I laughed with relief, and gratefully told the mortician, who was in fact a young woman, that she had done a 'professional job'. The mortician puffed with pride at my compliment and showed me the picture from *Vogue* she'd used as a guide. Berenger was unrecognisable, but when was she not unrecognisable under all that thick make-up and tricky lights and digital doodling with her flesh? I suggested the mortician sprinkle the casket with 'Eau de Berenger' to cover the smell of formaldehyde. It would cover the smell of anything.

There were only about thirty people present at the funeral. I managed that by faxing 'confidential' information that it was to be held on Wednesday when in fact I had scheduled it for Tuesday. I had seduced one of Berenger's publicists to my cause by keeping her busy with plans for a memorial service later in the month. It was a subterfuge that was sure to arouse bouts of hysterical abuse from A-list personalities not familiar with being excluded from anything newsworthy, but the thought of finally excluding them from something made me secretly pleased.

The whole service, non-denominational, was delivered with antiseptic pragmatism in a Second Avenue funeral parlour. I had chosen a place that disposed of bodies, not one that would save Berenger's eternal soul. Aaron arrived with a nurse at his side who pushed a wheelchair, in which he refused to sit. He was dressed beautifully in a dark suit but his chin was rough with grey stubble and his skin had a jaundiced cast. Throughout the short service he stared fiercely at the arrangement of oriental lilies behind the speaker's podium as if defying the lurid pink centres to give up their perfume. But I knew there was no chance of that—the lilies, like all the other flowers in the room, were plastic.

I took pleasure in this, the seediness of the funeral home. The dark red curtains lining the walls had the sheen of synthetic velvet, the worn rugs on the floors were from China, not Istanbul. The tables were chipped veneer, the chairs moulded wood in a heavy Italianate style, the altar cloths yellowing vinyl lace. Everything looked washable, and I imagined a crew of peasant women in headscarves coming in to scrub the smell of death away after we had finished.

Among the mourners were Alison, front row, clutching her Mala, a string of bohdi seeds. An impatient Erik, his hand twitching like a gunfighter to get to the cell phone bulging in his pocket and make arrangements that would ruin another few teenagers' lives. Several of Aaron's friends, none of them under sixty, including a famous producer, a famous protege, a famous soprano and a famous hotelier. Lilian Gessman in a dramatic black cape, fussing over Aaron's seating arrangements. Aaron's retired housekeeper, Frances Feeney, her faded orange head bent sorrowfully but her bright patterned suit screaming the contempt in which I knew she held the deceased. Darien Apps, in a purple hat that spiralled to heaven. Carla Fracas in silver velvet robes with a harness of crystals around her neck. Two young girls, one about thirteen, the other about eight, who might have belonged to anyone. And Detective Breen, the snoop, pretending to be paying his 'respects'.

As the small chapel filled, I scanned the crowd for any sign of Berenger's mother, Chantal. I was curious about her. I had left word about the funeral with some taciturn farmhand, but she had never called back. I imagine the newspapers had the same response, because no photograph of the grieving mother, wistfully holding for the camera a photograph of her precious daughter in ballet tutu, had been published.

I always assumed Chantal possessed some kind of flaw that was fatal in Berenger's eyes, such as a little too much plumpness around the waist or a manner of dressing that employed copious amounts of floral fabric, trailing shawls and a straw hat. I knew that Chantal managed a farm and that her first husband, Bill, had been killed in a bad tractor accident when Berenger was young.

There was a matronly woman standing at the back of the chapel whom I did not recognise and I was about to approach her, when a petite woman in a slim, sky-blue wrap dress under a fox fur coat came down the aisle towards me.

'You must be Nile. I'm Chantal.' She held out a tanned hand. She looked barely older than Berenger, although I suppose she must have been at least forty.

I knew not to look for familial similarities between Chantal and Berenger. But the adoption people had done a good job. Although much smaller than her daughter, Chantal had the same huge, hungry eyes. Her hair had once been a monochrome of dark brown, I was sure, but now it was frosted with ash blonde and set in voluptuous curves. But where Berenger's skin was a luminous pale, almost powdery, Chantal's looked like it had been washed with gold. There was a smattering of freckles across the bridge of her nose. She smiled warmly at me as she gripped my hand and the skin above her lips puckered into a dozen deep lines. She was a smoker, probably a ferocious one, I could see that. She bore an uncanny resemblance to an actress whose name I could not remember but who was often cast in European movies of the seventies as a sort of free-living American *femme fatale*. In fact, Chantal had the kind of look, slightly tinselly, that suggested too many afternoons sunbaking and chainsmoking on the deck of a yacht moored off Capri.

I didn't know what Berenger's adoptive father, Bill, had looked like, but I could bet he was long and lean and, as Berenger shot up in girlhood, people would have exclaimed, somewhat foolishly in the circumstances, 'Ah, yes, we see where she gets her height!' Where she got her height was a mystery.

I once asked Berenger if she had ever thought of looking for her birth mother, but she just snorted and said, 'What, and have *two* like Chantal?'

Chantal let go of my hand. A pearly little bag snuggled in the crook of her left arm. She looked down at her blue dress and her eyes twinkled with amusement. 'I'm not a fan of black. It makes one look like a Mediterranean widow, doesn't it?'

A style that would *not* be inappropriate here, I thought. Everything about Chantal looked expensive—the cluster of rings on her fingers, the manicured nails, the perfectly applied make-up—and the surprise must have shown in my face.

'Grapes. We have a vineyard,' she smiled, reading my mind. 'We employ over three hundred pickers in season. Of course, it suits Berenger to make out that her mother is white trash.'

'I'm so sorry about Berenger,' I said, mustering up as much sincerity as I could. 'She loved you very much.'

'Well, that's crap!' Chantal exclaimed, and it was almost a laugh. Heads turned. She smiled at me apologetically. 'But I appreciate it anyway.'

'Where would you like to sit? I can take you over to Aaron.'

'Oh, no, I don't want to get into that!' She chuckled again. 'I'd be much happier up here by myself. I can slip out quietly when it's over.'

'We're having a—well, a wake, I suppose, at Aaron's place uptown. Not in SoHo where they lived but...'

'I couldn't possibly go. I'm not very good at sad things. I just wanted to know that she was...gone. I wanted to see it for myself.' She crossed her arms and gave a deep sigh. 'Hard to believe, isn't it?' She made Berenger's death sound no more disturbing than a sprinkle of snow in April. 'I knew it would end like this.'

'You did?'

'It's terrible to dislike your child. But she was never very lovable. She was difficult, sulky. As a baby, she was not affectionate. And then at five she started waking up several times a night, with nightmares, headaches, you name it, anything to get attention, to take me from my bed. This lasted right up until she was about ten. It killed me, with the farm and all. It drove Bill to drink. And my new husband, Steve, he wouldn't have it. He'd brought himself up by his bootstraps, he was not tolerant of need. She kept on demanding, demanding, until there just wasn't any more to give. I was glad when she got into that modelling thing at fourteen. I took her to the agency myself.'

'Why are you telling me all this?'

'Well, you're a trustworthy girl, aren't you? You look it. It's not as if you're the press.' She tossed her head challengingly.

Her flippancy was starting to get on my nerves. 'There must have been good memories.'

'I don't want you to think I don't feel *something* for her. I read these stories in the papers all the time about unhappy young girls, delivering babies in their bedrooms without anyone knowing, or killing themselves in suicide pacts with their boyfriends...it makes me cry. But Berenger's not one of those, is she? The Lord gave her a good life, he gave her beauty and

59

determination and she trashed everything.'

'But surely you must have been proud of how well she did in modelling?'

'Why? What did it have to do with me? Her genes were programmed before I ever laid eyes on her. None of it—*this*—is anything to do with me. It never has been. She always went her own way and didn't care a damn what I said.'

She fished a lace handkerchief out of her bag and closed the snap shut. 'I suppose I'll be needing this, won't I?'

'I don't know that you will,' I replied.

She gave a coy little smile. No doubt the flirtatious one she used on all those farmhands to get them to pick quicker.

She held out her hand to me again. 'Well, if you don't mind, I'll take my seat, then.'

I watched her arrange herself on a chair, handkerchief poised in front of her face. Her skirt rode up on her thighs. What a waste, I thought, that there are only geriatrics, homosexuals and spinsters here to admire those elegant knees.

I don't know how we got through the service, but we did. There was hardly a wet eye in the house. Chantal watched Berenger's coffin disappear—to make certain, I suppose, that her daughter was well and truly disposed of—and made a smooth getaway.

I never heard from her again, but I bet Aaron did. I bet she went through every financial transaction with a fine-toothed comb, trawling Berenger's life for salvageable bounty. Mother's little dividend. Jewellery. Paintings. Designer clothing. There was probably a team of lawyers working around the clock right now on her behalf. But she wouldn't get as much as she thought. I'd called Housing Works before the funeral and arranged for them to pull up their truck outside the loft and load it with clothes, accessories, perfume, comic books and her vast collection of beanie babies. I was in a charitable mood. I had no right to do it. And that made me feel better.

The next day, Berenger was sitting on my desk, a pile of dust in a shoe box. Aaron didn't want her, so I gave her to Darien who I knew would make a dramatic gesture with the ashes.

Fling her far and wide, I urged, and make sure the wind is blowing out to sea.

You could say, I suppose, that I have not had much luck with employers. They tend to die on me. In my last year at the local comprehensive, I worked Saturdays selling wedding bands to gullible couples at a place called The Vow Exchange on London Road, in Morden, where I'm from, a nothing place of parklands, railway yards and brick maisonettes, famous only for being at the end of the Northern Line. I'd been at The Vow Exchange for eight weeks when the owner's girl-friend, who supervised the shop, died of complications from breast-augmentation surgery. He closed the shop that very day and sent us our severance pay by messenger. His wife wouldn't even allow him to go to the funeral.

My grandmother, who grudgingly fed and sheltered me when I was a teenager and showed less interest in my development than she might a lodger who paid for room and board, suddenly wanted me to stay close to home when it was time for me to go to college. My grandfather, Malcolm, was recovering from a stroke and Jean had decided he might 'go' at any time. I had been good for nothing up until then but now she saw a purpose for me—widow's companion.

I had been a bookish student at school but my grades weren't good enough to get me to Oxbridge, so I settled for Merton College just up the road. I enrolled in Art and Design, the only course that was vaguely appealing, but could have chosen Leisure and Tourism or Gardening and Horticulture or Musical Instrument Repair. It was that kind of place. Later, when the inevitable question came, I could always say I was 'sent up to Merton' and everyone would assume I meant the distinguished Oxford College.

My parsimonious grandmother miraculously agreed to pay for an extra course I took in town in secretarial studies. It was tedious enough until the gruff old cross-eyed bastard who supervised our speed-typing lessons got run over by a Robertson's jam truck one morning outside the Morden pub on Central Road, having dropped in for a bracing pint before another challenging hour with our perky little group of aspiring real-estate agency receptionists. We collected a few pounds for a wreath but none of us felt inclined to attend the funeral in Clapham.

In the end, there were no secretarial positions in small businesses in Morden anyway, all of them filled by wives who came in to help their husbands struggle through. I found myself a badly paid sales job in a discount bookshop on Crown Lane where I spent three years reading my way through my own personal degree course in English literature, five novels a week on average. I gobbled them up, everything from *Tristram Shandy* to *Trainspotting*. I might have stayed there longer, except that our smiling manager retired, only to be replaced by Jay Stockdale, known as Jay the Weed, a randy creep with oily dreadlocks who used to pin me against the boxes of books in the basement and breathe into my face with his rancid pot-breath and try to put his hands in my bra. I wasn't sad when he fell from a ladder and fatally collided with the hard metal edge of the CONTEMPORARY FICTION: K–Z shelf, fissuring his skull. The local constabulary questioned me for hours about Jay's drug habits, and they did it unpleasantly, as if I were the mystery supplier of the wad of hash they found in his back pocket. They brought in a thug from the CIB who called me 'girlie' and took gobs of wax out of his ear with a matchstick. I've never liked the police since.

When the fuss died down I found a job in South Wimbledon

as nanny to little Elisabeth Westbrook, the sweetest baby on earth, and I spent five happy months with her, cradling her in my arms and crooning 'Poor Baby Bunting', the one nursery rhyme my mother had sung me, and listening to her gurgle as I pushed her pram back and forth over a rock under a tree in the pocket-sized garden. But her father spoiled it all the day he drank too much chardonnay and plummeted from the sundeck, nearly taking me and Elisabeth with him. The police came again and the mother blamed me. Needless to say, I didn't leave with a reference, although the disaster was hardly my fault. I still miss Elisabeth.

That's when I took stock. I was smart and wasn't unpresentable, but I was twenty-three and still living with a grandmother who called me names like 'lazybones'. Now without a job, I'd lie on my bed and read all day, or go to the park when the grumblings at home became too loud. I wasn't antisocial, I had friends, but I couldn't ever take them to the house at Netley Gardens. My grandmother had predicted a dull, stupid life for me and I was proving her right.

One day one of the girls who'd been in my secretarial course announced she was leaving for New York because there were lots of jobs there, they loved the British, practically fell at our feet when we opened our mouths. When I told my grandmother I had saved some money and was leaving for America, instead of the expected outburst she just folded her arms and said, 'Good riddance.'

My friend was right. Despite a dismal lack of references, I was an attractive commodity in New York because I was from London. (Well, near enough to Big Ben for Americans, who have no sense of geography.) I could put on a jolly good accent, which compensated for everything else about me. Most of my early jobs involved answering phones, where my (to my ears) tortuously fake posh accent could be used to prestigious effect.

I shared a minuscule Carmine Street apartment for a while with a debutante-type whose name I'd learnt from someone with whom I'd shared a tiny table at Tea and Sympathy, the Greenwich Village tea-shop where all the ex-pats flocked for Yorkshire pud and Bird's custard. She didn't like the look of me, I could tell, until I mentioned I had been to Merton and then she perked up. She was out every night anyway and left me cheery messages such as GARBAGE OUT! DEFROST FRIDGE! and IN HAMPTONS FOR WEEKEND! After a couple of months she cocktail-partied her way into her dream job on a fashion magazine and dumped me and Carmine Street for a more fashionable address on Avenue A.

I found a cheap one-room apartment on 83rd and York. To supplement my income I babysat for a professional couple who lived a few blocks away. She was an entertainment lawyer and he was something at Morgan Stanley and their rambunctious twin three-year-old boys never saw their parents. I always took over in the evenings from an exhausted Caribbean nanny and left when the parents came home from work at ten or thereafter. As it eventuated, the mother had negotiated the terms of Aaron's book contract and knew he was looking for an assistant, so when I mentioned that I was looking for a day job, she thought of him immediately.

Of course, I didn't go to Aaron as a babysitter, but it ended up that way.

What living person has not heard of Aaron Karsner? Not only could his songs be heard in the rarefied atmosphere of the theatre but on film and on television, as the theme music for sitcoms or in commercials for recreational vehicles and for airlines that promised superior in-flight comforts and prettier flight attendants. There were documentaries about him and conservatories named after him and, even in Morden, he had his own section in the local music store. I was so terrified of meeting him I almost didn't make the call.

But he sounded kindly and I was relieved. He didn't sound frail or doddery at all, as the entertainment lawyer had led me to believe. She told me that Aaron hadn't written a new lyric for a decade. He had dried up. He was a dead leaf that hadn't yet lost grip of the tree. I wasn't too sure I wanted to be the one to shake it.

But, when I met him, he jumped up from his chair, showed me around his enormous apartment and bombarded me with questions about London and the theatre and books I had read. I was the one who felt doddery afterwards. He ran hoops around me.

He was fit. He told me he walked in Central Park every day. He ate and drank moderately. He didn't smoke. His only sin was the occasional pinch of snuff. I thought that quaint.

Of course, this was well before either of us met Berenger, who managed to age him more in one year than nature had done in the preceding eighty.

Aaron hired me on the spot. He didn't seem fussed about immigration status. He knew someone who would fix that. I tried to give him as much information about myself as I dared, but he brushed it away.

'I know when I can trust someone,' he said.

And so I began the daily hike from 83rd across Central Park to Aaron's apartment in the San Remo on Central Park West and 75th Street. A great gothic pile, the building looms over Central Park like a Gotham City version of a Greek temple, a seventeen-storey limestone and terracotta monolith complete with ten-storey shafts on top crowned by colonnaded towers and copper lanterns at its pinnacle.

I had never been in anything like it. Aaron had moved into his eleventh floor, eleven-room park-view apartment in 1948 and wasn't to budge until Berenger prized him out of there fifty years later. I spent my first week wandering through the maze of rooms marvelling at the audacity of them, the elaborate carpets, the walls hung with important paintings and photographs of illustrious people and the haphazard mess of books and manuscripts thrown about the place like scattered cushions in a harem. The view over Central Park stopped my heart. It was spring then and the foliage of the tallest trees had underskirts of pastel blossom. Aaron never went out on the balcony, but I threw the doors open whenever I could and drank it all in. I don't care what anyone says about New York air, from the eleventh floor of the San Remo it's like perfumed silk.

My job was to transcribe the hour-long tapes Aaron would make religiously each night for his memoirs. This would take me until midday and then I'd deliver the transcripts to him and he would call me back at about two to go over the revisions. We were often interrupted by people calling to pay their respects but mostly we were alone, except for Aaron's housekeeper, Frances, a good-hearted Irishwoman with hair the colour of pale marmalade, and a talent for baking the puddings and cakes that were the only things I missed from across the Atlantic.

It was almost perfect. I felt like I was part of a small family for the first time in my life. Frances would knit me gloves and make me soup when I had a cold. Aaron would give me books and pour me a 'nightcap' before I set off home. He began to include me in the decision-making about personal things in his life. What gift should he buy for Lilian's birthday? What was my opinion of that new score someone had sent him? How could he graciously decline an invitation to a certain dinner party? He was the first person I'd known who had acted as if they believed I was possessed of sensitivity and taste. I was flattered.

But he was not without his moods. Some mornings he would be irritable and, as the hour approached for his afternoon nap, which he generally took at four, he would seem distracted and agitated. Several times he snapped at me and I quickly learnt to stay out of sight at these times. When he awoke he was unfailingly energetic and expansive and it was easy to forgive him his ill-humour.

I once summoned the courage to ask him why he had hired me.

'I find your naivety refreshing,' he said.

I took it as a compliment.

The memoirs progressed slowly. After six months we had

reached only as far as Aaron's teenage years, as he had the habit of changing his story over and over again to accommodate different estimations of himself.

'Oh, I sound too sensible there,' he would say. 'Let's make me into more of a *rascal*.' And he'd remember an incident where he threw a brick at a tenement window or stole a ride on the back of an ice-cart or ran away from home and slept under the Brooklyn Bridge all night. I knew he was fashioning his story the way my great-aunt in Kennington made bridal gowns—a nip here, a tuck there, a need to let out the fullness in some other place. It is the kind of revision every life can use.

Aaron was a great man, a genius, and yet I held my own with him. He would occasionally chastise me for the wrong spelling of names but he never once suggested in his manner or speech that I didn't belong by his side. He enjoyed my company, found the expressions that I used, such as 'queue' or 'flat out', unaccountably amusing. And he trusted me.

They say that if your house is burgled, no matter what you do afterwards, you can never get rid of the sense of being defiled. That's how I felt the day of Berenger's death, after the police had gone through my bedroom looking, I suppose, for drugs. I stood there, shaking, while they systematically tossed it. They pushed aside the magazines and records and video cassettes without even glancing at them. They paid no attention to the photographs I had stuck on the wall. They were looking for chemicals and needles and lengths of rubber tubing, not schoolgirl fantasies.

They searched the whole building, except for Aaron's study, out of respect—Alison's kitchen, my office, the sofas in the sitting room, even the soil of the potted trees in the hall. They bagged every bottle of pills they could find. They ran gloved fingers between the floorboards and under the mattresses and in the crevices on top of bookshelves, as if they were performing a furtive sexual act.

After the funeral, the three of us, and Lilian, who made daily pilgrimages, tiptoed around the loft as if it were a maiden who had been violated and we were the appalled parents. I couldn't sit in a chair without feeling I was doing irreparable damage to something intangible. My body felt as heavy as a wrecking-ball in a paper house. I could not work, I could not sit still, I could barely eat. At night, I was kept from sleeping by a sinuous curl of sound that wound its way like ribbons through my ears: Wake up. Niley. Hear me. Listen. Try.

Some days I felt I would go mad if I didn't escape. But it was just as bad outside. We were kept informed daily of the police investigation into Berenger's death, but there was nothing conclusive, which left the tabloids free to concoct elaborate scenarios of hatred and lust and scour the earth for garrulous acquaintances to fuel the fires of fiction. I couldn't pass a newsstand without a lurid detail from one of Aaron's divorces or some pious anti-drug comment from one of the AA modelling alumni leaping out at me. I had been lucky in escaping the scrutiny so far, but I wondered how long it would last. They'd already combed through Alison's celebrity-studded past (THREE STARS DIE IN BERENGER COOK'S CARE!) and were currently focusing on poor Helen Martin, a deranged fan who had twice broken into Berenger's old apartment in NoHo in search of souvenirs and was now serving a sentence in a psychiatric institution in New Jersey. (STALKER FREE ON NITE OF SUPERMODEL'S DEATH!)

Despite what they imagined, the press had not created Berenger. She had created them, to do her bidding. Where she beckoned, they would follow. They thought it was the other way around. But no-one who saw Berenger give an interview to a worshipful journalist or flick a little smile at a waiting paparazzo ever had any doubt. She took delight in seeing them drooling over her. And they were drooling now. How she would have loved it.

But I hated it. I had never got the knack of them, these scribblers who felt they were superior to everyone else because a cluster of tiny letters on a page of glossy paper or newsprint happened to spell out their names. Because a few choice words tapped out at night with a cigarette dangling from their mouths could undo presidents...or supermodels. What kind of meal would they make of me when they got round to it? I dreaded that day more than I dreaded anything.

I feared that I didn't have the resources to protect myself, short of disappearing off the face of the earth. I rarely answered the phone now, just screened the calls and wiped them off, but when I repeatedly didn't respond to callers, they'd find other ways to intrude on my life, like sending messages disguised in flamboyant arrangements of flowers or, in the case of one journalist, climbing up the fire escape and tapping on the window. A squad car was posted outside and the crowds had long gone but that didn't mean we weren't surveyed and speculated about twenty-four hours a day, not the least by the police.

I went out as little as I could, the hood of one of Berenger's sweatshirts over my head. As long as I was not identified exiting or entering the now-infamous Wooster Street building, I could pass invisibly out in the world. Or so I thought.

The shock of the cold air, followed by the warmth of a cup of tea, revived me each time. I tried three different cafes during the week of the funeral and no-one recognised me. I became more confident and started to think of ways I could become permanently invisible.

I scrunched myself into a corner in the front room of Lucky Strike, a cafe on Grand Street, turned my face away from the window and opened a copy of one of the free weekly newspapers, flipping quickly through a self-proclaimed 'definitive' version of Berenger's death. Even in the headline they'd got it wrong—BERENGER'S DOWNWARD SPIRAL INTO DRUGS AND DESPAIR—which didn't bode well for the other seven pages of the article.

I was turning to the travel section when someone pressed his body against the edge of my small table. I looked up, expecting to see the waiter.

'"Nile"—now that's an interesting name. Did I ever ask you about it?'

'Shit!' I cursed.

'Don't be like that. Can I sit down?'

I knew it was useless to say no. He'd do it anyway. I closed my eyes. I didn't want to look at his grinning face. I knew he'd be grinning.

Josh Gruen.

He would have been forgettable, except that his name was attached to an article that had run in the *New York Times* magazine about six months before and ever since then I'd noticed his by-line popping up in various publications on articles about models, rock stars, young actors and smacked-out writers who had turned their brief life stories into lucrative screenplays. He'd treated the interviews like therapy sessions, therapy for *him*, and we'd learnt more than we ever needed to about Josh Gruen's financial woes and sexual insecurities in the course of his stories.

After Berenger's marriage to Aaron, the *New York Times* magazine had sent Josh to follow her from show to show, to count the number of cigarettes she smoked and the lines of cocaine she snorted and—no doubt this was his secret brief—to snoop on her conversations with her husband in order to report the inside story on the bizarre marriage of the century.

Josh wasn't really a journalist, nothing so sleazy, he made that clear in all his stories, just an earnest, creative soul who'd written a bestselling novel about water-divining in Wisconsin, or something like that, which made him the perfect candidate for an assignment on a spoiled eighteen-year-old whose naked bottom appeared on the side of city buses all over the nation. He didn't look more than eighteen himself and I remember him telling Berenger, in his ingenuous way, that he didn't know anything about the fashion business but thought Berenger was awfully pretty and would like to hang out with her for a while.

Whenever he'd finished asking her the day's quota of charmingly loopy questions such as If You Were Stranded On A Desert

Island What Colour Nailpolish Would You Want To Have With You? he'd bail me up in the make-up tent or in the restaurant booth while she was distracted and present his hidden agenda: what was she *really* like? Is she really adopted? Does she know her true parents? Do she and Aaron have separate bedrooms? How much money did she make last year? Come on, she must be shooting smack to keep herself that skinny, all the girls are doing it? Is it true they inject it into their toes?

I'd supply the official version. Loyal as dogs, people like me were there to supply official versions.

The article when it appeared surprised no-one, least of all Berenger, I suspect—a sickeningly sermonising confirmation that God's In His Place and All's Right With the World, that teenage models are still stupid, that old men do embarrassing things, the moral being that Jimmy and Bobby-Jo Everyday are much better off hanging loose at the mall than swooping around the world in supersonic jets, commanding the best tables at fashionable night-clubs and getting to eat fried chicken at the White House, that a good education and an honest day's work are ethically superior to standing on a square of white paper all day, chainsmoking Marlboro Lights, swilling champagne and putting your head down the toilet after every meal to purge the three arugula leaves you just ate for supper.

The article made Josh Gruen's reputation. Certainly, after-wards, he seemed to have cornered the market on model interviews. I saw him backstage a few times, following some other hapless girl around. And I once overheard him saying into a microphone, 'Models are a hobby of mine.'

I sighed and opened my eyes again.

He was grinning. 'That's better.'

I considered him. He was short and wiry with a crop of curly hair the colour of Callard & Bowser toffee, which stood up from his ears like a swirl of shaving cream. He was wearing a chocolate-coloured knee-length leather coat, the collar of which panned out flamboyantly across his narrow shoulders. A pair of granny glasses with amber lenses were perched on his freckled nose, obscuring the colour of his eyes. He looked like a refugee from Carnaby Street in 1965.

Josh pulled out a chair and it scraped against the tiles. I gritted my teeth. I had a cup of tea in front of me, or what passed for tea here, a wet bag with a dangling tag that read 'English Breakfast'. He motioned to the waiter for a beer. Then he extracted a small leather case out of a pocket and offered me a cigar.

I didn't even bother to shake my head. What was New York coming to? When I'd first arrived three and a half years earlier, you had to tread carefully in the streets to avoid used condoms. Now it was cigar butts.

The waiter brought Josh's beer and, I thought, sneered at the cigar. He was probably the last artist–waiter remaining in SoHo.

Josh took a couple of puffs of the cigar and then smashed it out in an ashtray on the table beside us.

I didn't say anything.

He leaned forward. 'So, what happened?' he asked me as if he were inquiring about nothing more than a missed appointment. 'Did she kill herself?'

I stared at my fingernails. I hadn't thought to change the nailpolish in the past week or so. Some of the black had peeled off in shards, like paint from a weathered fence.

'Oh, come on, Nile. We're old friends.'

I scraped at a thumbnail.

'OK. Be that way. I'll tell you what I know and then you'll feel so grateful you'll tell me what you know.'

I kept scraping.

'They haven't released the Medical Examiner's report, but unofficially they're saying she died of postural asphyxia, which means she took so many drugs when she fell asleep she couldn't move her head off the pillow. She had six different active intoxicants in her system, including cocaine, MDMA, alcohol, Rohypnol and Sanorex, a slimming drug. Can you believe that? A slimming drug! Now, given that you were her babysitter—'

'Look, Josh, whatever your name is—'

'Yes?' He folded his arms on the table in front of him and looked at me eagerly.

'Leave me alone.'

'I can't.'

'Why not?'

'I am indefatigable.'

'I don't want to talk about it.'

'It might help to open up.'

'Since when have you been a therapist?'

'I'm only trying to help.'

'Help yourself you mean. Are they going to pay you thousands to come up with another character assassination?'

'You're mad at me about that story I wrote.' It was a statement, but there was a hint of surprise in it.

'You made Aaron look like a fool.' I glared at him.

Josh held my gaze. 'It wasn't me who made him look like a fool. He went a long way towards doing that himself.'

'You don't understand anything.'

'Then explain it to me.'

'No.'

'I'm going to write something whether you talk to me or not. So let's stop playing this game. Is it about money? How much do you want?' He picked a packet of Sweet 'n' Low out of the sugar jar and tore a corner off it.

I was about to protest and then I thought, if I set a price, he'll go away.

'Twenty thousand dollars,' I said.

He turned the Sweet 'n' Low packet upside down. 'Maybe.'

'Maybe?'

'Maybe there are people who will pay that. But I don't work for those kinds of people.'

'I wouldn't talk to you for fifty thousand,' I said, rebuffed.

'Why not? The tabloids have already done their worst. The whole of America thinks she was a drug-crazed bisexual from outer space. What more can I do?

I watched as he carefully poured the grains of powder into a smooth circle that was slightly ovoid in one corner.

'Damn!' He threw down the empty packet and put his finger through the sugar, messing it. 'Giotto could make a perfect circle every time.'

'With Sweet 'n' Low?'

'You know, I did it once. It was beautiful. You couldn't see where I'd begun and where I'd ended.'

Just like me.

We looked at his sugar scrawl for a while. I could swear it formed a 'B'.

'Look, Nile,' he said. 'I just want to know some answers. Help me out, will you?'

'Why should I?'

'Because if you don't I'll draw my own conclusions.'

'Go ahead, then.'

'OK.' He folded his arms and leaned back in his chair. 'Conclusion one: Berenger did not leave a suicide note, therefore she didn't kill herself.'

'She could barely write.'

He ignored me. 'Conclusion two: death appears to have been hastened by a lethal mix of chemical substances, therefore her death was not natural. Conclusion three: her personal assistant, after discovering the body, didn't call the cops for half an hour, therefore she was covering up something—'

'Wait a minute—'

'Conclusion four: Berenger's rumoured not-to-be-ex-boyfriend gets arrested on some small-time possession charge, therefore the cops need an excuse to haul him, therefore he's our number-one suspect. What else? Oh, yeah. Conclusion five: the circumstances of the death are vague, therefore the media have licence to invent whatever stories they like. Conclusion six: you are sitting with a young writer of scrupulous ethics who writes for a dignified magazine intent on publishing the truth and who is about to pay for your cup of tea, therefore you should give him an exclusive interview about your life with Berenger and what you know about her death.' He stretched his arms and inter-locked his fingers behind his neck. 'Convinced?'

'I don't see how I can help you,' I lied. 'I was just her personal assistant.'

'Don't give me that. You went everywhere with her. You made all her arrangements. You sat next to her for hours on planes. You probably wiped her butt whenever she needed it. She must have confided in you.'

'Well, she didn't.'

'Not good enough. I'm convinced you're the clue to this, Nile. And I'm going to keep buying you cups of tea until you give in.'

He signalled the waiter.

'Please,' I said, weary of all the badgering. 'I'm just not that interesting.'

He turned back to me and gave me a salacious look. He didn't have to say anything. I knew what he was thinking: it's the plain ones you've got to watch.

I got rid of him by promising to meet him at Lucky Strike the same time the next day. I said I'd think about talking to him.

Not bloody likely.

I knew I had to get out of SoHo. I told myself it wouldn't be forever. It would be just until…but my mind staggered at the 'until'? Until what? I couldn't bear the hope and the threat in the word.

I ordered another tea and the Last Artist–Waiter smiled effusively at me. He'd worked out who I was. I could see the girls behind the bar casting glances at me. I buried myself in the real estate listings of the *Village Voice*.

I didn't want to share again but I couldn't afford even $1000 a month for 350 square feet in a fourth-floor walk-up on Delancey Street, a relative bargain. I wanted less than that, and more. My eyes kept straying to advertisements for apartments on the Lower East Side and Chinatown. My *heart* kept straying there. But they were all $3000-a-month factory floors or shares with non-smoking vegetarian tattoo artists who were seeking room-mates with 'tolerance'. All my tolerance had gone down that rattling conveyor belt with Berenger's body.

I scanned the Shares section three times. Pages of them. 'Pretty' prewar apartments. 'Lovely' lofts. 'Beautiful' parlour floors. Busy, interesting people who wanted busy, interesting room-mates. No smokers, drunks, drug addicts, psychopaths or wallflowers who would mope around the house all day in their fluffy slippers. Well, that cut me out.

In America they call these places apartments, but in Britain we call them flats. By the time I'd finished with the real estate listings, flat is what I felt.

And then I spotted something that had possibilities, in the 'furnished rooms' section.

Magdalen House. Christian women's home. Clean, linen provided. No men, no smokers please. $147 per week incl. tax. Apply to 462 West 22nd Street...

I tore it out and got up to find a phone.

he next morning, I walked out of 89 Wooster Street carrying a backpack, nodded a greeting to the police officers drinking coffee in the resident kerbside squad car and strode to a place where I hoped they would never find me.

I didn't say goodbye, I didn't leave a forwarding address, which made me, I suppose, a sort of fugitive. I wasn't thinking of changing my life. I just wanted...time. I didn't want to be BERENGER P.A. any more. I didn't want to know what she knew.

Was it cruel to Aaron to leave without explanation? That morning I had watched him read the morning newspapers, which Lilian had censored with a marker pen, and then shut the door on him. I didn't intend to hurt him, I think I had already done that, but I couldn't implicate him in my flight. He had enough to bear.

I took only those things that would fit in a backpack, and layered trousers, skirts and jumpers under my coat. I didn't want anything of Berenger's, not a thing that had brushed her skin or been touched by her fingers or held in her vacant gaze. I was superstitious, the Celt coming out in me, and I held within me an ancient fear that the souls of dead people are linked to the things they owned in life, that spirits inhabit favourite armchairs and childhood toys and drinking mugs and if you happen to take possession of that object the spirit will take possession of you. I don't know if I got this story from some old crone at the

Morden pub when I was a child or from the fertile mind of some television writer, but I didn't want to take any chances. I thought in having nothing of Berenger's I was rid of her.

Idiot.

As I strode toward the subway, I caught sight of myself in the shining window of a clothing store. A dumpy little figure in a long coat and beanie. Mouse hair straggling out on to my collar. A round face that either scowled or sulked: a milkmaid with a sneer. Peasant eyebrows that ran together when I frowned. English complexion—good. English teeth—bad. The smile was nice, when I meant it. Pretty was not a word that came to mind. I was dour and stodgy and lacking in grace. I was Wednesday's Child, full of woe. My mother had sealed my fate when she dumped me on the world. Why couldn't she have waited a few more days? Bonny and blithe I could have done with. Fair of face too. Oh, how it would have been different if I had been fair of face.

Magdalen House was geographically only a mile or two away from SoHo, but stylistically it was the moon.

I stepped out of the taxi on 22nd Street and looked up at the facade. It was a handsome old townhouse, with a stoop, constructed of pink bricks and set back from the street as if the whole building were blushing. And blush it might—the house was the dowdy sister in a row of elegant residences with buffed brass door knockers and shiny windows sashed in velvet. I liked it straight away.

I humped my backpack up the stoop and pressed the bell. The heavy old door buzzed open and I entered a small, shabby foyer with a cluster of cane chairs around a coffee table and a dusty rubber plant in a Chinese pot at the bottom of a flight of curving stairs. There was a reception hutch with pigeonholes behind it but whoever had buzzed me in was nowhere to be seen.

I stood at the desk and waited. It was covered in neat stacks of pamphlets. Menus from local restaurants. Discount theatre tickets for *Phantom of the Opera*. A flier for a warehouse sample sale, two weeks out of date. A photocopied picture of a rabbit with some mechanical contraption affixed to its skull, exhorting concerned citizens to attend a 'Cruelty Free Rally' outside the offices of a beauty magazine uptown.

I remembered those animal liberationists, the way they would target Berenger, wait for her outside film premieres or fashion shows, toting buckets of red paint and placards of skinned mink carcasses, the way they would shriek abuse and raise their fists and try to douse her with paint, which would inevitably end up on me and the security guards, while Berenger glided by, immaculate.

I didn't blame them. They felt betrayed by her. She had been their poster girl for a while, rather going naked than wear fur. If she wasn't the most eloquent of spokesmodels, her body was, posed on the sides of buses and pasted on walls all over the world. And then she changed her mind. She agreed to model for the famous Milanese furrier Fendi and, after a barrage of criticism, professed she didn't know the company made fur, thought the furry things she wore down the runway were made of cotton or nylon, fakes. As the world listened incredulously, she hardened her stance, wearing extravagant fur collars in public wherever possible. 'I didn't, like, strangle the little things with my own hands, did I?' was her grouchy justification whenever asked. 'It's not like killing your pet or anything. They don't have names.'

'That's one of Bernadette's little projects,' a husky voice said suddenly. I looked up to see that a tall woman with shoulders like a football player had appeared behind the desk. She held out a big hand. 'I'm Sister Pansy,' she smiled.

'Sister Pansy?' I was dumbfounded. She didn't look like a nun to me. She had hard lacquered hair and thick streaks of creamy blue eyeshadow across her lids and powdered-down beige lips. She was wearing a clinging jersey dress in a dazzling abstract print. She looked more like Jacqueline Susann than Julie Andrews.

'Terrible, isn't it?' she laughed. 'But all the best ones were taken. Marigold. Jasmine. Delphinium. Rose. We're named after flowers. Don't know why I didn't join an order whose sisters are named after precious stones. My real name's Beryl, you see.'

'That's nice,' I said limply, although Beryl seemed just as bad to me.

'No, it isn't. I *despised* it. I changed my name to Amber as soon as I got out of the clutches of my pious old mother. It worked better for my career. There I was, Liquid Amber, up on the theatre marquee.'

'You were an actress before...'

'Before I became a bride of Christ? No, honey, I was an exotic dancer. And you know what? I still don't think it was such a bad gig. I mean, I was glorifying the body God gave me, wasn't I? But I don't say that too loudly around here. Sister Impatiens is a bit of a prude.' She raised an eyebrow. 'I'm shocking you, aren't I? Don't worry, we're all reformed around here. Reformed hookers, reformed thieves, there's even a reformed nun! That's my little joke. She was actually an Episcopal nun and she changed sides. Said we had more fun.'

'How many nuns are here?'

'Oh, only about six or seven of us. We live next door, in the house with the wisteria vine. *Much* nicer than here. The mother ship's in Connecticut, a huge old mansion, chandeliers in every room, even the bathrooms. You have to say this for the Catholic church, we really know how to live it up. Have you checked out some of the jewels those bishops get to wear? I mean!'

She tapped an inch-long flamingo-pink fingernail on the side of her cheek. 'Now, you're the girl who called about the room, aren't you? I can tell by your accent. You haven't been here before? You look familiar. Where are you from?'

'Liverpool,' I lied.

'Like the Beatles, you mean? Can you sing?'

'Me? No.'

'That's a pity. We could use some good voices.'

'For the choir?'

'God, no.' But she didn't elaborate further.

'What do you do for a living?'

'I'm a secretary.'

'Oh? I haven't heard that word in *ages*. They're all executive assistants or P.A.'s these days, aren't they? That's admirably old-fashioned of you. Sister Forsythia will be pleased. She's got a bee in her wimple about feminists. If she had a wimple, that is. Who do you secretary for?'

'I'm looking right now. I just left my job.'

'Why? Sexual harassment?' She looked excited at the prospect.

'No, my employer died.'

'Oh, how awful.' She peered at me. 'Say—I know who you are!'

I looked at her in horror.

'You're that girl in the newspapers.'

'Please don't say anything.'

'Why would I do that? I bet you've suffered enough. I love the *Star*, don't you? I think there's a small picture of you some-where around here.' She started rummaging around underneath the counter and pulled out a stack of newspapers. 'Let's see. Oh, yes.'

She pushed the front page of the *Enquirer* at me. There I was, looking shifty, coming out of the door of the Wooster Street loft. Judging by the crowd captured in the edges of the frame, it was taken two weeks before, the afternoon of Berenger's death, when I had slipped out of the building to see Addam. The photograph was arranged in a collage with a larger snap of Aaron taken at the funeral and a picture of Berenger with a champagne bottle in her hand at a party. LOVERS' TRIANGLE? the headline bleated. Jesus. How did they come up with these things? It was never a triangle.

I averted my eyes. 'Put it away, please.'

'I understand.' Pansy briskly folded it in two. 'I tear up photographs of me these days. Now, tell me, do you need a job?'

'If you're worried about the money—'

'Why would I worry about that? The church is loaded. And we aren't exactly crawling with guests. Most modern girls don't want to stay in a fuddy-duddy place like this where you can't smoke and booze and you have to sneak your boyfriends in through the laneway. There *is* a gate out there, you know.'

'I don't have a boyfriend.'

She gave me a disappointed frown. 'Oh, well...Down to business, then.' She opened a ledger and started flipping through it. 'You know, it just so happens that our biggest room is available. Now, of course, there are other people who have priority but none of them is here right now. It would be easier all round if we could pop you right into it. You'll get some dirty looks, of course, when they find out. Are you game?'

'Really, I don't mind a small room,' I said. And I didn't. I wanted the plainest, dingiest, smallest room they had. It was penance for what I had done, what I had become.

'And that's why I'm giving it to you! I can't stand people who *demand*. When you get to know the others, you'll see what I mean.'

'How many rooms are there?'

'Eleven. Four on the second floor. Four on the third and three on the fourth. The room I'm giving you is at the front, second floor. The heater clangs a bit but it's cooler in summer. Are you staying that long?'

'I don't know. Possibly.'

'Well, you can pay by the month or the week. If you pay by the month, you have to give us a month's notice. By the week, a week's notice. There are absolutely no men allowed in the rooms, although, frankly, I would turn the other cheek if it were up to me. No smoking, no alcohol, no cooking. There's a maid service once a week, just to vacuum and dust. There's a laundry in the basement, coin-operated. Does it sound boring enough?'

'It does,' I smiled.

'Good, then let's go look.' She unhooked a key from a board behind her.

'Room two. This way,' she said, heading for the stairs.

'And, oh,' she said brightly as she placed a size-ten heel on the bottom step. 'We have a resident ghost. That doesn't bother you does it?'

'No,' I said. 'I don't believe in ghosts.'

Sister Pansy showed me to Room Two, which she called the 'antique' room.

The single bed in one corner was little more than a cot, regulation-issue narrow, with an etched-glass mirror hanging from a chain over it and, below that, a tiny wooden crucifix. There was no bathroom, just a long walk down a dank hall that smelled of synthetic lemon. There was minimal furniture in the room and most of it was scarred with age. A green vinyl reclining chair was placed in front of a small table which had an old television set on it.

'I don't know if that thing works,' Sister Pansy said.

'It's all right,' I said. 'I don't want to watch television.'

'There's a big cinema complex around the corner, then. I bet you like going to movies. If you're ever looking for someone to go with, check with me. If it's got Bruce Willis in it, I'm your girl. Anyway, if you want anything, just yell.' She put her hand on the old doorknob. 'By the way, I should warn you—the animal liberationist, Bernadette, lives next door. If you've got any fur, I'd be careful when you wear it. I still can't get the gum out of my fox jacket.'

'I don't have any furs,' I said. 'I live a very plain life.'

'Well, then, you should be the nun!' she laughed, and was gone.

I went to the window and yanked aside the heavy cotton curtains, which were printed with stylised scenes of Roman soldiers on horseback, carrying spears. The window was an old-fashioned casement type, grimy with dust. The street was quiet, lined with leafless grey trees. An old woman, hunched over so that her torso was almost parallel to the street, dragged a loaded shopping cart down the block and stopped to talk to an elderly man who was sweeping the pavement outside one of the town-houses across the road.

Good, I thought. Nuns, spinsters, old people: no-one could possibly guess that I would be here. It was the dullest street on Manhattan. Everything I needed was within a few blocks... almost everything. I knew Sister Pansy wouldn't tell. She was the kind of woman who liked a secret. I'd keep a low profile and wait for all the ill winds to blow over, which they surely must. My life would be simple again, free of moral compromise. I could reclaim myself.

As I moved my hand to close the curtain, I caught sight of something shimmering in the stark branches of a tree. I rubbed some of the grime off the window pane with my forearm to have a clearer view. For a fleeting moment I thought I glimpsed a little girl, sitting on a branch, swinging her legs. I saw a white arm, bleached as an old bone, and long hair trailing like dead mistletoe. Strange, I thought, for a girl to have climbed so high. And then I took in the sparkling blue of her dress, the dainty little shoes on her feet. A sense of dread came over me, as if someone had laid a heavy hand on my shoulder. I was unable to move, my eyes fixed on the tree. And then, as quickly as she appeared, she was gone. I was staring at a plastic supermarket bag caught on a branch and ruffling in the breeze. As I stood there, slowly compre-hending, the little old lady dragging her shopping cart looked up at me and gave a start. From the way she scurried off down the street I could tell she thought she was looking at a ghost.

In the week after I arrived at Magdalen House I didn't venture far. I kept the curtains drawn and slept for the first two days and nights, only occasionally woken by the clanging of the old steam heater as it kicked in when the temperature dropped to freezing. I had been designated a thin acrylic blanket and a pillow as hard as a stack of wet newspapers but still I slept. I hugged myself tight with my sturdy arms as if I were embracing oblivion.

Outside the periphery of my seized-up brain there were noises. Rapping on the door. Cars honking in the street. Music coming through the walls. Bitter rain on the windowsill... tapping on the panes. But still I slept.

My sleep was heavy and peaceful, uncluttered by dreams. But I finally awoke to the pain of bereavement, to a world that seemed grey and morbid and without hope, the murky negative of the albescent life I lived, for a fleeting moment, when I first worked with Aaron.

In the days after that I'd get dressed and sit in the grimy window, staring at the eventless street, invaded by the sound of Berenger's mean little voice:

'Oh, did I hurt your feelings? I didn't mean to. I'm sure you're very attractive. To someone.'

'You're mine now.'

'I knew he didn't really go for you. He doesn't look at you that way. People were laughing.'

'Who's that frump?'

I thought they were just the slicks of old conversations long washed away, skid marks and smears that would fade with time. The longer I kept living the longer she would be dead. It was the best reason to go on.

I rallied, and started venturing into the street, a block at a time. I'd pull my knitted cap down over my head and the collar of my coat up around my neck and skulk around the neighbourhood, mostly in search of food and mostly at night. I craved the comfort foods of my uncomfortable childhood, sweet, creamy, milky things like tapioca pudding and baked caramel custard, yeasty, mushy, sugar-glazed things like sticky buns and soft apple turnovers. It wasn't the most challenging of tasks. I was living in a country of adult-sized babies still seeking the breast who needed to keep their mouths occupied with wads of soft food. Every second store front was a treasure trove of grease and fat and sugar. Pizzas melting with stringy mozzarella. Burgers smothered in mayonnaise. Chewy bagels smeared with peaks of cream cheese. Twinkies and Little Debbys and tubs of Haagen Daaz. I didn't have much of a figure to begin with; there was something liberating about watching it slowly disappear for good.

I'd bring my shopping back to my room and fish the plastic tubs of carbohydrate from their brown paper bags, free them from the clumps of paper napkins and plastic cutlery and paper-covered plastic drinking straws, and spread everything out on the threadbare rug, like a Turkish feast, except instead of olives and smoked eggplant and fragrant lamb, there would be yellowing creamed rice with nutmeg on top, crusty, cold, orange-coloured macaroni cheese and jelly ('Jello') swirled with toothpaste-white cream out of a can. It was all delicious.

I grew to like the austerity of my room—the dingy aluminium lamp that gave off a tea-coloured light and was screwed, lopsided, into the wall above my bed, the crusty windowsill shedding dirty paint like bark, the bookcase held up by cinderblocks and its dozen tired paperbacks, the narrow rust-painted wardrobe with the door that wouldn't close and the half-scraped-off magazine page of David Cassidy shellacked to the side of the dresser. I was phoneless, laptopless, fashionless and free.

I'd hung my sheer blue dress, two long skirts and one jacket in the wardrobe and arranged my extra pair of boots underneath them. I'd lie on the bed and admire them hanging there, behind the unshuttable wardrobe door. My few other things, some underwear, a big sweater, some shirts, I'd managed to fit into the top drawer of the dresser. I felt proud that I had so little. The less...*stuff* I had, the more whole a person I would become.

I wasn't penniless, although my savings had virtually vanished since I began to work for Berenger. She never carried money and so I was always reaching into my pocket. I didn't always remember to get reimbursed. But when I peeled off the lump of cash for Sister Pansy, one month's rent in advance, I smiled because it was my money, not Aaron's or Berenger's or that of some Japanese account executive who handed over to us thick envelopes of $500 bills.

Sister Pansy had looked at me curiously as I handed her the wad of fifty-dollar notes.

'Well, I have to say, you're the first customer I've had who actually seems *glad* to be parting with money.'

'That's because I want to pay,' I replied. 'I want to pay for everything.'

'Confession is cheaper,' she advised.

At the end of the first week, I ventured out by day. I avoided those places where I might have been known. The 26th Street flea markets where Berenger sometimes dragged me on Sundays. Pier 57 where the photographic studios were. Barnes & Noble, where she'd autographed her beauty book. Twilo, where some magazine had thrown a party for her and she never even turned up. The art galleries down the street which were crowded with fashion types on weekends. That restaurant in an old parking lot, where she'd thrown a martini at a startled young waiter and then proceeded to lick it off him.

Instead, I hid myself in the cinema, with a tub of popcorn soaked in butter-substitute. I wrapped myself in scarves and sat in the park on Tenth Avenue with the other derelicts. I went as far as Strand Books, where I huddled amongst the shelves in the basement until I became dizzy with disconnecting words.

I became bolder in the second week. I uncovered my face,

and scoffed fried dough at the Twin Donut with its pink tables in full of view of Ninth Avenue. I walked down Fifth Avenue to Washington Square and up Eighth Avenue to the old flower market. I bought a tiny tree fern from the garden centre and put it in my window with the curtains boldly opened wide. I went into Old Navy and bought a sweatshirt with a hood.

I tried as best I could to avoid meeting people, although Sister Pansy kept trying to introduce me to some of my fellow lodgers. I'd always say hello and then walk away. They seemed to accept my coolness good-naturedly: I was British, I was an eccentric. I didn't know if the police were looking for me or if they had lost interest. I glimpsed the tabloids at the checkout at D'Agostino but they seemed to have lost interest too.

I should have been relieved, but instead I felt vaguely insulted. I didn't want the scrutiny of the police or the press or that smart-arse Josh Gruen, but I didn't want to be yesterday's fish-and-chip paper either. Having printed my picture, the newspapers had taken my soul—and then pulped it. The knowledge made me feel more forlorn than I had before.

One day, soon after, as I was walking along 23rd Street, I caught a glimpse of myself in the window of Haagen Daaz. Every part of me that used to suggest 'female'—the lumpy hips, the heavy thighs, the swelling breasts—was being merged into a single smooth ovoid, like the Goodyear blimp that billowed overhead on fine days. But it didn't disturb me. I wanted to be round. Being thin was sleeping with the enemy and I had done too much of that.

A poster advertising a new icecream flavour caught my eye and I stopped suddenly. The person behind me ran smack into the back of me, catching my long skirt in their foot. There was an almighty yelp as I stepped on the paw of a dog whose lead had looped around my ankle. I bent down to make sure the pup was all right and I realised it was Astor the Wonder Dog, a miniature schnauzer of my acquaintance, and attached to him at the end of his lead was his human, Darien the Wonder Model, who was looking down at me from her great height with her mouth wide open in an exaggerated *haute couture* interpretation of Munch's *The Scream*.

'Nileeee,' she shrieked and heads turned. (But she was used to that.) 'Ohmygod!' She yanked Astor up in the air by his lead and kicked him behind her like he was a scrunched-up Coke can littering the sidewalk. 'I caaaaan't fucking believe it!'

I could. I knew I would run into one of them one day. But I counted on them being too myopic to see me, or to ignore me if they did. After all, I couldn't get them twelve-day bookings in Mustique with Mario Testino or this year's Versace campaign with Avedon. I no longer knew the name of a good psychic or a hot new trainer. Whatever interest Darien Apps had in me should have died with Berenger.

The first time I laid eyes on Darien she was standing in the middle of a crowded tent in high heels but nothing else, one hand archly on one naked hip, the other hand raised and gesturing aggressively at her lurid thatch of dyed red pubic hair.

'Publish *this*, you fucker!' she was shrieking at a photographer who had his camera poised to flash. 'I *daaaaare* you!' It was explained to me later that the photographer was from a magazine that had recently trashed a whole photo shoot featuring Darien because she wasn't 'sexy' enough.

I remember being absolutely flabbergasted at Darien's concentration-camp body, at the goosefleshy texture of the skin, its grey colour, and the tiny purple spider-veins that ran up and down the back of her legs. She had an angry appendix scar below her stomach and a rash of freckles on her sunken chest.

But, then, she was my first naked model. I soon became

accustomed to the hairy forearms, the jutting hipbones, the pimply cheeks and the rippling stretch marks—startling imperfections so easily disguised by a designer outfit or a make-up artist's brush or, when all else failed, the careful dabblings in Photoshop by an attentive hand.

I thought, more than once, of the unfairness of it all, how freaky girls like Darien didn't have to be beautiful in real life to be beautiful in photographs or under tons of make-up on the runway. The only reason you'd give Darien a second glance on the street was because she was so spectacularly *ugly* and yet, here she was, a paradigm of 'modern' beauty, and all because some woman-hating photographer had concocted a fantasy in his head that women with jawlines like Easter Island monoliths were 'fabulous' this year.

The accolade 'fabulous' was the 'whatever' of the fashion world, a deliberately nonspecific standard that need never be explained, the secret Mason handshake that only the initiated understood. And who were these initiated? No potent and impressive brotherhood of maguses, I can tell you, but a scrawny bunch of girls my age in pale pink lipstick and a seedy group of middle-aged men with lenses between their legs. 'Fashion' beauty was the kind that never gave you anything back. It never put its arms around you or stroked your hair. And you never wanted to reciprocate. You never wanted to touch it back, like you might have wanted to reach out and touch Greta Garbo, or any of the kinetic, intelligent beauties of the screen. A magazine beauty was as flat as the paper she was printed on. She was a four-colour process, that was all.

But there she was, the girl who won *Esquire* magazine's year-end Living Skeleton Award an unprecedented three times, beaming down at me as if I were the casting director for Christian Dior.

'My God! You look a wreck!' Darien grabbed my arm and then bent forward in that ridiculous ritual of making kissing sounds against each of my ears, especially as I knew she despised me. 'We'd heard you'd gone *underground*,' she whispered conspiratorially. 'Have the cops arrested you yet?'

'Look, Darien—'

'Oh, not that we think you did it! That's ridiculous! It just looks bad that you wouldn't talk to any of the newspapers. Particularly when everyone else did.'

'I noticed.'

'You did? Did you see the *Star* last week? They ran that old Skrebneski of me in a bikini. The whole thing's like totally cheesy but do you know what the circulation is? The agency's having a *fit* of course because "It's ruining your upscale profile blah blah blah" but I say *fuck 'em*! I'm sick of being an old couture hag anyway and a bit of sleaze never hurt anyone in this country. I told the agency, "So long as I didn't kill the bitch, what's the worry?" Anyway, my booker went *white*. I think the old cow actually thinks I did do it! That'd be a laugh!'

'Darien, could we just move off the street a bit?' A crowd was gathering.

'What? Oh, sure. What about a coffee at Twin Donut?'

I didn't seem to have any choice in the matter as Darien clutched at my arm and dragged me and Astor the Wonder Dog two doors down into the diner with its big windows onto Ninth Avenue. She grabbed a table near the counter and waved me on to the seat opposite her.

The guy behind the counter started yelling at her to get the dog out of there, but Darien just flapped her wrist at him and said something that sounded like 'Oh, foofoofoof!' Immediately, she spilled the contents of her carpet bag all over the counter and was scrambling through the debris looking for something. She pounced on a beaten-up softpack of Marlboro Lights, shook it frantically and snatched a cigarette, thrusting it between her teeth. She rummaged some more and then whirled herself around so that she was facing the few other customers, mostly men, nursing coffees in booths.

She managed to project her voice even though her teeth were still firmly clenched on the cigarette.

'Well, how do you like that? Not a fucking gentleman among 'em! You miserable pack a jerks!'

'Darien!' I hissed, thinking I was about to witness a bunch of rednecks rise from their seats and beat Darien to death with chains. But only one of them looked up from his cup, like a startled rabbit.

'Oh, foof!' She swung back towards me and spat her cigarette out. It landed on top of a ziplock bag of dope she had made no effort to hide. 'Doesn't anyone fucking smoke anymore?'

'Not in here, Miss,' said the guy behind the counter who had been watching her closely. 'You're gonna have to leave if you wanna smoke.'

Darien made a growling sound. 'I can smoke anywhere I fucking like, Mr Donut Man. Because I am a *super*model. You hear? A *super*model. And you wouldn't have a fucking business if we *super*models didn't come in here once in a while and eat your crummy donuts.'

'Take a hike, lady.' The counterman was expressionless.

'Foofoofoof to you!' She waved her arms above her head like a child trying to scare a yard of chickens.

'Let's go somewhere else, Darien,' I said, knowing full well that somewhere else it would be the same.

'No way!' she said emphatically. And then, in a stage whisper, 'Don't worry. He knows me.'

Sure enough, the guy came back, silently placing a powdery donut in front of each of us before he moved off to take another order.

'You *seeeee*,' she gloated. 'You got to come out with us *super*-models more often…Oh, sorry, I forgot.' She looked sheepish. It was the first time I had ever seen her look sheepish. It only lasted for a second—she started shoving the donut into her mouth in one piece, powder settling all over her chin and down the front of her pale blue cashmere coat. I watched this performance in astonishment: she sucked the donut down like an anaconda might devour a live goat.

She pointed at my donut, while her mouth was still full with hers. I shook my head quickly. She grabbed it greedily with her hands, tore it to shreds, the dark jelly squelching between her fingers, the powder flying all over the counter and then bent down to place it in front of the Wonder Dog, who snuffled the whole thing in a few slurps.

How Darien kept her figure, if figure was what you called it, was beyond me. More than once I thought of that kid's game, Pickup Sticks, when I looked at her. She was all bone, ligament, tendons, connecting tissue. There was no flesh. Even her lips were thin. In fact, I would have considered her exceedingly ugly, especially with that long, oval face and that slightly bug-eyed stare, except that Berenger once set me straight: 'Oh, she's plain as poop, but she's *so* couture!' If being 'couture' meant looking like a wire coathanger, then I could see why Darien was so in demand. She was a collection of angles. Even her hipbones (there were no hips) jutted out like something to which you might hitch a horse.

Darien sucked the jam off her fingers and started shovelling the spilled contents of her purse back into it. A tube of something rolled on to the floor, but she ignored it.

'I still think it was a bad move, Niley, running away like that.'

'I didn't run away.'

'Well, it looked bad. Just the other day I heard two fags arguing about you. "Oh, it was the assistant," says one. "No it was the drugs," says the other. "Give up, girlfriend, I know for A Fact it was the assistant. The bitch had a real jealousy problem, you know?" And blah blah blah. You can't imagine what they're saying.'

'What else are they saying?'

'Oh, I can't be bothered filling you in on all *that*,' she answered infuriatingly. 'I've gotta go. Gotta catch a plane to Miami in the morning. But I just wanted to say to you—get yourself a publicist. Here.' She dragged out one of her model composites, rescued a purple marker pen from her bag and scrawled a number across a full-length photograph of herself with her hands circling her tiny waist. 'Call mine. Peggy. Of course, she's too major league for you, but she's sure to know someone. You could make yourself a fortune selling your side of the story to one of the papers. Heaven knows, everyone else did!'

'I don't have a side to tell,' I protested.

'Bullshit! Everyone's got a side to tell. And they're telling it!' She reached down and untangled Astor the Wonder Dog's lead from around the chair. 'Come on, genius. Mamma's got a plane to catch. And—' she looked up at me with a big grin—'a boy to fuck.' She waved boldly at the counter guy. 'Bye, Mr Donut Man!' He was standing with his arms crossed over his big gut but I could perceive the hint of a smile lurking amongst all those chins.

Naturally, she didn't leave any money and didn't intend to, so I scrambled for my wallet and paid at the register. Darien sailed out the door with Astor tugging at the lead, but when I caught up with her outside she was suddenly stony-faced.

'I know you don't approve of me,' she frowned. 'But who the fuck are you? I didn't have a fucking friend in this business 'cept Berenger. And then she goes and leaves me behind. The bitch *owes* me. That's why I sold those fucking pictures. So don't you go getting all superior on me for it. It was you who fucking pushed her over the edge. Don't think I don't know it. I was watching you. You *betrayed* her, you little slut.'

She wound Astor's lead around her fist so tightly she almost choked him. The tendons in her long neck strained like white string. She'd had her sugar hit and now she was ready to let fly. 'You're just damn lucky I didn't tell the cops,' she snarled. 'Not that I give a fuck about you. But I don't think it's any of their business. Don't think you're going to get away with it. If there's any fucking justice in this world, Berenger's going to come back and haunt you to your grave. C'mon, Wonderboy.'

She jerked at his Gucci collar and was off at a giraffe's stride down the avenue, head in the air, before I could say anything.

arien's swift and merciless appearance almost undid me. I was the wallpaper no-one notices until it starts peeling off in strips. I was trying to patch myself together but people kept coming up to me and tearing off corners. Erik, Josh, now Darien. I wasn't sure how long I could hold together.

I should have stayed in my room after that. I should have sat on my bed with a stack of books and waited out the months. My food could be delivered. This was New York after all.

But I couldn't stay still. My stomach felt like a cave full of moths. That night I paced my tiny room, back and forth over the threadbare rug. I couldn't quieten the voices. *It was you who fucking pushed her over the edge. When he's fucking them he's thinking of me. I've done a terrible disservice to you, Nile. Don't look at me like that. I did a bad thing to you.*

I must have fallen asleep eventually. When I woke up it was just dawn. The cold winter light washed the room a faded blue. I got up on my knees and pushed the curtain aside to see what kind of day it was.

There, etched into the grime and dust on the dirty window pane was the word 'Berenger'. I stared at it, confused. I couldn't remember doing it, but I must have scrawled it during the night. And then my intestines curdled. The word had been written backwards.

Which meant it had been written from the outside.

I never intended to walk to the subway and get on the C train the next morning. I found myself in a carriage crammed with people in dark coats before I even became fully aware of what I had done. As we jerked from stop to stop I thought of staying on the train and seeing where it took me, but I got off at 72nd Street at the last minute.

It wasn't far from there to the San Remo. I stood across Central Park West looking up at Aaron's apartment. Something white fluttered on the balcony, a curtain from an open window perhaps. Was someone up there?

It was cold and I couldn't stand there forever, looking for a past I could never reclaim. Reluctantly I turned my back and drifted eastward across the park. I formulated the vague intention of spending a few hours in the Metropolitan Museum, consoling myself with things that were undoubtably dead, like the Egyptian mummies or the spirit of nineteenth-century romanticism. But instead my feet took me right across the park, across Fifth Avenue, past the bastions of art to the bastions of commerce on Madison Avenue. It was an act of masochism but I was powerless to stop myself.

I hated that smart street. The women in their furs and winter tans, the braided doormen with their obsequious smiles, the merchandise that mocked my size and my isolation from the ranks of the rich. I hated the big emporia the most, the granite buildings as frosty as cold storage, with hatchet-faced sales attendants standing impassive as butchers, at counters like marble dissecting tables; men and women with wrists as thin as boning knives and stringy sheep's membranes for lips—behind them, the slabs of black silk suits and sides of sanguine gowns strung heavily on racks like so many carcasses of beef.

Whenever Berenger dragged me on shopping excursions, I'd stay in the car, inventing important phone calls that needed my attention. Occasionally I would have to go in search of her when she didn't return in the designated time. As I fought my way through the hawkers spritzing perfume and pushing miracle skin creams, I always felt like Jesus with the money-lenders in the temple, cursed with the overwhelming urge to smash their stupid displays and scatter their evil merchandise to the four corners.

But I was still vulnerable to their poisonous overtures, so when I drifted into Barneys on this day, like a zombie answering a shaman's drumbeat, and a woman approached me for a 'complimentary make-over', I allowed her to lead me like a lamb to a stool, push me down on it, and drape my shabby coat with a protective white cloth.

Picture me sitting there, the matted sleeves of my brown wool coat pushed up, while the saleswoman applied slashes of colour to the smooth underside of my forearms, demonstrating the options before she painted my eyelids and cheeks, running the pads of her fingers along the palettes of shadow and then along my arm in stripes, gripping my wrist, with those rainbow talons, like a store detective taking in a resisting knicker-thief for questioning. When she first did this, I did in fact panic, thinking she was going to cite me for some fashion-code violation—the pilled black sweater, for instance, or the failed experiment with chalky red lipstick. I began to relax only when the robotic sales pitch started up. The Latest Shade. You Must Try. It Looks Wonderful. Special Offer. I knew this stuff by heart. The threat of menace turned merely patronising. Patronising I can deal with. I have had enough practice.

I'd lose the pink eyes if I were you.

What?

You look like a rabbit.

I shook my head to clear the static.

'Something wrong?' asked the saleswoman indifferently.

'No...I...'

And that's when Berenger's feet materialised. Those pretty shoes that had to be cut off with shears. Then the ankles thin and bleached as dry twigs and the little bony mesas of knee, connected by calf-bones brittle as driftwood.

I didn't know what I was seeing at first. I thought something was wrong with my eyes, that I had been staring down at the hairs on my arm too long, the streaks of red and pink, and when I looked up the imprint of them was still on my retina, like that scene in the Hitchcock film when Gregory Peck's mind flashes back to a skiing accident after he sees the mark from the tines of a fork on a tablecloth. I turned my eyes away, blinked, and then looked up again.

Our grotesque heroine was perched on the woman's shoulders, the stringy ghostly legs draped like sweater sleeves down her washboard chest. My mind did not instantly register 'Berenger' but I knew something very bad was happening. There was the tinkling sound of laughter ricocheting inside my skull. There was that little voice. *Niley*. There was the expression on the saleswoman's face as she registered the alarm on mine.

'What is it?' the woman asked.

If I had a thought then it was: I don't want to see this. But my eyes involuntarily travelled up above the saleswoman's frowning face. It was like sitting through the gory bits in a movie—your brow is cupped in your hand, your eyes averted, but despite yourself you find yourself peeking, always at the very worst moment. My uncontrollable curiosity had led me to view throats cut ear to ear oozing curtains of plasma, slashed wombs gaping disembowelled foetuses that resolutely sucked their thumbs, shrunken heads with protruding eyes, corpses dissected neatly in two, eyes gouged, brains frying like eggs on hot black bitumen and now, most horrible of all, Berenger's miserly, bloodless face.

She was using the saleswoman's head for a prop, her right cheek resting in her right palm, the other hand casually plucking at the wretched woman's hair without, I noticed, disturbing any of it. At first I thought, I'm not mad, it's just an apparition, it's the lingering image from those bus-side jeans advertisements, where she rides the thick neck of that poor, tortured cowboy, tangling her fingers in his hair and laughing with a generosity she never had in life. (They widened her tight little mouth on computer, painted the sparkle into her eyes.) It was just a photograph. I had not had enough sleep and my mind was randomly associating.

But if it was an advertisement I was looking at, why was it kicking its legs and making fizzing noises?

'Is there something wrong?' the saleswoman repeated, dropping my arm now she suddenly realised she was demonstrating her exorbitant make-up to a bag lady.

Something wrong? echoed this thing that might or might not have been Berenger, curling a sickly lip in a face that was bleached as an old shell. Her eyes were milky and unfathomable, slimy as oysters, her hair a writhing seaweed of light. It was impossible to look away.

I began to feel the breath go out of me. It was like this monster was sucking the sound out of every living creature, the mewling noises out of babies' throats, the hiss rising up from the gossiping lunchers in the store's swish restaurant downstairs, my own thin voice out of my gaping mouth. Not only could I make no sound myself but I could see the curlicues of other sounds rushing past me, as if I were swimming in a deep ocean, buffeted by shrieking currents.

It was no apparition. I thought I'd rid myself of Berenger and yet here she was.

I think you should sit down, you know. The voice appeared to come from Berenger, even though she didn't open her mouth. It was sharp, panicked, not sympathetic. I was suffocating in sound, the thud of my heart as it strained against my chest barely distinguishable from the hiss of the bile that rose to my throat.

I felt myself drop to the floor.

Get a doctor! A customer is down! She was speaking under water, the voice deepening and breaking up into choppy waves until it became a soft roar. There was scuffling and the sound of stools being moved.

Come this way, Miss. I sensed firm hands on my shoulders and pressure against my back and everything went inky, there was the sudden hard flash of revolving glass and I was on the street, crouched on the edge of the gutter, spewing gritty vomit onto the greasy tyre of a stationary black stretch limousine.

'I'll call you a taxi, Miss,' said a voice that was no longer Berenger's. I looked up. A dark-suited security guard towered above me.

She's dead, I repeated to myself, feeling pedestrians give me a wide berth. What I have seen here is the lingering imprint of a soul long sold to the devil. She can't hurt me. She can no longer manipulate me. She cannot take from me what I have.

I managed to sit up, spat, and felt better.

I wiped my mouth with my technicolour forearm and looked curiously at the tyre. Green bile was splashed all over it. Berenger was the acid at the pit of my stomach and now it was all over Madison Avenue. Which seemed entirely appropriate. I struggled shakily to my feet, not one passer-by apparently feeling the obligation to assist a female who was not wearing a mink. There was a man in a braided coat hovering, but I shrugged him away. I didn't want to gratify any phoney shows of kindness. He just wanted me banished from in front of his windows. (Puke and ponyskin do not go.)

I steadied myself and trudged down to the subway station, raw but purged. A panhandler dressed as a court jester cheerily accosted me on my descent. I gave him the brush-off and then felt guilty. We fools should stick together.

It didn't take long for the feeling of dread to envelop me again. On the train downtown, I stared at the carriage windows, at the names and scatological words scratched into the dirt. The angry capitals echoing the reverse BERENGER I had discovered that morning on my own window now unnerved me more. Was it possible Berenger herself had written it with those skeletal fingers? I pulled my vomit-splashed coat around me and closed my eyes hard, trying to banish her horrible face from my consciousness. But, even with my mind closed against her, she invaded me, not only those ghastly white eyes, that snarling mouth, but the metallic echo of her little voice, and the cloying cloud of 'Eau de Berenger' that had filled the air at Barneys. There it was again, that stink of synthetic flowers…I opened my eyes wide in shock to find a lavishly perfumed blonde woman edging away from me to another part of the car.

On the cross-town bus I put my head against the cool glass and watched 23rd Street glide past. Every now and then a remnant of Berenger—a bus-shelter poster, a fifth-storey billboard, a restaurant where she liked to eat—slid by. I had steeled myself against these images before, but today I felt incapable. It was if I had unlocked the cover of a secret diary and the pages were fluttering open for all to see.

I must have slipped into a kind of trance. The bus hit a bump and I awoke with a start, just in time to catch a glimpse of wild, dark hair and a ghostly face moving with the crowds on the street. The spectre drifted out of sight and I leapt up from my seat and pulled the cord. I had to know if she was following me. I pushed my way off the bus and on to the street, searching frantically. And then I saw her ahead, the mass of brown hair bobbing as she turned into Seventh Avenue. I ran to catch up with her. She looked sideways at me and scowled. Her face was pitted with acne scars.

I stood and watched the girl go, her long coat flapping at her ankles, her ropy hair flying. She was not Berenger, but Berenger had spawned her just the same. The girl had created herself in Berenger's image, craving her 'look'. She had painted her skin white and her lips crimson, grown her hair long, and starved herself to achieve the required pallor. There were thousands just like her in this city, countless more around the world. They wafted down the avenues and emerged from subway stations with huge eyes and haunted, hungry looks.

Berenger's wraiths, I called them.

Berenger was known as The Wraith long before I met her, long before she rose from her death bed and came like this to haunt me.

She had a way with her, up there on the catwalk, that set her apart. She would appear at the top of the runway like a startled creature caught in headlights or a nervous child at a recital pushed on stage by an unseen hand. There would be a moment of hesitation and then she would start walking, not big strides towards the end of the platform where the important editors sat, but a kind of walk that would meander everywhere, often right to the edges of the runway, as if she were in some kind of trouble—some trance from which waking was not assured. Often she would come perilously close to falling right off it and indeed once she did, tumbling into the elegant lap of American *Vogue*'s European editor-at-large, a mishap which made the front page of newspapers all over the world. (Naturally, she had planned it all along.)

Up there, her long dark hair flying around her head like tumbleweed, her emerald eyes smudged with some make-up artist's interpretation of a week-old black eye, she was a figure straight from the Bronte sisters' moors, the poor mad wife in the battlements, the wilful beauty standing on a cliff, trailing wisps of fabric like lost hope.

In life, she played the spectral thing to the hilt. No wonder she was so good at it when she died.

This was one of those fortnights in fashion history when crushed and broken females were in favour, when every women's magazine you picked up featured editorials of models crumpled, like the dead, in doorways, on linoleum floors, in the trunks of cars or else propped up against unmade beds in seedy motels or bedsits, their eyes ringed with scorch marks of eyeshadow, the pupils dully staring, the limbs contorted, like discarded porcelain dolls or repertory Ophelias in some housing project update of *Hamlet*. These girls, most of them animated teenagers away from the camera, were required to be blank and motionless in front of it, and lie around in $3000 dresses in fake drug-induced comas, looking like they were waiting for an off-camera child molester to come and finish them off.

There were protests. One women's group managed, very publicly, to storm the offices of a high-circulation fashion magazine and hold a tumultuous press-conference by phone from the boardroom it had usurped, crying foul at the depiction of teenage girls as junkies, whores, human debris. Another army of incensed mothers-of-teenage-daughters infiltrated the daytime talk shows and waved pages from fashion magazines at applauding audiences. A bus-shelter jeans campaign featuring fifteen-year-olds in sexual situations was systematically defaced by persons unknown, who signed their graffiti NO!LITA. And then a French fashion photographer of minor importance was arrested in Miami when it was discovered he had kept a naked twelve-year-old girl chained to the legs of a table in his darkroom for five days and his perversion instantly became emblematic of the whole fashion business.

When Berenger started modelling, at the age of fourteen, there was another, more famous, model who had already been scandalously launched upon the fashion world. She had been given by the press the name The Waif, for her forlorn expression and diminutive size. Like The Twig in an earlier generation, she was sweet and human-scale. (Although the humans she was on scale with were undeveloped nine-year-old girls.)

The Waif bore the brunt of the outrage. Naturally fragile and anaemic-looking, with those big doe eyes, she could pose as the perfect victim. Those torn-out pages from fashion magazines waved on television by irate mothers were almost always of her, shivering, arms crossed over bare breasts, in white cotton kiddie briefs. While they were waving pages their poster girl was earning millions a year.

Berenger's first agency saw her as a variation on this theme.

105

Little victim Berenger, beautiful but ravaged, a broken blossom, crushed eggshell, shattered crystal. The modern ideal of a young white female. It took her second agent, Erik Sklar, to distinguish that she was different, to discriminate the quality in her that made her...tough. She had the resilience of madness in the way she would stare at the camera, half-crazed, so that the viewer of her photographs would often have the uncomfortable feeling of being sucked right into the frame, of being pulled into the unfathomable vortex that was Berenger's tiny brain.

Erik refused all work for her that would pose her as vulnerable, taught her how to exaggerate her walk and pump up her pout, brought in the experts to dye her hair black and powder her skin white, engaged a photographer with a gothic turn of mind to make her a new composite—and launched her on the world as a fully fledged monster.

A fashion critic from the *New York Times* first drew the comparison. The Waif has a competitor, she announced, after Berenger's first big season in Paris. 'There is a new "It" girl on the scene, only fifteen years old, and fashion spectators can't get enough of her, the way she rambles down the runway, taking three times as long as any other model, and stops, dazed, in front of the photographers, while the other models pile up behind her. The young model Berenger's novel approach to walking the gamut is causing an amused buzz amongst the audience but much consternation backstage as more established models threaten to walk away from shows unless the new girl is cancelled.

'But,' the fashion critic continued, 'she is the most interesting thing to come out of a dull season and prominent designers are clamouring to sign her up for fall advertising campaigns.'

'She has a very fresh look, which we like very much,' a garrulous Karl Lagerfeld told the critic. 'Not this victim look at all. Very romantic, I would say. And a bit scary, you know, like she should be locked up in a mental asylum. It's very *dangerous*, very *modern*.'

'She is not a waif, exactly,' concluded the writer, 'but more of a *wraith*, a six-foot-tall, 120-pound, wild-eyed, haunting beauty. She might have a touch of madness in her eyes but everyone who looks at her gets dollar signs in theirs.'

And so, The Wraith she became.

omenica was hired by Magdalen House to clean our rooms once a week. *Clean* is probably too generous a word. She would strip the sheets off the bed and then do a rough approximation of remaking it, never tucking in the side that was pushed against the wall and more often than not putting on the pillowcase inside out. Her vacuuming technique resembled someone trying to chase a mouse with a stick. She had a few turkey feathers taped to a wand which she used to move the dust around on my bookcase. I would have been suspicious that she'd plucked those feathers herself if I could have imagined her doing anything so strenuous.

Following her 'housekeeping' session Domenica would sit on my bed and proceed to spill cigar ash down the front of her apron and on to my rug while she indulged in some therapeutic griping about our benevolent landladies. She would complain about Sister Forsythia's zealousness in keeping track of the cleaning supplies and Sister Impatiens' latest punishing schedule. After lighting her cigarillo, she always slapped her chunky thighs with the heels of her square hands and began her litany of grievances with a high-pitched Central American 'Eh?'

I listened, sometimes for half an hour. I listened because Domenica's shrill accounting of trivial insults and injuries sounded as beautiful to me as…one of Aaron's lyrics. I loved to hear about lost keys and spider veins and suspicious-looking bed linen, sticky with the stains not generally made by single celibate women. I loved the stories about blocked toilets and the non-appearance of window cleaners. The light-fittings that were impossible to reach and the furniture that broke your back. Domenica's words would always brush past me like a fragrant warm breeze. She talked about dishrags and frying fat and babies with the croup, elastic stockings, corrupt priests and the new Metro cards. Nowhere, in any of this, was there whining about the weather in Paris, the fit of a gown for the Academy Awards, the timing of a dinner party in Milan, the crowds at a nightclub, someone else's million-dollar contract, the lack of sparkle in a stone from Van Cleef and Arpels or respect shown by a dresser at a fitting, the unhappy ending of a 150-page novella it had taken six months to read.

When I came back that day from Barneys, jittery and desolate, I threw off my coat and lay on my bed, like a corpse in a pine box waiting for Judgment Day.

All right, Berenger, you win, I thought. I'm not going to spend my life wondering if you're following me or not. Come and get me. Come right through that door and scare me to death. I'm ready for you. Whatever you are, you're stronger than I am.

But it was Domenica who came through the door, dragging her upright Hoover.

'Ju OK?' She was startled when she saw me. 'Ju got hangover?'

'No,' I said quickly, fearing one of Domenica's headache remedies. 'Just tired.'

She nodded as if this made sense at two in the afternoon and emptied her apron pockets of rags and tins of furniture polish that had never seen the light of day, excavating a crumpled packet of cigarillos which she shook.

'Ju mind?' she asked and didn't wait for an answer before pushing my feet aside and collapsing on the end of the bed with a sigh.

'Eh!' groaned Domenica, getting comfortable. 'Is cold here.'

'It is?' I asked carefully. The heater was clanking away, but she was right. It was cold. A hoary coldness that tingled the fingers, spiked the tip of your nose.

'Sure thing,' she insisted jovially. 'Ju got draft?'

'I had the window open,' I lied.

'Why ju gonna go and do that? Is freezin' jor ass off out there.'

'I smelt something burning,' I improvised, as Domenica expertly clicked a Coca-cola lighter and sucked deeply on the fine brown stick. I looked back at her and saw that her head was veiled in a rising curtain of smoke. But there was no sign of Berenger, only Domenica sitting on the bed in her embroidered Mexican smock, a Panamanian scarf tied jauntily around her throat to disguise the creases in her neck she called her 'curse rings', and her gaily knitted Peruvian socks puddling around her ankles, exposing flesh-coloured cotton tights from Venezuela, all these—including the contraband Cuban cigarillos—gifts from sisters flung about Latin America, sisters who were, respectively, married to a diplomat, a plantation owner, a straw-hat manufacturer, someone known far and wide as The Guava King and a famous nightclub entrepreneur, while Domenica was stuck with a no-good lazy layabout bad-ass hypochondriac Americano who drew several fraudulent disability pensions each fortnight.

'Smoke,' she repeated, nodding her head sagely. 'Ju smell smoke? Is no smoke.'

'Well there might have been smoke,' I said defensively. 'It might have been you smoking in the corridor.'

Domenica looked horrified. 'Me? Eh! Smoke in the corridor? No way! Why ju think I sittin' here? That Sister Impatiens march me right out door and into Welfare!'

'Well, anyway, I smelt smoke and I opened the window. You really think it's cold in here?'

'Like Sister Pansy's titties!' Domenica thought this was funny and threw her hands in the air, sending a column of ash tumbling on to the floor. She considered the ash for a moment and then rubbed it into the rug with her foot.

'Domenica, do you believe in ghosts?'

'What ju mean?' She sounded offended.

'No, not the Holy Ghost, I know you believe in that.' I paused while Domenica crossed herself. 'But, you know, *angry* ghosts, vengeful spirits that come back to haunt you?'

'Haunt?'

'You know, seek revenge because, well, you've done something to them?'

'Ju crazy!'

'You think so? You think I'm crazy to believe in them?'

'Everybody believe in ghosts! Eh? I got ghost like ju can't imagine! Big, strong, *sexy* man, come every night and lie on top of me. Not that it do me no good! About as good as no-good layabout husband! Eh?' At this, Domenica looked crestfallen. She scratched her neck under the scarf and blinked at me. 'So ju got ghost.'

'What makes you think that?'

'Girl like you, should be talking of boyfriend, beauty parlour, new Madonna record'—she crossed herself quickly—'not crazy old man hangin' round bathroom.'

'What crazy old man?' She was frightening me.

'*Ghost!* Ghost who hang around young girls' bathroom! Ju seen him too. Number seven, she seen him last week. Sister Pansy chase him with Bible. Make terrible mess. Guess who has to clean? Little bits of glass from here to wazoo. Pickin' 'em out of bathmat for—'

'Hang on, hang on, hang on!' I resisted grabbing her and shaking her. 'Which ghost is this?'

'Sure thing! Dirty ol' man in bathroom, come for look at young girls' panties. Then dead nun in hallway, fourth floor. She come out of wallpaper, big stain on it like dog been there. Can't scrub it out for nothin'. I say to Sister Impatien', why ju want me to rub out dead nun? I get rid of stain, get rid of old lady. Then where she go? And Sister says to me, like she a saint or somethin', "She go to *heaven*, Domenica" and I say "Then why ain't she there now, Sister? What's so good about stain in the wall when ju could be up there feastin' with angels? Why hang round old boarding house when ju could be lyin' on a cloud doin' nothin'?" And Sister Impatien' say, "That's enough, Domenica" and I gotta go get the Fantastic again...Which ghost ju seen?'

'I didn't say—'

'Come on. Ju don't have to say nothin'. Ju look like...ju seen a ghost!' She guffawed at her own joke. The cigarillo had gone out: she stuffed it into her apron. 'I tell ju what. I fix him for you.' She wagged a finger at me. 'No trouble at all.'

I looked at her suspiciously. Domenica had, in the two weeks I'd been there, insisted she treat blisters on my heels with chilli oil and an aching back with poultices of banana skin. In her lexicon of healing, headaches were to be cured with little dolls placed in your shoes and heartaches with braided corn silk tied around your wrist. What remedy would she come up with for a ghost? The *wrong* ghost?

Domenica lifted herself up from the bed and moved towards the bedhead. 'Ju watch,' she said, as she grasped the bottom of the mirror and lifted it from the wall, turning it so that the paper-lined back faced the room. She rubbed her hands together and plopped back down on the mattress. 'Easy,' she grinned.

'That's it?' I asked.

'In this room, sure thing. No more ghost.'

Could it be this simple? 'What did you do?'

'Everybody know that death come through mirrors. I jus' make sure he can't.'

'I never heard of it!'

She smiled condescendingly. 'But ju a *heathen*.'

'Domenica,' I said urgently, 'Are you telling me that if I turn that mirror to the wall, the ghost can't come into the room?'

'Ju have any other mirrors?'

'Just one small one, in my bag. You think I should get rid of it?'

'No, no. Is not necessary. Jus' keep closed.' She made a gesture like a clamshell closing with her palms.

'So the ghost can only come into a room through a mirror? And if I keep all the mirrors closed or against the wall, it can't come and get me?'

'In here,' she said. 'But what ju gonna do about all those mirrors out there?' She waved a chubby paw at the window. 'Ju gonna break all the car mirrors and the store mirrors? Ghosts come in and out like this all the time. Ju can't change what God only can change. But ju keep this room nice and safe. Ju get rid of that mirror.' She stopped and rubbed her chin. 'I take if ju like.'

'But what about the ghost?'

'I'm not frightened of no ghost,' she shrugged. 'Maybe dirty old man come and lie on me too?'

I've always hated mirrors, hated looking at a reverse me. Looking at someone who, despite being much plainer than I'd ever admit I was, stares back with unshakable smugness. ('Don't we look haggard today?' she might ask, or 'Gone up another dress size, dear?')

The old mirror that Domenica had turned to the wall was relatively benign, I supposed, the speckled backing of the glass showing through in places like an explosion of galactic gases, concealing more than it revealed. You could look in this mirror and not see much, which was a blessing. It had a nice anthropomorphic vertical stretch, too, which turned my bumps into graceful, if blotchy, curves. I quite liked the mutant me in it— longer through the body, my face sprinkled with the gravel rash of mouldy silver foil, my hair a whorl of misty cloud rather than the usual bedraggled soup of string. In this mirror, I almost looked like a sprite carried in by a storybook tornado, a bug-eyed waif trailing rags in the snow...a pale spirit roaming the earth at night.

God help me.

Berenger had a special relationship with mirrors, never being able to pass a reflective object without striking a pose. She lingered in front of them, pouted into them, cocked her eyebrows and turned her hips. Sometimes I would catch her frowning, not at her own reflection, but at something beyond that, as if she were receiving a morse code from the other side and its interpretation eluded her.

How many times had I talked to Berenger's reflection in the mirror, while she was having her make-up done or checking her profile? Hundreds, thousands? I probably knew her likeness better than I knew her real self. Maybe in the end, her likeness *was* her real self. All that was left in the physical body was the ghost.

I told Domenica I didn't want her to take the mirror. She looked at me as if I was a fool. To appease her, I gave her a scarf I'd never liked. She brightened up and dragged the vacuum cleaner out into the hall with her, dropping some of the contents of my wastepaper basket on the carpet as she went.

When the door closed, I curled up in the corner of the bed where it met the wall and waited. If Domenica was wrong, Berenger would be back in no time to irritate me. If she was right, I could sleep the sleep of the dead—who, being ghosts already, cannot have haunted dreams.

Domenica was wrong.

'Hi.'

That's all it took, no dramatic slow fade-in. She was there, fully formed, between blinks of my eyelids. As casually as if we were girlfriends on a sleep-over confiding stories of true love.

'Well, don't look so pleased to see me.' She was actually smiling—little, pointed, milky fox's teeth, still too small for her mouth. 'I mean, you're hardly Miss Popularity. Stuck with talking to that old washerwoman all day.'

'Just tell me what I have to do to get rid of you,' I said more calmly than I felt, as if it were possible to negotiate with a phantom. Despite the control in my voice, my arms were goose-flesh. My heart was thumping. Even the hairs in my eyebrows prickled with static electricity.

It's just Berenger, I told myself. It's not some unknown terror. You know how to handle her.

Berenger popped a piece of ectoplasmic bubble gum. 'What makes you think I'm going anywhere? Like, it took me a lot of effort to get here.'

'To get here?' I asked incredulously. 'Why would you want to do that?'

'Beats me,' she said, looking around the room. 'What a dump!'

I suppose to anyone peering through the window, the scene would have looked perfectly normal. Berenger had alighted on the end of my bed, her legs reconstituted and gaily crossed, her chin resting perkily on her wrist. While I couldn't say that she was flesh, exactly, there seemed more of her than there was before, as if the artist who had begun to sketch her had hastened back and filled in more chalky details. She was still wearing what she died in: a mini-dress, fringed with sequins, stained bright red on the torso, under the breasts and over the belly. You could see the red stain even though her tangled hair, the outlines of her arms, the bony knees, the dainty little shoes, the details of her dress (blue in life) were all a cloudy white. Stains like that you can't get rid of, even in death.

It was just like old times, back in Berenger's bedroom, me taking her through her schedule for the day. Except, of course, that she had died almost four weeks before. This was a fact, unrefutable. I'd run my hands through her ashes, held her tiny bird bones in the palm of my hand.

'You are a figment of my imagination,' I said boldly. 'You are less than nothing. Just a part of my brain with a hiccup. A headache, that's all. I'll take an aspirin and you'll go away in the morning.'

My courage faded as quickly as it had come. I looked on,

appalled, as her eyes grew, like headlamps coming towards me. I scrambled into the corner of the bed, hitting the back of my head on the wall. 'Don't hurt me,' I begged her.

'Why would I want to do that?' she asked, her voice tinny as a bell.

I could think of a few reasons.

Fortunately, she didn't seem to expect an answer. Her attention span had not been improved in death. She rose from the bed and wafted over to the mirror Domenica had turned to the wall, tracing the back of it with one finger distractedly. I can't swear she floated, but I can't say she took any steps. 'Turn this thing around, will you?' she demanded.

'You mean you can't?'

'What do you think I am, a poltergeist? I want to look at myself. I want to see what's happened.' Her blood may have ceased pumping, but it seemed her vanity was alive and kicking.

'But...aren't you afraid of the mirror?'

'Why?'

'Won't you get sucked into it or something?'

'Oh, *that*. You listen to too many fat women.'

'So it's nothing to do with mirrors? You being here?'

'I don't know why I'm here!' She stamped her foot, like she always did. Except that this time she was not stamping it because a limo was too short or the clouds had drifted in when she wanted the sun. And, of course, there was no real foot there to stamp.

'You don't?' I wriggled from the corner of the bed where I had been cringing and threw my feet on the ground, wanting to get closer...but not wanting to. I was trembling so much the bed squeaked like a cornered mouse. Despite everything that had happened between us, I decided to go along with it. If it was my mind playing tricks I had nothing to fear.

'I don't understand this. It seems to me you are dead. You have been dead for more than three weeks. So where have you been? Hanging round some backstage dressing-room eaves-dropping on what they're saying about you?'

Her eyes flashed like light bouncing off glass. 'What are they saying about me?'

'That's more like it! Really, Berenger, I thought they might have improved you down there in hell, but I can see that you're as stupid, vain and paranoid as ever.' And, I thought, you can no longer fire me for saying it.

'Listen to me,' she said, 'There is only me and you. There is no-one else. I've never seen any stupid God or any stupid Devil. The only hell I know is this stinking room. If there's an Other Side, tell me how to get there. If you can't, shut up and turn the mirror around.'

I couldn't argue with that. As I waded across the room towards her, it occurred to me that turning the mirror around might be the cruellest thing I could do to her. After all, she had, as they say, lost her looks. The thing we are told to be most afraid of. Even those of us without many looks to lose. Of course, Berenger, at nineteen, had barely *found* hers, but they were all she had.

'Are you absolutely sure?' I asked. I was blindly groping around in my dark grab-bag of attitudes—meanness seemed to be the one I had clutched and brought out into the open air.

'Yes,' she nodded grimly.

So I turned the mirror.

She gasped.

She had lost her looks, all right. There was not a vestige of her in the mirror at all—not a single wavy line, not even a drift of mist of the sort that clings to gravestones in horror movies.

'I can't see myself! But I can see my arm when I do this!' she cried out, holding her hand in front of her face and examining it. 'And I can see my feet!' She looked down. 'And you can see me, can't you? You knew it was me!'

'I can see you perfectly. What there is of you to see.'

'Then tell me!' She was right in my face and I was suddenly shaking like a leaf that knows a hurricane is heading its way. 'Tell me what you see!'

When Berenger was alive—well, when she wasn't dead, or

undead, or whatever this creepy manifestation might be—
she was forever demanding that we ('we' being a great scattering
of people from those indentured in service to her to some
awestruck waiter who had happened to take her fancy while
he was flourishing the pepper grinder) tell her how beautiful
she was. She didn't fish for compliments, she *trawled* for them.
She might disguise it as a question about some new model or
the other ('What do you think about Lizzie Ward? Don't you
think she's pretty?') and woe betide the person who agreed
with her. You were supposed to say that Lizzie Ward had a wide
nose, or too much hip and that you couldn't understand what
had come over the Jil Sander people for giving her the whole
fall campaign, Lizzie Ward's ugly face wasn't going to sell a
single belt loop. And then you were to praise some campaign
that Berenger had just done, provided of course that it wasn't
one that she hated. Her ego was like an immense house full
of secret passages.

Standing in front of the old mirror then, she reminded me
of the Bad Queen in *Snow White*. Mirror mirror on the wall,
who is the fairest one of all? Funny, that we'd come round to
that again.

'Tell me.' It wasn't exactly a command. If I hadn't known
better, I might have thought the tone was imploring.

I am forever a coward. I could have told her that the peerless
skin had sunk into her face, pushing the outline of those praised
cheekbones upwards like the chalky shelves that run along some
ravines, that the bee-stung lips had shrunk away from the teeth,
that the slender nose was now bloated, thanks to the way she lay,
face down, in death, that her hair had been carefully combed by
an undertaker into last year's bouffant, rigid as brick around her
face but matted and wild at the back where she was enfolded in
satin on the ultimate Bad Hair Day. Her body seemed cobbled
together from bits of life, bits of death and bits of funeral parlour.
It did not make sense to me. But I was trying to make sense out
of the senseless.

But I didn't tell her any of this. Not from kindness but from dread. 'Look at it this way: they always *did* call you The Wraith...'

Brilliant.

t had grown dark before I realised it, but I didn't need any light. Berenger was still standing by the mirror, staring into it. The effect was the exactly the same as when you stare into a bald light bulb for several minutes. She was *seared* into my eyeballs.

I closed my lids tight and the image remained. To think that when I was a child I imagined things that glowed in the dark were wonderful.

We had both been silent a long time. (Perhaps two days had gone by, a week: what difference would it have made to my life anyway?) The effect of this was to lull me into the sensation that Berenger was something benign, like an architectural feature of a room—say, a broken sash on the window or a door off its hinges—that you mean to do something about but can never get up the energy to fix. Maybe if I could walk out into the corridor and down to the bathroom, she'd just hang there quietly.

'Don't do that!'

I nearly jumped out of my dehydrated, pitted, cellulite-positive skin. Somehow I had made my way to the door, reaching out for the higher of the three security chains, a gesture that Berenger apparently didn't like because she was a tidal wave once more, surging over her boundaries.

'Bloody hell!' was all I could hear myself saying as her radiation filled the room. She sent out flares like sunspots and I ducked. And then suddenly the burst of heat dulled as quickly as it came.

'Neat trick, hey?' She smiled like any teenager.

My mouth was still flapping like a fish on a deck. I reeled it in. 'Why did you do that?' I gasped. 'You could have blinded me!'

'Oh, I thought I was only, you know, a figment of your imagination,' she sneered.

I looked at my forearms. Some of the hairs had been singed, reduced to fuzzy bits of stubble that reminded me of a teddy bear I once owned that liked to take his tea and cakes a little too close to the electric heater.

'Bloody hell!' I said again. 'I thought you couldn't *do* anything! You couldn't move that mirror!'

'Heat I can do,' she grinned. 'Cold, too.'

'I was only going to the loo!' I chastised her.

'Don't do *that*,' she smiled, 'There's a loopy old man in there who tried to put his hand up my skirt.'

'What old man? There's no old man here!' God: Domenica's ghost. 'You can see other ghosts?'

'Oh, sure, lots of 'em,' she said, and then made a laughing sound, soft as a silver chain bracelet rattling. 'You always did believe everything I told you.'

I've never responded well to being mocked, even by a thing that isn't really there. I had the overwhelming urge—one I had suppressed for a year—to punch her smack in the middle of her jaw, the dimple beckoning me like a bullseye. But I'd never before punched a single thing and I didn't even know how to make a fist, so I instinctively tried the next best thing—to scratch her eyes out. I flung myself at her, across the room, and, as my fingernails clawed at her, I felt myself enter a clammy space, not warm, not cool, but *moist*. I went through her and out the other side. My arm tingled as if I had fallen asleep on it and developed pins and needles.

There I stood, with one arm in Berenger up to the elbow and the fingers of my other hand scratching at the back of her head.

This was closer to her than I'd ever intended to be. I pulled back in shock and shook my hands, willing the blood to start pumping again.

I looked at my reddening palms in amazement. Berenger wasn't solid of flesh, but there was still substance to her. I could feel her when my arm went through her. She wasn't just air. She wasn't a vacuum. She was less than a person, but more than my guilty imagination playing tricks on me. At that moment I understood something that made me shudder to my unbelieving toes: she was *real*.

'Why me?' I asked her, unable to halt the defeat creeping into my voice. 'I meant nothing to you.'

I was slumped on the floor, my back to the door, and she was doing some sort of hovering thing, her outlines softly pulsating like an electric angel on top of a Christmas tree.

'Oh, I tried everyone else,' she pouted. 'But they couldn't see me.'

'What do you mean?'

'I mean I did all this stuff—' She started shooting fireballs again and I cringed. 'And they didn't even *notice!*'

Despite myself, I was sympathetic. I know what it's like to be ignored. They call you a wallflower, but you always feel like a weed. 'But what about Aaron? I can't believe he didn't see you!' I thought about the broken man I'd closed the door on, crumpled in on himself.

'He looked right through me, the stupid old fool!'

I had to remind myself that I was talking to a pile of sparrow bones and ashes, sealed in a casket, some of which—the parts that weren't sprinkled by *Vogue* cover girls over the sea at Montauk—were kept in a crematorium at a Queens cemetery. Otherwise I would have killed her.

'What about Darien, then?'

'Look!' She scowled like Tinkerbell having a temper tantrum, minus the pompoms on her shoes. 'I tried *everyone*, all right! Even that stupid little haircutter with the bad skin—'

'Harry,' I reminded her.

'Harry, whatever,' she said crossly.

'Who else?'

'Carla, Anna, Nathan, Mario, Naomi, Karl, Erik, Walter, Lee, Patric, Kevyn, Stephen, Andre, John, Susan and Keith, Marc and Massimo, Helmut and Edward...' She was shouting with frustration by the time she finished reciting a list of the alumni of the fashion world, all of them her Very Best Friends.

'And you tried me *last*?'

Her eyes dimmed. 'Yes.'

'And I was the one who saw you,' I said more to myself than her.

'Yes.'

I closed my eyes and grimaced and my whole body groaned. What did I do to conjure her up when I thought I'd so permanently put her away? 'Please tell me I'm not stuck with you.'

She just stared at me, the uneasy stare of someone who has had the same realisation. Then, out of nowhere, she started wailing and the sound unfurled like a cheap effect from a third-rate werewolf movie, except in Berenger's case she sounded more like a *werehare* caught in a trap, a tinny, keening yowl. My first thought was, what will the neighbours think, knowing there was a rabid animal liberationist right next door who was always slipping pamphlets under my door, gruesomely illustrated with photographs of cute chimpanzees with vices attached to their skulls or lovable hamsters wearing globs of eyeshadow. 'I don't want to die!' she whined.

'Well, I've got news for you!' I snapped back.

'I don't want to die—and I'm not going to die!'

Had there ever been such self-delusion? 'Face it, you idiot!' I felt my nails digging into my palms. My neck was going to snap if I clenched the muscles any tighter. 'You are already D-E-A-D!'

'Oh, no I'm not!' Suddenly there was a tinkling lightness in her voice and the pointy teeth reappeared. She looked more sinister when she smiled. 'And you can't make me go away!' she crowed. 'You can't do anything! Because wherever I've been, I'm like—*back*!'

I don't know why I did it, but I jumped to my feet and grabbed a vase of half-dead tulips that had been sitting on the dresser for days. I tossed the contents—rubbery flowers and putrid water— at Berenger's grinning face, hoping, I suppose, that she'd melt like the Wicked Witch of the West when Dorothy threw the bucket of water at her. Instead, the foul-smelling mess splashed all over the floor and I was still looking at Berenger—and thinking about how I was going to explain the smell to Domenica. I thought too much about explaining myself to others, which is why I was alive and feeble and Berenger, who was dead, was charged-up like a nuclear reactor.

'You missed!' she jeered. She had obviously given up on the Poor Little Me angle: it only ever worked on men anyway, the corpulent, cigar-chomping cousins of lingerie manufacturers who would hang around on shoots, the preening, queeny boy bookers at the model agency who would run her dirty errands, the prissy, preppy journalists who would plead for her in print. The blue-eyed, self-infatuated pop icons who needed bruised beauty to bolster their torn-teeshirt fragility. The elegant, ancient geniuses who…If there was kindness in a man, Berenger could sniff it out, toy with it and turn it sour.

'Look.' I was madly thinking of something that would convince her to go away, trying to use all my powers of logic— ha!—with a *thing* that was entirely illogical. 'Surely it's nicer where you came from? The spiritual dimension? Floating around on clouds and going where you want without a heavy old body to tie you down—'

'*Heavy?*' she flashed. 'I was, like, never *heavy!*'

'You know what I mean. You can go where you want and it doesn't matter if there's a big fat banker with garlic breath sitting next to you on the Concorde or you got wasted the night before and have to spend all morning with your head down the toilet. No more getting stuck in traffic on your way to Heathrow. No more 5 a.m. calls. No more dieting and no more leg waxing. I bet there are no sick bags in the Twilight Zone! If I were you, I couldn't wait to get back there!'

'Well, you've got it all wrong!' She was extremely agitated. 'I can't tell you, Niley, how horrible it is out there!'

'What do you mean?' I asked carefully. I was still holding the vase in front of me like a weapon, but I couldn't deny I was fascinated.

'Well, the first thing I know,' she said confidentially, almost eagerly, like she was back at Veruka gossiping with the other juvenile delinquents, 'is that I'm in the Prada store...'

'Hold on a minute. You mean, you didn't feel yourself die?'

'That's what I'm telling you! It was all so ordinary. Like, you know, when you're really fucked up and you wake up and you don't know where you are? So, I just thought maybe I'd had a really good night, you know, and I'd woken up with the headache of death...'

'Funny about that.'

'...but it was all *wrong*. Like, what am I doing in an empty store? Me? Like without any security? Any fans? Any sales assistants sucking up to me?'

'At least your brain was working—it must have been working overtime to sort that one out.'

'I didn't sort it out until I looked in your mirror! Not really. I couldn't understand, at first, why the world was empty—there wasn't *anyone* at Chaos, can you believe it? Times Square and no people! The Bowery and no bums! And then I was at home, and there weren't any people, Alison wasn't in the kitchen, and I was mad for a moment—why weren't you all at work? And I stood in my room for the longest time just, like, looking at the bed.

'And then suddenly I was somewhere else and then somewhere else, like I was...a card in a pack being shuffled, or something. I went to all these places we'd been to before, so many

125

places I can't count them. Remember that market in Turin where they painted my feet blue?'

'Tunis,' I corrected her.

'Whatever. That big wall in China where the camel spat at me?'

Oh, yes, how could I forget that camel's finest hour?

'And those pointy rocks in that desert somewhere? That really high mountain? I went so many places! I saw palaces and cathedrals and walked on pink sand beaches. And it was all *boring*. As boring as when I went to all those places before. Except there weren't any cute boys to play with.'

I tried to ignore the raw infidelity that always made me fume. 'But you *did* see people? You saw Aaron. And Harry. And *me*?'

'That was the funny thing. I began to see that I...wasn't dreaming or having a bad trip. The thought just came to me, what if I'm dead? What if *everyone else* is dead? But there weren't any bodies piling up in the streets, you know, and if they had all been zapped, then where were the aliens?'

That B-grade brain had clearly not improved by being Embraced by the Light.

'And it was so cold, even in the deserts, even in the tropical rainforests. I could see the sun and the rising heat but they didn't warm me. And then, slowly, I started to feel this...current...of warmth, maybe not warmth, but like a warm breeze without the temperature. I knew it was warm and I knew it was running next to me like a ribbon, but I couldn't touch it. Sometimes it would come so close it almost brushed my skin, you know, even though I knew I didn't have skin now, not really. I could see the bones, and then they weren't even bones, just shapes of bones. And this breeze would like play with me, tease me, lick at me, wherever I went. I can't tell you how badly I wanted to grab hold of it! Like a lifeline! That's what it was—a lifeline!'

'And you did? You did find a way?' Despite myself, I had to know.

'Suddenly it blew really hot. I couldn't feel the heat, but I knew it was hot. And thicker. Thicker, like mud. And I was pulled into it and I was scared that I would melt. And then, you know, I was with Addam. Just like that. In a hotel room somewhere. London, I think.'

At Addam's name I gritted my teeth.

'And there were two girls there. *Little* girls. Like fifteen years old.' She said this with disgust, forgetting—or just omitting?— that she too was barely that when she first met him. 'But they weren't doing anything, you know? The girls were asleep, tucked up in the bed like children, the sheet folded high under their chins. It was sweet. And Addam—well, he's lying in the middle of the carpet, on his back, his arms and legs stretched right out like a star, but he's not asleep, he's just staring at the ceiling, at a small chandelier in the middle. At first I think he's off his face, but he's breathing easily, he's relaxed, like he's in a trance.

'"Addam?" I whisper to him, really gently, because by now I've worked out it might be frightening for me to appear like that. "Addam?" I'm so close to him, I can count the moles on his belly. He's got his teeshirt rolled up over his chest and he's wearing Stephen Sprouse jeans I've never seen on him before. You know, the really great ones with Warhol print? Anyway, he's unbuckled the belt and pushed the jeans down over his hips and I reach out to trace the line of black hairs where they disappear into his underpants—'

'Spare me the details.'

'There *are* no details!' Her eyes were like plates of glass. 'I can't feel him and he can't feel me! I am nothing to him! He doesn't know I am there and there's *nothing* I can do to make him see me! And I say, at last, "Oh, Addam, you must have loved me so much to call me back like this!" And just for that instant I know he hears me, he clenches his fists a fraction, his eyes go hard as rocks.

'And all of a sudden I'm thrown off him by a force like a bolt of lightning. I'm thrown on to the ceiling—kind of *into* the ceiling—like when you ride the Screamer at Coney Island. And then I'm out of there—like, *completely*...

'And everywhere else it's the same. I am shut out. The air around Aaron is…you know when you burn your hand on ice? Carla is so deep in meditation with her stupid yoga master she has no time for me. Darien's in therapy, blocking me out. Patrick just keeps taking the same picture over and over again and won't look up from his camera no matter what I do. And every time I get close to them, physically close to them, I'm stung with this heat that's like a lash, and I have to back off.

'And the rest of them—I can see them now. It's like seeing people is a language to be learnt. Like when you suddenly say '*une cafe creme, s'il vous plaît*' without thinking of it in American first, it just comes off the tip of your tongue? Suddenly I've, like, crossed over into the world and the people are back and I can walk among them and even though they can't see me I can see anyone I want! Did you know Mina's screwing Jean-Claude? I couldn't fucking *believe* it!'

Her eyes were shining really brightly then, like when she'd been out bingeing and had woken me up in the early morning with some drug-addled idea for redecorating the White House or getting the Dalai Lama to model for Versace.

'Was my funeral really wild?' she suddenly asked. 'Were there, like, *godzillions* of people?'

'Oh, weren't you there?' I asked, just to push one or two of those thousand hyper-sensitive buttons. I always sought refuge in wit when I was frightened out of my mind.

'I tell you—!'

'All right, all right! I get it! It was a private funeral, actually. Simple—but stylish. Aaron wanted it that way.'

'He *would*.' She sounded peeved.

'I suppose you would have liked something more festive? Well, I assure you, there were people dancing on your grave.'

Fortunately, this went over her ectoplasmic head. I didn't have the energy to duck any more fireballs. 'Was there lots of stuff in the papers about me? Did I get a, like, *People* cover?'

'I could probably dig up the odd five hundred articles, yes.

I'm sure they're still coming. The *Enquirer* has a new revelation each week.'

'About *what?*' She looked pleased.

'Trust me, if you had been alive, you would have enjoyed it.'

'Niley?' She was suddenly very quiet. 'Are you sure I'm really dead? Like, if I can't remember dying how can I be dead? I don't get it. Isn't someone supposed to meet you on the Other Side? A spirit guide or something?'

'Berenger, that's all just mumbo jumbo.'

'No, it isn't. It's what the book said,' she said petulantly, curling up a top lip that wasn't really there. I wondered, for a moment, where all that collagen went.

'Which book?' I asked her, thinking, I suppose, that she meant the Bible.

'The one Darien gave me!' she told me crossly as if it was the only book in the world.

That book. I remembered it well. What was it called? *Heavenly Creatures?* No—*Heavenly Visitors.* A book by a clairvoyant about the spirit world. All the models were reading it. Along with *The Celestine Prophecy. Talking to Heaven.* Oh, and the novelisation of 'Sabrina the Teenage Witch'.

'You see, Niley, everyone has a spirit guide. They're there to help you, like, adjust to the other life. They wait for you with open arms at the end of the tunnel of light. They take your hand and show you your life—and death. I've seen pictures of it. But where was my person? Why wasn't she there? Did she miss our appointment because she was, like, running late? Is she looking for me now?'

'Perhaps she can't find you until you go back up there— wherever that is,' I suggested hopefully.

'Don't you see, I can't! Do you think I want to be stuck here with you and your boring life? I want to be up there with Kurt Cobain and River Phoenix. Like, *partying.*'

I watched as her outline started to break up, like the interference in a television signal, bursts of static that shattered into tiny shards, reconnected, and then fractured again. I allowed myself to hope that she was about to leave me to resume her paranormal hitch-hiking, but she re-formed in front of my eyes a moment later, almost completely whole, except that her right arm was missing from the elbow down. 'You see,' she said, her eyes shining like silver coins.

I don't know how long we stayed like this, staring at each other in mutual dismay, she hovering above me like the Christmas star, me on the floor like a broken doll.

Eventually, a little voice spoke my name.

'Yes?'

'How did I die?'

The question startled me. 'What do you mean, how did you die?'

'I don't remember anything.'

'You don't?'

'I told you!'

'But you must have remembered something.' I tried to stop myself from shaking. Did she really not know?

'It's like I'm...blank.' She frowned, even though she didn't have a brow.

'What about the drugs?'

'What drugs?'

'You don't remember taking any?'

'No! What's the big deal about drugs?'

'Berenger, drugs probably killed you.'

'Probably?'

'You went unconscious and suffocated in your pillow.'

'I did? Cool!'

'You're sure you can't remember? Can you at least remember the party?'

'What party?'

'Where you wore that dress.'

She looked down. 'I died in this?'

'And you can't remember going to bed?' I swallowed hard.

'And if you were alone?'

'No…I got out of the elevator and…'

'And what?'

To my horror, she suddenly started to hyperventilate. *Uh, uh, uh.* I always hated it when she did this. The choking sounds would turn my stomach. In life, she could hold her breath until she went purple, then blue. Until she got her own way. In death, there was no colour to underscore the lack of oxygen, but her eyes were bulging, her fingers clawed at her airy neck, she had gone rigid with panic. And suddenly she was hanging from the ceiling, like a corpse at the end of a rope.

Uh, uh, uh.

I wildly looked around my room for a paper bag for her to blow into. I knew there was nothing there, not even one of those plastic supermarket bags that snag on everything. Domenica, who hoarded everything, had taken them with her.

Uh, uh, uh.

'Breathe into your hands!' I shouted at her from force of habit. I jumped up on the bed and lunged at her, my hands on her shoulders, where her shoulders should have been, shaking her. But of course there was nothing there, at least nothing you could touch. My hands went through her and I walked off the end of the cot, thudding heavily to the floor.

I sat there for a while. What was I thinking? She could hardly suffocate. She was dead. I threw my head back against the edge of the bed and suddenly laughed, an asylum cackle I hadn't heard from myself in a long time.

'Why are you laughing?' she whined from somewhere above my head. 'It's not funny being dead.'

'I'm sorry, I'm sorry.' I tried to calm down. 'It's just that I've never tried to save a ghost's life before.' I gave another involuntary snort and then looked quickly up at her to check if I'd offended. I could do without being barbecued again.

She wafted above me, her arms folded across her misty chest. The cloying smell of rotten roses was seeping from her fleshless skin, the stench of a grave her cremated body never saw. 'You've got no right to laugh at me. It's your fault that I'm dead.'

I swear even the hairs on my toes stood on end. 'I don't know what you mean,' I said slowly.

'Oh, yes you do.'

'I wasn't there, I swear.'

'You swear?'

'Yes. Absolutely. I wasn't there.'

'Well, that's my point, then. You should have been there. You were supposed to protect me. That's what I paid you for.' And then she came right at me, her arms outstretched, her fingers clawed, her teeth bared, her eyes like sharp tacks in their sockets. I flung an arm over my face to protect myself but it did no good. I could feel the bones of her small hands on my skull, crushing it. 'I hate you!'

'I didn't do anything!' I screamed.

'You didn't look after me! You were supposed to look after me! You let me die!'

'I didn't mean to! I didn't mean to!' I shouted back at her, my body rolled up in a ball. 'I didn't mean for you to die!'

'There's something you're not telling me.'

'No there isn't!' I sobbed into my sleeve.

'There is! You're hiding something. You have to tell me, Nile!' Her fingers dug into the bruised pulp of my brain. 'Tell me!'

'I don't want to!'

Her voice was little more than a whisper, reedy-thin. 'You can't hide it from me, Niley.'

'I'm not hiding anything,' I said weakly.

'I'll make you tell.'

'You can't.'

'Oh, yes I can.'

I curled up into a tighter ball, bracing myself for another outburst of phantasmic rage. My heart and my brain were pounding together. A dankness cloyed the air and choked me.

If she hurt me, how long could I hold out?

And then, suddenly, I felt her shift away. My brain still thudded in its skull but the pressure had gone. The room turned cold again. The scent of rotten roses disappeared and I could smell Domenica's disinfectant in the hall.

I turned my neck slowly, raised my arm, and looked behind me. I pushed myself up off the floor, not quite believing what I saw. Or didn't see.

'Berenger?' My mouth could barely form the words.

There was no answer. The room was as Domenica had left it, slightly dusty and spectre-free.

I sat on the bed and breathed the disinfected air with relief. Berenger had gone.

But in her place, in the deep recesses of my mind now liberated from her spiky chatter, the memories slowly seeped back.

can hear Addam's voice, now, on a scratchy radio playing somewhere down the hall, sandwiched between the shufflings and shoutings of people going to and from their cells. It's the third song of Addam's the DJ has played tonight, all of them ballads. She must have a thing about him. Like all of us.

I know this song by heart. Not just the lyrics, but the phrasing, the sound his breath makes under the words. The way his voice softens on 'sweet' and hardens on 'leave' and shatters into prisms of sorrow on 'lost'. Here, in my cell, I can sing a perfect duet with him. My voice can still wind its husky arms around his slender melodies.

And I wonder if we can be together again.

In the first year I worked for Aaron, I met Addam exactly once. There was no love lost between them, as I was soon to find out. I can hardly bear, even now, to think of it, how I must have seemed to him.

One afternoon, I was passing through the hallway of the San Remo apartment, holding a cup of tea in one hand, a newspaper tucked under my arm, when I saw Addam, who had been visiting his grandfather, standing at the front door, staring at the doorknob as if he had never seen one before.

He was wearing a flea-bitten old coat with a fur collar and

ragged jeans over scruffy sneakers. He had a knitted beanie in his hand which I supposed he was going to pull down over his face once he left the building to hinder anyone recognising him. Aaron lived on the street where John Lennon was shot—spooky territory for any rock star.

I hesitated for a moment and then walked toward him.

'Can I help you?' I asked, thinking he couldn't work out which way the door unlatched. I wasn't completely ignorant of modern music, I knew who Addam was, I knew he visited Aaron infrequently and that there was something…difficult between them. I had kept a low profile the other times Addam was at the San Remo. He probably didn't know I existed. Aaron never introduced us and scarcely spoke about him afterwards. I thought the problem was that Addam didn't pay him enough respect. But it was more than that. It was much more than that.

Addam didn't look up. 'No…thanks. I'm just…' My presence barely intruded on whatever was preoccupying him. I stood there awkwardly, waiting for him to turn the doorknob. Eventually, frustrated, I reached for the knob at precisely the same moment he did. Our hands touched and I pulled back, embarrassed.

'Sorry,' I said.

He straightened and turned to me. 'It's OK.'

Most people never see Addam close up. His face is usually framed by television screens and CD boxes and the sharp edges of magazine pages. I suppose you could look at Addam's face this way and think, dispassionately, 'What a handsome young man!' or 'Isn't he nice looking?' But, in the flesh, calm appraisal is impossible. He has the kind of face that makes you blush and then look away. It *hurts* to look at him.

He isn't pretty or Adonis-like, the kind of prissy, granite-jawed man's face they love in Versace advertisements and gladiator movies. His face is not 'rugged' or 'cute' or any of the other cliches of the day. He cuts his hair himself, hacks it, really, and the truncated curls are disarmingly ragamuffin. His eyebrows are thick and unruly and pitch up towards the corners, making him look mournful or wry, depending on what the eyes are doing. And it's what the eyes are doing that matters most. You can't look into those eyes and come out alive, as they say. They are wide-set and almond-shaped and glacier-blue. He has pale olive skin and black hair all over but those eyes are blue. A combination not unknown in the history of man, but on Addam they are a shock, a shock to find a grungy young man with the eyes of the angel in *Barbarella*.

He knows how to use them, of course. He hasn't sold ten million records on his songwriting ability alone.

Now I am sounding like Aaron…

When Addam turned and looked at me and mumbled, 'It's OK', I was like roadkill in his gaze. I had to avert my eyes, the power of his face was so disturbing. My hand started shaking so much my teacup rattled right off its saucer onto the carpet and my newspaper fluttered, like my heart, to the floor.

'No, I'll get it!' I shouted, panicked, as he started to bend down. I kept my eyes on the floor as I scrambled the newspaper together and collected the cup. When I got to my feet, I dared raise my eyes only so far as his neck, taking in the leather cord knotted around it.

'I'm sorry,' I said, mortified.

'No, I'm sorry,' I heard him say and his voice sounded…kind. 'I was just trying to get out of here.'

'Let me,' I offered, eager to show I'd recovered, that his beauty meant nothing to me. I reached past him again and jiggled the knob until the door pulled inwards. Outside, in the hallway, a maid was vacuuming.

'Great,' he said, shuffling his feet.

'My pleasure,' I made an effort to say brightly, hearing the servant come out in my voice.

He must have heard it too, because he took a step towards the open door, then turned back to me and hesitated. 'Wait a minute,' he said, distractedly. A hand went to his jeans pocket and emerged with a crumpled bill. He took my free hand and pushed the money into it. 'Well…thanks, again,' he nodded and was gone.

I looked at the five dollars in my hand.

He thought I was the bloody scullery maid.

There had been other men in my life. Oh yes. All of them bastards, none of them counting for anything. Least of all being remembered by me. I can't even speak of them in the same breath as I do Addam. But then, there is no-one I can speak of in the same breath as I do Addam. Not even Aaron, now.

It was infatuation. It couldn't have been love. I didn't even know him. He took one look at me and I was a goner, as they say. There was nothing poetic about it. He touched my hand by accident. I felt as if I had been burnt. And I had.

The *chance* of something between us was enough. A tingling kind of hope that I carried with me each morning on my long walk across the park. Would Addam visit today? Would he stop and talk to me? Would he start to look for me, seek me out? Would he one day let me touch his lips with mine? It wasn't very much to hope for but it was enough. Enough to drive me mad.

I didn't know it then, but I had made a choice. Between Aaron and Addam. It was either one or the other. But for a brief moment I thrilled to the possibility I could have both.

Until Berenger came along.

There was one hitch in my plan for a future with Addam: he didn't come back to the San Remo for months. I worked up enough courage to mention his absence to Aaron, but I got such a black look in return, I kept my own counsel.

Now is the time to introduce Baby. I have been putting her off. She is not the worst mother in this story, but she still makes the top five. She pisses it in.

Mostly I succeed in putting Baby out of my mind. But she's

part of this whole mess. Addam, Aaron, Baby, Berenger—they're all intertwined. Next time round, I'll choose my acquaintances from the other end of the alphabet.

Baby is, in real time, fifty-one years old but in her mind she is eternally twenty-one and still living in the East Village fucking every green-haired musician who ever took the stage at CBGB's in the seventies. Fortunately, she now lives on the west coast, near Berkeley, a long way from here, although I imagine she is winging her way to my cell right now, digital video strapped to her wrist, with plans for a documentary on the women who kill and the men who love them for it, or something equally asinine. She will come to me because she's another person who thinks she owns me, thinks my life story, now that it has suddenly become intriguing, is her own personal property.

It doesn't matter that people think I'm a killer. What matters is that I'm *her* killer.

Baby says she is a film producer but almost the only thing she has produced in her life is a set of lyrics to a song that has become a seventies classic. Whether she actually wrote those lyrics or not has been a matter of dispute for some time. The rock band she collaborated with said they only gave her a credit on the album cover because they wanted to 'shtoop' her. The last judge who heard the case ruled against Baby, his opinion being that the chorus of the word 'Baby' at the end of every verse was insufficient proof in itself of Baby's contribution.

The only other thing that Baby has produced, as far as I know, is Addam.

Baby met Addam's father, Kurt, at the landmark MC5 concert at the Fillmore East in 1969. She was twenty-one and he was thirty-two.

'Hi. I'm with the band,' is how Baby supposedly introduced herself that night backstage.

'I *am* the band,' is how Kurt supposedly responded.

There was an element of truth in that. Baby told me Kurt was 'Doc' to most of the people who knew him in those days, the keeper of the stash that everyone needed to kick themselves along, the spectral being in the shadows who was always there with his little black bag and a fixed smile. The band wouldn't, couldn't, go on without him.

Baby says that Kurt was a mathematical genius who had calculated a life plan for himself based on a complex formula involving numbers, that drugs were just a 'phase' in his plan and that he was moving on to real estate when all the numbers added up to nine. She says that if Kurt were alive today he'd probably be some computer mogul like Bill Gates. But as far as anyone knows Kurt never did make it out of the seventies.

I don't know how long the affair between Baby and Kurt lasted, but I have worked this out: Baby must have become pregnant around March 1970. Kurt disappeared in August that year and never saw his son, Addam, who was born on 8 December. Baby was not all there either. She has concocted an elaborate story about drug lords killing her lover, for how else could she explain that he turned his back on her and their infant son? In doing this, she has turned Kurt into a troubled saint like Iggy and Lou and Jimi and Sid and all her fantasy fucks.

Aaron doesn't talk about Kurt. I've heard people try to open him up about it, but he cuts them dead. I pricked up my ears once when a conversation with a group of visitors dangerously turned to Kurt and Addam. Aaron mumbled something about Addam not having Kurt's 'genius'. That Kurt's mating with Baby had muddied the splendid Karsner gene pool. Everyone laughed, thinking Aaron was joking.

But he wasn't.

Baby came to stay with Aaron from time to time. Strangely, Aaron didn't seem to mind the intrusion of a woman whose relationship with his family could be called tenuous at best. He tolerated her where he found other, more reasonable people, intolerable. I supposed she was his last link to Kurt.

Baby's excuse for staying with Aaron was that she couldn't bear to stay in Addam's 'dump' under the Manhattan Bridge—she who said she had once gone unwashed for a week after fucking Sid Vicious. So she would arrive with her laptop and a suit bag full of tight jackets—either red, black or leopard-print—and proceed to drive Aaron's housekeeper, Frances, crazy with parcels that had to be delivered, drycleaning that needed collecting, and 'urgent' phone calls that were expected and had to be redirected to her mobile.

Baby was, at that stage, doing pre-production on a feature-length documentary about how rock-star girlfriends are misunderstood. (As Berenger would have said, *duh*.) She set up office in a booth at the Odeon and came home in the evenings to smoke a couple of joints before going out to a series of bars and nightclubs to meet with more 'contacts'. Her major complaint was that the Upper West Side was too far from Tribeca and this was a complaint she made very loudly when she was suffering from a sore head, which was most mornings. Despite the attempt to wear hosiery that displayed no holes and carry a briefcase with a bronze name plaque, Baby's taste for animal prints and studded leather labelled her forever, *groupie*.

After the first time Aaron vaguely introduced us, she laboured under the misapprehension that I worked for her as well. That I was part of the Karsner package deal. Baby started sending me a steady stream of e-mail when she went back to California—scripts for me to read, letters to type, errands to run, clothes, books and CDs to buy for her and ship—all conveyed in the kind of coochy-coo language that might have worked in the days when she didn't have a face like cracked vinyl.

Aaron told me to humour her. He gave me a raise on top of an already generous salary, which I supposed was Baby-sitting money. But that meant I had to pay some attention to her demands. The easy ones, like putting in calls to Harvey Weinstein at Miramax (never accepted and never returned), I performed routinely and efficiently. Once or twice I obtained for her a lipstick you could only find at Patricia Field. But after reading the first draft I ignored all her attempts to get me to help her edit her script. It made absolutely no sense. The rock-star girlfriends were supposed to be the heroines of the piece, but all they seemed to do was lie around in druggy semi-comas accepting golden showers from security guards. In Baby's limited universe, this was probably a noble act.

The truth is, I was happy to humour Baby. I couldn't stand her, but she had one overwhelming point in her favour. She was Addam's mother.

The e-mail was flashing at me when I arrived at Aaron's apartment one morning, a long six months after the humiliating incident where I'd first met Addam:

> ...oh and another thing—that boy-child of mine brought some slut up here last weekend when i was doing my thing at sundance and she had the great fucking idea to take SIDS SAFETY PINS right off the mantel where you know its kind of a SHRINE. You've got to get them back for me darlingheart. boychick is AWOL and i am desperate. i don't know the whores name but she's the sulky one on that fucking huge billboard at LAX...

I should have trashed the message straightaway. Baby on a bender. It would blow over in a week. Sid's safety pins probably weren't Sid's safety pins anyway. No more than Joe Strummer's guitar string was Joe Strummer's guitar string. If Christie's ever came along to catalogue her holy relics the question of provenance could never be addressed. Who could tell Sid's safety pin from one bought last week at Woollies?

Much later, I read an interview in *The Face* where Addam said that Baby had lived for years amidst hundreds of disintegrating boxes of guitar picks, paper napkins encrusted with saliva and dried vomit, cigarette butts, soiled Y-fronts, balls of pubic hair combed from beds, crumpled plane tickets, fading polaroids, rusting razor blades, tubes of hair gel and ripped fishnet tights. As a free-roaming, effectively abandoned toddler, he'd over-turned a few of the boxes one day and then sat contentedly down on the rag carpet in the mess he'd made to eat his way through a box of crunchy things, which turned out to be 'Joey Ramones' toenails, you stupid kid!' according to an hysterical Baby when she found him about a day later.

I tried to ignore Baby's message, but she sent it again, three times. Which forced me to do something. And which, I fear, forced everything that came afterwards.

Of course, Baby knew 'the slut's' name, she was being disin-genuous. I was the only one in the world who didn't. I never read fashion magazines. They were below contempt. They made me feel off-kilter, like when you're in the street on a windy day and you have to lean this way and that just to keep standing.

I did look up at billboards, occasionally, and glance at the posters on bus-stops. But the models on them were faces that didn't deserve names. Why should I care who these men and women were, blown up to six times human size and yet still not a pore in sight?

As far as I knew, Berenger was a gun.

After reading Baby's fourth e-mail, the first thing I did was call Addam's personal assistant, Trini, with whom I'd spoken on several occasions, mostly to pass on messages from Baby to her son. Baby, having neglected Addam for a good twenty of his twenty-seven years, was showering him with attention now that he was fast becoming the rock star of her dreams. I had hoped each time I'd called Trini that there would be an excuse to reach Addam directly but she was an effective watchdog. This time I had an idea.

'Trini,' I asked, 'where can I find Addam today?'

'He's in the studio. Can't be contacted. Why?'

'Baby.' That's all I said. It was enough.

Trini groaned.

I don't know why I wasn't straight with Trini. I don't know why I didn't say, 'Trini, Addam's girlfriend has got something of Baby's. Do you know how to reach her?' That would have been all. I could have circumvented Addam altogether. But, of course, I didn't want to circumvent Addam.

'It's OK,' I lied. 'Baby's got something of Addam's she wants me to return. Actually, it's something that belongs to Addam's girlfriend.' And then I added casually, 'The one who was in California with him.'

My fishing expedition paid off. 'Berenger?' Trini sounded surprised.

'Who's she?'

'You're kidding! Jees, Nile, you've been working for that old guy too long.'

I bit my tongue. I wanted to say: he's sharper and sprightlier than *you*.

'She's, like, a *supermodel*!'

'And what's that when it's at home?'

I could hear Trini sigh before she said, patiently, to the crazy Englishwoman, 'Like a model only more famous. She dated Ethan Hawke, pre-Uma. And that old guy...um, Gabriel Byrne...no, not him. Who the hell was it? Anyway, she's really really gorgeous and she makes big bucks. Addam likes that. He likes rich women, 'cos otherwise he's afraid they're after his money.'

'Well, you know, Trini, I don't exactly keep copies of *Vogue* in my bathroom.'

'You're the only one who doesn't! Anyway, you don't need to, she's all over the place. You must have seen some billboard with her picture on it. I've gotta say this, Addam likes models. He doesn't care what colour they are or what height. Most of 'em tower over him anyway, when they wear heels. I don't know what all this stuff about rock stars and models is anyway? Both of 'em must be out of it most of the time. Must be like two twigs rubbing themselves together. Maybe that makes fire. Hey, you know, I might be right!' She seemed very pleased with her analogy.

'What's Addam's schedule this week? Is he seeing her?'

'You suddenly working for the *Star* or something?'

'Trini, I just want to get this thing back to...Berenger was it?'

'Oh, yeah. What'd she leave behind, anyway?'

'Just some make-up I think.'

'Oh, don't worry about it, then. She must have loads of that stuff.'

'I think there's some jewellery too,' I said quickly. 'Something important anyway.'

'You want me to give it to Addam to give to her? I'll send a messenger.'

'No. I can do that. I'll get the messenger.'

'You know, I think Addam said he was going backstage tonight at a fashion show to watch Berenger.'

'How do I find out about that?'

'Dunno...hang on, I've got one of her cards round here some- where. Addam gave it to me. In case. In case of what I don't know.' I could hear her rummaging around her desk, which I imagined was a trash heap. That would go with Addam's image. 'Got it!' She gave me the details. 'You should see this card. It's all, like, magazine covers and a Chanel ad. You *do* know what Chanel is, don't you?' Before I could answer she added, 'Just kidding!'

Trini was so perky I could have strangled her through the phone. I said goodbye and called Berenger's agency. I had, I said, an urgent package to deliver to Berenger from Addam's mother. The telephonist suggested I drop it in to the agency's Greene Street office and started to give me the address but when I interrupted her and said it was imperative that I gave the parcel to Berenger myself she went all tense on me and put me on hold. I imagine she had me tabbed for a stalker, or something, so I hung up.

The whole subterfuge was ridiculous. What would I say when I met Berenger? *Give Baby back her safety pins or she'll stamp her foot?* And what would Addam think of this? Far from being impressed, he'd think I was a lunatic. According to Trini, he already thought his mother was one. I was prepared to lie for him, do anything for him if it came to it, I already knew that, but I wasn't going to risk losing his respect before I even gained it. had to think of something else.

And then Trini called me back. 'Addam just called in and I told him about Berenger's jewellery. He said if you're sending someone backstage tonight, would you do him a favour and send the manuscript he gave Aaron to read a few months ago? He says Aaron will know what it is. I'm going to leave the name at the door. What name will I tell them?'

'Oh, just use mine,' I said casually.

I believe you make your own fate. How was I to know I'd just made mine?

ryant Park was once a sleazy patch of drug-dealer territory on the corner of 42nd Street and Sixth Avenue,
but now it is an entirely salubrious picnic spot where
twice a year the fashion shows are held. When I got out of the
taxi, with Addam's parcel under my arm, I was surprised to see
two huge tents pitched on the lawns and hundreds of people
milling about at the entrances. I had to ask a security guard
where I could find the backstage. He looked at me dubiously and
pointed to an opening at the rear of one tent, where camera
crews were waiting. After the girl at the backstage door had spent
about twenty minutes screaming into her set of headphones, I
was waved off on a journey through a labyrinthine corridor
which opened up on to the back of the stage and a scene of
pandemonium the like of which I'd never experienced before.

When I was about five my mother had decided, in one of her
hare-brained schemes, to take us on a ferry ride to Calais for the
day. Almost as soon as we left Dover the boat threatened to sink
in the Channel and we had to be evacuated. I can't remember
much except the screaming and the pushing, but the effect of a
few hundred people scrambling about on deck was nothing
compared to the panic induced by the prospect of the curtain
going up, so to speak, in five minutes, on a roomful of half-naked
females who still had curlers in their hair.

I looked around for Addam but didn't see him. I had

absolutely no idea what Berenger looked like and I had just assumed, as she was a famous model, that she would be radiantly pulsating at the centre of the room, lit by Klieg lights. But as I tried to push my way through the crush of boys in teeshirts flourishing cans of hairspray and video crews hunting last-minute interviews in packs, I found I couldn't easily distinguish who were the models and who were not. There were young girls sitting at mirrors, there were young girls standing behind them, young girls leaning on tables puffing on cigarettes and young girls cross-legged on the floor chugging champagne. Most of them looked like children, too young to wear anything that might remotely be called 'women's fashion'. But I didn't know then that twelve-year-olds have the most prized skin for modelling anti-wrinkle creams: after that, it's all downhill. With the bright slashes of blush across their cheeks and their hair pulled tightly back into high ponytails, they reminded me of a ballet class backstage at a graduation performance.

I was almost knocked unconscious by a heavy cameraman wielding video equipment and then virtually trampled to death by the two women who galloped after him. I decided sticking to the edges of the tent was a better tactic than taking my chances in the melee. I found a tucked-away tent-flap and shared it with a plastic garbage can full of ice and Diet Coke and a rack of clothes. From this vantage point I was directly opposite the plywood staircase that led to the stage with good views of the make-up and dressing areas. If Addam were to appear I was sure I would see him instantly.

I clutched Addam's manuscript tightly under my arm. I wondered briefly whether it might be an autobiography like Aaron's. It was wrapped in wrinkled brown paper and tied with rough twine. The only thing written on the paper was a tiny annotation on the top left-hand corner, DEVIANT, with a date that was several months old. When Aaron had handed it to me, he'd said, almost absent-mindedly, 'I suppose the boy wants a comment,' but added nothing else.

147

A petite girl in a leather jacket carrying two paper cups of coffee frowned at me disapprovingly. I supposed I wasn't wearing the right clothes for her tribe. I'd changed into a long green skirt and burgundy shirt and struggled with some mascara, but the effect seemed to be the opposite of everyone else's. Most people were dressed for summer, not for hanging round a drafty tent in chilly spring. Little transparent tops like underwear, very tight stretchy teeshirts, chunky sandals and tight pants with wide bottoms, everything in crayon colours, made them all, to me, look like the animated characters from Gumby.

The girl came back past me. Under her leather jacket she was wearing a short lace dress and spike heels with laces round the ankles. She frowned at me again and said, 'You better not stand there. Neena's coming.'

When I looked blank she said, as if to a small child who has been discovered stealing biscuits from the pantry, 'It's *her* rack. You're in her way.'

I edged closer to the garbage can. I think the girl would have preferred me to be in it. The rack did indeed have a torn piece of paper with the word NEENA sellotaped to the top bar. Stuck to one end was a sheet of polaroids of a model in various outfits. In every one of them she was making a lewd gesture.

The din in the main room suddenly got louder. A stage manager called out, 'All right, everybody, five minutes!' Some models had already started getting into their outfits, with the help of dressers, but most of the others had been hanging around in the make-up tent gossiping or earnestly trying to formulate responses to the video journalists' relentless questions, which hung in the air like lunatics' nonsequiturs ('I'm desperate to know, what colour is that?' 'Is back-combing *back*?' 'I didn't know you were from Texas!')

I felt like an idiot standing there in my dowdy clothes with the parcel under my arm and a grimace affixed to my lips. What on earth had I been thinking about, coming here? I was surrounded by beautiful, half-naked girls. If Addam saw me in this company, I would look worse than plain. I'd look like a toad. I was feverish in my warm clothes and I could smell the perspiration on me. I knew the sensible thing would be to get out of there quickly, take the manuscript and call Trini in the morning with some explanation. I had engineered the meeting, but now I realised it was all wrong. Why would Addam care whether it was me who brought the package to him or a messenger? I hadn't been thinking straight. I should have suggested I deliver it to his place. At least that way there might have been a chance he would have focused on me. But here, in the midst of all these ravishing teenagers, what hope did I have of drawing him to me? I wasn't experienced in these things, except in the most fundamental ways. No-one had ever courted me, so I didn't know how to court anyone back.

Before I could move, I was suddenly pushed back against the tent by an expulsion of air. Girls started running out of the make-up area and into the dressing-room, some still trailing hairdressers and boys with big brushes of powder. A six-foot-tall girl stopped right in front of me, pulled off her top, wriggled out of her skirt and, half-turning towards me, tossed her clothes at me, expecting me to do something with them. I stood there helplessly while the petite girl zipped her into a pair of tight trousers. The model bent over and the girl slid a sleeveless top over her head. The model wriggled into it and smoothed it down. All the while this was going on the long cigarette in her mouth was dangling ash.

The model braced herself by the clothes rack while her dresser attached a pair of stiletto-heeled sandals to her feet and buckled them. Next, the dresser took a scarf and threw it around the model's neck. She stood back to survey her work. A small youth with ruffled hair came up and tweaked the scarf and went away again.

I thought about dumping the model's clothes and going to hunt for Berenger but I was momentarily distracted by the sight of Darien—I didn't then know her name of course—stripping for the photographer, her brutally thin body repulsively on show. And then a screaming match broke out between a handsome young Hispanic man and a girl with diamond clips in her hair over a beaded cardigan a model was wearing.

'I still say it's *wrong!*' the girl shrieked, tugging at the cardigan hem. 'It's not *fierce* enough!'

'Eet's *perfect!*' the man snapped back. 'A leetle beet lady, a leetle beet whore.'

That a bit of fabric sewn together by some illegal immigrant in a Chinatown basement could cause so much passion! You have to wonder at it.

'D'you wanna know what I think?' sighed the model, looking bored.

'No!' they screamed at her in unison.

'Get it together folks!' No-one seemed to pay much attention to the stage manager, who was standing on a platform looking harassed. Across from me, a huddle had formed around a young model who was looking uncomfortable as an Asian seamstress sewed her into a pair of trousers. A female stylist was tugging at a leather halter around her neck.

The boy with ruffled hair was standing at a distance, contemplating the fitting, one hand combing his sideburns nervously. The stylist stood back, frowned and addressed him. 'That's the best I can do. She's a fucking size two, for chrissake!'

'I hate it,' the boy groaned. 'She looks like an effing scarecrow. Don't we have a spare jacket or something? What about the plaid?'

'Lydia's wearing it. *Track marks*,' she added ominously.

'Fuck it. Hasn't she heard of snorting it? Tell the bitch to do what everyone else does and put it up her nose.'

The diamond-clip girl had obviously been listening in. 'Why not take this beaded cardigan?' she called out. 'It looks bloody awful on Maggie.'

'No! No! No! Nono!' shrieked the Hispanic man.

'Let's try it,' said the boy. 'Calm down will you, Carlos?'

As the cardigan was handed over and the girl beamed smugly, Carlos kicked the trash can furiously. I had to jump not to be splashed with flying water. He shot me a poisonous look as if I too were disputing his judgment about the state of the universe.

And then the mood in the room shifted suddenly. People stopped what they were doing and even Carlos forgot about his tantrum. I followed their eyes to where Addam was being helped through a flap at the back of the tent by a security guy in a dark suit and head mike. Addam had his head down as he stepped over a pile of discarded shoe boxes. Behind him, holding his hand, her long hair over her face, was Berenger. I knew instantly it was Berenger because I *had* seen that heart-shaped face before. And I knew by the reaction in the room. People were just staring. 'Ohmygod!' whispered someone behind me. '*Trouble.*' I shrunk back in my corner, embarrassed. Would he notice me cowering there? Although I felt like all the eyes in the room were on me, of course they were not. The focus of everybody's attention had turned back to the boy with ruffled hair who I'd assumed by now was the designer. He pointedly ignored the newcomers, fiddling with the buttons of the disputed cardigan.

'Scott?' asked the girl who was standing with him.

'Tell her to get fucked,' Scott said.

The young model he was fitting was turned towards Berenger, who had now taken the lead and was dragging Addam in their direction. Scott crossly tugged at the cardigan to make her turn back towards him. Addam was smiling and a blonde guy with dreadlocks gave him a hi-five, but I couldn't read the expression on Berenger's face as the crowd parted for her. It looked sour to me.

'Hi Scott,' she said sweetly to Scott's back. 'Where's Orlando?'

'He's busy with someone else's fucking hair,' he replied, still with his back to her.

'But I'm ready now,' she continued in that sugary voice.

'I just cancelled you,' Scott said grimly, turning around. There was an intake of air all round.

'No you didn't,' said Berenger casually.

'The fuck I didn't.'

'I'm here. You can't cancel me.'

'You're fucking two hours late.'

'You're mistaken, Scott. I'm always, like, last.'

'Not for my show.'

'Is that my outfit?' She glared at the young model, who looked on the point of tears.

'Not any more. Angela's wearing it.'

'Angela's not wearing it if she wants any more bookings in this town.'

I almost laughed at the excruciating cliche, but no-one else did.

'She looks fucking horrible anyway,' Berenger went on. 'If you send her out in that everybody's going to piss themselves. Now, where's Orlando?'

'I don't mind,' Angela said limply, although you could tell she did mind. It was probably her big break.

'Shut up!' Scott snarled at her. Angela's big eyes flew open and then she began to weep, copiously. No-one comforted her. She used the sleeve of the cardigan to wipe her eyes. It came away smudged purple.

'Now look what you've done,' smiled Berenger. 'You've ruined her make-up. It's going to take hours to fix.'

'Bitch,' Scott said, but I could feel he was capitulating. He said it without much venom.

'You're going to be paying for me anyway, baby.' Berenger gestured to a girl to take her leather jacket. 'So you might as well, like, get your twenty grand worth. Now where is fucking Orlando?'

With that, everyone went back to what they were doing. I couldn't believe how easily they all gave in to Berenger. Angela, sniffing, handed over the halter to Scott as if it were a hot potato. She stood there, trembling, one arm across her boyish chest, while the seamstress started ripping the stitches she'd just sewn into the pants. Without missing a beat, Scott went over to a table where jewellery was laid out and selected a neck piece for a model in a long tweed dress. He no longer looked angry, nor even vaguely disturbed. Berenger was whisked away to a mirror, where several people started working on her at once. Someone lit her a cigarette and she stuck it in her mouth greedily. Only the stage manager seemed to be having an apoplexy, as he tried to line up stray girls by the stairs.

Addam had hung back behind Berenger the whole time. I watched him walk over to a table and grab a bottle of champagne. He wasn't particularly tall, short of six foot, but he had that hollow, hunched-over posture that very tall people develop. His face looked strained, deep lines under the eyes, shorter, pinched ones above his nose. I noticed, for the first time, that he had a severe limp in his right leg. If you scan the fan pages on the internet, you'll find reference to an interview Addam once gave to *Spin* where he claimed that Baby only finished knitting one tiny little bootee before he was born and the unfavoured leg shrivelled in protest. He was joking, of course, but the fans endow his crippled leg with magical properties, as though he were a modern Merlin come to life. Maybe they are right.

I watched him take the bottle over to where Berenger was sitting at the make-up station and pour some champagne into a paper cup for her. How I wished he were pouring it for me. He sat beside her and put an arm around her neck. The video crews circled them and a woman with a microphone was crouched beside Addam firing questions at him. He seemed happy to oblige. Berenger was smiling all the while as people tugged at her hair and attacked her face with brushes. She looked triumphant. The admiring glances he gave her made me feel sick. I hated her more in that minute, I think, than I did at any time later.

All this took another twenty minutes. Addam's manuscript felt heavy under my arm. I could have slipped out easily. There was now such a crowd gathered around him he would never notice a negligible figure like me. But I didn't go. I was powerless. The dictionary definition of 'glamour' is to enchant with evil intent. I was enchanted by these glamorous people. And I only half sensed it was evil.

Someone had started playing some upbeat rock music very loudly out in the auditorium. A female producer in a pants suit came back from out front and, jerking two thumbs in the air, screeched excitedly, 'Quentin and Mira!!!'

'Go! Go! *Go*!' screamed the stage manager to the first of the models in line. He put one hand in the small of her back and pushed. At the same time, Berenger got up from the make-up station and strolled over to her rack of clothes. The moment she reached it, three people fell upon her, helping her out of her clothes and into the re-adjusted pants and the halter top. She straightened the halter herself and balanced on a dresser's arm while she slid her feet into spiky high heels. Scott came over and threw a lei of beads around her neck. She grimaced and pulled two strands back over her head and thrust them at him.

'Amy!'

'Darien!'

'Maggie!'

The stage manager was calling the girls in groups. The first ones out were already coming back, unbuttoning their outfits as they clattered down the steps in their heels. I was in awe of how they could do that and not trip. One of the producers was standing at the bottom, holding out cups of champagne and lit cigarettes for the girls to snatch as they ran past.

One girl waved a fake-fur wrap over her head and giggled, 'Anyone need some pussy?'

When Darien came back out, she walked so slowly that the two girls behind her ran into her.

'Hey!' yelled one of them.

'Move that big butt!' teased the other.

'Kiss my ass!' Darien grinned and patted her leather-clad backside.

'I done that *already*,' called a model decked out like an African princess. 'Done taste so good!'

Darien wiggled her tongue lasciviously at her as she went past.

'Kristina!'

'Kelly!'

'Berenger!'

Berenger walked carefully up the stairs and then disappeared between two flaps. When she came back she was flushed red. She grabbed the arm of the model in front of her.

'Don't you *ever* do that again!' she snarled.

'What'd I do?' The young girl looked bewildered.

'Fucking did two turns at the end. I almost ran into you!'

A producer diplomatically wedged herself between Berenger and the model and handed Berenger a cigarette, allowing the other girl to escape. Berenger took a puff and threw the cigarette down. Addam was standing by her rack, smiling. She threw her arms around him and gave him a showy kiss. I looked away.

Berenger had two more outfits. As Scott was helping her into the next one, she started to whine, loudly enough for a good part of the room to hear. 'You always give *me* the shitty clothes. Just because I look good in everything.'

Her last dress was a showstopper. It should have looked ridiculous—a sheer Chinese sheath on a girl with an Irish complexion—but she carried it off. She managed to look savage and ethereal at the same time. But she clearly wasn't happy with the transparency of the fabric.

'These nipples are going to cost you an extra grand each,' she scolded Scott. He laughed, but I wasn't as sure as he was that she didn't mean it.

'Kiara!'

'Ling!'

'Berenger!'

Berenger grabbed Addam's arm and took him with her. Addam shrugged his shoulders exaggeratedly to indicate a stage appearance wasn't his idea, but you could see he was pleased.

She dragged him up the stairs and they disappeared. You

could hear the crowd whistle, even over the music. The rest of the models followed them, in clusters, tripping and giggling. Then Scott went out, with his right hand over his heart, looking relieved. The unseen audience cheered like a football crowd.

They all returned a few moments later, in scraggling fits and starts, joined by a rabble of audience members and a whole army of security men. Berenger posed with Addam for the backstage photographers and then she went to change. He brushed off the rest of them and sat on the top of the stairs. Someone handed him a jug of vodka and he took a swig. Most of the crowd had emptied off the stage and followed the models into the make-up room. I supposed there was a celebrity or two amongst them by the way the paparazzi were weaving and ducking.

Despite how I felt about myself, I couldn't leave Addam alone up there. I needed to make him turn his head and look at me. It was a need as fundamental as the blood pumping through my heart. I went around to the side of the staircase and put my hand on the railing. My head was on a level with his crotch: not an advantageous position to start a conversation. 'Addam?' I asked nervously.

'Yeah?' He sounded irritable. I suppose he thought I was going to ask for an autograph.

'Addam. I'm Nile. From your grandfather. I've got your manuscript.'

He looked down at me with sudden interest. 'Oh, yeah,' he said more brightly, an eyebrow devastatingly raised. 'I know you. Where is it?'

I felt myself blush deeply. I passed the manuscript to him under the railing. He handled it tentatively for a moment, took a deep breath, and untied the string. He shuffled through the pages anxiously and then looked back at me, curiously. 'He didn't leave a note?'

'No,' I said. When I could see that Addam looked crestfallen, I added, 'But he's been very busy lately.'

'Sure,' Addam said bitterly.

'No, really,' I said. 'He's working hard on his memoirs. It takes a lot of energy. He's an old man.' I felt a twinge of betrayal at the last statement, but for some reason I felt a stronger need to mollify Addam. My loyalties were already shifting.

'Ever since I was a baby he's been an old man. It's just a fucking excuse.' He suddenly glared at me. 'Who are you anyway, running his dirty little messages for him?'

'I—' I was speechless at the unfairness of it.

'You tell him from me that I don't need his shitty approval. And if he expects me to come visiting—'

'Oh, but I know he really really enjoys that.' God, I was starting to sound like Mary Poppins.

'Do you?' He looked at me sardonically. I couldn't interpret the hard look in his pale turquoise eyes. And I didn't get much of a chance before we were joined by ten purple-painted toenails in a pair of platform shoes.

'Addam, I'm starved. Let's get outta here.'

'Yeah, OK.' He stood up slowly, hitching the manuscript under one arm. I was now face to face with two pairs of shoes.

There was a pause while they got tangled in each other. And then they started down the stairs. When they got to the bottom, I could see Berenger tuck her arm into his and lean close.

'Who was that *frump*?' she said so loudly I think the whole tent heard.

The next morning it was Aaron who looked agitated.

'Did the boy say anything?' he asked me as soon as I came in.

'He seemed to expect a note or something from you.' I looked at him directly. 'He seemed upset.'

'Well, what does he expect me to say? He's had the nerve to write a piece for the theatre. It was a load of hogwash. Musically immature and lyrically moronic.'

'Maybe he wanted a few pointers from you?' I suggested gently. 'Maybe he wanted his distinguished grandfather's help?'

Aaron snorted. 'What he wanted was to show me he could write three hours of musical theatre. If musical theatre is what you call it.'

'He wanted to impress you.'

'Well, he failed. Ever since these garage bands started up in the sixties, they killed songwriting. Every idiot with a guitar thinks he can write a song these days.'

I could understand that Aaron might be frustrated by this, but I didn't see why he was being so ungenerous with his grandson, when he was always dictating painstakingly detailed letters of encouragement to young composers. He was clutching the wide arms of his mission chair tightly. I asked him if he needed another cushion but he shook his head impatiently. We were about to start work on his teenage years, which I knew included a devastating bout with The Consumption, as he still called it, and I assumed he was tense about this. But when I started setting up the tape recorder he waved it away.

'How does the boy look?' he asked suddenly.

I stopped fiddling with the tape and looked at him. His washed-out grey eyes held mine keenly. Aaron had rarely engaged me in so personal a conversation before. 'Good,' I said uncertainly.

'Healthy? Does he look healthy?'

'Absolutely. He's got a new girlfriend.' I didn't know why I added this bit of trivia: Aaron disapproved of gossip. But he looked interested, so I went on, because he seemed to expect me to. 'She's a model. A spoiled brat I'd say. You should have seen—'

'Never mind that,' Aaron interrupted. 'Is the boy in love with her?'

It wasn't a question I cared to answer, so I said lightly, 'Well, you know Addam better than I do.'

'I don't know that I do.' He said this mostly to himself.

'He likes models,' I rabbited on to fill in the awkward silence, repeating what Trini had told me.

'And who told you that?' Aaron said sharply.

Chastised, I responded, 'It's common knowledge.'

'Common knowledge? You put too much store in it.' Before I could protest, Aaron added, 'So you think this one's special?'

'Well, I don't know—' I was struggling with Aaron's sudden interest in Addam's love life. It was not a subject I was willing to talk about in depth. I was still smarting from Berenger's insult, 'frump'.

'And she's mad about his money?'

'Oh, I don't think so at all. I don't think money's got anything to do with it.'

Aaron made a dismissive sound and sank back into silence. I put the tape recorder back in the drawer.

Eventually he said, 'I want to dictate a letter.'

For a moment, I hoped that the communication was for Addam, but Aaron launched into diatribe against a producer who was angling to put some of his songs with a book about the Wall Street Crash of '29. He hated to be thought of as a dinosaur from another era. What was offensive about this proposal in particular was that Aaron didn't even write his first published lyric until the middle 1930s and the biographies refer to his 'golden age' as the period from 1946 to 1962. Even this irritated him, because he believed he did his most inventive work in the seventies and eighties. A musical about the Crash was an anachronism as well as an insult. I winced at some of the language he was using.

'Is the boy in love with her?' I couldn't get Aaron's question out of my mind.

Aaron subscribed to a service that compiled, on a weekly basis, anything in the international press relating to himself, his songs or productions of works. I didn't think the service had been required to work too hard—there had only been a trickle of items in the first few months I'd worked for him—so I didn't hesitate to request a search of Addam–Berenger material.

Naturally, I didn't tell Aaron about it.

The material on both of them, together, was surprisingly scarce, although individually they each stacked up an *Encyclopaedia Britannica* of clippings. There were a few smug photographs of them together at parties and openings, as published in various social pages, a couple of snippets in the gossip columns, an interview in *Scene* where Berenger alluded, casually, to 'hanging out' with Addam, and a couple of larger pieces about Detox's musical history. The rest I later pieced together from snatches of conversation I'd overhead at parties and fashion shows.

I sat up in bed on successive nights with a thick stack of photocopies. According to several clips, Berenger had met Addam on the set of one of Detox's videos. I was curious about it, but there seemed no way to get copies of old videos, apart from calling Trini, which I was reluctant to do. I found a picture of them on the set, Berenger huddled on a flight of stairs, a coat over her shoulders and a cigarette in her hand. I couldn't make anything of her except that the length of arm that emerged from under the coat was as skinny as a spider's leg. Addam was standing beside her, one hand lightly tangled in her hair. It was a gesture of such tenderness I could hardly bear to look at it.

Months later, Berenger played the video for me one night.

It had been Detox's third big hit. The band was approaching critical mass, where celebrity and notoriety—not the same thing at all in my book—intersect. They'd had their obligatory fatal drug overdose—the bass player, naturally enough—and the obligatory arrest for smashing up a hotel room. There were the obligatory starlet girlfriends and the obligatory stretch limousines idling in the gutter all night, the drug and booze binges and the spewing down the front of an entertainment reporter's jacket. The keyboard player had been arrested for shoplifting in Virgin and a back-up singer had made a speech at a press conference in Paris denouncing the French government for its policy on Algeria.

None of this had touched Addam, from what I read. He

didn't steal and he didn't overdose and didn't seem to care much for politics. Where the other members of Detox always managed to be captured by the photographer's lens when they were lying around hotel rooms with their eyeballs rolled back into their heads or straggling through airport concourses making V for Victory signs, Addam would be snapped, looking moody but dapper, outside the Armani shop on Rodeo Drive or contemplating the meaning of life, in a perfectly pressed Helmut Lang suit, on the end of a pier on the Hudson River.

Detox's third video featured Addam in a dark suit and bare feet, stumbling, crawling and scratching his way across a street laid deep with broken glass. Much was made of the fact that it *was* broken glass, not barley sugar or plastic or whatever they use in stunts, and that Addam had refused a double for the close-ups where his feet and hands are torn and bleeding. But he didn't have any sensation in his bad foot anyway and a few lines of coke probably took care of the rest. He walked over glass all right, and he did it for two days, because it made a good story and good stories sold records and sold records made you rich. He also had a damsel to woo.

Berenger was sixteen. She was already 'super', as these things go, because a girl can go from zilch to super in the instant it takes to appear spectacularly in one fashion show or be booked for Italian *Vogue* by photographer Steven Meisel. But Berenger wasn't so super that she was beyond taking a small role in a rock video by a hot new band. According to interviews at the time, Addam had seen a picture of Berenger in a magazine and had wanted her for the video. Berenger's agent, Erik Sklar I assumed, had indicated she was unavailable and then had done the deal at the eleventh hour, provided Berenger could choose hair and make-up, wardrobe, and stills photographer, and that there would be on hand plenty of that Swedish water that comes in a blue bottle and has to be hand-tapped, whatever, and specially imported. The Gotham column of *New York* magazine strung a whole column out of that bottle of water.

So there floated a contractually satisfied Berenger at the end of the glass-strewn street, sepia-toned and draped in a wispy piece of tulle. A wind machine had tormented her hair into Medusa's locks and she undulated her arms in some sort of attempt (I supposed) to be a spooky seductress, but which looked to me to be a wooden response to a drama coach lurking behind the scenes somewhere and calling out, 'More *arms*, ducky! More arms!'

She was to get better at this spectre thing.

When Berenger played this video for me, I told her it was stupid. 'Why would Addam walk over glass on the road for you, when you can plainly see that the footpaths are fine? Look— there's no glass at all where you're floating.'

'It's, like, *agorical*,' she sniffed.

I watched Addam stumble, bloodied but distressingly handsome, towards the outstretched arms of Berenger about five more times that night. He never made it. As he came within a whisker of her, Berenger disappeared in a puff of dry ice, leaving a bereft Addam to stoop down, pick up a broken bottle and fade out with the glass poised as if he were about to cut his wrists.

'Isn't he romantic?' Berenger said wistfully as she rewound the tape.

I don't know why I showed Aaron the picture of Berenger on that magazine cover. I think I half-knew it would precipitate something. I wanted something to happen. I wanted Aaron's world and Addam's world to collide. And then, I thought, I could have both of them.

'Look at this,' I said to Aaron, one afternoon, bringing the latest *Harper's Bazaar* into his office with his papers. 'That's Addam's girlfriend.'

Aaron glanced at it and looked at me curiously. 'You think I'm being unkind to my grandson, don't you?'

'No…I didn't say that.'

'No, you didn't, Nile, but I can see it. Do you think I should make amends?'

'What do you mean?'

He didn't answer, but asked, 'How about a dinner for Addam? Do you think that will work?'

'I...suppose so,' I said.

'A dinner,' he mused, more to himself than me. 'That's what families do, isn't it?'

How would I know? I felt like saying. I never had one.

I had thought all along how *sad* it was that Aaron's only blood was Addam and they weren't speaking. And now the old man wanted to put his little family right again before he died.

'A dinner sounds a very good idea, Aaron,' I said.

What did Aaron see in Berenger? She was only a photograph on that *Harper's Bazaar* cover, with two dimensions; a third if you counted the Estee Lauder advertisement on her back. She was wearing a 1930s-style chiffon gown, a 'tea' gown I think they called it, and the ruffled sleeves and layered hemline fluttered in a delicate breeze. To say that she 'wore' the dress or that it 'fluttered' was actually a misnomer for she neither spoke nor moved nor did any real breeze brush the surface of the page to play with the gossamer fabric. She was trapped there, or her image was, caught like a flower in a press, painted over with layers of hard glaze. She did not move, she did not give: the active party, the giver, was the observer, whose eyes and brain did all the work of connecting a blue dot there, a pink one here and interpreting them as 'girl', 'dress', 'fragile', 'beautiful'.

She was just a rash of pixels. If you magnified the page she would disintegrate into a million little points in clusters of light and dark. She would not look pretty, not even particularly like a girl, but more like the suburbs of Los Angeles seen from the air, or the weave of nubbly fabric, or the gases in space exploding at the dawn of time. She would not look human at all. She would be flat terrain for the mind to travel over. And the mind could take many paths.

Aaron's mind was like a blind man's hand, constructing her

substance from the braille of her surfaces. My mind registered nothing but a teenager in a pale yellow dress, although this is not quite true, because the picture triggered memories of excruciating humiliation too. The embarrassment of hand-me-down dresses, of the bi-annual visit to Oxfam for my seasonal wardrobe. But Aaron's mind found something exquisite in the picture, as if it had been staggering along a dusty road and suddenly stumbled upon a lush and intoxicating garden.

Berenger's image was a memory, a longing that tugged at his heart. At least that's what I thought when he asked if he could keep the magazine.

Aaron became morose in the few days after I showed him Berenger's picture. It didn't help that women, young women, were on his mind. We had reached the part of his memoirs where he had married his first wife, Ada, a few scant weeks into 1935. She'd been a chorus girl in a show at the Adelphi and had gone off on a road tour three months into the marriage and had never come back. I think Aaron was still embarrassed that the marriage had taken such a predictable turn. But he was only nineteen. The magic age for everything in this sorry tale.

It was Aaron's second wife, Madeleine, who was Kurt's mother. She was five years older than Aaron and had been a model for the photographer Paul Outerbridge, whose fleshy nudes had caused something of a sensation in the New York of the 1920s and 1930s. Through Outerbridge, Madeleine had developed an interest in photography and had talked herself into a cataloguing job at 291 Fifth Avenue, Alfred Steiglitz's gallery, there being precious few jobs in photography for women, even as assistants, in those days of heavy cameras and a weaker fair sex. The young Aaron, flushed with his first songwriting success, met her there in 1937, when he came to approve the print Steiglitz had been commissioned to take of him for *Vanity Fair*.

Aaron had a framed platinum print wrapped in a blanket in a

closet. It was an Outerbridge portrait of Madeleine. In it, you could only see her dimpled buttocks and thighs, clad in a coarse pair of stockings. It used to hang in Aaron's study in the San Remo apartment, but Berenger took offence at it when they moved to SoHo and Aaron hid it away. I was there when Berenger screwed up her face and called the soft white flesh 'gross'. I think Aaron hid the picture, not to comply with Berenger's wishes, but to shield the naked Madeleine from further abuse.

There were other photographs of Madeleine, many of them, because Madeleine was her own favourite subject, pre-dating Cindy Sherman by almost fifty years. Her earliest photographs of herself are soft-focused, romantic portraits, often shot through mirrors or dirty windows. In most of these, she is reclining passively, strung with flowers and looking with amusement at herself, the photographer. They are quite beautiful.

Madeleine died of breast cancer in 1940, when she was thirty and Kurt was only three. Aaron told me that in her last two months of life Madeleine took hundreds of photographs of her bruised and distorted right breast, intending them for an exhibition. He destroyed them when she died.

She was a sharp beauty with that bobbed coiling hair, dark fierce eyebrows and, judging by snapshots other than her own, an apparent taste for wearing men's suits. Compared with the fluffy chorine Ada, and Aaron's third wife, the sturdy hausfrau-socialite Margaret, who ruled over his domain with lacquered orthodoxy, Madeleine seemed modern and forward. I imagined a young woman who was passionate and intelligent and unflinchingly loyal. Nothing like Berenger.

She would have made a good mother for me.

Margaret was another matter. She was the daughter of a famous bandleader and a second-string torch-singer. She had had some ambitions to be an actress, but once she became the wife of a songwriter rapidly accelerating towards celebrity, that seemed to satisfy her. Too much talent in one family is as bad as too little money—Margaret seemed to recognise this. Apparently, she did have talent, loads of it, for hosting glittering musical soirees, charity luncheons, after-theatre suppers and summer festivals in the gardens of their house at Cape May. No doubt Margaret's prowess as a networker helped accelerate Aaron's career: already, in August of 1943, when they had been married barely a year, *Harper's Bazaar* was profiling the couple as the leaders of America's 'Treble Clef Societe'.

In 1941, Aaron wrote the book for his first major Broadway revue, *Mantilla*, and, despite unenthusiastic notices from critics confused by its Spanish Civil War setting, by late 1943 it was still playing to sell-out houses, mostly prompted, I suspect, by Margaret's brilliant skill at ingratiating herself with the wives of the nation's press barons and therefore assuring that her husband, her homes, and her gilded hairdos got constant play in the newspapers and journals of the day. The clippings of Aaron and Margaret—mostly of Margaret in the 1940s—fill several books, which she religiously chronicled right up until her death from heart disease in 1978, at the age of sixty-four.

In her pictures, Margaret is always dressed formally and smartly in skirt suits and strong shoulders, with her yellow hair braided across the top of her head like a Swiss milkmaid. She looks smug, bossy and bovine and I can't get out of my head an image of her lying on a coroner's slab with her cholesterol-choked arteries exposed, a thick layer of cold white fat wrapped like a blanket around her heart.

Aaron's marriage to Margaret post-dated Madeleine's death by two years. There was no time for mourning with a young boy around who needed a mother. Aaron admits that Margaret's appearance—on top of a piano at a cocktail party given by Oscar Hammerstein for his son—was extremely convenient. She was two years older than he was and twenty-six when they met, but had no inclination to have children of her own.

I don't know what kind of marriage it was, but it lasted almost forty years. Aaron seemed alternately fond and sullen when he spoke of her. I got the feeling that she railroaded him into being content with her, even if it ran against his naturally vexatious grain.

Although the quote has been attributed variously to Dorothy Hammerstein and Nancy Olson Lerner, I believe it was Margaret who, having overheard a dinner companion congratulate Mrs Richard Rodgers on her husband's having written 'The Bloom on Your Cheeks', interrupted the conversation indignantly with 'Richard Rodgers didn't write "The Bloom on Your Cheeks", my husband did! What *your* husband wrote was the dum-dum-dum-dee-dum!'

Consider, then, Aaron's fourth wife, on the night they met.

It all happened so suddenly. For weeks, Aaron had said nothing about his idea to invite Addam and Berenger to dinner and I hadn't dared ask. I eventually forgot about it, knowing in any case it wouldn't include me—although I had planned, if the occasion arose, to work late.

With her usual element of surprise, Baby unexpectedly turned up at the apartment one day, accompanied by several suitcases and many silver camera cases. She said she was on her way to Connecticut to grab an interview with Patti Hansen before the Stones went on tour again, although I suspected from her later telephone conversations this was news to Patti. Her documentary was progressing: there was interest in it from some women's film fund. Did I think it would be more 'commercial' if she included some 're-creations' using actors? She'd found a young boy out in Oregon who was the spitting image of Iggy, same body, really *incredible*. She was currently lodging in her cabin and instructing him in…the art of being Iggy, I supposed. She was going to talk to Addam that very night about producing the soundtrack for the film. Addam had admitted to her he was still dating that bitch…and, oh, by the way, she had found Sid's safety pins in the cat's tray…and so on. I learnt all this in Baby's first five minutes in the third bedroom, where I was helping her unpack.

'OK. You can level with me,' Baby said as she watched me hoist one of her suitcases onto the bed, her arms folded across a black leather biker's jacket with zebra lapels. 'What's Aaron up to?'

'What do you mean?' I asked, genuinely surprised.

'The invitation to come and stay, the dinner tonight.'

'What dinner?'

'The dinner with Addam.'

I hadn't really been listening to her. I had been imagining how I might talk her into allowing me to come with her to her meeting with Addam that night, which I assumed was going to be at his place.

'Addam's coming here?' I asked, suddenly panicked.

'Well, don't sound like you don't know anything about it. You're Aaron's personal assistant for fuck's sake. Don't you have to organise the food or something?'

I took a deep breath. 'I work with Aaron on his book, Baby. I don't organise food.'

'Well, you organise food for me.'

'I make restaurant reservations when you're in town. I don't even do that for Aaron.'

'But he doesn't go out, does he? He just sits in that room and broods.'

'He has visitors. He has students. Just last week Julie Andrews came to talk to him about some project.'

'She did?'

'James Levine drops in all the time. Steve Sondheim, Freddie Ebb—'

'Do you think she'd read my script?'

'Who?'

'Julie Andrews, of course!'

'You mean the *rock groupies* script?'

'I never fucking use the word "groupie".'

'Isn't she a bit old?'

'For what?'

169

'For a part?'

'I was thinking of her for narrator.'

'But what's Julie Andrews got to do with'—I was going to say 'groupies'—'rock and roll?'

'God, don't you understand anything about the film business? I need a *name*.'

I didn't respond. I had the suitcase open and I shut it again and went to the door. 'If that's all,' I said, in a very good imitation of a ladies' maid. If Addam was coming I had to go and do something about my hair.

'No, no, it isn't!' She sounded upset that I was leaving. 'You've got to tell me about tonight.'

'But I don't know anything.'

'He insisted Addam come. He insisted that slut come too. Addam didn't want to for some reason, but I twisted his arm. I mean, what if Aaron wants to talk about his will?' She started pacing up and down across the front of the bed. 'He's definitely up to something. Maybe he's going to give it all to some charitable institution. Ten-year-old cellists with leukemia in Siberia or wherever. You sure you don't know anything about this?'

'Cross my heart.'

'It's not about me. It's about Kurt. It's Kurt's money and it should go to Addam. He was taken from us both so early…it's up to me to make sure some good comes of *something*. How much do you reckon Aaron's worth?'

I found this conversation grisly. 'I thought the material world didn't concern you.'

'Oh, for Christ's sake, get real! Of course I don't care about the money. Addam's got plenty of money already. This is a *spiritual* quest. We're not going to have closure until Addam gets his father's legacy.'

That word. Closure. People were obsessed with shutting things. But it was always after the haemorrhaging had begun. 'Closure of what?'

But Baby didn't choose to answer. Instead, she fell upon the suitcase and started rummaging through it. 'What the fuck am I going to wear?' She took out a stack of print leggings and dumped them on the bed. 'What about this?' She held up a red leather bustier with laces at the back.

'Baby, if it's only a family dinner…'

'But it isn't.' She looked at me with irritation. 'I don't know why he insisted that Addam bring that whore.'

'Whore?' I had visions of Addam arriving with a hooker on each arm. The hookers would be dressed in red and black lace mini-slips. Exactly like the garment Baby was holding up in front of her now.

'The whore who stole Sid's pins, of course!'

It took a while to register. 'But you said the cat—'

'Do you think lace is a bit overdressed?' She smoothed the mini-slip over her belly.

'Not *that* lace,' I told her honestly. She put down the slip and picked up a floral thing with ruffled sleeves which looked like it might have been snatched from a five-year-old's trunk. 'Betsey Johnson,' she explained.

'Don't you think it's a bit young?' I asked.

Baby glared at me.

'Well, unsophisticated…'

'Exactly how old is this girlfriend of Addam's?'

'Berenger? Seventeen? Eighteen? Why?'

'I don't want to fucking look like Grandma Moses next to her, that's why!'

I looked at Baby with her dreadlocked red hair, her diamond nose stud, the dangling pink plastic pacifier hanging from her ear, the zebra-print tights that matched her jacket, the almost non-existent leather skirt and the high-heeled wooden Candies on her feet. 'Baby,' I said. 'There's no chance of that.'

I would normally have finished with Aaron by late afternoon, but Baby had kept me so busy arranging her agenda, I was still

171

there at seven doing her chores. In a voice dripping with ulterior motive she informed me that she had asked Frances, the housekeeper, to set another place for me at dinner. 'I want you as a witness,' she said.

I could feel myself blushing deeply just at the thought of being seated with Addam and Berenger. I told Baby I had nothing to wear: she told me it didn't matter. I don't suppose it did, for me. But I didn't want Addam to see me in my awful day clothes. I asked Baby if I could borrow a lipstick and she smiled magnanimously. Finally, she got all gussied up in something that looked more suitable in the sleazy meat-packing district than the respectable Upper West Side and then paced the Persian carpets nervously, like a hooker who hadn't made her night's quota of tricks.

They were late. Not late, as in twenty minutes late.

Late, as in two hours late. Baby's mascara was halfway down her cheeks by then and she had downed more than one or two whiskies as well, but Aaron sat inscrutably in his recliner rocker the whole time listening over and over again to a demo of a new musical someone had sent him. The screeching chorus set my teeth on edge, especially when the Space Shuttle was about to explode. I could have done without the grating finale, as well, about Christa McAuliffe being a little cutout star in the sky. My guess was that Aaron had chosen to listen to this particular stinker on this particular night just to irritate Baby. Uncharacteristically, Baby said nothing, as if she were frightened of offending him. The truth is, Baby couldn't tell a stinker from a work of art anyway.

I had stayed in Aaron's office nervously shuffling files as long as I could and then I tried to busy myself in the kitchen with Frances, clanging pots and pans and moving the pre-prepared meal from bench to bench to give the appearance of being busy. Frances, who had prepared several of Addam's favourite dishes, was getting more and more upset by his non-appearance. 'I miss the chance to cook for the boy,' she had told me earlier. In the end, I was forced to join Aaron and to watch Baby pace woozily back and forth.

I was more strung out than all of them. 'I think I better go home,' I told Baby at 10 p.m. 'It's late.'

'It's not late!' Baby protested, a little unsteadily. Nothing was ever too late for Baby, not ordering up food at 4 a.m. or arriving for a meeting a day after it was scheduled or thinking about conceiving another child at fifty.

Aaron was about to say something when the intercom buzzed.

Baby raced to it. 'Send them up!' she yelled and started straightening the straps of her slip as if she was about to go out on her first date. She looked over at Aaron nervously. He was leaning back in the chair with his eyes closed.

They came through the door giggling. Addam had one arm flung around Berenger's neck, leaning into her so hard she looked as if she might stumble. She had a hand over her mouth, her head nuzzled into the space between his chin and shoulder, as if she were whispering to him. She didn't look at anyone in the room, just let Addam lead her. For a moment, I thought she might have been injured or sick and started to pull out a chair. But the amused look in Addam's eyes made me stop.

'Sweetheart!' Baby wobbled up to them and the three of them hung in space like sideswiped ten-pins. I couldn't tell who was the most fragile or the most drunk. I would have taken a bet that Berenger, in her impossibly high spiky heels, would have been the first to slump. Most people made that mistake. She was about as frail as a steam tanker. But I wasn't to know that then.

'Sweetheart.' Baby kept on pawing at Addam's shoulder but he ignored her, guiding Berenger towards Aaron, who still had his eyes closed as if he were asleep, but I knew he couldn't be. At his age, sleep is like a light coating of dust, easily blown away.

Addam stood in front of Aaron, his grin unreadable. Baby hovered in the background like someone waiting for a piece of priceless china to fall off a mantel. I was frozen behind Aaron, wishing the bookcase would swallow me up. I knew I was smiling like an idiot but my muscles wouldn't relax into a form more natural. Berenger was making little hiccupping noises into Addam's shoulder, occasionally punctuated by a snort as whatever was funny about the situation got the better of her. She looked like something Addam had found under the bridge, with her ragged, thin dress and her straggly long hair. Addam, on the other hand, was wearing a suit and tie so ostentatiously conservative I knew he was sending up the formality of the occasion.

'Old man.' It was more of a command than a question. When Aaron didn't respond, Addam nudged his highly polished leather slipper with his toe. I was astounded at his rudeness and looked at Baby to see how she was reacting. She looked blank: the couple of joints she had smoked on the terrace had kicked in.

For a long while Aaron did nothing, just sat there with his eyes closed.

'Aaron, Addam's here.' Baby almost sang it, as if Aaron had already been packed away to a nursing home and this was visitors' day.

'Yeah, your guests have arrived,' said Addam.

Aaron suddenly opened his eyes. 'Is that so?' he asked and sprang to his feet so lithely that Addam had to take a step back. Berenger jerked her head up and for the first time I got a look at those astonishing green eyes. Aaron saw them too—I could see something like shock pass across his face. But he composed himself and gave her a radiant smile. 'So, this is the breathtaking creature who has won my grandson's heart!' he exclaimed with what I knew to be exaggerated courtliness, but could see Berenger thought was normal octogenarian behaviour. He reached for Berenger's hand and she flinched and then gave him a quizzical smile as he raised the back of it to his lips and kissed it. I had seen Aaron do this before as a kind of formality but never with so much feeling.

'Hi,' she said weakly.

'Addam tells me you are a model,' Aaron continued. I doubted whether they had ever had a conversation about Berenger and Addam looked for a moment like he was going to contradict Aaron, but he just smirked and shrugged. 'You must be a very good one.' Aaron still had a grasp of Berenger's hand and she contemplated it with revulsion mixed with a spark of approval, I thought. She looked plaintively at Addam.

'I've gotta go to the bathroom, Addam,' she said suddenly, as if none of us existed. She tugged her hand away from Aaron. He stared at the air where it had been with something like disappointment.

That's when I knew we were all in trouble.

'Want me to come too?' Addam asked.

'Pleeeeese?' she implored with a kittenish smile.

'Excuse *us*,' said Addam with a mean smile and led Berenger into the hall.

'Well!' Baby slurred, suppressing a yawn. 'She's got the manners of a fucking cockroach. Anyway, she's not *that* good-looking. You said she was good-looking.' Baby turned to me accusingly.

'Did I?' I asked.

'She's rather pretty all the same,' Aaron commented. He was silent for a moment. 'You can tell Frances we're ready to eat.'

I had my doubts about that, but I went into the kitchen anyway.

Fifteen minutes later, Baby had flopped into a chair at the head of the table and Aaron was still poised behind the carver waiting for Addam to return. He was standing very rigidly, as if steeling himself for something.

Baby threw down another whisky. 'I don't know what they're doing.' She waved her glass in the air and, ignoring me altogether, said to Aaron, 'Send Nile to find them, will you?'

Aaron nodded at me and I went dutifully. You can imagine how thrilled I was at the prospect of retrieving the couple of the year. As I walked along the corridor, I feared I'd stumble over them tangled in some kind of modern sexual position that involved multiple orifices and the painful use of various odd-shaped apparatus.

The small guest bathroom lay in a kind of dogleg off the main hall. I could hear whispering as I approached. 'Addam!' I said very loudly. I didn't want to find them up against a wall with her legs wrapped around his neck. 'Addam!' There was a scuffling sound and then I heard Addam call through the bathroom door, 'Fuck off!'

'Dinner is served,' I called out. Dinner is served! I sounded like a butler in a film. I was ready to turn on my heels but Addam suddenly opened the door a fraction and stuck out his head. I couldn't see Berenger. 'We're coming, OK?'

'All right. But the food will get cold.' Brilliant. I am a brilliant conversationalist. Addam rewarded that comment by slamming the door in my face.

But they did appear in the dining room a few moments later. I can't say they looked any more dishevelled than they had when they left the room, but something had passed between them. Addam looked smug.

Berenger, however, seemed confused. She took one look at the place settings and declared, 'Oh, but I never eat sitting down!'

I'd never heard such a thing in my life and I'm sure Baby and Aaron hadn't either by the looks on their faces.

'What does she mean?' Baby asked Addam.

'We want to stand up,' explained Addam, his eyes gleaming. 'Both of us.'

'But *why*? I don't get it.'

Berenger tugged at Addam's sleeve. 'I can't eat sitting down!' She sounded panicked, as if we were going to strap her to a chair with spikes protruding from it. But it was nothing to do with the chair, or any chair for that matter. Berenger did indeed always eat standing up at other people's homes, even though she sat quite happily at restaurants. It wasn't some special quirk of her digestive system. If you sat down and food was put in front of you, people noticed if you didn't eat it. Later on, I always had to make it clear to people who wanted Berenger for dinner that she would only attend buffets.

'Of course you can't eat sitting down!' Aaron made it sound the most natural thing in the world. He rose from the table. 'We will all stand.'

Baby screwed up her face. 'What?'

'Come on,' said Aaron and it wasn't a suggestion but a command. 'We can't upset this poor child with our uncivilised eating habits.'

Baby pushed back her chair and staggered to her feet. I helped Frances hand out plates of chilled soup. Addam raised an eyebrow at the bowl I handed him. 'It looks like my dinner did get cold,' he smirked, but his pale eyes were friendly and there might have been an apology in them.

'What's in it?' Berenger asked me, eyeing the white soup suspiciously.

'Potatoes, leeks and cream, I think,' I answered, looking at Frances, who nodded.

'I don't eat dairy.' Berenger turned away in disgust. Models never eat dairy, I was to learn. They don't eat wheat, either. Or yeast. Or fat. Or red meat. Except when all these things are present in a Big Mac.

I noticed that no-one much touched their soup and that Frances took away full bowls. The meat course didn't fare much better.

The conversation staggered on for a while. Aaron asked Addam politely about his forthcoming album and Addam answered him politely. Addam inquired about Aaron's auto-biography: Aaron made dismissive noises. Baby got in a few sentences about her film.

'Tell me, Berenger, what kind of music do you like?' Aaron asked.

There was a lengthy pause where you could actually see the cogs of her brain turning over the words 'music' and 'like' before she finally responded, 'Like, Marilyn Manson?'

And then Baby managed to get Addam involved in a conversation about the soundtrack of her film. I could see the dynamic of the room change. Two sets of couples, A and B, were forming. I, the 'N', was nowhere in this.

Aaron took Berenger over to the piano and sat her down at it. He leant over her shoulder to demonstrate a couple of notes. She was looking at him with what I thought at the time was stoned incomprehension. And then he played a few bars of something she seemed to recognise. She moved over and let him sit beside her.

Addam kept looking back at them while Baby talked. Aaron was now playing the score from *Little Women* which he and Arthur Keane had written in 1957 and which had been made into a film in 1960. It had been a phenomenal hit and the songs had passed into the cultural language like those of its contemporary, *My Fair Lady*.

Remarkably, Berenger started singing. A plaintive little voice, reed thin, that swiped at the low notes like an inept batsman. But, as approximate as her musical ability was, her grasp of the lyrics was faultless. Despite the cocktail of chemicals that was undoubtedly at that very moment playing tag with her brain cells, she managed to get Amy's third-act song word-perfect.

If Aaron seemed delighted, Addam was astonished. She probably just hummed his songs.

She giggled. 'It's, like, my *favourite* song. I sang it all the time when I was a kid. Kind of like "Raindrops on Roses" but sadder. I always wanted to be Amy.' Well, *that* made sense. When every little girl worth her Brownie stripes wanted to be Jo, Berenger related to the vain, vacuous Amy. 'I used to tie a tablecloth around me at the back like a…bustle?…you know, and dance around the house.'

'How marvellous!' exclaimed Aaron. He turned to Addam. 'You didn't tell me we're about to have another musician in the family.'

Addam coloured. I knew he was about to say, 'We're not' but

Berenger got in first. 'Addam, you didn't tell me your grandfather wrote *songs*.' She said 'songs' as if they were the most admirable things in the world, which perhaps they are.

'Lyrics my dear,' Aaron patiently explained.

'The way he spoke I thought you must have been, you know, ga-ga.'

I think we all gritted our teeth at that.

'Did he?' asked Aaron, looking at Addam.

Addam had adopted a nonchalant pose. I didn't like him at that moment.

'Well, he may be right,' Aaron sighed theatrically and gave Berenger one of his expansive smiles. 'Maybe I *am* ga-ga, as you so charmingly put it.' But there was a hard coal of ill-humour burning behind his gaze.

Baby made a strange sound, half cough, half strangled whine. I think we all knew something was happening, but none of us was perceptive or sober enough to interpret what it was.

'Let's go, Berry,' said Addam suddenly, moving away from Baby. 'We got things to do.'

But Berenger ignored him and kept her huge, shining eyes on Aaron. 'Did you write "The Rain in Spain"?' she asked breathlessly, as if no-one else was in the room. 'I, like, *really* love that one too.'

woke up in my room at Magdalen House confused, unsure how many hours or days it had been since Berenger had horrified me with her ghastly manifestation. I could still hear her thin little voice, accusing me. 'You can't hide it from me, Niley.'

I slowly became aware it was morning. The curtains over the window were bunched up, allowing the morning sun to project the shapes of leaves and branches on to the wall and momentarily trick me into thinking my reconstituted friend was still wavering there, staring back at me. The tangled branches were her wild hair, the gleam reflected from parked cars her savage eyes. As the shadows played in front of my eyes, I thought: was she any more than this?

The world seemed normal. It was still cold. Out the window, people wore coats in the street. My bed was in the same place. The heater still clanged. There was no backwards 'Berenger' etched into the dust.

I thought she had been real. Not a real person, a real phantom. But I had been seduced by phantoms before.

When I was a teenager, I would be visited, nocturnally, by a boy who professed love for me. Each night that he came he would be in a different guise. He would be blond, he would be dark. He would have brown eyes, he would have green. He would be wearing jeans, he would be wearing a peasant's smock, like the yokels in the pastoral romances I hid under my mattress. What was the same in every dream was that I was sick with love for him and he was sick with love for me and during the course of several thousand rapid eye movements we would lie together in the grassy knolls and fragrant gardens of my dreamscape and he would cover my face with kisses and I would stroke the long tendrils of his hair and I would feel the palpable warmth of him, the real flesh on mine, the real wetness of his lips and of the cartilage in his bones. And there would always come a point in the dream, as I was falling into his well, that my rogue consciousness would stray from the heat of him to the actual dampness between my thighs and I would think 'I don't ever want to wake up' and then, of course, I would.

And that's how it would start, the desperate attempt to slide back into the dream and reclaim him, my eyes squeezed tight, my head wedged under the pillow while my conscious mind roamed the landscapes of my imagination, disconsolately collecting memories of him like daisies, but never managing to piece together anything but a dull semblance, without the smell or touch or fire of the lover I had created wholly out of air.

And I would go crazy for the loss of him and thrash in my bed and soak my pillow with tears. I would be inconsolable. But the day would come and my sorrow would become heavier and then sink altogether. By day's end I would be free of him. I would feel nothing for him. And in some ways that was worse.

I looked out the window to the branches of the tree that still held the tattered plastic bag I'd mistaken for a child. The morning light was cold blue, as if a storm was coming in. The bag twisted in the wind, puffing out like a comic-strip ghost crying 'Boo!' I stifled a tortured sound, both giggle and shriek. I was being haunted! And by a child-woman I could put my arm through. By the memory of a lover who once appeared in the night. By the phantom sounds of babies crying and demons screaming. By a plastic bag, for Christ's sake.

I could have laughed but I stood there by the window and cried.

When eventually I went downstairs that day, Sister Pansy said to me, cheerfully, 'You look like you've seen a ghost!'

My legs dissolved under me and I sat down heavily on the steps. 'Is it that obvious?' I asked.

The good nun rushed over to me from behind the desk and started fanning me with one of the animal liberationists' pamphlets. 'There, there,' she said, taking my hand. 'She won't hurt you, you know.'

'How do you know that? You don't know what she's like.'

'Oh, yes I do. I've had my altercations with her. She's just stubborn, that's all. She refuses to believe she's dead.'

'That's what I don't understand. How can you not know you're *dead*?'

'Oh, from what I hear, most of them can't remember the moment of death, so in their minds they haven't died. Many of them are doomed to repeat the last thing they did before they passed into eternity. Like crossing the road, or taking out the garbage. Unless, of course, you can get a spiritualist to talk to them and convince them to go over to the Other Side.' She sighed. 'We've had three spiritualists come and talk to Eglantine but she refuses to go.'

'Eglantine?' I asked, not understanding.

'That's her name. I suppose you saw her up on the fourth floor? It scared the shit out of me the first time she came through that wall like that.'

Oh, Eglantine. The dead nun Domenica has seen.

'Poor thing. She was shot in the corridor when she tried to stop an angry husband who was looking for his wife. This was in 1947. There's a stain on the wallpaper that's her blood. In fact, the bloody wallpaper was stripped off and replaced but the stain just keeps on coming through no matter how many times we replace the paper. Spooky, isn't it?'

'But you haven't seen any other ghosts...lately?'

'I've got my hands full with Eglantine. Now, you don't look too upset. I'm glad you're sensible. Most girls who see her go completely to pieces.'

I'm sensible, I thought. I'm not going to go to pieces over Berenger either.

Sister Pansy helped me to my feet. 'In a place like this,' she said, 'girls imagine a lot of things. All alone in those dreary little rooms. It's unhealthy, if you ask me. But Eglantine's the only real ghost we have. She's even on the Haunted Manhattan walking tour. They're here at three every Saturday afternoon, standing on the pavement outside, pointing at our windows.'

'People come *looking* for ghosts?'

'You'd be surprised what people come looking for.' There was a soft rustling behind us on the staircase. Sister Pansy looked up and smiled. 'Oh, here's Ayesha. I want to introduce you. You're neighbours.'

I turned and looked straight into the most unfortunate face I'd ever seen.

Ayesha Bhargava. I winced every time I saw her, this diminutive girl with the face and neck that melted together like warm icecream and the right eye permanently closed by a cascade of scarring that stretched across her face like the taut fingers of a pink rubber glove. It was difficult to imagine she was pretty once, before her father arranged her marriage to Vir Bhargava, a forty-six-year-old taxi driver from Delhi, before the sister-in-law decided the dowry was not enough and conspired with her brother to throw burning oil on his young wife and free him to find another bride. Before her mother and father disowned her as damaged goods.

Ayesha carried a crumpled picture of her wedding day everywhere with her, the creases in the black-and-white photograph carefully smoothed out and pressed between thick plastic, and you could see her teenage face radiant with happiness, the eyes huge and limpid, the nose pert, the mouth curved like a wave— every feature in its place, perfect, hopeful, and unsuspecting of the terrible act that would soon come and ruin her life. Ayesha was nineteen years old and beautiful then but that is not why she carried the photograph with her. It was to remind her of her husband, Vir, whose forgiveness she sought every waking moment.

Despite Ayesha's 'accident', as she insisted on calling it, which ravaged forty-five per cent of her body—her face, shoulders, torso, hands and feet—she still felt guilty for fleeing to America. She had a well-meaning and well-connected cousin, Revi, who owned an Indian restaurant on 5th Street and who, outraged by the old ways of his homeland, sent Ayesha a one-way ticket to New York and sponsored her visa. Ayesha worked in the restaurant, hidden away in the steaming kitchen, and slept on Revi's floor in the house in Astoria he and his family shared with another 5th Street restaurant dynasty. But, after she was only there a few weeks, her cousin's wife had asked her to leave, Ayesha said, because she frightened the children.

I struck up a friendship with Ayesha soon after Sister Pansy introduced us that day in the lobby. I'm ashamed to say I was drawn to her because of her melted face. I had lived for months with a famous beauty who could barely tolerate a cuticle that was starting to shred, whose last scheme, before death did its own radical cosmetic surgery, was to have the wrinkles in her earlobes removed by laser beams. And here was Ayesha, a monster, a thing that children hid from on the street, with her sweet ways, her unselfishness, her politeness…her calm. She had been the same age as Berenger when she was scarred for life, but the vicious act hadn't scarred her soul. She was not mean, vain and neurotic. She was the un-Berenger.

Ayesha was strangely philosophical about her appearance, the glutinous skin that looked like it had been painted on with a palette knife, the caul over one eye, the crippled hands. 'Beauty is terrible, Nile,' she would say, as if she was relieved to be rid of it.

When I went to bed that night I kept on every light in the room, including the beam of a flashlight I'd bought during the day, in the hope that brightness would dissuade visitations by any creepy teenage ghosts who might be in the neighbourhood. I suppose my behaviour was preposterous. But so was the idea of a ghost in my room.

I had barely settled under the blanket when a tapping sound started up on the door. I froze. The tapping persisted. I cautiously climbed out of bed and stood by the door, breathing shallowly, for several minutes before I dared investigate. Ayesha was astanding there in the corridor, beautifully fleshy and whole. With a sigh, I let her in. She asked if I had something that might help a pain across her forehead. I think she was often in pain but bore it without complaint. She seemed very embarrassed to be asking a favour of a stranger and, when I obliged with two Advil, behaved as if she were beholden to me. She brought me flowers the following day and for the next week would knock on my door every time she was venturing outside, to see if I needed anything from the store, the magazine stand, the market. I knew she would have gladly travelled all the way to Coney Island to get me a Nathan's Famous hotdog if I had asked.

I'd never had a real friend before. My grandmother wouldn't let me bring friends home from school in case they messed up the house. At college, the girls shut me out, as if I were a stain that would ruin their immaculate boy-catching outfits. I rarely went out to the pub after work because I didn't drink. And in those first few months in New York, my scintillating socialite room-mate kept me well out of view when anyone visited, like a secret, mutant sibling. I used to sit and watch Berenger and Darien with their heads together, gossiping, as if they were an alien species. I didn't understand the concept 'girlfriend'.

But Ayesha was uncomplicated by the usual female vanities. She rarely had a hard word to say about anyone. Whenever she visited my room, she filled it with chatter about things she thought wonderful about America, like donuts and rollerblades.

185

It made me believe, for a moment, that these things were wonderful too.

I clung to Ayesha's friendship because her bright prattling filled the spaces in my head dangerously vulnerable to invasion. When Ayesha talked, there was no room for Berenger.

But I couldn't shake off the feeling that Berenger was listening to us, biding her time. More than once, I felt I was being followed down the street. I sometimes got goose-flesh for no apparent reason. As I lay on my pillow at night, I could feel little fingers prickling my scalp. I slept with the light on and checked the window each morning for nocturnal scratchings. Nothing. Berenger didn't make a peep. But that didn't mean she wasn't there. Her silence was not empty. I could feel her hostility in startling ways. Every time I touched a door handle or a metal railing, for instance, I would jump with the shock of static electricity. I knew it wasn't the ion-charged winter atmosphere. It was Berenger, reminding me she was there. Waiting.

Sister Pansy had been fretting about my antisocial ways, and thought I needed a job. It just so happened that Ayesha's boss, Dr Susan Mackie, an anthropologist who was writing a book about women in India with Ayesha's plight, was looking for a new research assistant. Ayesha and Sister Pansy conferred on this, without consulting me, and decided I was perfect for the job. Ayesha presented to me my appointment for a job interview, which had been written into Susan Mackie's diary in her own hand, as proudly as if it were a seven-layer cake she had baked herself.

'I don't need a job, thanks Ayesha,' I told her, although that wasn't true. If I were to survive, I had to do something. But I didn't want to be exposed to all the inevitable questions. Still, Ayesha looked so crestfallen, I changed my mind. Who would recognise me in a stuffy academic's office?

The interview was so speedy, I hardly remember it. Susan Mackie didn't seem to have a clue what to ask me. She looked at me, held out her hand, and said with a smile, 'You'll do.'

I suppose I do look like I'll 'do' in these circumstances—like a librarian, or an office manager at best. You could imagine me tucked away amongst stacks of books or poring over the month's ledgers. I may not be snappily dressed but I am solid and reliable. And these days I come cheap.

Ayesha had a passion for Krispy Kreme donuts which came hot off a conveyor belt in a shop right near the subway. She ate three of them every morning for breakfast, I discovered on our way to work that first day. 'You'll get fat!' I teased her, and her one eye would look at me cynically, as if she couldn't believe I'd think she'd care about getting fat.

Ayesha was afraid to go on the subway alone, fearful of being teased by gangs of gigantic schoolboys in puffy down jackets, drooping denims and Jansport backpacks, so she collected me for the ride downtown every morning at nine. She always draped her face in a sari under a big tweed coat and stared at her crippled hands while the C train lurched to the World Trade Centre. Even when she was chattering away to me about *True Romance* magazine, she kept her eyes downcast. I, on the other hand, was always surreptitiously scanning the subway car for signs that my fellow travellers might recognise me. No-one did.

Dr Susan Mackie's office was on Vesey Street, tucked away on the fifth floor of a beaux arts building populated mostly by insurance brokers, travel agents and trust-fund kids playing at being multimedia moguls. The building looked over the grave-yard of St Paul's chapel, with its chalky, ancient headstones eaten to thin tablets by acid rain, and spindly cherry branches that tapped against each other in the wind. Susan's office, being at the back, didn't have the luxurious view of rotting crypts and mouldering piles of autumn leaves that a prime lease affords: but given that she was writing a book entitled *The Incendiary Wife: A Social History of the Burning Brides of India*, she hardly needed to be reminded about human mortality. But for Ayesha, who inhabited the tiny outer office with an old IBM clone and a telephone, and for me, forced to share a windowless broom cupboard with several stacks of undisciplined files, a view even of a rooftop airconditioner would have been better than the fluorescent half-light we had to endure.

We would unlock the office before 9.30 and Ayesha would go straight to her desk and wait for the phone to ring. My job was to plough through transcripts of tapes Susan made on her last trip to New Delhi, back in August.

At ten or eleven, Susan Mackie would push open the door to the outer office and dump her usual jumble of manuscripts, books and overflowing handbag on her desk.

'I'm sorry, guys, I'm *sorry*!' I would hear her exclaim breathlessly as she came in. She was always flustered when she arrived. That's because she was a thirty-eight-year-old single mother, the kind that never married, and the mere existence of two-year-old Rufus meant she was incapable of leaving her Park Slope row-house in the mornings without forgetting something and having to go back, or finding herself on a train that wasn't delayed by a suicidal schoolgirl. I don't think Susan was actually ever sorry about being late, because being late was part of her person, like the tiny strawberry birthmark on her jaw. What she was mostly sorry for was *us*, her two scarred refugees in their airless boxes.

'I've gotta get us another office!' She would slump into a squeaky desk chair and wipe a strand of bouncy chestnut hair out of her eyes. She was tall and rangy and square-jawed, like that actress in the *Alien* movies. She swivelled her chair around, surveying the piles of manilla folders which were set to topple from the shelves at any minute and sighed, 'We gotta get a system here!'

That, of course, was my role, but all I did once I started was work through the backlog of tapes. Susan's disorganisation extended to hiring me for one job and giving me another. She had, apparently, already missed three deadlines on the book. I could feel another coming on.

That first morning on the job, I stayed in my cupboard as Ayesha filled Susan in on the morning's solitary phone call, from Rufus's shrink. I hadn't laid eyes on the child at that point, so I wasn't sure whether Susan gave birth to a son or a social experiment. But I was rooting for the latter—having not found a man who was perfect in every way for her, she was trying to create one of her own.

Rufus was born on a dirt and dung floor in Fatehpur in Rhajistan and spent the first few months of his life carried around in a sling while Susan visited hospitals, government offices and slums. Ayesha told me that Susan believed Rufus needed to be exposed to female suffering at this early age so that he could grow into a man who was sensitive to the political oppression of women worldwide. Personally, I thought she was more likely to create a pyromaniac who got his kicks from setting fire to women—a gynopyromaniac, perhaps?

Later in the morning, Susan called me into her room for a chat. Despite the child who had to be delivered to the nursery school each morning and the general disorganisation of her office, Susan always managed to look...I suppose sexy is the word, if you happen to like women in slim jackets and micro miniskirts who wear spiky heels to show off their fabulous legs. I looked at Susan's legs (it was virtually impossible not to) in their unblemished hose and thought, underneath it all you have the same priorities as everyone else. Your son may indeed be the next incarnation of the Dalai Lama, you might be on your third book about dead, oppressed women, but what's really important to you is to be admired for your legs.

'Look, I'm sorry about all this mess,' she said, as I stood in the doorway. 'Why don't you sit down? Oh, well, maybe the edge of the table?'

I did what she asked and pushed a stack of *Atlantic Monthly*s to one side. A pile of folders toppled to the floor. Susan didn't even notice. The space in her office was always in this kind of flux: shove, spill, topple, fall.

'So, how are you enjoying it here?' Her chumminess seemed forced.

As I'd only been there two hours, I really couldn't say. 'It's fine.'

'But I've noticed you look a bit…disturbed?'

'Well, I'm not. I'm fine.'

'I'm sorry I've thrown you in at the deep end, but with a May deadline…'

'It looks interesting.'

'It is, isn't it?' She brightened up, pushed her chair away from the desk, and flexed a slender ankle. 'I was researching my second book, on *sati*—you know, the widows who are incinerated on their husband's funeral pyre, none of them do it voluntarily of course, they are *obliged* by custom, men's custom… where was I?…Oh, I was travelling near the Chinese border in Kashmir when I came across my first burnt bride. She was seventeen years old and, even though a neighbouring couple were in the room at the time when her husband set her alight, they were too frightened of him to report it to the police. Did you know that poor families routinely murder their infant daughters because they know they will be unable to come up with a suitable dowry when she is of age? The lack of dowry brings more shame on the family than murder…But so many babies are dying there, what's one more? That's the attitude of society. It makes me *ill* to think of it. So'— she slapped her hands on her taut thighs—'I decided to do something about it.'

She smiled at me for a few seconds. 'Ayesha tells me that you used to work for that model who killed herself…Berenger, wasn't it? It must have been very sad for you.'

I could have killed Ayesha at that moment. Or perhaps Sister Pansy, who had no doubt filled Ayesha in on my sorry little story. 'Very,' I lied.

'It must have been awful.'

'It was.' That part was true.

190

'Was she very unhappy?'

'It was an accident,' I said, defensively.

'Of course, of course. But drug overdoses are rarely *really* accidents, are they? The subject always has underlying problems, maybe she even had a death wish.'

I did not!

I tried to block out the voice that crept into the space between my cranium and my brain.

'It's astonishing how many really lovely girls have a serious lack of self-esteem.'

Who is this woman?

I could feel those tiny skeleton fingers digging into my skull. 'Go away!' I said to the air.

'What?' asked Susan Mackie, frowning.

'I'm sorry,' I said. 'There's a mosquito.'

'This time of year?'

'Maybe it's been trapped here since summer.' Keep talking, I thought, say anything. Don't let that other voice in.

'Maybe. I suppose the place isn't that clean…'

Find out if she can see me.

'No!'

'Well, I'm sorry about it, but with my budget I can't afford a cleaner.'

Find out if she can see me!

'Don't be ridiculous!'

'I'm sorry you feel that way.' Susan sounded peeved.

'No…no,' I said, not wanting her to misunderstand. 'I didn't mean you.'

'Then…who? Is something bothering you?'

'I'm fine.' But I wasn't. I wasn't by a long way.

'Do you want some water?'

'No thanks.'

Tell her I'm here.

'She'll think I'm mad.'

You are mad.

Was I?

'Nile?' Susan leapt to her feet and hovered, not sure what to do.

I closed my eyes and try to channel Berenger out. 'Is there anyone else in this room?' I asked Susan with great effort.

'You mean now? Well, Ayesha's stepped out…'

'No-one but you and me?'

'No. Why?'

'See!' I hissed at Berenger, every nerve-ending in my body shrieking. 'Now, piss off!'

'What do you mean?' Susan was now indignant.

'And don't come back!'

'Nile, I really think you should—'

'And stay out of my room, too!'

'If you feel that way…' Too late, I watched Susan back away against the door.

'No!' I yelled at her, realising what I had done.

'It's OK, Nile,' she said, making eye contact with me. 'I'll just get Ayesha. She'll know what to do.'

I watched Susan slide through the door. I stood there, trembling.

'Berenger?'

In front of my eyes, a stack of papers tumbled off Susan's table and thudded to the floor.

I knew that was Berenger's answer.

had been working for Aaron at the San Remo for a year and a half when I was woken one night in my 83rd Street apartment by a call from a drunken newspaper columnist who claimed he had just been with Berenger at a nightclub and that she had told him she was unofficially engaged to marry Aaron. Could I, as Aaron's personal assistant, confirm? I told him I could not, slammed down the phone, and then wondered how he got my number.

I lay there awake, fretting over how suddenly vulnerable I was. The press knew my number! I felt exposed, as if a barrage of telephoto lenses were pointing at my window. I thought those days were long over. But then I realised this wasn't what I was fretting over at all.

Berenger and Aaron? Surely he meant Addam?

Since that tense dinner three months earlier, I hadn't heard a word about Berenger. As for Addam, the only mention of him in the household was whenever I downloaded Baby's illiterate ramblings in cyberspace. I had to be content with sneaking the occasional glimpse of his picture in issues of *Rolling Stone* and *Spin*. The sensible part of me scoffed at my fantasies about a man who would never see me as anything other than the lackey of his grandfather, but the part of me with imagination skipped all the practical considerations and went straight to the consummation.

A few weeks earlier I'd noticed a small column in the arts pages of the *Times*—

Talks are under way between theatrical producers Lenrick and songwriter Addam Karsner, lead singer of the band Detox, to bring Karsner's rock opera, *Deviant*, to Broadway. After a reading of the musical at the packed WPA theatre last Friday evening, which featured the talents of Karsner pals Fiona Apple and Iggy Pop, Lenrick president, Theo Handesman, announced that the company is looking for a suitable theatre to mount the production and is considering the feasibility of restoring the old Starlight on West 39th Street for the purpose.

Insiders report the musical is about a rock star and a fashion model, with Miss Apple considering the role of the latter. Will Mr Karsner star opposite her? 'Addam is not even considering it,' Handesman said. 'He has said all along he wants Trent Reznor to play the lead.' But will the diminutive Miss Apple make the grade as a fashion model? 'Well, there is Kate Moss,' Handesman comments. 'She's tiny too.' Word of mouth is that the musical transcends its cliche-ridden subject matter. 'It's brilliant!' said pal Madonna, who sneaked into the WPA theatre for the second half of the Friday night reading, toddler Lourdes asleep on her hip. 'It will be the next *Rent*.'

I clipped the story from the paper and placed it in the folder on Aaron's desk where I put anything I thought might interest him. He made no comment about it during the days that followed, and I didn't dare mention it. So I continued my molish ways, transcribing and filing and helping Aaron raid his memory for anecdotes to include in his book.

One afternoon, he called me in to the study to ask me for a phone number. There was a young woman with him, whom I took to be one of the frequent students from Juilliard who came to interview him for their course work. Aaron introduced us. Her name was something old-fashioned, like Thelma, but she had rings through her nose, dangling what looked like silver fish, and a shaved head. She looked at me with arched plucked eyebrows as if my presence mystified her, but I supposed she was simply so dazzled by the great man that all other creatures on earth had ceased to exist for her at that moment.

While I was writing down the number on the legal pad Aaron kept beside him for notes, Thelma was enthusing about some production she'd seen at the Roundabout. Aaron was silent, a small flicker of amusement playing at the corners of his mouth. I knew he hated this particular production, a 'song cycle' about the 1932 garment-workers fire, which he found pretentious and, worse, unmelodious (his usual complaint). Thelma started to pick up on his disapproval a few sentences into her spiel. Her eyes started darting about the room uncertainly and she floundered for a minute before changing in mid-review to what she thought was a safer subject. 'You're Addam Karsner's grandfather, aren't you?' she blurted. 'You know, the one in Detox?'

'I'm well aware of who he is,' Aaron said coldly. A smile was stretched across his lips but his eyes were opaque.

Thelma took the chilly smile for encouragement. 'Of course, you do, I'm so...*duh!*' She raised her mascara-clogged eyelashes to the ceiling to express in a shrug what words could not and chomped on her purple-stained bottom lip. 'He's like really *dope*. I have all his CDs, even that unplugged one with the two live long-plays. It's really hard to find. I think "I Eat Myself" is the greatest song ever written! It's so *sad*.'

I pretended to keep writing, even though I had long since finished jotting down the number. From where I was bending over, next to him, I could sense Aaron's rigidity. He was absolutely still, like an old lion ready to pounce on an unsuspecting scrub turkey, of which Thelma was beginning to remind me.

'I mean, it's fabulous news about *Deviant*, isn't it?' she continued, oblivious. 'Some of the students at Juilliard went to the reading and they said it was absolutely brilliant! Like the best thing they'd ever seen. He's so incredibly talented, he must get it from you!' She looked up brightly, expecting Aaron to be pleased with the compliment.

Aaron closed his eyes. Thelma took that for assent.

'To be only twenty-seven and have your first Broadway production! It's like Jonathan Larsen, isn't it, only I hope Addam won't die!' The reference to the untimely death of the author of *Rent* made me cringe. Aaron had privately called *Rent* a 'cacophonic soap opera' and 'a great argument against finding a vaccine for AIDS', which even I had thought a little harsh.

'Well, that was a stupid thing to say,' Thelma said more to herself than to Aaron. 'Of course he won't die. He'll probably live to be as old as you.'

'Thank you,' said Aaron, bowing his head.

'How old were you when you had your first Broadway show, Mr Karsner?' There seemed to be no end to Thelma's asininity. 'You were like *young*, weren't you?'

'Twenty-two,' Aaron replied dryly.

'Cool!' said Thelma. 'You know there are twin brothers at La Guardia High School, they're only fifteen, who are updating Dante's *Inferno* to like the *seventies*. They've finished *Purgatory*. It's like set in a disco.'

'That must be hell.'

'Yeah! It's getting so's you're old hat at twenty! I better hurry up. I'm eighteen. That's almost over the hill these days.'

I had to intervene. Aaron was gripping his left wrist so hard with his right hand I thought he might snap it. Later, after he had abruptly terminated the interview with the confused Thelma and I had found my chair beside him, ready to take notes on the manuscript, he said playfully, 'In my day, students were just as stupid.'

'What do you mean, in *your* day? You've got a lot more days in you yet.'

His wry smile withered. 'You disappoint me,' he said, and his eyes drifted away from mine. 'I haven't lost all of my marbles you know,' he went on. 'You talk to me like some damn nurse in an infirmary.'

It was the first time Aaron had spoken to me in this way, as an equal. He'd always been, I suppose, a little patronising. But now he was speaking as if I was an irritating spouse of whom he'd long grown tired. In a peculiar way, I was flattered.

'Do I? I'm sorry,' I answered. 'I didn't mean to.'

'You're all the same. Even Frances, who must be sixty if she's a day. You all treat me like a senile fool who's ready to be shipped off to the retirement village...or the grave.'

'But I don't—'

He waved my protests away with a delicate hand. 'I have the same brain that I had when I was twenty—a *better* brain than when I was twenty because I exercise it every waking minute of every day. This body may not have the strength it had then, but my eyes haven't failed me, thank God, and I can still manage those wretched subway stairs. Although you may find this hard to believe, I'm not ready for diapers yet. I intend to live as long as Irving did—*longer*!' He meant Irving Berlin, who had died at 101. 'I intend to die of old age when I'm *old.*'

I was about to protest that he wasn't old, but of course that was precisely what he meant.

He hadn't finished. 'You find that surprising, don't you? That I don't think I'm old?'

I began to say no, then took a deep breath. 'Yes,' I said truthfully.

'Good girl,' he nodded, satisfied. 'I can feel the difference in my body, of course, even in small things like holding this book on my lap. It didn't just sneak up on me. One day I was leaping up all those stairs at the Paris Opera and the very next day I couldn't get out of this chair. And there are times, like this morning talking to that foolish young girl with those things in her nose, that I feel as old as Methuselah. What a stupid girl! To have the gift of a voice and to want to waste it on...*pop* music.' He spat it out. 'Oh, I know what you're thinking,' he continued. 'My lyrics are "popular" too. But there's a difference. I didn't get where I am now by writing *down* to my audience, to their basest needs and emotions. I wrote *up*! Up to their hopes and dreams. But this generation, your generation if I might say so, Nile, wants to deny everything we did, make music that has no melody and films that have no plot and books that have no point. The girls dress in sacks to deny their beauty and the boys wipe themselves out…No, no, don't interrupt.'

I was about to open my mouth to agree. I'm sure he thought I was going to contradict him.

'Old people all say that, don't they? That the younger generation is stupid, inarticulate, ill-mannered and morally bankrupt? But has there ever been a more stupid younger generation? When we were young we fooled around, did wild and crazy things. We'd had a war, seen our fathers and sisters and school friends wiped off the face of the earth. God was trying to show us how worthless we were. And so we had to fight back to prove Him wrong! Everything we did was to prove our worth, whether we made great art or music or built enormous skyscrapers or founded huge corporations. We were optimistic, despite everything. This generation is stupid because it's so *pessimistic*. To be alive and to be depressed about it—' His face contorted in disgust. 'But this all confirms what an old fogey I am, doesn't it?'

'No, I understand what you're saying.'

'I might look like an old fogey—and sound like one too—but I'm a young person in an old body. Age means wisdom, and I am not wise, Nile. I am still capable of foolish things. But I can't win. When I was young they called the same foolish behaviour *immaturity* but now they call it *senility*.'

That afternoon, as if to taunt him, Aaron received a call from his editor, a young man called Fleischer Row. (Aaron secretly called him 'Fleischer & Row' because he was so self-important 'he acts as if he owns the wretched company'.) I'd spoken to him on the phone but we'd never met because Fleischer usually preferred to have his conferences with Aaron at some fashionable literary hangout downtown where he could keep his own personal humidor and his own personal bottle of Le Taroquet 1938.

I didn't know how old Fleischer was, but he always sounded as if his voice had just broken. 'How is the Living Legend today?' he asked me in a tone that was just on the wrong side of respectful.

'Fine, Mr Row,' I said curtly and handed the phone across the desk to Aaron.

Aaron mumbled the usual pleasantries. I knew he didn't like Fleischer and found his insatiable appetite for gossip a chore. From the gist of the conversation I could tell that Fleischer wanted to reschedule their next lunch. But I pricked up my ears when I heard Aaron say, 'Oh, is that so?' He sounded cautious, and didn't look happy, although I imagined he would have been overjoyed to learn that he had escaped this month's ordeal with Fleischer. 'I see. I promise you I will think about it. Goodbye.'

Aaron put down the phone and shrugged his thin shoulders. 'It seems as if we are not "sexy" enough,' he told me.

I asked him what he meant.

'It appears as if I am not writing a book that will attract enough young readers, especially young females. As Fleischer & Row so succinctly puts it, all my readers are dying off. So we need to "sexy" the thing up, bring in more gossip. Could I relate some stories about Jack Kennedy, for instance, he still goes down well. And perhaps I could make some more of my relationship with my brilliant grandson? In fact, why don't we divide the book into two parts—the first one being my meagre life and times, the second one My Life With Addam Karsner, young, handsome, romantic rock star? We'd swing a lot of Christmas sales with that angle.'

'That's ridiculous!' I commented loyally, although underneath I was thrilled by the prospect of having to collaborate with Addam.

'Is it? The last time I had lunch with Fleischer at that infernal greasy spoon, the whole restaurant overhead the woman at the next table exclaim as I sat down, "Is that Aaron Karsner? I thought he was *dead*!"'

'But, Aaron, it's *your* book, you can write what you want. It's your *life*. I find it fascinating.'

He looked at me steadily for a while. 'You're not a normal young woman, are you Nile? You don't go in for that drug business and you don't spend all your money on clothes and going out to nightclubs chasing boys. You prefer to while away your days with a decrepit old thing like me. I imagine you don't even have a boyfriend, do you? At least, I've never heard you chatter endlessly about such a person, like any other young girl might do.'

'I've had boyfriends.'

'Of course you have! But sex is not a priority for you, Nile. I can see that.'

How? How could he see that?

'May I venture to say it's in the way you dress. You go about in head scarves and hats that conceal your young face. You are always sensible, bless you, Nile, but there is not a single thing about you I could call…flirtatious. I'm afraid that sex appeal is something on which we both miss out.'

I wasn't really listening to him. I was flabbergasted by the turn the conversation had taken. Was I as dreary as all that? As unattractive? Aaron, a liver-spotted arrangement of bones whose hands shook when he was holding the telephone, thought of me as a sexless drudge because I was serious and dutiful and wore clothes that did not distract from the job at hand. The unfairness of it stung like lemon juice on a wound and I had to blink back tears of despair.

'Now don't get offended, Nile. I'm sure you could be a pretty young thing if you decided to work at it. But you have other values, and I admire you for that. Now, let's go back to that manuscript and see how we can make it sexy.'

Aaron seemed unexpectedly chirpy all of a sudden, as if a

heavy weight had been lifted from him. He had, after all, unburdened all his frustrations on me. But I knew he didn't mean to hurt my feelings. He misunderstood me, that was all.

Months later, after they'd been married, I found out what had gone on between Aaron and Berenger while none of us was looking.

I was sitting with Berenger in the Air France lounge at Charles de Gaulle airport watching her down glass after glass of champagne in preparation for the flight. She was starting to get maudlin about her life and so I distracted her with some comment about a party she had been invited to in New York the next night.

'I'm going to take Aaron,' she said.

I looked at her in surprise. She rarely took Aaron to anything social.

'Don't look at me like that!' she snapped. I could feel heads turning, if they weren't already, to look at the loud and semi-inebriated supermodel.

'You think I ran after him, don't you?' she asked.

'I didn't say that.'

'But you thought it, didn't you? For your information, he called me. Like, I wasn't expecting it. I only took the call because I thought it was Addam.'

'But why on earth would he call *you*?'

'He happened to find me *fascinating*. That's what he said.'

'So he asked you on a…date?'

'He said he'd like my opinion of the book he was writing. That he thought I'd have something interesting to say about it. So I went.'

'But why?'

'Because he made me feel *smart*.'

'So you went there and read the book? Just you and he sitting by the fire sipping sherry with the grandfather clock chiming?'

'Very funny. I did read it. But it took me a few visits.'

'A *few* visits? How come I didn't know about any of them?'

'I came late at night. You weren't there. He didn't ever say a word about you.'

'But Addam knew you were going?'

'No. I didn't tell him. Things, like, weren't so good between Addam and me then.' She hiccupped.

'But I don't understand it. Why would a girl like you want to spend all those hours with a man like Aaron?'

'Why would a girl like *you*?'

'That's different.'

'You just can't accept that Aaron preferred my brain to yours.'

'Oh, that's what it was, was it? Your *brain*?'

'As a matter of fact, it was. My conversation always cheered him up. He'd, like, have a dull old day with you and that creepy housekeeper and I'd come along and make him feel better. I could tell him, like, *everything*.'

'Like about you and Addam I suppose.'

'In the beginning I did tell him about Addam. He was very kind. He listened to me. It wasn't like, "Oh, Berenger, shut up!" or "Oh, Berenger, what would you know?" I get that all the time, like I was five years old or something. He told me all about Addam's childhood and why he acts like he does, all the women and stuff and why he's so *hard*. And he told me I shouldn't take it. I was too beautiful and too clever. That I should respect myself more. And, like, everyone else is always trying to put me down like I'm *too* beautiful and *too* famous and so I need to be slapped around a bit, but Aaron, he was respectful to me and it was nice.'

'He was nice. So are all grandfathers. You've never had a grandfather so you wouldn't know. Being nice is no reason to marry him.'

'Isn't it? No-one had ever been nice to me before.'

'Oh no? What about the clothes, the trips, the people kow-towing to you at every opportunity—'

'You think that's *nice*? That's...*phoney*. They're not giving *me*

202

things or inviting *me* places. They're inviting *Berenger*. She's different from me. I have to put her on every morning before I go out and push her around with me like some kind of fucking old aunt in a wheelchair. She's a drag. Aaron liked *me*. He didn't want the whole fucking star trip. He wanted me sitting in his room, on his big old sofa, just talking about whatever came into my head.

'Don't you see, Nile, someone being nice to me is the most romantic thing that ever happened to me? You take niceness for granted because you think it's ordinary, that anyone can be nice. But you show me who is ever really nice. It's all fucking surface where I've been. No-one is ever nice without a reason.'

'So it all comes down to Aaron being, what did you say, cosy? Only you could reduce him to the status of a stuffed toy. He's a *genius*, Berenger, he's not something you pick up at the Disney store.'

'Well, he didn't like being a genius. You all made him feel like a fossil, with this genius stuff. I don't know what a genius is.'

'Precisely.'

'You don't get it do you, Nile?'

They called our flight number, but not before she took another gulp of champagne.

Then there was the phone call from the drunken journalist. Aaron marrying Berenger? It was inconceivable. Inconceivable that a man like that, with all his gifts, would waste his time on a pouting nitwit whose idea of an intellectual challenge was probably filling out an immigration card at the airport. (I was right about that.) Was it all to do with how beautiful she was?

Beauty is skin deep, they always say. But 'they' don't mean it. They only say to it to make plain girls like me feel better, make us feel that beauty is something inconsequential that can be blown away like face powder. But beauty doesn't just brush the surface, it gets *under* your skin, spreads like a fungus, takes hold in such a way that you can turn yourself inside-out trying to scratch it away. I was disgusted that Aaron had fallen for an absurd teenager's pretty face but, in the end, was I any better? It wasn't Addam's mind I was infatuated with after all.

Aaron pre-empted any discussion of the marriage rumour. The first thing he said when I walked into his study that next morning was, 'Well, it seems we're going to have a wedding.'

'Yes,' I said, and it came out sharp as flint. I avoided his gaze and started rummaging through some papers.

He didn't say anything but I could feel him watching me. His breath rattled in his chest like a stone in a bellows. 'You don't approve, I take it.'

'No...I do. Congratulations,' I said dully, stacking papers that didn't need to be stacked on top of each other.

'No you don't,' he continued. 'You think I'm an old pervert, like the rest of them.'

'I didn't say that!' I could feel myself flush deep to the follicles of my hair.

'You didn't have to. But it's what I want.'

'I'm sure,' I replied tersely.

'I'd like to have your best wishes.'

I stopped what I was doing. He was looking at me brightly, even with amusement.

'You do have my best wishes.'

'I don't think so. I don't think so,' he shook his head. 'What can we do to win you over?'

'We?'

'Berenger and myself.'

'Oh.'

'You will keep working with me even though I'm no longer a crusty old bachelor?'

'I—I don't know.'

'I don't want you to get put out because there'll be another young lady in the house.'

I knew even then that Berenger was no young lady.

'Are you...I mean, is she...?' What I was trying to say was *Are you going to live together? Is she going to share your bed? Have you already had sex? Are you capable of it?* But, of course, I said none of this. What I did blurt out was 'Is she going to wear a wedding dress?' As soon as I said it I went crimson.

Aaron thought this was very funny. 'I hope she's going to wear a wedding dress! My other wives did.'

I recovered as quickly as I could. 'What I meant to say—is it going to be a big wedding?'

He smiled benevolently. 'The answer is yes. And why the heavens not? It's the last wedding I'm going to have!'

There was nothing I could say to that.

I was stung at first. I couldn't suppress the feeling that Aaron had betrayed me. We were happy as we were. Why did he need a wife? He had Frances and me. Why did he need to complicate things with a little brat who had already had her claws in Addam? I thought of Addam pouring champagne for her in that tent, putting his arm around her, tangling his feet in hers. And then, suddenly, an astounding thought occurred to me: if Berenger is marrying Aaron, where does this leave Addam?

t wasn't a wedding. It was a photo opportunity.

I didn't have much to do with the arrangements. Aaron seemed determined to keep me out of it and I knew better than to ask him questions. I don't think Berenger knew I existed. She was out of town most of the time, but when she did visit Aaron she usually arrived as I was leaving or, if she was in Aaron's office, I made myself scarce.

The subject of the wedding rarely came up directly between us. In fact, as far as I could see, it held little interest for him, apart from keeping Berenger happy. Whenever I did overhear her trying to rope him into a discussion about guests or catering or which publication was likely to offer the most for photographs, he would demur with, 'It's your wedding, dear.' Berenger seemed to be launching herself into the event like a child planning for her eighth birthday party, while Aaron was the distant relative who was footing the bill but not intending to take part.

A public relations company had been engaged, ostensibly to keep the media at length, although in reality it was working hard to 'package the concept' and sell it off in small increments to the highest bidders. Occasionally the chief publicist would get through to me at Aaron's when Berenger wouldn't return her calls and she'd launch into a blow-by-blow description of the negotiations before I managed to squeeze in the suggestion that she was speaking to the wrong person. She'd hang up on me without apology and then call back an hour later with another update. I had the feeling she needed a sounding board, and I, of course, was the perfect plank.

And so I got to know all the details. *Harper's Bazaar* was to be allowed the official wedding party fashion spread, to be photographed the week before the ceremony, with *Bazaar* editors styling the clothes that Berenger and her four bridesmaids would be wearing. Every detail was to be pre-produced, from the masses of flowers on the church pews to the celebrant's Gucci heels, which replaced the shabby suede flats that the stylist deemed unsuitable. The happy bridegroom refused to take part in this exercise but was considered superfluous in any case. 'This is a *fashion* story, after all,' the publicist pointed out to me in one of her monologues.

In Style was to cover the wedding itself and various other publications were parcelled out pieces of Berenger, who gave prenuptial interviews by phone from places as inaccessible as the plains of Bosnia, where she was undertaking a high profile tour of land mines with a French pop star and the President of UNICEF. When asked by one journalist why she and Aaron had chosen to be married by a celebrant rather than a priest or rabbi, Berenger responded, 'Well, I'm, like, a *heathen.*'

The location of the wedding, a deconsecrated chapel on an estate in East Hampton, was supposed to be a secret, but only for as long as it took the ink to dry on the invitations, which were sheets of apparently plain paper typed with a few cryptic details.

'Like the invitations to Helmut Lang's shows, when he did them in Paris,' I overheard Berenger explaining to Aaron one afternoon when I was in his study in the San Remo. She produced a piece of paper. 'It's really cool. When the girl on the door shines a special light on it, a little HL appears, which makes it authentic. We could have a little B and a little A.'

'Dear, it's a wedding not a nightclub,' Aaron commented, without looking up from the manuscript he was reviewing.

'But you want it to be *fun*, don't you? Not like those other boring weddings you had.'

The journalists pursued Addam for a comment about the marriage from the start. The clipping service sent me some passing references to him. He'd been accosted by a columnist from *Page Six* at Asia de Cuba and had announced, 'I'm very happy for both of them.' And then, in an aside, he had told a companion, 'They deserve each other,' which, of course, the journalist picked up.

I'd been bold enough to ask Baby how Addam had taken the news. She said he had been 'heartbroken'. I hurt for him but I was overjoyed that Berenger was out of the picture. Then Baby added that Addam seemed to be healing pretty fast, that he had a new girlfriend already—the 'voodoo goddess', as she called her. I was stunned, although why on earth I should have been I don't know. Did I imagine he'd wipe his tears away and come to me?

I knew Addam was invited to the wedding but even Baby didn't expect him to come. The eighty invitees were asked to keep mum about the details, but seventy-nine of them seemed to think this meant unloading the information on only one or two select gossip columnists, as opposed to the usual practice of issuing a blanket press release announcing their inclusion in the 'wedding of the year'. One newspaper printed a map of East Hampton with directions to the site.

The one guest who did not talk was me. I was shocked to receive, in the mail, the sought-after piece of folded white paper with the black-light sensitive 'AB'. I didn't imagine that I would make it to the A list, but here it was, a sheet of paper sitting on my dresser. I kept on folding it and unfolding it for days. The morning after it arrived I thanked Aaron shyly and he said, 'It's nothing at all. I thought you'd like to see the old codger make a fool of himself.'

Baby, of course, was beside herself. She veered between being thrilled that she was connected to such a media maelstrom ('It's just like when Mick married Bianca!') and worried about what Berenger's new status would mean to Addam's inheritance. She sometimes called me three times a day, mostly to make certain she was getting an invitation. She wanted to make a documentary of the wedding, but I believe Aaron put his foot down.

'But I'm virtually the mother of the bride!' she wailed. I don't know how she worked that one out. As far as I could see, she was only the mother of the ex-boyfriend of the bride or the ex-defacto-daughter-in-law of the groom. In fact, there was no 'mother-of-the-bride', which might have increased the chances of Baby achieving her wish to be part of the bridal party. I discovered this when I was walking past Aaron's sitting room one day on the way to the bathroom and overheard Berenger whining about who would 'give her away'.

'But what about your stepfather?' Aaron was asking.

'Oh, he can't come.'

'Why not?'

'Some farm stuff, I don't know.'

'Your mother, then? She could give you away.'

'She can't travel.'

'Why not?'

'They can't come, OK?' Berenger sulked. And, right then, I knew: she didn't want to ask them. She made them sound like simple farm folk, and she was ashamed of them. Not that it mattered: with Baby there, there'd be more than enough mother to go round.

'I suppose I could ask Richard.'

Aaron just garrumphed. Whoever Richard was, I thought, Aaron didn't like him.

'I only slept with him *once*.'

Erik Sklar ended up giving the bride away. Even though it was the middle of winter in a garden barely sheltered from the icy blasts of the Atlantic Ocean by a few low bushes of oleander, Berenger wore a dress of strapless lavender satin, lashed about the waist with black lace, above which her small round breasts were forced almost to her throat. It was more suitable for a bordello in Kansas City than a beachfront wedding on Long

Island, I thought, but I was merely an observer. I did know, however, that a European designer who needed the exposure in America had paid her $30,000 for the honour of having her appear in his dress.

A few months later, *In Style* magazine reported that the wedding looked like a Revlon advertisement, the bridal party was so full of famously made-up faces. This was hardly surprising since the bride earned her living *being* a Revlon advertisement, as did two of the bridesmaids.

I recognised Darien Apps, even though I had last seen her stark naked. The three other bridesmaids—a tangle-haired redhead, a platinum blonde and a moon-faced African—looked as if they had been selected purely for contrast to Berenger's dark hair. I think I was right about this, for later on, when I was with Berenger backstage, she barely ever gave them the time of day, except for the most fleeting of air kisses.

The bridesmaids wore sugary colours that matched the frosted almonds piled high in glass bowls on the tables at the wedding feast afterwards: actually 'feast' was a misnomer, the menu consisting of minuscule chilled crustacean appendages prepared by a famous Japanese chef, silver buckets of glistening fish eggs—three kinds—and a tossed salad of bitter endive, tiny rounds of chocolate cake the size of subway tokens and hundreds of splits of Krug, which everyone sipped through straws. The four girls stood around patiently in their wispy dresses in the frigid air, the thick hairs on their bare arms (a sign, I learned later, of the nervous disorder anorexia) standing up like spiky dune grass, their perfect white Revlon teeth chattering, as the celebrity photographer, a bespectacled paparazza who specialised in back-stage shots, dashed around among them, shooting not only faces and poses but obscure details like the Union Jack on the back of Baby's leather jacket—Sid's, she said—and the vertiginous heels of the celebrant's shoes, which I suppose justified the *Harper's Bazaar* stylist's insistence on them.

But of course models were used to standing around in the

cold, waiting. It was the toughest part of their job, this limbo land between preparation and performance, the empty hours or minutes with nothing to do but chainsmoke Czech cigarettes, read novelisations of 'The X-Files', peruse magazines in search of their own faces and indulge in listless small talk. Even though I knew little about the fashion business then, I had no doubt the bridesmaids had all performed the wedding scene before, if not in outfits for magazines that specialised in perpetuating the myth that a beautiful bride is a happy one, then for those annual spring fashion spreads, where they would be posed in fluttering floral dresses on lawns under sprawling oaks, giggling behind mani-cured hands or twirling parasols gaily, Pekinese puppies romping at their heels and a groaning gingham-clad table of summer sweetmeats they would never eat laid out under a pergola in the unfocused distance.

Berenger looked sublimely happy standing outside the church with her spray of lilies—funeral lilies I noted—and her accessorised maids-in-waiting. But who could tell if the blush on her cheeks was from modesty, excitement or Lancome Pomette rouge?

Aaron was another matter. Although he was accustomed to media attention, it wasn't of the same kind. 'These damn vultures, wanting to know what I'm wearing,' he mumbled to me one morning before the wedding. 'A dark suit for Christ's sake! What happened to the old questions like "What are you working on now?" or "Tell us what really happened with Ethel Merman!" They don't even want gossip anymore. They just want clothes!'

On the day of the wedding, standing around outside the chapel waiting for Berenger, Aaron looked less impressed with 'clothes' than ever. I knew that Berenger had arranged for him to wear a collarless Armani tuxedo and, even though he looked striking in it, he wasn't happy about it. 'Might as well put me in a sandwich board with the damn designer's name written all over it,' he said. Aaron was standing very erect, fingering his shirt collar as if it were too well starched, and I noticed that there were make-up stains on the sharp white cotton. His skin tone

211

was that peculiar shade of orange you see on television people. His eyebrows had been darkened and his upper lids smudged with black pencil. He looked like a music hall comedian—or a corpse dressed for an open coffin by a Mexican undertaker.

Frances was fussing around him and Baby was vamping for the cameras and I noticed Aaron's lawyer—later to be mine—Sidney van Doren, among the group. But the groom's side of the church would have been very sparsely populated if the other guests had paid attention to wedding protocol. Berenger's friends spilled all over the place, taking their cue, I noticed, from the invitation and dressing in the kind of dark, skimpy, glittery clothes I imagined they wore to nightclubs and parties in big Manhattan lofts, the kind of clothes in which you guzzled martinis and snorted cocaine and indulged in hasty sexual acts in public places. But what did I know? I had bought a new dress for the occasion but now I deeply regretted that my choice of colour had been brown.

What can I say about the ceremony? It was short and strained, as if everyone just wanted to get it out of the way. But then, from what I've seen, all weddings are like that. Aaron was motionless throughout, but Berenger fidgeted, blew air kisses, swivelled to wave at various people and pouted for a group of male models in a front pew. At one point, the make-up artist jumped up from his seat to correct the amount of shine on her face. The celebrant made a short speech about love being ageless, which made everyone cringe. When Aaron took Berenger's face in his hands to kiss her, I looked away.

The photo session outside afterwards was about three times as long as the ceremony. These people knew their priorities. By the time the wedding party traipsed into the marquee for the reception, Berenger was starting to look testy and Aaron seemed drawn. The bridesmaids had wilted and Erik Sklar was talking intently into his cell phone. Only Darien Apps looked radiant, but that might have had something to do with her frequent absences from the long table.

There was no-one but an enormous woman wearing too much jewellery at my table when I went to sit down. She seemed much more interested in the sugar almond centrepiece than in me. She grunted when I took my place, crunched a handful of almonds, and followed that with a martini chaser. I introduced myself as Aaron's assistant.

'Oh yeah?' she said, marginally more interested. 'Whaddya think about all this then?' She wasn't looking at me as she spoke but heaving her huge body from side to side to try and get a view of the room from her disadvantageous position.

I started to say something suitably positive but she spoke over the top of me. 'I was s'posed to be up there on the big table. I was s'posed to be a bridesmaid. But they couldn't find anything to fit me! Ha ha!' Her laugh sounded hollow, malevolent. I assumed she was humiliated by the rejection, but she added, 'And aren't I glad of it! It's a *joke*.'

'It is?'

'Course it is! He'll be dead in six months, after she's finished with him.'

I have to say I was shocked. 'What's she going to do to him?'

'She'll drive him crazy, you'll see. He'll just give up the ghost. Silly old fart.'

'He's not a…fool,' I felt obliged to say, although I was having my doubts.

'Oh, no?' She picked up a fork and pointed it at me. 'Just see how quickly he goes and gets a heart attack. I'm a healthy young woman and she gives *me* palpitations!'

'Healthy' was not the first word I would have applied to this woman, who seemed out of breath merely from the effort of picking up her cocktail glass. 'Are you her cousin?' I said. I thought 'sister' might be stretching it, although I didn't know.

'Ha! Look at me, whad'ya think?' She puffed out her cheeks to make herself look even more grotesque.

'Well…'

'There's a similarity in the eye colour, you mean? Hers are

emerald green and mine are sewer green? Yeah, everyone says that!' She put down the fork and reached over for another handful of almonds. The table shifted. 'I'm just sick of people saying we look like twins!' She snorted and a fragment of almond shot out her nose.

Frances, dressed very smartly in a blue tweed suit, which looked startling with her marmalade hair, was ushered into a seat next to my expansive companion. I watched her cringe and take a position sideways on her chair, as far away from the heaving bosom as possible. She nodded at me. 'Hello,' she said, appraising the woman beside her.

'Shelley.' A hand like a small pillow shot out in Frances' direction. Frances took a finger tentatively and shook it. 'With two e's. Like Shelley Winters. Who are you?'

'I'm Frances Feeney. Aaron's housekeeper. Who are *you*?'

After all those years with Aaron, Frances had probably endured her fair share of overpowering females and did not look the slightest bit perturbed.

'Oh?' Shelley looked at me as if she were puzzled at the question. 'I'm Berenger's booker.'

'What's that?' asked Frances. 'It sounds like something they do to prostitutes.'

That sealed it for me—now I knew Frances didn't like Berenger. And why should she? She'd be picking up pantyhose off the bedroom floor now.

'You mean, like "Book 'em, Danno!" Ha ha. Never thought of it that way. What I do is take all Berenger's bookings for work—modelling work. I'm like air traffic control, I get her here, I get her there and I make sure she never crashes. That's what they said about me in *Esquire*. You saw that story on Berenger last year?'

'That must be very interesting,' said Frances, her eyes drifting back to the bridal table, where Darien Apps had flung an arm around an awkward Aaron.

'Yeah, it's cool. I give the best phone in New York. That's

what they said about me too.' She suddenly slapped one cheek with a beringed hand. If her cheekbones hadn't been so well padded the chunk of amethyst on her index finger might have inflicted a serious bruise. 'Oh, my God! Will you look who's coming this way!'

Frances and I followed her stare towards the middle-aged Japanese couple who approached.

Shelley hissed behind her hand. 'That's Mr Takanata from the cosmetics company. He's her biggest client. Hardly speaks a fucking word of English. I should've looked at the placecards before I sat down. Shit, I'm slipping. He's the one who keeps me in cat food, so we gotta be nice.'

Mr Takanata and his wife, who was wearing a canary yellow suit and a black hat with a veil, bowed and sat down. Shelley took over the formalities. 'Mr Takanata, Mrs Takanata, I'd like to introduce you to…everyone.'

We spent a good deal of the next few minutes all smiling desperately at each other. I wondered who the remaining three guests at our table would be. I was hoping that we would be rescued by some of Aaron's theatre friends, but the placecards merely said 'RESERVED'. It was clear to me I was in social Siberia, banished to the worst table with the most dire set of companions. Even Frances, who could usually be relied upon for a bit of bright chatter, went all quiet.

'Well,' Shelley said cheerfully to the smiling Mr and Mrs Takanata, 'It looks like we're the geek table!'

I never understood why Addam came. He came late and he came with two beautiful and famous women, whom he wore on either side of him like wings. The other wedding guests, by their excited gabbling, seemed not to be able to decide who was the most fascinating of the new arrivals—the 'heartbroken' Addam, who surely should have stayed home to lick his wounds, the politically outspoken Haitian singer in full African garb (Baby's 'voodoo goddess' I supposed) or the young actress who specialised in roles in independent films and had recently been dumped by her movie-star boyfriend.

Shelley dropped her spoonful of seaweed and salmon roe before it reached her mouth when she saw Addam. 'Oh, my God!'

He was making his way through the room slowly, stopping at every table to embrace various people as if they were long-last friends, when I had no doubt that he had probably seen most of them in the past week. His companions did the same. They were as colourful and animated as a Punch and Judy show, bobbing up and down in the dispensation of their affections, which even I could see was somewhat indiscriminate.

Addam made a big show of going up to Baby and kissing her on both cheeks. Then, in what I'm sure was calculated to look like an afterthought, he leapt up to the long bridal table and shook Aaron's hand fiercely. He reached over and took Berenger's hands in his in an operatic gesture, which resulted in smatterings of applause from his audience.

And there was no doubt at this point it was *his* audience. What a performer, I thought, watching him with admiration mixed with some repulsion. He's almost as good at it as her, playing bride up there, with the wedding cake and the plaster groom, and sucking champagne through a straw. Berenger looked puzzled at Addam's flamboyant gesture, as if he were a strange creature she had never seen before. He knew better than to linger and moved on to the bridesmaids who greeted him with enthusiastic giggles and embraces.

Aaron smiled magnanimously throughout. Well, I thought, he's the one marrying Berenger after all. He doesn't need to stake his claim.

Now the 'RESERVED' card made sense. Shelley held it up and waved her bangled arms in the air in an attempt to catch Addam's attention. When he did eventually reach us, limping more exaggeratedly than I'd noticed before, he kissed Shelley on the cheek and whispered something in her ear, which made her beam. But the seat he took was between me and Frances.

This was the last thing I expected. I clasped my hands in front of me and looked at my plate, my heart pounding. I could feel myself go crimson from the ears up. I heard myself swallow and I was sure the whole table heard it too. If we were the 'geek' table, as Shelley had proclaimed, why were Addam and his glamorous companions seated here? Unless, of course, the person who arranged the place settings was making a point.

'No!' Shelley groaned and patted the chair on the other side of her. 'Sit here Addam!' He ignored her. Shelley sighed and introduced him around.

He gave Frances a kiss. I raised my eyes briefly and his flickered. 'Nell,' he said to me, mishearing. 'How are you?'

'Nile,' I reminded him. 'Like Cleopatra.' It was always a stupid thing to say. I no more looked like Cleopatra than Frances did.

'It suits you,' he said chivalrously, and then complimented Frances on the colour of her outfit.

'You must have gone to charm school since I saw you last,' Frances quipped.

'Yeah, sorry about that. Was I that bad?'

'You were bad,' said Frances dourly. 'Look what happened.'

'So whaddya think, Addam?' Shelley shouted across the table. 'Am I gonna to be booking her out for nine months?'

Mr and Mrs Takanata smiled and nodded knowingly, but they were clearly unaware of the drift of the conversation. Addam lightly stroked the base of the empty glass in front of him in a nonchalant gesture, as if he were considering her grotesque question very seriously. Under the table, I could feel the vibration of his leg. It briefly brushed mine and in one instant I felt the current of his voltage race through me.

I must have started, because my right hand flew out and I knocked my glass of dark red claret clear across the white table-cloth. It pooled in front of Addam and splashed into his lap and across his shirt, which happened, of course, to be white.

I couldn't have done more damage if I had tossed it at him in a fit of rage.

Everyone jumped up simultaneously. Frances started dabbing at the shirt with her napkin.

'Salt! Get some salt!' shouted Shelley.

The Takanatas clucked sympathetically.

Addam held up his hands and said, 'I'm fine. I'm fine.'

By now guests at the other tables were standing to look.

'I said I was fine!' he snapped at Frances as she dabbed her napkin down his leg. She stopped, appalled, and I could see the tears well up.

I stood there stupidly. Stupidly, stupidly. I could see Addam's face colouring. I knew this was not the kind of attention he wanted.

'I'm sorry,' I said quietly but no-one heard me. Then, as quickly as they had risen, people started sitting down. Addam pushed his chair back and hobbled off to the bathroom, brushing off Shelley's attempts to come with him and help. The guests went back to their plates of grotesquely deformed seafood. A few minutes later, I excused myself and went in search of the ladies room, which was in the main house adjoining the marquee.

I stood in the opulent bathroom staring at myself in the gilt-edged mirror. There was a smug gold cherub carved into the top of it: I felt as if he were blowing raspberries at me through his little trumpet. My bloodshot eyes disappeared into the upper creases of my cheeks, which were blotchy from tears. My lips, always on the thin side, were now no more than a twisted scratch of brown. No matter how I tried I couldn't make the edges turn up. I looked like I'd been mangled in a car wreck.

I wet some toilet tissue and dabbed cold water over my face to try to reduce the puffiness. It didn't work. I sat in a toilet stall for twenty or thirty minutes, taking deep breaths. No-one came to find me. I couldn't see how I could go back to the table without everyone knowing I'd been crying. But I couldn't see how I could get away from the place, either, without a car.

I needn't have worried. By the time I slipped back to the table, I found that the voodoo goddess had taken my seat and was engaged in a rather physical tete-a-tete with Addam. One of the other model bridesmaids had come to sit next to Shelley and Mr Takanata was in a conversation with Erik Sklar. No-one noticed my absence or presence. I might have been the ghost in this story.

Frances was absent, so I took her chair, trying to turn it so that I didn't have to face Addam and his girlfriend who, I'd noted earlier with growing dismay, was not only beautiful but wickedly funny. As I moved it, it tangled in the legs of Addam's chair. He looked up at me, an eyebrow raised. He hadn't been very successful at getting the wine stain off his shirt—it swam across his chest like a watery stigmata.

He smiled as I sat, and reached across his girlfriend to touch my hand. 'Thanks,' he grinned and nodded subtly in Shelley's direction. 'You saved me.'

'From what?' I asked dumbly.

'From myself.'

Long after his hand had gone back to whatever it was doing under the table with the voodoo goddess, I sat and stared at my own as if his touch had left a psychic imprint on me. My grandmother had once shaken the gloved hand of Mrs Thatcher and had vowed never to wash her own again. Ridiculously, that's how I felt right then. I wanted to put my hand to my own lips and kiss his touch. I knew I was a clumsy, dowdy girl in a brown dress, whom he had already forgotten. But it didn't lessen the longing. In fact, it made it stronger. An exquisite tension was developing between my fantasies and the nothing I could realistically expect. I think I loved the longing as much as I thought I loved him.

The wedding dragged on to a desultory conclusion. As the wedding cake was being distributed, Addam stood and said his goodbyes. Frances scolded him for leaving before the bridal party.

'Hey Nile!' Shelley yelled as Addam started to move away.

She called my name so loudly the crew of a ship on the horizon could have heard her.

'You've gotta take your wedding cake and put it under your pillow so you can dream about the man you're going to marry.'

I smiled weakly at her, mortified.

I believed at that moment that everyone in that tent must have known which man I hoped it would be.

agreed to stay on as Aaron's assistant after the wedding. I told myself that Berenger would make no difference. She wouldn't impinge on me, having no interest in Aaron's work. I tried to avoid her in those first weeks and mostly I was successful. Berenger was away on location seventy per cent of the time. The days she was home she either slept in late or was picked up for a job in a limo at 6 a.m. I was always gone before she came home. The only evidence of her being in residence were the trails of clothing and shoes thrown all over the apartment before a harried Frances could get to them and the invasion of fashion magazines on coffee tables that once held only the *New Yorker* and *Playbill*. Once or twice I ran into Berenger in the hallway and she looked right through me. I didn't think she even noticed me. I was wrong.

It was about six weeks into her marriage to Aaron when she acquired me. I was helping Aaron find a missing letter in his study, when Berenger, who had been sitting on the desk all the while swinging her legs and sucking on a Spice Girls lollipop, suddenly pointed at me and announced to her new husband, 'I want one of those.'

One of those she got.

I protested vehemently at first, horrified at the thought that I would have to spend my days with this revolting teenager, who already I could see was imperious, temperamental and manipulative. I didn't know anything about fashion, I told Aaron. But he seemed as determined as she. It made sense, he said. We were getting to the final chapters of his book, he pointed out, none too subtly. He might not need me full-time after that, but this way I would be assured of a job. I felt like I had been handed a morsel on a plate while another, more delicious dish, had been taken away.

'It's a wonderful opportunity for a girl like you,' Aaron said, trying to appease me. 'You'll get to see the world.'

A girl like you? 'I don't know how I feel about the world,' I admitted.

'Nonsense! You'll have a wonderful time and I'll rest easy knowing she's in your care.'

It didn't occur to me then what he meant.

Aaron allowed her to take me to Paris the very next weekend. She'd been booked for an advertising campaign which was to be shot on location. The shoot would take one day and, after that, Berenger would make an appearance on a television variety show and then we'd return to New York.

Berenger hadn't slept a moment on the eight-hour flight to Paris and that meant I hadn't either. She usually took the Concorde but it had been overbooked and the client ('that bitch!') hadn't screamed loud or long enough to get us bumped back on. Obliquely, it was my fault, because my job was to fix these things, but I was new, I didn't know, and she forgave me this time.

As soon as we boarded the plane, she started complaining. We moved seats twice, the champagne was 'too warm', even though she'd downed three glasses before she thought to make a fuss, the seat coverings itched, the chair wouldn't recline enough, her headphones were louder in the left ear than the right, the cutlery was dirty, the engine was making a 'funny' noise, the flight attendant was ignoring her, the man in front smelt of garlic, she didn't like the choice of films, she didn't like the interior colour scheme.

I realised almost immediately that she was scared of flying. She had put away so much alcohol, she should have been snoring like a publican the moment we were strapped into our seats. Instead, she sat perfectly upright, gripping the armrests and, when the plane started down the runway, *me*. She was white and her eyes were fixed on the back of the chair in front of her as we lifted into the air. I could hear her counting under her breath. It was months later that she admitted she'd once been told that the most dangerous time after take-off was the first thirty seconds, and so she always counted to sixty just to make sure. I was surprised she knew how to count that far.

When the plane levelled off she slumped, but dug her nails into my forearms any time the jet made the slightest vibration. She fidgeted the whole way—hopping in and out of her seat to go to the bathroom, constantly rummaging through her bag or the seat pocket for misplaced sunglasses, magazines and breath mints, flicking through the video menu agitatedly as if trying to summon up a favourite movie (*Pretty Woman, Casper, Mars Attacks*), picking up *People* magazine before throwing it down with a sigh, calling for an extra blanket and then feeling too hot. I could see the flight attendant wanted to strangle her, as did the elegant, sleep-deprived woman behind, but the Armagnac-swilling German opposite leered approvingly throughout, and even passed her a sick bag when she started to make gagging noises during a mild bout of turbulence.

She would not let me read my book, a biography of Leonard Bernstein, because she didn't have a book to read. It wasn't fair, she said. When I asked her if she'd forgotten to bring one, she answered, 'Oh, I only read books when I know the writer.'

I was impressed, thinking that she might have been having secret correspondences with Pynchon or Salinger, when she added, 'You know, like Kate's book or Claudia's or Ethan's. It's kind of more interesting that way. Otherwise, books are just *pages*.' She seemed to think she'd made a brilliant critical statement and that satisfied her for a while, until they brought supper and the linen napkins scratched her cheek.

There was no client or agent to meet us at Charles de Gaulle, although there was a driver with a sign that had her code name, the unimaginative 'Miss Smith', printed on it. She thought it very witty. But she was bubbly in the car on the drive into Paris, the relief of being on *terra firma* again.

'We are going to have *fun*, Niley,' she giggled, flapping a long arm out one window. 'I am so glad to get out of fucking New York.'

This was a woman who had been married six weeks. 'What about Aaron?' I asked. 'Won't you miss him?'

'Oh, *yes*.' She adopted an exaggerated upper-crust accent and clasped her bosom theatrically. '*Desperately*.'

Later, I knew what she meant. She missed Aaron, all right, but she missed the boy who delivered the groceries, too. Aaron just happened to be her number one Adoring Fan. She basked in his floodlight. But she also basked in the lesser lights, the small smittances, the mortal boys on the streets and in shops who gave their hearts to her so cheaply. At Charles de Gaulle, at the baggage carousel, I could see her looking under her dark glasses at businessmen, backpackers, even a Catholic priest, hoping to catch them sneaking a furtive appraisal of her. If she could catch a penis rising inside a pair of trousers, all the better: she'd even, on occasions, point it out.

'I *hate* French men!' she declared in the limo and I could see the driver take a sneaky look at her in his rear-vision mirror. 'They're so…*arrogant*.' This certainly didn't stop her from flirting with at least a dozen of them—porters, waiters, policemen, dog-walkers, desk clerks—before she collapsed, exhausted, on her king-sized hotel bed.

There were white oriental lilies in her room, big clouds of them, when we arrived that first time. In my room, there were delphiniums, out of season and even when I took a stem out to investigate it, it didn't drop a single blue petal. We were connected by a white and gilt door which she wouldn't allow me to lock and we weren't there five minutes before two bellboys were knocking at her door with more floral tributes. She fell on the cards greedily and then, disappointed, tossed them in the baroque litter bin. I never found out who the flowers were from.

A maid insisted on unpacking. Berenger announced she wanted to sleep for two hours. I found her chamomile eye-mask and then left her lying fully clothed on the bed, still in her pointy-toed shoes, which poked up above the carved bed end like grey kitten's ears as I closed the adjoining door behind me.

I put my vanity case on the spindly desk the hotel had placed by an open window. It was the middle of the day and the white voile curtains billowed into the room. I could hear birds and two maids calling to each other from opposite sides of the courtyard. I took a deep breath and stared back into the room, at the splendour of it, at the eggshell blue coverlet on the bed, the pale silk lampshades, the brilliant white bathrobe folded on a footstool, the heavy gold tassels on the brocade curtain sashes. Even the soap seemed rare and exquisite, like an ancient tourmaline washed smooth and round by a deep Amazonian river.

I can't pretend I wasn't seduced by Berenger's Paris that first time. I had been to Paris once before, when I was a student, but never to Berenger's Paris. My Paris had been fleabag hotels with tile floors and quarter-baths up several flights of stairs so narrow they had to be negotiated sideways. My Paris had been baguettes eaten on park benches and one cup of coffee a day. My Paris was full of bookstores and street markets and cathedrals, of wobbly bicycles on cobblestones, dog shit underfoot, and the cool marble hallways of museums.

But in Berenger's Paris everything was *charmant* and *genial*. Maids picked up after me; black cars idled in the gutters while I talked on the phone. I was sent bottles of perfume, silk scarves in flat boxes and teeshirts with 'Pret-a-porter-automne-hiver-1998' printed on them. In time, my own flowers arrived, smaller bouquets than hers, but expensive ones nonetheless, often featuring strange root vegetables or cabbages in witty, odourless arrangements.

But, of course, it was not me, Nile Kirk, who was deserving of all this consideration. They were wooing Berenger and I was inseparable from her. I *was* Berenger, the dull, corporate part of her who made all the arrangements and cleaned up the messes. I was the one you had to appeal to if Berenger was threatening to walk off the job or if you needed her a day earlier in Buenos Aires. She had the Fat Booker, her publicist, and her manager, Erik, but they were mostly in New York, whereas I was always on the spot, available and conciliatory and, at first, pathetically eager to help.

She set me straight about that a few weeks into our relationship, when we were back in New York. I was trying to accommodate a journalist's request to meet her over coffee for an interview. I'd been back and forth to Berenger with suggestions for places and times but she'd always been non-committal.

'Look,' I finally said in exasperation, 'Cathy's getting pissed off. She'll walk away from the interview.'

'Good,' said Berenger.

'Good?'

'I don't want to do the fucking thing.'

'But I've spent all this time trying to help get it together!'

'Niley,' she frowned at me. 'Your job is not to help, it's to *hinder*.' She said this grandly, as if she'd read it off a poster. 'It, like, doesn't look good if I'm easy to get.'

All these people, the journalists, the designers, the maitre d's, the account executives, the hotel managers, the photographers, the magazine editors, the stylists, the boy hairdressers, the girls who did make-up, the variety show hosts, the television producers, the nightclub owners, the model agents, the Latin playboys, the German catalogue kings, the English book publishers, the Brazilian society hostesses, they humoured me to get to Berenger; I hindered them from doing so. That was the dance we danced.

I was only learning the steps that first trip to Paris and I thought it was the light fantastic.

The Arenes de Lutece in the Latin Quarter once seated 15,000 spectators who came to the amphitheatre to watch Christians get shredded by lions. Berenger, standing with her spike heels firmly planted in the reddish soil and clawing the air while two giant wind-machines lifted her hair into airborne tentacles, looked like she'd be more than a match for any lion, even if the black-slashed eyes and the stripes of rouge seemed better suited to a bit player in *Cats*.

They had been shooting the campaign all day and I'd spent most of the time on the Roman version of bleachers—cold stone steps—taking calls for Berenger on her Motorola. She snatched it back off me every time they had a break and more than once got into a fight with an editor who tried to take it from her when photography began again.

All day, people kept appealing to me to 'do something' about Berenger, but I was still too raw and didn't have the faintest idea what was wrong. In some ways, everything seemed 'wrong'—the hours spent on make-up, for instance, the summer clothes Berenger was wearing in winter, or the regular disappearance of the photographer—but I grew to learn that these events were normal. It was all painfully slow and the rhythm was excruciatingly stop-start. Berenger would be standing there, her gown finally blowing in the direction the photographer wanted after an hour of the crew fiddling with the wind-machine, and then the hairdresser would have to fix a single hair that had fallen over one eye. Berenger would pose again, and the make-up artist would duck into the frame and powder her nose. She'd take up her pose once more and the light would change. A single picture could take three hours and Berenger would have to be ready to perform throughout. I could understand why she got testy: her whole young life was whizzing past while some technician tinkered with a light.

I was saved from having to 'do' anything at all in the end by Berenger's sudden interest in one of the photographer's assistants, a scruffy young man named Christophe with a tattoo of an ankh on the back of his neck. Berenger soon had him fetching her bottled water and holding her hand while she changed shoes and even, once or twice, scratching between her shoulder-blades when her skin itched. I was effectively redundant for the rest of the day, and I dared to sneak a tour of the crumbling arena. It was a relief to have a stone wall to look at.

At the end of the day's work, despite all the spats, the group seemed reluctant to split up. We all piled into our respective cars and taxis and piled out again into a Middle Eastern restaurant on the opposite side of the city. The restaurateur moved a couple who were already tucking into plates of couscous to another part of the room, and laid out a long table for us with a flourish. I was seated between the photographer, who asked me one or two polite questions in a heavy accent that was not French, and the fashion stylist's assistant, Cleophee, who had canary-yellow hair and contradicted everything I said.

Berenger was seated next to Christophe. Every time she took out a cigarette, he would light it. I've never seen her smoke so much. She refused food but insisted on feeding Christophe by fork from the big central tub of saffron-flavoured vegetables. They all downed lots of Spanish rose. I declined.

Berenger had one arm slung around Christophe's neck, leaning into him sleepily, when the hair stylist, Riccardo, stood and proposed a toast to the absent designer, 'who is paying us three times what we are worth!'

The fashion stylist leaped to her feet. 'To Bruno!' she said, tipping her glass in the direction of the photographer and sloshing the contents over an abandoned plate of roast lamb. 'Who's *worth* three times what he's worth!'

Bruno acknowledged the compliment with a nod.

'To Amanda!' said the stylist's assistant pushing her chair away from the table. '*Salope!*'

'To Cleophee!' grinned Amanda. '*Cunt!*'

There was applause and stamping of feet. We were making so much noise, other diners in the restaurant had turned to listen.

'To Berenger!' Christophe raised his glass from where he was sitting, obviously not daring to untangle himself from the advantageous position he found himself in. His eyes betrayed the fact that he couldn't believe his luck.

'To Berenger's *husband*!' Riccardo said waspishly, and sat down.

There was silence. Christophe looked at Berenger in bald astonishment. I would have thought that news of Berenger's scandalous marriage had been flashed around the globe, but perhaps the Bruno–Christophe juggernaut had spent the past few weeks in a yurt in Mongolia.

Christophe recovered quickly. '*Ouias*! To Berenger's *marie*.' He gave a wobbly grin and held up his glass again. I could see him thinking, Who is this husband? and, more importantly, *Where* is he?

Berenger gave Riccardo a black look that should have shaken him to his bones. She said to Christophe, 'Your fucking glass is empty.' She shook a cigarette from its pack and waited while he composed himself enough to strike a match.

'Why don't you show us your ring, Berenger?' Bruno said casually.

'Yes!' said Amanda quickly.

Berenger shrugged and held out her hand while she took a deep drag from her Gitane. Smoke shot from her nostrils as if she were a comic-book dragon.

'Ooh, it is beautiful!' gasped Cleophee. '*C'est quoi?*'

'It's a star sapphire, you dope,' interrupted Amanda, poring over the stone. 'We had them from Cartier for Mugler, remember?'

'It looks like a…lightning?…trapped in a *bague*,' Cleophee cooed. All hint of her foul mood had disappeared now.

To me, the smooth grey-blue cabochon the size of an olive,

with its six points of milky light, looked like one of those X-rays of breast cancer they show young women to scare them. I wondered if Aaron had made the same observation, and if it had pained him when Berenger took him to Fifth Avenue to buy it. She didn't wear a classic wedding band and the star sapphire looked to me like any chunk of agate you could pick up from a street vendor on Washington Square. No wonder Christophe had been hoodwinked.

'*C'est combien?*' Cleophee asked, wide-eyed.

Amanda kicked her.

'It's OK,' said Berenger proudly, wiggling her fingers. 'One hundred and fifty-three thousand.'

'Francs?'

'Dollars.'

Cleophee sighed. '*Merveilleux!* Could I try it on, please?'

I think everyone was surprised when Berenger answered, 'Sure' and pulled the ring off her finger.

Cleophee took off her skull ring and dumped it on the table. She carefully slid Berenger's sapphire past the knuckle and held her hand in front of her. 'Oh, it is too big, I think,' she said with disappointment, as if she had expected Berenger to tell her to keep it.

'Let me try,' said Amanda greedily, and grabbed Cleophee's wrist like she was one of the ugly sisters fighting over the glass slipper. Cleophee teasingly jerked her arm back with a giggle. We all watched aghast as the ring flew off her finger, hit the table and disappeared under it with a clunk.

Cleophee was on her hands and knees first. And then we all were, including Berenger. Riccardo was giggling helplessly and Amanda was repeating 'I'm sorry, I'm sorry' under her breath as we scrambled around under the table. We found crumpled napkins, hairballs, Metro tickets, stray carrot chunks and a small packet of powder someone had dropped, but no ring.

Berenger was crawling around, making strange noises. I had to drag her back into her seat. She thrashed about in her big handbag looking for her Rescue Remedy. The manager and the waiters joined in. Other diners started looking under their tables. Several guests and a few drinkers at the bar had paid their tab and exited while the hunt was going on: later, it occurred to the owner to ask that no-one leave the restaurant, but by then it was far too late to have stopped anyone scarpering with the gem.

We searched for forty-five minutes. Bruno insisted the manager call the police. By then, Berenger was sobbing into Christophe's lap; he was stroking her savage hair. It was a Pre-Raphaelite melodrama, worthy of Holman Hunt. Cleophee was still down on her hands and knees obsessively, but Amanda was nursing a drink in the corner, staring blankly.

Four squad cars came and twelve police. We might have called it overkill: but perhaps a supermodel in distress was an international incident and, anyway, more fun than rounding up illegal North Africans in Belleville and clubbing them senseless. The police politely patted down the pockets of the customers still in the restaurant, questioned the kitchen staff and daintily lifted up the tablecloths. I had been voted chief witness, and by the time I had given an English-speaking inspector all the details, the restaurant was empty. Where was Berenger?

The car was gone and I hailed a taxi—the police, with all those cars, could not offer a lowly assistant in teeshirt and jeans a lift.

Back at the hotel, I knocked on Berenger's door, but there was no answer. I had the Motorola, so she was out of reach. I went to bed, but didn't sleep, wondering if I should phone Aaron, or if Berenger had already done it. Around 2 a.m. I heard some scuffling in the corridor and what sounded like Berenger's door thudding shut. But I went to sleep after that and woke with the birds at six. I spent three hours transcribing another of Aaron's tapes, because I remained his creature, too. I was like a time-share apartment that could be meted out in small parcels of days.

Berenger phoned me at ten. The police had contacted her. I bowled thoughtlessly into her room expecting to find her dressed and ready to leave for the television studio, where she had a rehearsal at noon, but she was practically naked, sitting up in bed with a breakfast tray on her lap and Christophe on his stomach beside her, snoring into the pillow. I could tell it was him by the inky ankh.

I collected myself. 'Doesn't he have work to do?'

Berenger ignored me. 'Those stupid cops,' she moaned, 'they want me to go somewhere and sign something.' She picked up a white bowl of coffee with both hands. 'Of course, I'm not going.'

The star sapphire gleamed at me sardonically. 'Your ring!'

'That's why I'm not going. Thank goodness I found it. I'm glad I didn't, like, count on the rest of you.'

'*When* did you find it?'

'I guess it must have, sort of, fallen into my bag.'

That was impossible. She must have picked it up off the floor, stashed it in her bag when she was digging out the Rescue Remedy and then sat back and watched us all get hysterical.

'Anyway, it's good news for you. I don't know what Aaron would say if I told him you'd lost it.'

'Yes, what *would* Aaron say?' I replied, pointedly staring at Christophe's sinewy back.

'Listen,' she said, dropping the cup and pushing the breakfast tray out of the way. She crawled forward on the bed until she was only a couple of feet from me and then squatted back on her heels. With the bruise over her left breast and the embroidered sheets frothing around her thighs, she looked like some depraved character from the Marquis de Sade. 'You're mine now. You work for me. Your loyalty is to me. I'm the one who's lending you out to Aaron to help with his book. So don't get any big ideas you owe him anything. He dropped you the second I said I could, like, use you. And if you think you can rat on me, think again. He doesn't want to know. About *anything*.'

Christophe turned over, groaned and flung an arm up to shield his eyes from the daylight.

'He's *nothing*,' she said, turning to look at Christophe with hard eyes. 'He's, like, just a fuck. I'm married to an eighty-one-year-old man. You go figure it out.'

They say you can feel your blood boiling in your ears. I felt like I was drowning in the Red Sea. I couldn't stand that she was doing this to Aaron...and getting away with it. She was right: if I told him, it would only bring him pain.

Christophe had dropped his arm and pushed himself up on to one elbow. He looked at Berenger expectantly. He hadn't seen me. 'Did I hear this word *fuck*?' he smiled.

'Yeah,' she said, leaping off the bed and tossing a pillow at him. 'Fuck off!' But she giggled as she ran into the bathroom and slammed the door.

I looked at Christophe and his gaze shifted to me. If he was surprised, he didn't show it. He made a gesture as if to pull the sheet up over his sluggish penis and then thought better of it. We might have stayed like that for hours except there was a knock on the door. 'That's the police,' I said and turned on my heels, but not before I had the satisfaction of seeing panic fill his eyes.

Aaron didn't want to know.

When I checked our hotel bill, I observed that Berenger had phoned Aaron twice. She had made fifteen calls to Addam.

Which was something I didn't want to know.

aron, bought Berenger a kitten as a coming home gift. It was a strange, hairless creature with spindly legs and flat ears: its high, oval eyes reminded me of those gentle space aliens who inhabit popular movies, the ones Berenger would later demand I take her to; the public screenings, where she'd wear dark glasses and concealing knitted caps and sit low in the seat with a tub of popcorn on her lap, sucking on Coke.

Its name was Yard, for Berenger was apt to tell everyone, 'It cost Aaron a cool yard!' It adored her in its highly strung, pure-bred way, and she adored it in hers, feeding it sugar cubes and caviar—it would eat anything except tinned cat food—and sometimes taking it with us, in a cage, to exotic destinations, where the hairdressers and editors would fawn over it, and where once, in Oaxaca, it had to be rushed to hospital in a coma from being fed tequila through an eye-dropper.

Fortunately, I was able to work with Aaron on his book—albeit in a continually interrupted manner—for the three days after our return from Paris because Berenger was busy with her twice-annual commitment to a large American apparel manufacturer, which involved standing on grey paper in various outfits and accessories, from jeans to evening wear, while her favourite photographer, Nick Standard, specially imported from London for the occasion, sweated away at making images that would please not only a battalion of corporate executives, art directors, marketing experts and media buyers but Berenger, her manager, her agent, her best friend and anyone else she cared to involve in the final approval of the shots.

I felt awkward being alone with Aaron now that I knew his wife of seven weeks was faithless. But Aaron seemed in high spirits in the mornings, and I assumed what Berenger had told me in Paris was true, that they had an 'understanding'.

On our fifth day home, we were off again to fulfil another contractual obligation, this time for in-store promotion of Berenger's fragrance at Neiman Marcus in three different states. Berenger was never happy on junkets like these. 'The thing I really hate,' she confided one night, as she took a bite of a $20 room-service cheeseburger, 'is that you never can have, like, a *relationship* with all this travelling. All the girls complain about it.'

'But you do have one, a relationship,' I felt obliged to point out. 'You're married.'

'Yeah,' she sighed and licked her fingers. 'But you know what I mean.'

One morning, after Berenger had been collected by a car to take her to Coney Island for a British *Vogue* shoot, Aaron broached the subject of her with me, for the first and last time. 'She's not giving you too much trouble, I hope?' he said, unexpectedly, looking up through bifocals from a transcript I had done for him the night before.

'No…' I said, unsure of what to say. She'd been giving me trouble, all right, but it was less about handling her than knowing what my place was in this puzzling arrangement. Aaron was partly to blame for this—mostly to blame, really—for passing me on like a chattel and yet still demanding my attention. But between them they paid me more handsomely than I'd ever been paid before.

Aaron was disciplined in his working habits, but Berenger was erratic and bloody-minded, and I never knew from one morning to the next if she'd require me to accompany her on a shoot, spend all day calling around the stores to find out who stocked an obscure brand of nailpolish she'd seen in some South African magazine, or take Yard to the vet for his shots. I knew I was to go with her when she travelled—someone needed to hold the passport and deal out the tranquillisers—but on the days we spent in New York she was occasionally distant and imperious, as if she realised I might not altogether be her devoted subject. I was sure she didn't entirely trust me, and would often say outrageous things to me in confidence just to test if I passed them on to Aaron. She was ridiculously transparent, I thought, in her petty manipulations, and this gave me confidence that I could handle her childish intrigues.

But perhaps she just didn't know what I expected her to expect of me. She wasn't that sophisticated, after all, and for every ounce of Beluga she would showily order in a restaurant while everyone was looking, there'd be a wad of bubblegum stuck under the table for the cleaners to remove. Her whole life seemed to be formed by what she'd seen in films or magazines, so she veered from treating me like a plantation slave to a cunning interloper who was plotting to take over her career and her fortune, as if we were living out scenarios from *Gone with the Wind* crossed with *All about Eve*.

Then there were the days when she'd be insistent that I come with her to the studio, or shopping, or to the beauty parlour. 'This is Nile, who does *everything* for me,' she would boast. Everyone else on a shoot would have clearly defined roles except the models' boyfriends, who hung around flipping through *People* magazine in the hope that the paparazzi had caught them with their famous girlfriends stepping out of some limousine at some movie premiere. I suppose I was the female equivalent of the model's boyfriend, except that I was being paid for my role as ego-booster. But perhaps they were being paid too.

Aaron seemed unconcerned about me being away for days at a time and waved away my apologies whenever I had to interrupt our work to take a call from a magazine requesting a comment from Berenger about her daily beauty routine or what she was currently reading or planning to do this summer. 'Oh, you just make it up,' Berenger would tell me, and I did, which in the long run was the best thing. 'My' Berenger would always credit the cosmetics company that paid her enormous retainer, and be 'absolutely riveted' to Thomas Pynchon's latest novel, even if it was 773 pages long, looking forward to spending summer with her family, thank you very much. Later on, when I was more confident, I became a fraction wicked about this and would quote Berenger as saying things like 'I'm going to spend the summer learning how to bottle fruit.' The magazines still reported it dutifully. They didn't care what Berenger said, as long as she said it to *them*.

So when Aaron asked me suddenly about my relationship with Berenger, I didn't know how to respond. If she was giving me trouble did Aaron really want to know? The question seemed more of a statement: 'I hope you're not going to tell me she's giving you any trouble.'

Which is why a tentative 'No...' seemed as far as I could go.

I didn't tell him and things went on. Berenger was not often home, although what was 'home' to her was ambiguous, too. She'd moved into the San Remo with Aaron, but kept her one-bedroom apartment in the Police Building in NoHo for those times, she said, when she was 'stuck' downtown. She apparently had told Aaron she'd sell it but, in the meantime, an assortment of models and their boyfriends seemed to be in occupation. I went there a few times on errands in the first month or so and was shocked at how much like a flophouse the apartment looked.

Despite the appalling condition of her own place, Berenger was constantly sniping about Aaron's San Remo apartment, claiming it gave her claustrophobia. She didn't like being there— all the 'old stuff' gave her 'the creeps'—and was in fact in residence as little as possible. She had cleaned out Aaron's closets, and a lot of Margaret's things with them, although the floor-length sable, which Berenger bizarrely loved to wear to her

3 p.m. breakfasts like a robe, stayed. She lived out of suitcases, as if the San Remo were just another luxury hotel, a pitstop on the way to somewhere else. Which it was.

They were moved to SoHo—for they hardly did any of the moving themselves—by July. Frances Feeney, who continued to disapprove of Berenger, refused to go with them and Aaron gave her what I believe was a generous retirement bonus, enough for her not to need to work for some time. 'Now you look after him,' she said to me as she tearfully watched the last of the furniture go out the door. 'I don't want to be reading his obituary next week.'

Aaron did resist the move, he did put up some sort of fight. After all, he had been living at the San Remo for more than half a century. In the end, Berenger had to recruit some heavyweights to bully him into doing as she wished. Even she could not uproot him by willpower alone.

Berenger arranged for Erik Sklar to come and have a little talk with Aaron. He arrived one afternoon in a peculiar grey suit with pockets that looked like they'd been roughly tacked on by hand, spent half an hour in Aaron's study, and left. Four weeks later Berenger had signed the papers on the loft and Aaron seemed resigned.

'It makes financial sense,' was all Aaron ever said about it to me, as we were packing up his manuscripts. I thought he sounded embarrassed to be so thoroughly railroaded into giving up his home.

The day he was moved in, Aaron stopped and stood in the middle of the loft, contemplating the space. 'So this is where I am going to die,' he said to no-one in particular. He was wrong about that.

Was it the strangest relationship in history? The gossip columns seemed to think so. And Berenger delighted in feeding them little morsels.

'My old man,' she called him in *Newsweek*. 'He sings me to

sleep at night,' she told *marie claire*. 'I never did like young men anyway,' she told *Details*, throwing out the challenge. 'I choose all my husband's clothes,' she lied in *Esquire*'s Favourite Women issue. 'We are looking for a house in St Barts with a cabana where my husband can write,' she informed *Hello!* 'Oh, I *never* wear make-up to bed,' she confided to *Allure*, 'It frightens my husband.' 'We have a *very* sexual relationship, actually,' she revealed to *Vanity Fair*. '*Not* that it's any of your business.'

WE DO HAVE HOT SEX!! was how the *Enquirer* reported it. The *Globe* slashed WE ARE NORMAL!!!! across a computer-generated picture of Berenger in bed with Aaron with rollers in her hair.

Normal? I lived with them and that alone was not normal.

It was Berenger, in her sweetest mood, who had pleaded with me to get rid of my apartment and move down to SoHo with them. 'Pretty please?' she cooed. 'You can have your own television!'

'But why?' I asked her. 'Surely you lovebirds want to be alone.'

She ignored this. 'You can have a housekeeper to pick up all your things and your laundry done and your meals cooked for you. And you can have the car when you want to go out of town.'

'I've got nowhere to go.'

'Well, you can find somewhere! It's all *free*, Niley. You won't have to pay for anything!'

Oh, yes I will, I thought.

'We'll give you a raise and we'll move all your things. Just say you'll do it! *Please!*'

I was resistant. 'I like living where I am.' I thought of the tiled hallway that smelled of fried plantains and the free-standing bath that served as a kitchen sink when you covered it with a piece of board.

'But it's nowhere, Niley,' she protested. 'You're not going to be taken seriously until you move downtown.'

'Not going to be taken seriously by *whom*?' I asked.

'By *everyone*.' She fluttered her purple fingernails. By 'everyone' she meant a few teenage girls, their hairdressers and a couple of fashion editors with alligator handbags.

'Aaron wants this?'

'Yes! Go ask him. I told him you could work later…' Her voice trailed off guiltily.

'So it was your idea?'

'*Both* our ideas.'

'I'll have to think about it.'

'Well, I wouldn't take too long about it,' she warned. 'We'll have to start interviewing other people for the job.'

This was the point where my common sense abandoned me.

Berenger's proposal seemed sanity itself on the surface. Since she had requisitioned me, I had barely seen the inside of my apartment. And, in truth, by the time Berenger made her suggestion, her *demand*, that I move to SoHo, I had already been spoiled. I had slept between heavy linen sheets at the Princepesa in Milan, slurped hot chocolate from bone china bowls in the garden terrace of the Ritz in Madrid and squatted on an electrically warmed toilet seat in my room at the Tokyo Four Seasons. The calamine-pink bathroom tiles, chipped Zabar's mugs and faded polyester sheets of East 83rd Street already had lost their competitive edge.

A few days after I moved in, Berenger went through my things and threw out most of them. 'I'm *editing* you,' she explained, as she tossed an Indian scarf I quite liked into the laundry chute.

And she began to donate her cast-offs to me like I was some needy charity. The clothes—size four—were far too small but we shared the same shoe size. And so I accumulated Walter Steiger lizard pumps that she considered 'too boring' and Yves Saint Laurent patent stilettos she thought 'too black'. None of these, of course, had she bought, but rather collected in various ways, not all of them, I thought, particularly ethical.

She expected to be given her choice of clothing at the end of a shoot and, if a designer or stylist were not forthcoming, she would boldly leave with the item anyway, daring anyone to stop her. Several times I heard her exclaim, 'Oh, this will be perfect for my niece' or her cousin or her father's aunt who had Parkinson's—all, as far as I knew, entirely fictional people—and in a blaze of generosity would leave with the garment tucked into her satchel. Once, in a shopping mall, she tried to walk away with a doll a little girl had given her to autograph until an indignant mother wrenched the toy back.

She threw me scraps and they were more beautiful things than I had ever dreamed of owning. The occasional sweater or stretch skirt fitted and even the odd jacket, if I didn't do up the buttons. The rest—including a Chanel pants suit she deemed 'too over', whatever that meant—hung opulently in my closet, set-dressing for the pantomime of Nile-Cinderella and her beautiful step-sister.

That is how I found myself, within a scant few weeks, wearing shorter skirts, tighter jackets and higher heels than I'd ever worn before. I found myself railroaded into a new shaggy haircut, which was pressed on me at a *Vogue* cover shoot by a haircutter who I discovered later was very famous—and therefore acted all the while as if I should be suitably grateful to him—and who cut my hair by standing some distance away and pecking at my head with silver blades. I had my eyebrows plucked and my black-heads squeezed but I turned down Berenger's offer of joining her at her bi-annual appointment to have her lips puffed—*slightly*—with collagen.

'I still think you should have come,' she told me afterwards. 'That thin-lipped look of yours isn't exactly *attractive.*'

'Thin-lipped suits me just *fine*,' I responded. 'You need me to be thin-lipped on your behalf.'

'Oh?' She seemed taken by this answer and chewed on her bottom lip momentarily, thereby undoing a considerable amount of the work that the clinic had done the day before. She never again suggested I have cosmetic augmentation, although there were a few hints about what a chemical peel might do for my complexion.

None of this was from the goodness of her heart. I knew she was ashamed of how I looked, although there was some cachet, I could tell, in me being 'intellectual'. I once caught her mouth that word to another model while they were both pointedly looking at me across a room. But the other personal assistants were tiny little things who wore their mistresses' Prada cast-offs with aplomb and fawned appropriately at the famous designers, the ones I always took for delivery boys. Berenger wanted a 'brainy' P.A.—God knows, the rest of them had barely passed their third-grade reading exams and one of them proudly told me she'd graduated from 'magazine school'—but she wasn't prepared to take the chance that people would think any less of her because of my ragbag appearance.

The trouble was, this brainy P.A. didn't have the brains to work out what was going on.

I was not me. I was no longer reliably plain Nile. I looked in the mirror and I was different. Not beautiful by a long way but *pleasant*. I was wearing someone else's clothes and applying someone else's make-up to a face crowned by someone else's hair-style and walking—awkwardly at first—in someone else's teetering heels. Even the perfume I wore was not my choice, but someone else's, and I no longer recognised my own scent. And a dangerous thing began. I moved to a new address and I found myself surrounded by gorgeous things that I did not own and did not earn and I started to believe that I *had* earned them and they *were* mine and that, because I earned and owned them, I was somehow *better*. Better than myself and better than other people.

I started dropping my clothes on the floor for the new house-keeper Alison Bow to pick up and sweeping noisily into restaurants with Berenger and her friends so that lesser people would stare and snapping at airline clerks and waitresses and cab drivers for the offences real and imagined that lesser people commit. I wasn't a monster like Berenger and I never meant to harm anyone, but I'd put on some of her vanity with her clothes, and breathed it in with her perfume, and I was intoxicated.

It only lasted a few months, but then, so did she.

I lived with them and there was nothing normal about it.

Days would go by when Aaron would barely see Berenger, even when she was in New York. He was an early riser by habit and went straight to his study once dressed, where he would stay until around eleven. Alison brought him fruit and tea on a tray and he'd work until two, when he'd have a light lunch and then a short nap. After that, if I was around, we'd put in a solid three or four hours together and then Aaron would retire to play the piano for a while before dinner.

Berenger would often leave for locations very early, flying out the door with her dark glasses on, munching a piece of dry toast and pulling on a coat, like a kid late for school. When she wasn't shooting or making a public appearance, she'd sleep in. I say 'sleep in' because she'd either be comatose on the bed, snoring blithely, or curled up in front of the television, watching some morning talk show, from where she got all her information.

'Did you know that 50,000 Americans last year were abducted by space aliens?'

Of all the members of our happy family, Aaron was the one who took up the least space. He napped frequently and there were whole parts of the day where he hid himself away in his study alone. His showbusiness friends came often at first, but this soon dwindled off. They were used to lounging around the piano on the old suede sofas, and were visibly awkward perched on the steel benches and the expensive creaking black leather sofas that Erik Sklar had insisted Berenger buy, imposing his cool Scandinavian taste on hers.

I could see, too, the looks of pity on their faces as they tried to understand why a man who had been to dinner at the White House eleven times, and had publicly out-shouted Ethel Merman at rehearsal at Carnegie Hall over the interpretation of a song, could so passively accept being shunted out of his comfortable home of fifty years and into this hard space that resembled, in its better moments, a temporary exhibition hall.

'It was time for a change!' Aaron clapped his hands and told the assembled friends at one housewarming soiree. Berenger was in her room watching a tape of *Scream*, and refused to come out until it was over. When she did finally wander downstairs it was almost twelve and she compounded things by greeting Aaron with a loud comment about how it must have been past his guests' bedtime and how 'naughty' it was for him to keep them up.

I watched as she downed three big glasses of her favourite drink—straight vodka with a dash of cranberry to make it pink—and then told everyone in earshot how cranberry juice was great for curing honeymoon cystitis and how she'd had a lot of that lately because she and Aaron had been fucking so much. No-one knew where to look and I could see the colour rise underneath Aaron's starched white shirt collar and then stop just below his ears, as if he had willed it not to reach his face.

The guests did leave soon after this, citing tiredness, even though I knew they were theatre folk and probably had hours in them yet and would go off to a local bar and dissect Aaron's predicament. They kissed the air around Berenger's cheeks and, I could tell, were longing to get into the elevator and get the hell out of there.

The last to leave was Lilian Gessman, Aaron's theatre-director friend. She stood at the door with her cane under one arm and patted Berenger on the shoulder (she couldn't reach her head), kissed me on the forehead and brushed Aaron's cheeks with her lips. She took Aaron's arm and slowed down to let Berenger and me step towards the elevator ahead of them. I saw her tuck her round body into the space under his arm and then stand slightly on tiptoes to whisper in his ear.

'Aaron, this is *not* normal,' she hissed in her gravelly voice.

It was not normal.

Aaron kept his San Remo apartment, although he closed it up, and Berenger kept her NoHo place and sometimes they found themselves in SoHo at the same time. While Berenger slept, Aaron worked. While Berenger worked, Aaron napped. While Aaron slept, Berenger went out to nightclubs. While Aaron played the piano, Berenger talked on the phone. While Aaron entertained his friends, Berenger watched *Scream*. Those were the physical parameters of the relationship.

They went out publicly together enough times to give the impression that they were a pair of happy newlyweds. They attended film premieres and charity balls and the launch of her new light fragrance, Voile de Berenger (it stank as much as the original 'Berenger', but in a watered-down way). Often I went with them—not, I think, because Berenger particularly cared but because Aaron needed someone to keep him company while she was off table-hopping and coke-snorting in the bathrooms.

I became the Berenger-substitute.

She would kiss his cheek showily and announce, 'I'm sorry, honey, I just have to go and see, like, a few people…' and she'd be off to another table or out of the place altogether.

Aaron would watch her go and then turn to me with that creaky smile of his and whisper, conspiratorially, 'Now, where *were* we?'

One person who watched us closely was Darien Apps. I often caught her looking at us across a room. She would bound up and take Aaron's arm proprietorially. 'Come on, Mr K! You can't talk shop all night!' she'd say gaily, passing me a hard look, and she'd whirl him off on her arm.

I think Darien must have had a word to Berenger, for she stopped being so generous with her husband. Not long after-wards, Aaron was invited to present the Tony Award for the Best Revival of a Musical and the televised event clashed with a fellow supermodel's twenty-first birthday party in London that Berenger said she 'would die' if she missed.

Aaron seemed unconcerned about not having his wife at his side. 'I'm sure Nile would love to come, wouldn't you, dear?' he asked me, rather too warmly, in front of her.

Berenger's look darkened under several layers of porcelain make-up. 'Nile's coming with me!' she snapped. 'I can't do London alone!'

'Why not? You did it alone last week,' I ventured, when Aaron said nothing.

'But I was *attacked*!' she whined.

She had been 'attacked' by a group of uniformed public school girls and boys who had spotted her stepping out of her car on Kensington High Street and had been so bold as to ask, a little rowdily, for an autograph. Berenger had panicked, jumped back into the limo and made the driver put his foot on it, all the way back to her hotel, from where she didn't emerge for twenty-four hours, despite a booking the next morning for British *Vogue*.

'It was like *Clockwork Orange*!' she told us, and anyone else who would listen. I silently chastised myself for having suggested she watch that video only the week before.

'Maybe Nile would actually *prefer* to go to the Tonys,' Aaron said quietly and I looked at him in surprise. Usually he didn't interfere with Berenger's decisions on when I should travel with her.

'Well, she *can't*,' Berenger snarled. 'I'm not going back to that hellhole alone. Why don't you take that Lilian? She looks like she could use a night out on the town.'

That was the end of the conversation. The one place I had so far avoided was London. Berenger went there infrequently because the British were never able to cough up the astronomical fees she demanded. I was glad of it. When I left London three years before, I hoped it would be for good. I'd come close only once, when the flight that was taking Berenger and me to New York from Paris had to make an emergency landing at Heathrow. We were stuck in the airport for five hours and I was almost as hysterical as she was. Heathrow was unnervingly close to Morden and I sat in the first-class lounge cringing every time I heard an accent that could have been from home. If 'home' was what you called it.

So I went reluctantly to London with Berenger, and Lilian accompanied Aaron to the Tonys. It was mercifully brief. I had a miserable time trapped in a damp Chelsea basement with two hundred stoned juvenile delinquents and then we turned around and flew back to New York again.

Lilian, I believe, had a ball.

In the beginning, Berenger's friends, like Aaron's, came to SoHo. I learned to avoid the big living area, where they'd all gather, lest I be roped into a conversation about *The Celestine Prophecy* or an argument about whether Sandra's nails looked better green or blue.

The entertainment wouldn't vary much: they'd get a delivery of pizzas and several schlock-horror videos and lie about the floor chainsmoking. Sometimes they'd invite a couple of masseurs to give them aromatherapy or a beautician to pierce those few body parts that remained unpunctured. But mostly they enjoyed being slobs, lying around with Cheezels crumbs down their teeshirts and Coca-cola stains on their jeans, chortling along with the homicidal Chuckie as he cut a swathe through suburban America with a hunting knife.

'It's just *normal* kids' stuff,' Berenger shrugged one night, when I discovered them all squashed, giggling, into a cupboard, playing 'sardines'.

It was not normal enough for her friends, though, who shortly stopped coming.

'That's a weird scene you live in, man,' a male model I was sure I'd never met before said as he shared the elevator of a Seventh Avenue building with me, where I was going to collect Berenger after a fitting at Donna Karan. 'It's like *spooky*.'

I think Berenger's friends felt as uncomfortable as Aaron's did. I could hear that male model telling one of his girlfriends, 'Like, who needs it?'

'It's like Heidi and her grandfather...'

'It's such a gross out, you know, the thought of her and him…'

'It's not sex, it's necrophilia…'

These were the snatches I overheard in bars and bathrooms all over town. It was the conversation not only of the moment, but the whole year. Other scandals would flare up and die out, while Berenger's marriage continued to be fodder for the minds of talk-show hosts and the programmers of 'E!' entertainment television, and the grateful hacks whose job it was to trawl the murky depths of human folly for fictions that would catch the eye at the checkout.

I suspected, even for Berenger, there were two marriages—the one at home and the one she read about or watched on television. There was always a pile of *Stars* and *Globes* and *Examiners* under her bed, illicitly stashed as if they were *Hustlers*, and she'd get me or Alison to tape the fashion programs and gossip shows if she were away. She would fast-forward through them on her return, claiming to be on the lookout for anyone to sue. I'm sure she found it much more interesting to watch her marriage on video than actually live it.

'Did you know we're a May–December romance?' she asked me once, having heard the expression for the first time. 'That's what Oprah called us.'

I was not immune from speculation myself. I used to lie in bed on the floor below them listening for muffled cries of passion, although in reality very few sounds ever carried through the layers of oak and pressed tin. Occasionally there would be a thump, but that might have been a drunken Berenger throwing a shoe at the wall.

I became aware, slowly, that she was the instigator of much of the affectionate activity between them. 'Honey?' she'd call from the bedroom, like one of those perky wives from a fifties sitcom. 'When are you coming to bed?' If we were working late in Aaron's office I would raise my eyebrows questioningly at him and he would turn, I thought, slightly pale.

And it was Berenger, despite her absences and her table-hopping, who went up to Aaron at the piano and sat on his knee, or reached for his hand and intertwined her arm with his as they walked the gamut of photographers at a film premiere.

At times like these, she was girlish around him, and even coy. The gestures of affection could easily segue into petulance if Aaron didn't immediately stop what he was doing and embrace her, but often her ardour surprised me with its intensity, and I could see it surprised Aaron too.

At times like these, I would think, she does love him.

I would look at Aaron's frail hands with their translucent skin stretched so tight over the bone the flesh underneath looked bruised and I would think of them on Berenger's milky thighs and a voice inside me that I couldn't suppress would join with all the voices and say, How could she?

When the question should have been, How could he?

henever I collected Berenger's messages from reception at whichever extravagant hotel we were staying in that week, there were invariably one or two from Addam.

That's nice, I told myself, they've remained friends. This was the naive Jane Ann in me speaking. But the more cynical Nile said: there has to be more to it than that. And so the little message slips tortured me more than Berenger's demands in the middle of the night that I phone Housekeeping to come and kill a fly in her room or change the wattage of a light bulb.

'Aren't you going to call Addam back?' I ventured one day, fishing.

'Why?' she scowled and snatched the messages off me. I knew the subject was forbidden.

I hadn't seen Addam at all in her company. But I feared that didn't mean anything. I had difficulty keeping up with her boyfriends. There were so many of them.

In San Sebastian, where we had gone for an international model contest, there was Camilo, whose family had produced wine in the Navarra region for centuries, and whose motor yacht was docked in the port for the summer. Every day he wore a different coloured Lacoste polo shirt, with the same style of pressed white canvas trousers, like the other deeply tanned young men who were hanging around the beach at La Concha, shadowing the young girls and their chaperones in the hope—no, expectation—of catching a ripe little fourteen-year-old from Poland or Albania when she fell off the vine.

But Camilo was a practised seducer. He wooed Berenger by buying out the fairground on the mountain for a night and taking her there alone to ride the old rocket ships and dodgem cars. While she was holding out for what she could get from him, he did the same thing the next night for a sixteen-year-old from Phoenix, Arizona, and her eighteen-year-old chaperone. Berenger was furious, but intrigued, and when a bomb, planted by a member of the Basque terrorist organisation, ETA, exploded in a bar in the Old Quarter and blew off a tourist's leg, she couldn't get on Camilo's yacht, with its uzi-toting body-guards, fast enough.

In Hong Kong his name was Michael Cho and he was the assistant food and beverage manager at our Kowloon hotel. He was a tall Chinese with a long, serious face and was always very formal when greeting us in the lobby in his black hand-tailored suit, though Berenger told me later he wore Superman boxer shorts, given to him by his fiancee. Michael would slip into her suite at night and they'd watch military announcements from the mainland on television or he'd unlock the door to the rooftop pool, which was closed after midnight, and they'd float naked in the terraced spa over-looking the harbour. Fraternising with guests was, of course, strictly forbidden and I have retained the lingering image of Michael's crimson face when Berenger gave him a passionate kiss, in front of other hotel executives, in the lobby on the morning that we were leaving. That was probably the end of Michael's career.

In Monte Carlo, she fell for the gardener who trimmed Karl Lagerfeld's palm trees. His name was Angelo and he was an Italian boy from across the border who came into Monaco on the back of a truck once a week with six others to care for a number of pedigreed plants. Berenger had been sunning herself on the terrace when she spotted the bare-chested Angelo shinnying up a tree. He was reluctant to come down and talk to her, so she flirted with him across the balustrades while he worked. That night, she skipped dinner at the Hotel de Paris with Helmut and June Newton, and took a truck ride to a village near Portofino with the Italian boys where they drank someone's grandmother's hazelnut firewater and went to an all-night discotheque that still had the original fake-fur-lined walls. She came back from Italy in a taxi and woke me at 6 a.m. so that I could pay the driver the 2000 francs she had promised him. All that she would say about her new paramour was that she didn't understand a thing he said.

In Turkey, he was the young falconer who trained the bird they attached to her wrist while she sat petulantly on horseback in Vivienne Westwood taffeta waiting with the rest of the crew for the sun to hit the horizon. The next day, she complained that the falcon sat on a perch and watched everything they did.

In Berlin, he was a bouncer at a nightclub, with dreadlocks down to his waist. In Cape Town, he was a tennis player who'd reached the semi-finals of the Canadian Open. In Corsica, he was a Finnish punk who slept on the beach in bicycle leathers. In Montreal he was a busker who performed excerpts from the Marquis de Sade with hand puppets. In Buenos Aires he was a dancer and in Havana he mixed cocktails at a *rhumerie*. In Nepal, he was, or so she said, a defeated candidate for Dalai Lama.

It was the United Nations of Berenger and even I didn't know how many members it had. There were many hours when she would disappear and come back looking smug and I had no idea where she had been or with whom. I suppose I wasn't a very good jailer, but I'd proved that early on in Paris when she took up with Christophe. From that point on, I became her accomplice.

I told Prince Albert's major-domo she had stomach cramps and the editors of Italian *Vogue* that she was upset over the loss of an aunt and I once wove an elaborate story for the photographer Mario Testino about how she'd been abducted by a crazed, but harmless, taxi driver who had taken her to the Bois de Vincennes and made daisy chains for her, which was why she was four hours late for a shoot.

Underscoring my sense of disgust at myself was the fact that Berenger needed no excuses. She knew photographers would wait hours, even days, to capture that heart-shaped face on film and art directors would trek across Uzbekistan if there was a chance she'd agree to their campaign.

She was smart enough to know how far she could push it, though. Once she was in front of the camera or up on the runway, and everything was to her liking, she was a consummate professional, simply because she knew, if she didn't give up her best angles, there was a chance she'd look bad in the pictures. 'Patrick? Is it time for me to put on my good face?' she'd ask kittenishly, from under a bank of lights. 'Or are you just doing another fucking polaroid?'

Berenger was not the most beautiful girl in the world, in my opinion, although she thought she was, and there were other, newer models, who were punctual, professional and far less expensive. Some of them probably would have looked better in the pictures, too. But this was all beside the point. 'I worked with Berenger today,' had its own special cachet to the countless satellites who depended for their livelihood on being in orbit around the hottest star in the galaxy.

There were people who refused to work with Berenger, like important art directors or stylists, but they eventually came round, if the money was breathtaking enough. So Berenger's temperamental behaviour actually became currency in itself, because the top people could use it as a bargaining point in their own negotiations: 'I will not work for that bitch for under twenty grand a day!' It was a kind of silent collusion, that suited all of them in the end, and even those paying the bills were boastful of how much Berenger and her entourage were costing. If you cost enough and were difficult enough, you were irresistible in that business, that is my conclusion.

I was not the only one aware of Berenger's infidelities. And so, at first, I was surprised that none of them found their way into the press. But then I realised that, even though people saw Berenger's flirtations, they didn't register them. They didn't register them, because they didn't count as anything more risque than sipping a rum and Coke or snorting a line or getting undressed in front of a whole pack of strangers. It was like lead actors having sex with each other, or rock stars running the gamut of groupies in a night: expected, encouraged and nothing to do with real life.

'Why do you think?' Darien Apps asked me through a haze of cigarette smoke one morning backstage. 'Why do you think Berenger is in such a good mood today?'

'I'm sure you're going to tell me,' I said.

'See that electrician over there, the one with the "Stone Cold" teeshirt and jeans?' She let her sentence trail off and raised a knowing eyebrow at me.

I must have made a face, because Darien put her cigarette out on the cover of someone's copy of *She's Come Undone* and scolded, 'Don't look so fucking po-faced! She's just a kid for chrissake! She's gotta have *some* fun.'

'She's a married woman,' I felt obliged to reply and I know I sounded priggish.

Darien lunged at a hairdresser walking by and gripped his arm. 'Hey! When do I get out of these rollers? I'm not a fucking pincushion!' Then she turned back to me. 'She's a married *child*,' she corrected me. 'She needs to be out all night taking drugs and going to clubs.'

'Who says she does? I never needed to.'

'And why is that, I wonder? I bet you didn't lose your cherry until you were like twenty or something. Or maybe you never did lose it? Maybe that's what's up with you.'

'What's up with me?' I was shocked. Shocked that Darien,

who was normally so affable, was attacking me, and on grounds that seemed so flimsy. When had I shown anything other than utter loyalty to Berenger?

'I've seen the way you look at her, those narrow little eyes. You shouldn't look like that, you know. You look piggy.'

I wanted to protest, but no words came out. I could defend myself on grounds of behaviour and intellect, but I was helpless when it came to the subject of my looks. I probably did look 'piggy'.

We stared at each other for a while until the hairdresser came back and said, 'OK Miss Thing. It's time for your closeup.'

'It's about fucking time. Who's the star around here?'

I never did think it was about sex. I thought it was about being *bad*. When you looked like an angel, being bad gave you an edge. It was the contradiction that was fascinating.

The drugs, too. They were bad things bad girls did. I didn't think she really needed to be 'out of it', as she said, so often. It was like blowing smoke in your parents' faces. It was the nineteen-year-old who was never going to die, guzzling vodka until it made her stomach bleed and gulping pills until she fell unconscious, or bingeing on hamburgers and milkshakes one day, followed by cough medicine cocktails the next.

Sometimes I was the sensible Big Sister who said nothing. 'Boy, does that crystal meth rock!' she'd say bleary-eyed in the morning. Or: 'That was the best fuck I ever had in my life!'

Challenging me. Saying: Miss Goodytwoshoes, look what you're missing out on.

Sometimes I was the Parent. 'Don't wait up for me!' Walking out, slamming the door. Or: 'Don't fucking tell me what to do!'

Challenging me. Saying: You're boring, pathetic, at my mercy.

And sometimes, only sometimes, I was the Best Friend. 'Do you think he's going to call?' Fretting, chewing her nails. 'How do

I look? Should I wear the red dress instead?'

Manipulating me. Saying: I need you, Niley. I trust your advice. And you have to give it to me because you are at my command.

I think, in being bad, she was only living up to expectations. Some time that first spring, after the trip to Corsica and the sullen punk with his heavy boots in the sand, Berenger was engaged to appear as guest speaker at a model search held at a barn-like convention centre on Manhattan.

These events are often referred to as 'cattle shows' and I could see why: herds of big-eyed young girls and their ruined mothers were channelled through the barren spaces like witless stock being moved from pasture to pasture, their over-painted faces (the mothers as well as the daughters) washed out by the neon lighting of the artificial environment, and their barely contained excitement at the possibility of being 'discovered' as the next Berenger causing them to whinny and flare like corralled young heifers smelling each other's fear. Even the makeshift stage, around the perimeter of which the model agents sat, looked like a cattle run and the girls who tried to stride confidently down it often stumbled or galloped awkwardly on their way to the end, where they were to pose for the judges.

The young hopefuls, or their mothers, who were probably more hopeful, had paid a substantial fee, plus transport and accommodation in New York, for that one walk down the runway in front of the gurus of the modelling business. Encouraged by small agencies in their home towns, girls who were too short or too plump, with braces on their teeth or blemishes on their cheeks, clumpy noses or eyes set too close together, long waists or thick ankles, thin lips or scrappy hair, these *plain* girls who carried within them the secret teenage desire to be adored and pursued were the ones who had been most vulnerable to overtures from adults who professed to understand the mystery of beauty and celebrity and who offered it all for a modest $165 registration fee.

I didn't like these events and this one least of all. The scouting agents seemed indifferent to the parade of teens trying to master walking in high heels and wearing a frozen smile at the same time. Sometimes they even openly mocked the more awkward girls. Maybe if you spend your life categorising most of humanity as visually defective, you develop a certain lack of generosity. Later, however, I began to understand things from the agents' point of view. I overheard one of the mothers collaring a scout as he excused himself from the auditorium.

'You didn't smile at my Laureen! Now she's crying so hard I can't get her out of the bathroom!'

The agent must have been used to these kind of accusations, because he answered smoothly, 'Well, you go tell Laureen that I did notice her. That's my job, to notice girls like Laureen.'

'You really did?' asked the mother, looking suddenly enthralled. 'Laureen 146? In the yellow satin dress?'

The agent seemed anxious to move on. 'Yes, ma'am. Now, if you don't mind—'

'Does that mean she's going to get a contract? You see, she's only fifteen and we've got to decide whether she'll finish school or whether—'

'Tell her to finish school,' said the agent.

'You mean…?' The mother was so needful she was like an open wound. I could feel myself wince and wanted to be somewhere else to spare her any more public humiliation, but I was trapped in a funnel of people slowly moving in the opposite direction.

'Look, Mrs—'

'Crystal.'

'Crystal. Laureen is probably going to be a brilliant student, but she'll never be a fashion model.'

Crystal looked flabbergasted. 'But the Carson model agency

in Gainesville took her on! She's already done a brochure for a shopping mall! Everyone said how pretty she looked!' Crystal's voice was reaching hysterical pitch.

'Crystal, calm down,' said the agent and put his hand on her shoulder. 'If Laureen wants to model for shopping malls and get some pocket money, that's fine. But she's not going to make it in New York. It's too tough here.'

'Tough? But she's *pretty!*'

'She's pretty but—'

'What's wrong with her? Tell me what's wrong with her!'

'OK, Crystal. The yellow satin dress, right?'

Crystal nodded.

'Let's see. She's too short for a start.'

'But—'

'And her nose is too thick at the bridge.'

'There's always—'

'And she's carrying too much baby fat.'

'She could diet?'

'And her skin is sallow. No cheekbones to speak of. Her posture is very bad.' He dropped his moderate tone and said pointedly, 'Is that enough for you?'

Crystal had gone quite pale. 'What if she did another course at modelling school? I always said she didn't pay that much attention—'

'Crystal, enough!' the agent snapped. 'Your daughter is never in a million years going to be a fashion model. Now, *you* get over it!' And he broke free.

'But what about Kate Moss?' Crystal called out to him as he pushed through the crowd. 'She was too short!'

Crystal's ambitions drained out of her with her colour. Later on, I saw her sitting with the woeful Laureen, staring sullenly into space.

'But what did I do wrong, ma?' pleaded Laureen. 'What did I do wrong?'

I felt for Laureen and her kind because most of these girls—

all of them, really—*were* lovely in a sweet gawky way, but not lovely in the way that could carry a $30,000 gown or a million-circulation magazine cover. Some actors devoured the screen like animals, and so the most successful models seemed to have some kind of wild creature in them, one that you could glimpse in photographs, as if it were clawing its way out of her eyes. Berenger had it: a whole safari park of them. Darien was a plain girl but she had the animal in her and it was the animal that made her a success, not the shape of her face or the roundness of her mouth.

One girl stood out from the others on this afternoon and several agents were vying to sign her up. I could see the less successful girls looking her over. 'What's she got that I haven't?' was writ large on all their faces.

She was, indeed, rather peculiar, with a tiny head out of proportion to her long, shapeless body, short red hair that curled around over-large ears and pale eyebrows that disappeared if you saw her from any distance. She had a homemade tattoo of a dagger above her left ankle. She looked to me like a praying mantis, an effect heightened by the lime green ribbed sweater she was wearing over her short skirt.

For most of the day, she sat on a chair, legs wide apart, jumbo ears plugged into a walkman, looking entirely bored. I think that's what did it for the agents. She *behaved* like a model already. And so they started treating her like one. Competing for her contract, they began by telling her how beautiful she was and bringing her cans of Coke from the dispensing machine. By the end of the day, one of them had arranged a date for her with her favourite young actor and another was dangling in front of her the keys to an apartment in SoHo.

'Yeah, but is it near a McDonald's?' she asked as she flicked cigarette ash into a plastic cup held by an agent on his knees beside her.

'Isn't she *fabulous*?' the kneeling agent said to no-one in particular, as if he were a first-hand witness to the miracle of the Assumption.

In that moment, I knew where Berenger had come from.

erenger had been dead four weeks. You'd think that fact alone would have made her a little subdued. But she was everywhere, insidiously, in my room and on the street, a face on billboards, a voice in my ear, a prickling of my scalp and, sometimes, at her worst, a thing with streaming hair and burning eyes that came in the night and prodded me awake.

I tried to ignore her. I turned my face to the wall when my room turned phosphorescent at night. I drew the curtains on the street, where sometimes her mournful figure would prowl, just to spook me. I walked quickly when she shadowed me, cursing her persistence. I blocked out her incessant whispering, the tapping on the pane, the occasional flares of heat when she grew impatient with me. I averted my eyes from the images of her, still fluttering on bus-stops and looming on billboards and smirking at me from every corner newsstand. I wrapped my eyes and bound my hands and stuck wax in my ears against her siren call. But I never stood a chance.

She had a whole bag of music-hall tricks she employed to attract my attention: eerie howling noises in the middle of the night, fluttering curtains when there was no breeze, doors that slammed by themselves, toothbrushes and other objects that would be misplaced and later found in unlikely locations. It's just your mind, I would tell myself, as I mounted a hunt for my keys for the third time in a day. But I found no comfort in this, that she was my imagination at work. What kind of mind would conjure up a horror like Berenger? I hoped, desperately, that I didn't have that kind of mind.

And so I lived in perpetual anguish, never knowing when she would appear, or in what guise. I awaited, apprehensively, the next ambush, the next time she would slip a comment in the space between my thought and my speech, the next time she would appear on the end of my bed, minus an appendage and popping bubblegum. It was the not knowing that unnerved me. I hadn't been able to control her in life and it wasn't proving any easier after death.

The night after her appearance in Susan Mackie's office, Berenger would not leave me. She drove me mad with her pacing. Back and forth, back and forth, like a sheet flapping in the breeze. I pulled a pillow firmly over my head, trying to ignore the presence in my room that never slept, but kept poking and pinching at my brain with sharp, invisible fingers. 'Piss off,' I said more than once to the air.

But it was no use. She was agitated, complaining. 'Why did I have to get stuck with *you*? It's boring here.'

'You're the one who is doing the haunting.'

'Who's to say you aren't haunting *me*?'

'I'm not the one who died.'

'Oh no? Then why can't you get a *life*?'

To the latter, I replied, 'I could ask you the same thing.'

'I can't just fucking float here all night with nothing to do!'

I hugged my pillow. 'Why don't you get Kurt Cobain down here? Start up a band? I can't sleep anyway with your whingeing.'

'It's not a joke! You're treating me like I'm some kind of…flower arrangement. Ghosts are people too, you know.'

I gave a snort of laughter. Ghosts are people too! She was hardly a person when she was alive. She was just the performance of a person. No, not even that. She was the performance of a performance. Berenger the psychodrama, on billboards all over town. If she once had human form it was long before I knew her.

'Stop it!'

'I'm sorry,' I said. 'I'm sorry I hurt your feelings. But don't you think it is ridiculous? Me, talking to the walls? Trying to have a logical conversation with a lump of ectoplasm—'

'I'm not a lump!'

'All right, you're not a lump. We've established that. You're not much of anything.'

'If I'm not much of anything, then why are you talking to me?'

Before I had time to reach for a book to throw at her, a fearful thumping began. It took me a while to register that the noise was not coming from inside my head but from outside, in the corridor, where usually all was peaceful at this time of night. The thumping was at my door.

'All right! All right!' I wasn't in the most tolerant of moods and I expected to open the door and find an enraged Bernadette waving a squashed squirrel that had been run over in the street by a car.

Ayesha usually scratched at the door like a mouse, but here she was, in cotton pyjamas, with her forearm raised, tearful, about to smash my door in.

'Ayesha!' I exclaimed and pulled her into the room. She waved a crumpled piece of paper at me. 'Nile, did you not see this?'

I took it from her. I could feel Berenger hovering over my shoulder inquisitively. 'Ayesha,' I asked. 'Is there anything different about this room?'

'No.' She wiped away a tear and look confused. 'What is it?'

I sighed and looked at the paper Ayesha had handed me. It was a letter, on plain paper, with an insignia of laurel leaves on top. I scanned it quickly. I could see why she was distressed. We were to be turned into a hotel, still administered by the nuns, but offering 'short-term accommodation' to single women, at double the rate we were paying now. The long-term residents, who paid by the month, were asked to nominate if they were willing to pay the higher rent or to vacate their rooms within thirty days. According to the letter, a state agency had ruled that the church was within its rights to evict us.

Ayesha bent over and picked up off the floor an envelope addressed to me. It had obviously been slipped under our doors by stealth when they thought we were all asleep.

'But Nile,' Ayesha sniffed. 'How could Sister Pansy do this to us?'

'Maybe it had nothing to do with her.'

Ayesha looked totally bewildered. 'But she is a *nun*!'

In Ayesha's mind, even though she was not Catholic, the nuns were living embodiments of God, and should therefore Know Everything. Compounding her distress was her touching belief that the government was another arm of the same deity, one that tended its flock even in times of deluge and drought. I had to explain to her that the nuns were called the Brides of Christ, they were 'married' to God, and she of all people should know what husbands were capable of doing to their wives. She should look on our predicament as a big hot vat of ghee from God.

She considered this silently and then went back to her room, to light some incense for Sarasvati.

I turned back to Berenger. 'So,' I said. 'What about rustling up a Heavenly Host or two? Surely you know someone who can exert some influence on the Catholic Church?'

She didn't take too kindly to that idea and poked out her tongue.

I flopped back on the bed and put the pillow over my head.

The next afternoon, I was standing on 22nd Street with fifteen other women, including one in a wheelchair, waving a placard that read BETRAYAL! and making outraged faces for a news crew from New York 1 and a photographer from the *Post* who had discovered us on his way to stake out a movie star who was supposedly having lunch on the sidewalk outside the Empire Diner.

I was waving my placard in solidarity with Ayesha, who had bravely agreed to be photographed in front of the building, scars and all, with Nola who was fifty-nine and had stomach cancer, with Keesha who was working for welfare cleaning the toilets at the Port Authority, with Bernadette, the animal liberationist next door, who had lived at Magdalen House since 1979 and must have been older than her waist-length locks and plastic dress suggested, and with Mary Ann who had threatened to jump off the Brooklyn Bridge because where else in this whole universe would she find a place for less than $450 a month?

I was as dismayed by the situation as the rest of them, even though, unlike the others, I could have afforded to rent my room at hotel prices once the church tossed out its burdensome congregation of cripples. But I liked the plainness of things as they were, the counting out monthly of small parcels of cash, the feeling that we were all rejects, cast-offs, losers. It was a sickness in me, I knew. But when you have walked around with big wads of other people's cash in your pockets and hopped on the Concorde as if it were a local bus, frugality seemed like something to cherish, an incredible luxury.

So I stood there for an hour or two with a placard reading BETRAYAL! That night Ayesha watched the news on the old Zenith in the communal lounge downstairs. Although we had been given a bare thirty seconds on the piddling local station, she and Mary Ann had already fielded dozens of calls from viewers enraged at our predicament. Ayesha blushed when she told me that one of them had called to ask her for a date.

I didn't get a date out of the screening, but I did get a visitor, two mornings afterwards, a visitor I cared for even less than I cared for my revised Berenger. Detective Ostrowsky, knit cap in hand, wearing a pea coat and cargo pants was standing in the corridor outside my door when I opened it. She looked like she'd just stepped off the Intrepid, although it was more likely she'd come from snacking at a diner, judging by the strand of tomato skin she seemed to have snagged between her front teeth.

My mistake was not slamming the door in her face. I just stood there, frozen. She seized the moment of my hesitation and put her foot on the bare rug inside the door and then kept on coming.

'You were supposed to keep us informed of your whereabouts,' Ostrowsky barked.

I could see she was still all charm. Maybe I didn't care for her so much any more. But it was too late, she was in the room and had pushed the door shut behind her.

'You can come in if you like,' I said between my teeth. As far as I knew, I didn't have any tapioca stuck in them, but anything was possible. I ran my tongue over my front teeth and Ostrowsky, noticing this, did the same. She actually blushed when she caught the tomato skin where it was hooked and put a fist over her mouth while she took care of it. That over, she looked around the room. 'So.'

'So? Is this an official visit?' I asked, noting the absence of a second officer. Didn't they travel in pairs?

'No. I'm just here for a girl talk. So this is where you've been hiding out.'

'I haven't been hiding out.'

'What do you call it, then?'

'Resting between engagements.'

'Is that so? You were supposed to—'

'Yes, I know,' I interrupted. 'Keep you informed. Well, I forgot. I don't see what difference it makes anyway. Berenger died weeks ago.'

'We still have some loose ends to tie up.'

'Oh?' I said this more weakly than I should have. 'Do you mind if I sit down?' I backed up towards the bed and set myself down on its edge. Big mistake. Ostrowsky was now towering over me. 'Would you like a chair?'

'No, thanks,' she replied, grasping the knit cap in both hands like it was my neck she was about to wring.

'What loose ends?' I asked faintly.

'How well do you know Addam Karsner?' she asked suddenly, her head on its side like an amused bird about to peck the life out of an innocent little groundworm.

'Aaron?'

'Addam,' she repeated.

'Oh, *Addam*,' I said dumbly. 'I know him well enough.'

'Exactly how well is that?'

I considered how to frame the answer. 'Well, he's—' No, I couldn't say that. 'He's—' I stopped again. 'He's Aaron's grandson,' I finally said, as if that should put an end to it.

'Were Berenger and Addam lovers?'

I weighed this one up. Ostrowsky probably already knew the answer. 'Of course. It was no secret. She dated him before she married Aaron.'

'Don't you find it strange?'

'What?'

'That she'd marry her lover's grandfather?'

'I thought we went over this before.'

'We didn't.'

'No, I don't think it's strange.'

'Addam Karsner is pretty gorgeous, though, isn't he? He's got lots of girls after him?'

'I guess so. He's not *that* gorgeous,' I lied. 'And he limps. Aaron doesn't limp.'

'I'm sure a lot of girls like that limp.'

'Maybe.'

'Do you know what Berenger was planning to do on the morning of 15 January?'

'Of course. She was taking a flight to Morocco for a vacation.'

'That's unusual, isn't it?'

'For her to take a vacation?'

'Uh-uh.'

'I suppose so.'

'Sources tell me, it was right before the Paris couture fashion shows. She usually modelled in these, didn't she?'

'Well, she cancelled out.'

'Why would she do that? Missing out on all that filthy money?'

'She didn't need it.'

'But she liked it?'

'Of course she liked it. Look, she only did a couple of the big shows anyway.'

'But she always did'—Ostrowsky took out a palm-sized notebook and glanced at it—'Christian Dior, right? She had a contract with him.'

'Not with Christian Dior. He's dead.'

'Just help me out here.'

'All right. I think she was going to fly back for that. For Dior.'

'On 18 January? Three days later?'

'She was used to it. She hopped on planes all the time.'

'But then she was going *back* to Morocco?'

'Yes, she had a shoot.'

'Why go earlier then? She had to come back to Paris and then go back down again. Surely it wasn't worth it?'

Actually I didn't know. 'Look, you've got to put yourself inside her head—'

You called?

I groaned and closed my eyes.

'What's wrong?' Ostrowsky sounded suspicious. And well she should have been. When I didn't answer she prompted, 'You were saying I should put myself inside Berenger's head.'

No thanks!

I made a tremendous effort to block out the voice. It was like wrestling with an octopus underwater. 'I was saying she didn't think about things the way we do. It wasn't always logical what she did. If she wanted to go some place, she just went. Even if it took two days to get there and she was only there for a minute. She once went all the way to Auckland for a weekend. She'd think nothing of going to London to go shopping. She'd go to Miami for a party.

She'd fly to Milan, even when she didn't have any work, to hang out with a few friends and watch TV in her hotel room.'

'You usually went with her?'

'Not always on those trips. I usually went when it was work.'

'So that's why you weren't going with her to Marrakech on 15 January?'

'That's right.'

You weren't going because I didn't fucking invite you!

'But you were going with her the second time, when she returned on 20 January?'

'No, actually.'

'Oh? That's unusual, isn't it?'

'A bit. She didn't always want me to come.'

'Do you have any idea why she didn't want you this time?'

'No. I suppose it was going to be too much fun.'

'Too much fun?'

'Forget it.'

Ostrowsky looked like she was sucking on a lemon. 'Why would this trip be too much fun?'

I kept my eyes glued on hers. That way, I could channel out some of Berenger's babble. 'Too much fun for *me*. You know golden sands, oases, souks, exotic cocktails…'

'Oh.' She looked thoughtful. 'Did you make her travel arrangements?'

'We have a travel agent.' I had no idea what Ostrowsky was getting at.

'Hmmm. Was she travelling alone?'

'As far as I know. She was being collected at the other end by her friends.' I stopped and examined Ostrowsky's face. 'She *wasn't* travelling alone?'

'No. Addam Karsner was booked on the same flight from New York on 15 January and was making a connection to London an hour after she was flying back to Paris on 18 January. Not under his own name, of course. We don't think it's a coincidence.'

I could feel the blood drain from my face. 'That's not true.'

Oh, yes it is. He was coming with me.

'But he couldn't have been!'

Yeah, well you're wrong.

'But why?'

We were going to elope.

'You couldn't elope, you idiot. You were married already.' But could she?

'Why do you say that?' Ostrowsky looked at me with beady eyes. What had I said? I tried to concentrate on her words.

'Addam Karsner had no reservation at any hotel in the country. That suggests he was staying with Berenger. Which suggests they were still lovers.'

'He could have been staying with friends.'

'Why would they travel together?'

'They *are* related...*were*...They were friends. We used to go to Addam's concerts.'

'We have reason to believe that Addam Karsner was involved in a relationship of a sexual nature with Berenger Karsner *after* her marriage to his grandfather.'

'At least she kept it in the family,' I said flippantly.

'So you know something about this?'

'I don't know anything.'

'I find that hard to believe. You were, from what I understand, the confidant of the deceased.'

I felt obliged to correct her, although I was not sure this was wise. 'I was her slave.'

'You sound resentful.'

'I was paid well.'

'So you did not know that she was having a relationship with her...grandson?' Ostrowsky smiled at her own joke.

'Step-grandson,' I said pointedly. 'No. I didn't.'

Liar.

I didn't, after all, lie between the sheets with you, I said to the voice in my head.

'You don't find anything unusual about the fact that he was

270

travelling with her on 15 January? That she didn't tell you that she was going with him? That she didn't tell her husband? The elder Mr Karsner claims to know nothing about it. If it was an innocent family thing, why didn't anyone else in the family know about it?'

Why does she care?

'What?'

'Yes?' Ostrowsky asked, leaning towards me.

'What has this got to do with anything?' I asked.

'I am just trying to piece together the deceased's state of mind before her death.'

'But why? Berenger died of an overdose.'

'Technically, she didn't die of an overdose. She suffocated on her own vomit.'

'Well, why does that need investigating? Aren't you people always in a hurry to wrap up a case?'

'Not me,' said Ostrowsky proudly and for the first time I caught a glimmer of the fanatic in her eyes. 'I don't like to see a young girl die like this without understanding why.'

'That's very conscientious of you.'

'Someone has to be. If we left it up to the boys—' She rubbed her face. 'Look, we've managed to keep this quiet, but I'm going to tell you. Berenger's death may have been assisted.' She waited for my reaction.

What does she mean? Assisted? What does that fucking mean?

'Calm down!' I was feeling as rattled as Berenger.

'I am calm,' Ostrowsky said. 'Is there any reason I shouldn't be?' She studied me for a minute. I'm lucky I'm English, I thought, she'll think my rantings are cultural.

She started to say something, hesitated, and then plunged in. 'In fact, we are certain it was. She snorted some heroin, amongst other things, and yet there was no...obvious residue anywhere. No plastic bags, no bottles of pills, no traces of powder on the bedside table, where we assumed she cut it into lines. Someone was there and cleaned up every trace afterwards.'

Smack? I did smack?

'Are you sure it was heroin?' I thought it had been cocaine.

Ostrowsky nodded. 'An especially pure dose, too. She was lucky she snorted it. It would have probably killed her if she put it in her veins.' She realised what she had said. 'You know what I mean.'

'She had this at *home*?' I'd never seen Berenger use heroin in any form. But what did I know?

'Absolutely.'

'But couldn't she have done it at the party and then got home and collapsed?'

'Not according to the M.E. She would have become unconscious almost straight away. Her driver, who seems a reliable sort, testified that she was conscious all the way home in the car, if a little tipsy, and walked into the building unassisted. We have several witnesses at the party who have corroborated that she wasn't more than a little intoxicated when she left the party. In fact, according to a few people she seemed quite capable of indulging in some public, uh, sexual activity with a young man before she left.'

'I saw you myself.'

'What did you see?'

'Nothing,' I said quickly. 'Couldn't she have cleaned up herself?'

'Impossible, according to Forensics. There was nothing in the trash and she couldn't have stayed awake longer than a couple of minutes, so she couldn't have discarded anything outside the apartment.'

'And you think Addam was involved?'

'He's a known user. They were former lovers...current lovers. They were related by marriage. We picked him up afterwards with some controlled substances on his person. He denied being there of course...'

Of course.

'It's not so unlikely that they were together, sharing,' Ostrowsky concluded.

'I think you're wrong. I don't think it was that way at all.'

'What way do you think it *is*?'

'Well, for a start, he wasn't with her.'

'We don't know that.'

'But you went round and saw him…afterwards?'

'He could have been with her that night, realised what had happened, that she'd overdosed, maybe they were snorting the stuff together, so he went home and pretended—'

'No,' I said. I felt overwhelmingly sad all of a sudden. 'Addam couldn't have been there. He wouldn't have left her. He's not that kind of person. He would have called someone.' I wasn't as certain as I sounded. I'd never been certain about this. And if he was going away with her the next day, surely it was possible he was there the night before?

'How do we know he didn't? That he didn't knock on your door and get you out of bed to help him cover up?'

'Why would I do that?'

'Oh, I don't know, out of some kind of affection for him? You seem pretty quick to defend him.'

'I just know him, that's all.'

'You were the one found with the body. You were more likely to be the one to have cleaned up.'

'But I didn't…I was in shock.' I thought it wise to change the subject. 'Have you spoken to Addam again?' I asked cautiously. When she nodded I asked, 'Well, what did he say? About the Morocco business.'

'He said he knew nothing about the booking to Morocco. He had no intention of going. He was solidly rehearsing in the studio for the British concerts.'

'That makes sense.'

'He denies being with Berenger the night of her death. He says he was home sleeping. Which, frankly, sounds phoney. I thought rock stars stayed up all night.'

'That's because you don't know any.'

'Actually, I do. When I was a rookie I used to do security at concerts.'

'Then you'll know they're comatose most of the time.'

She actually smiled. 'What about the husband?' she made the transition smoothly, still smiling. 'You were close to him. Did he ever speak to you about his wife, his grandson? Do you think he had any inkling they were having an affair?'

'*If* they were having an affair.'

There was a silence. Berenger, too, was strangely quiet.

'Look, Detective,' I was now anxious to get her out of here. 'Have we finished? I've—'

She came over to where I was sitting and traced her hand lightly over the magazine pages I'd ripped out in a frenzy and stuck to the wall after Berenger's first appearance that day at Barneys. I'd forgotten that they might seem a bit...peculiar to someone else.

'What's this?'

'Just decoration.'

'Are they all Berenger?'

'Yes. That one's her friend Darien Apps.'

'I recognise her. But you've...defaced them.'

'Not really. I've just put funny moustaches on them and, you know, coloured in their eyebrows, given them pimples, that sort of thing—'

'But you've scratched out their eyes.'

'I suppose I got carried away.'

'Carried away?'

'Didn't you do that when you were a child? Scribble on photographs?'

'When I was about three, yes.' Ostrowsky homed in on a *Vogue* cover of Berenger romping in a garden with three cute puppies. 'She looks almost innocent in this one.'

'Almost,' I agreed.

'Except for the noose you've drawn around her neck.'

Ostrowsky stood straight and crossed her arms over her chest. 'You know, the world would be a better place without this stuff.'

'What stuff?'

'Junk like this. Magazines. These pretty girls with big cheesy

274

smiles on their faces like there's not a problem in the world. Do you know how many battered wives we see because the husband suddenly gets the idea he should be married to Cindy Crawford and not some poor worn-down soul who has borne him five kids and doesn't have time to take care of herself? Just last week we had a homicide, this childcare worker puts a restraining order on her ex-husband and he doesn't like the idea so he comes up to her in the street, shoots her right through the heart, point-blank, like an execution. Drops the gun and waits for the cops. Seems they got divorced because he was always after her to do her hair this way or that, buy this face cream or that lipstick, go on this diet or join that gym. He told the cops she'd look "more beautiful" dead. That they'd have to groom her before they put her in her coffin.'

'I thought they usually wanted their wives to look like *Playboy* centrefolds.'

'Yeah, but they want to have sexual relations with the centrefolds, they don't care about dating them, marrying them. If you've dated enough guys you'd know that most of them are looking for girls who look like *that*.' She flicked a finger at a *Harper's & Queen* cover. 'They think they *deserve* them. Try to find a guy in any of the five boroughs of New York today who doesn't think he'd be better for Claudia Schiffer than David whatshisname. The ugliest jerk in the world, his gut hanging over his belt, thinks he's the perfect mate for Claudia Schiffer. Where do these guys get off?'

Ostrowsky sounded as if she had some personal experience with this.

'But men don't read those magazines, women do.'

'And the woman feels she's less of a woman because she doesn't look like that, so she suffers from low self-esteem and leaves herself wide open to let some perp come in and bash her up.'

'And you're saying he bashes her up because she doesn't look like Cindy or Claudia or Berenger?'

'Exactly.'

'But you're wrong. You know why? Because beautiful girls are getting bashed by their boyfriends and husbands too. It happens all the time. I've heard stories of lots of models—'

'Really?'

I looked at Ostrowsky's blazing eyes. This confidential girl talk had just been a ruse to get me to reveal more than I wanted. She was all tricks and techniques. But I knew something then: she was floundering. She didn't have a clue. It was all speculation. She had grabbed hold of the wagging tail of the dog but it wasn't leading her anywhere.

'Detective, we could chat all night, but do you have any more questions to ask me? *Relevant* questions?'

She was slightly startled by my abruptness, but covered quickly. 'Yes,' she said. 'Why are you protecting them?'

'"Them"?' I kept my eyes wide and innocent.

'They haven't done anything to warrant such loyalty as far as I can see.'

'Well, I don't know what you're talking about, but that just happens to be my business, doesn't it?'

'I don't think we've discussed what your relationship was with them. Exactly.'

'"Exactly"?'

She folded her arms across her chest in a satisfied manner as if to say: I got you. 'You weren't having a sexual relationship with Aaron Karsner by any chance?'

'*Addam?*'

She smiled. 'Aaron.'

I breathed a sigh of relief inside. 'Did he tell you that?'

'No.'

I looked her straight in the eye. 'Then you have your answer.'

'We have been talking—'

Suddenly, I'd had it with her. 'Look, Detective Ostrowsky…'

'Grace.'

'You've been doing all the questioning. Can I ask you one thing? One simple little thing? Something that has been bugging me along?'

276

'Shoot,' she said, looking at me curiously.

'What do you get out of this?'

I told her she should arrest me, or leave. Maybe she thought the girl-talk thing would work. Two plain girls together bitching about one beautiful one. But I was alert to the game. I'd played it all my life. Condescension. People thought they could get around me by appealing to a perceived need for companionship. She's dowdy, they'd think, and studious, so she mustn't have many friends, therefore we can wheedle our way into her confidence by flattering her with our attention. She'll be so pathetically grateful for the gesture, she'll do whatever we want.

People thought they could get around me, and I let them.

The popular girls at the comprehensive would do it. In a group they'd come up to me at recess. 'Nile, why don't you come and sit with us...' And there'd be some friendly chatter and then, 'Nile, we were wondering...' Could I help with a maths project? Could I introduce them to a boy in my class? Could I stand lookout for them while they went into the shed for a fag?

I did what they asked, affably. I didn't seek their friendship or need it. I knew they were snickering at me behind my back, but I didn't care. I made myself hard. They were just pretty schoolgirls, destined for childbirth and varicose veins and a life spent watching 'East Enders'. I was something else altogether. Not that I knew then what that something else might be. It was just an idea, not even enough of an idea to make a shape out of it. I hadn't counted on it involving dead bodies. But I suppose most people don't count on life turning out the way it does. I was no different in this.

When Ostrowsky left, I turned to Berenger. She was sitting at my feet, smoking agitatedly. Not a cigarette. Just smoke.

'I, like, never took smack. It scared the shit out of me. Addam knew that. You've got to call him.'

'What?'

'Well, I can't, like, get on the phone and call people. But you can. You can do it for me. Just like you did before, you know?'

'Now, wait a minute,' I said. 'I don't work for you any more. I don't have to do anything.'

'But I'm haunting you!'

'So?' It was easy to be brave when she was like this, like the monster she was in life, not the one she was in death.

'So you have to do what I say!'

'Why? Why do I have to?'

'Because you feel guilty about me.'

She was never as stupid as she looked.

'All you have to do is call him.'

'No.'

'Why not?'

'I'm not doing your dirty work for you again. That's over.'

'Look at me,' she said, shrugging a tattered shoulder. 'What can I do that's dirty?'

I thought about succubi and incubuses that come in the night and entwine you in their wispy embrace. I thought about Addam lying there on that mattress on the floor and Berenger's white fog covering him, entering him, overwhelming him.

'Can't you get him to come here? Then I could appear…with you…and talk to him. And if he couldn't hear me, you could speak for me. I've seen it in the movies.'

I remembered that film. She'd watched it four times one night, and went through two boxes of Kleenex, as she came down from whatever combination of pills she had swallowed before dinner.

'If you don't help me I won't go away.' She was trying blackmail now. It was so predictable. 'I'll drive you crazy.'

'So what's new?' I needed to sound as if I didn't care.

If she knew I cared, she would find the softness in me and enter that way. I didn't want to open that door, even a crack.

'Please,' she whispered. 'Please call Addam.'

'What am I going to say? Hold on a minute, Addam, while I put a ghost on the line?'

'Tell him about me. Let him know...I, like, love him.'

I looked at her, or what there was of her. At this moment she was moist eyes and wild hair and hungry teeth. And the outlines of hands clasped tight, beseeching me. 'No.'

'Nile, he hates me and I don't know why! I can't remember!'

'Concentrate, then.' I rolled over on the bed, and pressed the pillow again to my head. I didn't want this conversation. I didn't want to know if Addam had been with her that night. I didn't want to know he was going away with her the next morning.

I suppose they call it denial.

had, of course, been disingenuous with Ostrowsky. I knew about Berenger and Addam. I knew when they met and where they met and how they got there. I made the arrangements and ordered the cars.

I even know when it started. It was the night Berenger thought her Gameboy was attacking her, shortly after I'd moved into the SoHo loft. Aaron was out, lending moral support to Lilian, who was addressing the 92nd Street Y. Berenger seemed miffed about Aaron going off with Lilian and had retired to her room complaining of sore underarms. I hadn't heard that one before.

A couple of hours later, she was on the phone, sobbing and entreating me to come to her room. Thinking something catastrophic had happened, I rushed upstairs to find an hysterical Berenger pressed into a corner under a window, holding the Gameboy at arm's length and shaking violently.

'It's snapping at me!' she screamed.

The batteries had evidently run down. One of the ferocious little icons kept blinking and fading, blinking and fading on the screen.

Berenger seemed to think the creature had some kind of grievance against her. 'It won't stop!' she wailed. 'It won't stop!'

'Give it to me,' I said calmly, as if soothing a tempestuous toddler, and I tried to take the device off her.

'No!' She held on grimly and pulled it back, cradling it against her chest and looking up at me stubbornly. Then she looked down at the Gameboy, shuddered, opened her hands and allowed it to drop to the floor with a clatter. She was so pale and sweaty that her skin had the texture and colour of a glazed donut.

'I want Addam!' Her eyes were wild and bright, fringed by wet lashes and globules of purple mascara. Snot had run down her nose and glistened in the dimple above her upper lip. I wanted to scrub her face with a handkerchief, scrub her face *off* with a handkerchief, if the truth be known. I was never very good with hysteria. I started to shake myself.

'I want Addam!' she sobbed.

'I can fix it,' I told her with the semblance of calm, but my voice was an octave higher than I would have liked. 'It's only the batteries.'

'What do you know?' She clenched her fists and looked at me angrily through tears. 'I want Addam! Addam will fix it.'

I was shocked. I knew she'd been calling him, from her hotel bills. But I thought there had been no physical contact. I hoped there had been no physical contact. But now, here she was, calling for him, and inconsolable.

'Addam will fix it,' she kept repeating. She sounded bewildered, and kept plucking at a scab on her knee.

I decided. 'I'll get him,' I said.

'You will?' She looked pathetically grateful.

I went and sat on the bed and took a deep breath. I dialled the number I had committed to heart.

'What?' answered a cranky voice at the other end. It was about 11 p.m. but I didn't think Addam had been sleeping.

I explained, keeping my voice level.

He didn't scoff, which was what I'd expected. 'All right,' he said. He hung up.

'Addam's coming,' I told Berenger.

'He is?' she asked meekly. She wiped her nose with her bare arm. 'Will he come before it eats me?'

I let Addam in fifteen minutes later. He was wearing a scruffy teeshirt and tight tartan pants. He barely looked at me, just a sideways nod, if that kind of thing is possible. I stood back, against the front windows. He went straight to where Berenger was crouched and knelt in front of her. 'Now who's attacking my little girl, then?' he asked gently, taking her hands.

Berenger glanced in the direction of the discarded Gameboy and shivered.

Addam followed her gaze. He suddenly dropped her hands and pounced on the Gameboy, and made as if he were wrestling with it. He rolled on his back, kicked his boots in the air, grunted and thumped the floor as though in a life-or-death struggle with a villain twice his size and weight. I watched, more appalled than amused.

Berenger's eyes were on stalks.

'Take this! And this! And this!' Addam stopped kicking and gripped the Gameboy in both hands and pretended to punch it. 'Aaaaargh!!!' He clutched his throat with one hand and pretended that the Gameboy was now strangling him. 'I'm...afraid...my dear...the fucker's got...the...best...of... me...aaaargh!' He fell to the floor, bucking, clutching the toy, in comedic death throes.

Berenger managed a smile.

Addam opened one eye and caught her at it. 'Funny is it?' he asked, mock-crossly.

'Yes,' she giggled.

'Shit.' He sat up. 'Thank Christ for that.'

He examined the Gameboy in his hand, shook it.

'Haven't you heard of Tamogotchis?' he asked her. 'They don't put up nearly so much of a fight.'

I left the room. I went downstairs and sat on my bed, thinking Addam would come and talk to me, to discuss Berenger's state of mind at least. But it was stupid to think that. What did he owe me? The last time I'd seen him I'd spilled wine on his white shirt. That made for strong emotional bonds.

I stayed there for a long while, maybe two hours, and then I fell back on the pillows fully dressed. I didn't blame him. It's always more fun in the nursery than downstairs with the nanny.

In the morning, Berenger was so perky she agreed immediately to a request by an AIDS charity that she donate some of her clothes to a celebrity auction. She approved the design of her new http://www.berenger.com website, without complaining about a single image and managed to have an entire telephone conversation with the Fat Booker without screaming obscenities. She was feeling so full of sweetness and light and chemical substances she insisted I spend the whole day with Aaron.

'Don't you want me to come with you to Balthazar?' I asked, referring to a working lunch Berenger was having with Dorothy Merkin, the ghostwriter of her book, which was imaginatively titled *Berenger's Big Beauty Book.*

'Why should you be bored to death too?' she responded, with uncharacteristic empathy.

'How is she this morning?' Aaron asked me when I took some transcribed pages up to his study. He seemed in rather a defeated mood, shaky and enervated, with beads of sweat on his brow. He had obviously slept in his study, judging by the crumpled rug thrown over the sofa. There were cigarette butts in the ashtray, which suggested Lilian had come back with him after the event at the Y. They would often talk for hours in this room and it usually annoyed me that Lilian kept him up so late when he needed every ounce of sleep he could get to deal with Berenger.

'How did Lilian's speech go?' I asked, not that interested, but wanting to give the subject of Berenger a wide berth.

'Brilliant!' he exclaimed, suddenly engaged. 'That woman can talk!'

I knew that.

'I have to speak with you, Nile,' she would lecture me on the phone. 'You mustn't let that child drain him too much.' Or:

'Those producers are taking advantage of him. I want you to make sure he talks to Sidney before he signs anything.' And: 'I'm going to take him up to Provincetown next week. The air will do him good. I want you to clear his agenda…'

'I want to send Lilian some flowers,' Aaron continued, 'Those blue things she likes.'

'Delphinium or larkspur?' I asked.

He waved a hand. 'Find out, will you?'

I did find out about the flowers—delphinium—when what I really wanted to find out was: did Aaron know about Addam's visit?

But, of course, I didn't dare ask, even hint, and the day went smoothly, thanks to Berenger's absence. Indeed, she was so absent that I had to field a call from an enraged Dorothy Merkin.

'I've been in this goddamn hole by myself for ninety minutes and the waiters are about to evict me to give some Hollywood hotshot my table! Where the hell is she?'

'Dorothy, I think you better leave,' I advised. 'She's probably caught up somewhere.'

'My ass!' cursed the ghostwriter. 'She can pay for this fucking bottle of Krug.'

'Send me the bill,' I sighed.

I ran into Berenger in the elevator around seven. She looked tired. 'Dorothy called—' I began.

'Don't give me that!' Berenger snapped before I could give her anything. 'I didn't have to go. The fucking book's finished anyway. She just likes to be seen with me. Stupid old cow.'

'Where were you?' I asked coolly.

'Shopping,' she said.

'So where are your parcels?'

'I had them sent,' she said, with a sneer, as if I were an idiot. It was exactly how teenagers talk to their parents, I believe.

'Don't forget you're going with Aaron to the theatre tonight.' I said this with some relish, knowing how she hated the theatre and tried to get out of these engagements.

'I feel sick,' she complained.

'Oh, no you don't,' I said.

She looked at me irritably. But she knew what I meant.

She went to the theatre.

Berenger's fragrance promotion schedule began to coincide with Detox's concerts, not only in New York and the European capitals, which were her frequent haunts, but in more unlikely locations such as Birmingham, Alabama and Vilnius, Lithuania. Was it a coincidence or simply an indication of the remarkable fact that there were places in the world where people enjoyed both listening to downbeat music and spraying themselves with Voile de Berenger? What kind of people could they be?

If I was travelling with her, she'd insist I come with her to hear Addam play. I feigned illness the first couple of times she asked me, but there was a limit to this excuse (although it was limitless when Berenger used it herself) and the third time I tried, Berenger gave me the peckish bird look and asked, 'Are you afraid of something, Niley?'

I had to go after that. It became easier after the first time, but I still couldn't shake off my embarrassment. Addam would smile at me but I'm sure he didn't have any idea who I was. I was out of context. I told myself I didn't belong backstage with Addam's camp followers, the young girls with barettes in their hair and skimpy halter tops and the boys who lounged in vinyl jackets and the haze of illicit smoke, any more than I belonged backstage at the fashion shows.

The frank display of sex disturbed me. The girls seemed to me to be all rolling bellies and bursting cleavages and moist, bruised lips. In public, the boys intertwined with them possessively, like young, sated lords of the manor who had had their way with the serving wenches. They lay around the green rooms and in the dark crawl-spaces offstage like worms at the bottom of a muddy river, wound around each other in mutual inertia, making little snorts and giggles now and then, one of them occasionally breaking away to stumble to the bathroom or the refrigerator.

This sluggish polyester octopus was unimpressed by—and maybe unaware of—everything except its own sticky centre, and that included Berenger and her followers. Her entourage invariably consisted of a dozen extras she had rustled up during the evening. She wore them like armour, a phalange of noisy, posturing soldiers who surrounded her like a flying wedge as she entered through the stage door, with me bringing up the rear.

I felt old and stale and disapproving, and watched myself slipping into the schoolmarm pose I adopted whenever I feared criticism. I could feel my jaw set and my mouth purse and my arms would automatically fly across my chest in the gestural equivalent of *So?*

Berenger would ignore the grunts and groans and walk through the reclining groupies like Jesus over water, trailing the twelve disciples. Addam, in the scrum, would seem as unaware of her as his flunkies were, until she stood right before him, an evil little smile playing on her lips. They wouldn't exactly address each other but Berenger would announce something like 'I need a drink' to no-one in particular and a plastic cup of something would materialise in her hand. Addam would nod his head and then go back to whispering in the ear of the boy next to him or stroking the hair of the girl tucked under his arm. Berenger would start to flirt with a member of her entourage, usually a good-looking boy she'd chosen earlier for this specific purpose, but sometimes a girl, just to shock, and she'd slowly get swallowed back up in the tentacles of her cheer squad. When the support band went on, Addam would disappear with his dresser to get ready, and we wouldn't see him again until he went on stage.

It was always this way, although occasionally one of the groupies would take exception to Berenger's presence, and would cause a minor ruckus, seething with foul language behind her back or, in one case, going so far as to throw a cup of vodka at her face. I was pleased to observe that Addam had no special girl, the voodoo goddess nowhere in sight, just a series of accom-modating females in midriff-baring tops, most of whom looked right through Berenger with unfocused eyes. But the girl who threw the vodka was alert enough to smell something not entirely familial in Berenger's behaviour, and the scent wasn't just Voile de Berenger.

I found it all really...predictable, how the girls clung to Addam. And I didn't much care for his attitude, the way he matched their dopey needfulness with disdain. But he was living in a loop that had been playing over and over since the sixties, when Mick did *Performance*, and through the seventies, when Sid killed Nancy, into the nineties, when Kurt Cobain shot himself in the mouth, a prescribed code of behaviour that valued pathetic attempts at anarchy over order, indulgence over restraint, slack-ness over motivation, cynicism over sentiment, perversity over honour, debasement over respect, hostility over friendship, and a shrugging nihilism above all. In picking up the microphone, Addam bought into a role scripted decades ago by gossip colum-nists he had never met, rehearsed for him by performers he had only seen in video clips and accepted as fact by teenage fans he would never know, except through their overwrought letters of undying love.

Do I sound jealous?

I could see Baby's hand in this, Gertrude schooling Hamlet in the expectations of his title. She knew all about the rituals of the court—the taking of young virgins, the personal vanities of the royal toilette, the opening up of veins to receive the consecrated sacraments—and she had trained him well. Addam had adopted all the narcissism that went with his elevated ranking and, it shocked me to realise it, the required callousness, too.

'But why can't I go with you to the party?' I once overheard a young girl implore as Addam was leaving through the stage door. 'I mean, like, we had a good time last night, didn't we?'

Addam shook his arm fiercely to get her off him and gave her a cold stare. 'That was last night,' he said and turned his back.

Far from being devastated by Addam's indifference, she followed him out the door. 'What about tomorrow night, then?'

Addam was aloof with Berenger in public, but I knew it was otherwise in private. He didn't send her packing, home to Aaron, as he should have. He wasn't the one risking anything. Berenger had more to lose, I thought, but she seemed to get pleasure from the risk. She would stand in the wings, smoking, her arms crossed in an attitude of impatience, her pointy-toed foot tapping. She was engrossed in Addam, even though her body language said otherwise. Her eyes didn't once leave him as he moved around the stage, even when the swivelling lights sent dazzling sunspots of bright colour across her line of vision. The stage would be flooded with purple, then red, then acid yellow, and all through it Berenger's eyes would move with Addam, gripping him.

I was watching Addam too, although with partly averted eyes. I found it painful to look at him limping around like that, even though I knew the limp meant nothing to him, no more than a cowlick might in some schoolboy's hair. But it gave so much poignancy to his performance I suspected he exaggerated it. In the louder numbers he would move all around the stage in an agitated manner, sometimes kicking at a wall furiously or dragging the microphone stand right into the wings. I wondered what particular demon made him so convincingly disturbed. And then suddenly the mood would change, the lights would mellow, he'd bow his head, wipe his brow with the corner of his shirt and take the microphone between his hands as gently as a lover. I'd bite my lip and have to look away, as his husky, tender voice filled the auditorium.

At moments like these, his emotional connection to his audience was something to behold, even when the sentiments expressed in his songs were manipulative and contrived. Whenever a spotlight swooped across the swaying girls I could see their faces shimmering with tears and their tight white fists clamped in their mouths as if to quell all the screams and sighs welling up inside. There were boys down there, equally galvanised, pumping their fists in the air through the angrier ballads and leaning amorously into the girls when the mood turned despondent. I think that while the girls saw in Addam some fractured romantic figure who was crying out for their affection, the boys heard their own sounds of confusion and anguish in his voice.

Whenever Addam crouched down with his microphone at the apron of the stage and sang directly to the fans in the first few rows, he always included the boys in this intimacy. He didn't sing just for the girls, but for all melancholy youth.

Crowned with the golden lights of the theatre, his face iridescent with sweat and the colour of his suit, which was inevitably purple or ruby or some other bloodstain, pulsing against the dark of the stage, he seemed radioactive. I didn't know what to think of his songs, whether they were bad or brilliant or mediocre. All I knew was that I wanted him more than did every sobbing girl in that theatre put together

'Ooh, I think he's eminently do-able,' I overheard some queeny hairdresser confide in a wardrobe person one night backstage.

'Get in line!' sniggered the girl with the clothes rack.

Which gets down to the truth of the matter. They were all in the queue, the ones who were attracted to his songs and the ones who were attracted to his looks and the ones who were attracted to his celebrity…and the *one* who was attracted to his danger and stood at the head of the line.

And I, Nile Kirk, was on that wretched line too.

A week went by after Ostrowsky's visit. I lived it in a daze. I couldn't believe that Addam had intended to flaunt his relationship with Berenger by running off with her like that to Morocco. I didn't understand why he would be so deliberately cruel to Aaron, even though he and Berenger had been sailing very close to the wind before she died. But it was one thing to be selfish and careless, another altogether to plot a public humiliation. There was no point in being so bloody-minded unless he really loved her. And I agonised over that.

'Were you going to tell Aaron?'

'It wasn't, like, his business.'

'So whose business was it? Your cat's?'

'Aaron didn't care.'

This was news to me. But I couldn't get another word out of her on the subject. And then Berenger vanished. Ostrowsky seemed to have put her in her own particular black mood.

Ayesha and I would sometimes have lunch in the graveyard of St Paul's chapel across from Susan Mackie's office. Even in winter, when the trees were stripped of their leaves, the smell of the mulchy soil and the mossy crypts had a certain bizarre cosiness. I was so tired from my nocturnal wranglings with Berenger I could have lain down happily on one of those grassy knolls, under a tombstone, and gone to sleep. Berenger didn't once trouble me there, but then, I didn't expect it. She had a child's imagination and was afraid of ghosts.

Lately, Ayesha had westernised herself. She took herself to GAP one lunchtime the week before and bought some baggy jeans and a sweatshirt, although she still wore sari fabric draped over her head. She was gaining confidence, I could tell. Sister Pansy had been promoting her as the spokesperson for the tenants at Magdalen House in their dispute with the landlord and, although I could see the cause was hopeless, I was impressed with the way she calmly and clearly put our case forward.

Ayesha offered me a clementine. She had pushed the sari down to her shoulders, the 'good' side of her profile facing me. I studied her downy jawline, the perfect shell of an ear studded with gold, the glossy black braid that curved around her neck. She had definitely been pretty, once.

'May I ask you a question, Nile?'

'Of course.'

'My new friend…Kevin…would like to meet you. I have told him so much about you. And he is very nice. He asks that you join us for dinner tomorrow night.'

I had been hearing about Kevin Kendricks ever since he called Magdalen House after seeing our protest on television. Ayesha was at first reluctant to meet him, but I think Keesha and Sister Pansy encouraged her to go out and 'make a new friend'. Make a new friend! What kind of man would seek out a tragic figure like Ayesha? And pursue her? Take her to dinner and the cinema? Buy her flowers and donuts? Make her feel special?

He had to be a creep.

I was an expert on creeps. I was a magnet for them. I never knew what it was that drew them to me. Perhaps I looked as if I might be grateful for their drooling advances. The pretty girls at school and at college had a way of deflecting unwanted attention that never worked for me. If I was cold and imperious, like them, the creeps would just get brutal. 'Who d'you think you are then, love? Bleedin' Marilyn Monroe?' they'd say as they grabbed my arm and pushed me into a corner. The pretty girls got respect for turning men away, but all I got was contempt.

So I learnt to give in. Not graciously. Why should I flatter them by making them think I enjoyed it? They didn't care anyway. A quick fumble in my blouse, a hand on my shoulder pushing me down, a fist in my hair yanking my face forward, a hasty unzipping of jeans. I didn't bite, I didn't gag. I became good at getting it over fast.

Sometimes they would buy me a coffee or tea, to butter me up first. Whenever I saw that coffee coming I knew what was in store.

And then I met a boy who wasn't like that. He was a veterinary student, smart, handsome and fastidiously well-mannered. He told me I had nice eyes and bought me three-course meals. And then he'd take me for a walk along Beverley Brook, holding my hand, and tell me all his troubles. There was no unzipping or pulling of hair. His fingers intertwined with mine and that was all. When I suggested I did for him what I did for the others, he looked away. I thought, is this respect, at last?

I have to tell this part quickly, or I won't be able to tell it at all. One summer night, as I was walking home from the Vow Exchange where I sold wedding rings on Friday nights, I was suddenly hooked around the neck from behind and dragged into a dark stairwell in a deserted shopping arcade. It happened so fast, all the air went out of me and I couldn't struggle. I was gripped around the waist by a strong arm and slammed into the concrete wall so hard it split my cheek. My hips wore the welts of his fingernails for weeks afterwards. I bled from every orifice. And when it was over I opened the eye that would open and saw his hand pressing into the wall above my head and, on his third finger, the signet ring his father had given him when he was accepted into college. He said nothing, withdrew and slipped away, but I knew he had wanted me to see that ring.

I wiped myself on my cardigan and threw it away. My grandmother barely listened to my story that I'd fallen down on London Road. I didn't say anything to anyone. He was my boyfriend, after all.

I regretted agreeing to join Ayesha and Kevin for dinner the moment she introduced me to him out on 22nd Street where he was waiting on the kerb with a cab.

He was moderately good-looking, in a shifty way, which made me all the more suspicious. He had the kind of mild, fair-skinned face that a refugee from northern India like Ayesha would find exotic. To my eyes, his face was too broad across the forehead and too wide across the mouth so that when he smiled he looked like an elastic band stretching. His hair, which was sandy-coloured, was slick, but wayward little tufts kept popping up here and there to suggest that much covert greasing had been done to conceal the fact that this was a head that had spent a lifetime shorn in a brutal crewcut. He was wearing the kind of anonymous dun-coloured trenchcoat the white-collar workers from Surrey wear when they commute on the tube into London every day. But it looked brand new: I guessed he was trying too hard to be respectable. You could tell, straightaway, from his ramrod posture and the bulk of shoulders, that he had done time in the armed forces.

Kevin stretched his face into what he thought was a smile and opened the back door of the taxi with a flourish. His chivalry did not end there: he helped both Ayesha and me to be seated comfortably, tucking her long skirt under her legs solicitously so that it didn't get caught in the door. Then he closed the door carefully and sat in the front next to the driver. He gave instructions and we lurched off into the glittering night, shimmering with promise for the love-struck Ayesha, who stared at the back of Kevin's head with a look of absolute adoration. I was sure she didn't notice the small patch of nude scalp, like a hatchet wound, where no hair grew.

Kevin placed his arm along the back of the seat and turned in profile to speak to us. He bestowed on me a smile that suggested I was the most glorious creature on the planet and then I knew it for sure: he was a phoney. No-one smiled at me like that and meant it.

'You ladies all right back there?' he asked.

'Fine, thank you,' I said, tersely.

The taxi bumped through the cobblestone streets of SoHo and my heart sank as we pulled up at a familiar restaurant, briefly Berenger's favourite, a theme park of pseudo Frenchness, complete with lace-curtained windows and waiters with starched tablecloths tucked into their waistbands as aprons. Three months before it had been impossible to get a booking here unless you were a model, a movie star, a designer or a trend analyst. Berenger and her friends used it as a cafeteria, smashed their cigarettes out in the Limoges ashtrays, stained the little espresso cups with pink lipstick and picked at the curly leaves of their *chevre* salads, whiling away the hours canvassing their favourite subjects—parties, boys, clothes, beauty treatments and beanie babies. And now, through some freakish coincidence, I was about to have to sit through another tedious dinner here. Kevin had managed to obtain a reservation, so I supposed that the girls had moved on to other free bottles of champagne at other restaurants, leaving the transiently hip SoHo establishment desperate enough to accept diners like Kevin Kendricks on a Friday night.

When Kevin jumped out of the cab and opened the back door for us, I briefly considered jumping out the other door and disappearing into the night. But Ayesha grabbed my arm as she slid along the seat and pulled me, gently, with her. I'd ruin her night if I ran off.

I watched Kevin count and recount eight single dollar bills and then reach into his pocket and add a fifty cent tip. He turned and saw me looking at him and averted his eyes.

When we entered the bustling room, I hung back, hoping no-one would notice me, but I'd forgotten how finely tuned the sensation-seeking antennae of a maitre d' could be. In one swoop, he genuflected in front of me, had his waiters remove a 'RESERVED' sign from a table, and ushered us to our seats. I was appalled that he'd placed me in the most prominent table, like a trophy. I could see the line of people waiting at the bar looking curiously at the three of us wondering what we'd done to get such special treatment. Gradually, I could feel all the eyes in the room on me.

Kevin immediately commandeered the wine list and ordered the cheapest bottle on it. The maitre d' interrupted the trans-action and brushed aside Kevin's choice, insisting on sending us, as an aperitif, a bottle of champagne, which was delivered in a silver bucket. Kevin looked agitated when the opulent bottle arrived and I resisted telling him that it would be complimentary. It was mean of me, but I wanted him to suffer for bringing me to this place.

Ayesha had never drunk champagne before and her cheeks flushed bright red after only a sip or two. Kevin threw an arm over the back of his bentwood chair and quaffed his drink debonairly. A pity some of it trickled down his chin. Ayesha didn't notice—her eyes were shining so brightly you could see yourself reflected in them.

Every time I glanced up from my drink, I caught someone looking at me. I was forced to concentrate on Kevin. He was no boy. He could have been anywhere from thirty-eight to fifty-two, I calculated, a fourteen-year span that might have included any number of wife beatings, date rapes, fondlings of young girls on trains and sex tours of Thailand. It might even have included a mail-order Filipino bride or two and who knows how many Vietnamese peasants left defiled and eviscerated in a paddy field.

'You ever been to Asia, Kevin?' I asked, innocently.

He fell into my trap, grandstanding. 'Why, sure,' he said, giving me a wide smile. 'One tour of 'Nam, Hong Kong, Bangkok, Penang, a cruise of the Pacific in '87...let's see, uh, Singapore, Kuala Lumpur when I was a kid, Manila three times, Jakarta...does Fiji count?' He folded his arms and leant back. 'Course, I never made it to the Indian subcontinent but, now I have met the lovely Ayesha, I truly wish I had.'

Ayesha beamed at this calculated piece of flattery. I felt sick to my stomach. 'And what do you do, Kevin, that takes you to such exotic places?'

'Components,' he said vaguely and reached over and squeezed Ayesha's hand. The fold of sari that covered her head slid off and pooled around her shoulders. She released her hand and reached for the fabric to veil her face again. Kevin snatched her hand back. 'Now, why do you want to cover that beautiful face of yours with a bit of old fabric? Leave it off so that I can enjoy every bit of you.'

Ayesha's scars reddened and she looked down at her place-setting, but I noticed she squeezed his hand back and her knuckles went white with the pressure of it.

'What kind of components, Kevin?' I insisted, knowing that Ayesha was impressed by components, the kind of components that are made in American-owned factories where her family and friends had toiled for years.

'Wire supports,' he said, smiling at Ayesha's raw, scarred forehead as she kept her eyes glued on her knife and fork.

'For construction?' I asked, feigning interest.

'You might say that,' he said briskly. 'Now, I wonder where our waiter is?'

He was changing the subject. 'Come on, you can tell us. You don't work for the CIA, do you, Kevin?' I asked lightly.

He looked at me and smirked. I had flattered him. Ayesha's head snapped up as she looked at him with even more respect, if that was possible. But I knew he was hiding something.

'Well, you know,' I continued, 'all those *components*. You could be making bombs, fuel lines, weapons…'

'Could be,' he grinned. 'But I'm afraid it's nothing as incendiary as that. Didn't you say you felt like seafood tonight, Ayesha? Why don't you allow me to order for you?'

'So what's the name of the company?'

'What?' His voice now had an edge to it. The kind of edge it had when he'd been drinking and his wife came home from work late and he was getting ready to punish her. I wanted Ayesha to hear it.

'I said, what's the name of the company you work for?'

'Well, you know, there are, uh, actually many companies. You ever heard of Lindaco? K.M. Technical?'

'No.'

'Well, then, Nile, I think that maybe it won't make any difference if I do impart that information. Let's get Ayesha something to eat. She looks as if she might fade away.'

'Wait a minute,' I said. 'Lindaco. That's that billionairess who owns all the lingerie companies, isn't it? Linda…I can't think of her name.' Berenger had been negotiating a contract with one of Lindaco's subsidiaries at the time of her death.

'Linda Remnick.' He said this curtly.

'So you work for her?'

'Yes I do, Nile.'

'And those wire components?'

'For lingerie, Nile.' He pronounced it 'lingeree'.

It came to me at last. 'You mean you make underwire for bras?'

'I *supervise* the making of underwire for brassieres among other things,' he corrected me.

'You do?' Ayesha looked at him bug-eyed. I hoped it was dawning on her that all this was a big act.

'It's technically much more complicated than you—'

'Oh, I know!' said Ayesha. 'My uncle works for Lady Godiva! Managing the factory that makes the…how do you say? Snips?'

'Snaps?' Kevin asked, his eyes gripping hers.

'Yes…snaps!' She laughed. I hadn't heard her laugh before.

297

It was a lovely laugh, like tinkling beads.

'Well, beautiful lady,' he slimed. 'I knew we had more in common than our lonely souls.'

This was sickening. I couldn't help myself. 'What makes you think she's lonely?' I asked crossly.

'Nile!' Ayesha looked embarrassed, but I was doing this for her own good.

Kevin continued to stare at Ayesha, stroking her hand. 'Anyone can see that Ayesha has not been…appreciated.'

Ayesha beamed back at him.

'She's appreciated,' I said. 'By lots of people.'

'Nile, I can see you are her friend, but that's not the kind of appreciation I was talking about. Male appreciation is what I mean. Ayesha has not been loved enough by men.'

'But what is wrong with him?' Ayesha was sobbing, back in her room. Kevin had escorted us to our elevator and kissed Ayesha's hand. Me, he had glared at, as if he wished I'd go up in flames. I didn't feel much better about him. Not only had he caused me acute embarrassment by exhibiting me in public but he'd acted towards Ayesha in a boorishly patronising way.

'He bought you a single rose in the restaurant for a start. You can't trust a man like that.'

'But why not?' she moaned, sitting on the edge of the bed and clutching the cellophane-wrapped rose to her breast as tightly as a nursing infant. 'It was offered to me and I said I would like it.'

'Any normal person would brush those rose-selling scum away. He wanted you to think he was romantic, but what's romantic about a freeze-dried rose?'

'A freezen…*frozen* rose is romantic when you have not been given one before, Nile.' She looked up at me defiantly.

'But that's my point, Ayesha! He knows that about you. He

knows you'll be satisfied with a six-dollar rose. None of those American girls would. He's being cheap. He sees you on the television and he knows you're unworldly and would be grateful for anything...a rose, a bottle of bad wine. Did you notice that, when he ordered for you, he ordered the cheapest dish on the menu. An omelette!'

'But I wanted an omelette!'

'No, you didn't. You only wanted it because he suggested it. When I insisted you try the Beluga, he went purple with rage. If you hadn't spent the whole night looking down at your plate, you would have noticed these things.'

'But I don't like it, the Beluga.'

'It doesn't matter. That's one thing I learnt from Berenger. Always order the best and you know where you stand. Kevin resented buying you Beluga, it was obvious. If I hadn't been there, he would have taken terrible advantage of you.'

'No, it is not true. He is always kind to me!' She was gnawing on the edge of her sari now. I felt sorry for her, but I had to tell her what I knew. To save her.

'Ayesha, he was taking advantage of you. How many dates have you been on with Kevin before tonight? One, two?'

'Two,' she said glumly.

'And where did he take you?'

'We shared a cup of coffee the first time. Here, on this street. He bought me a Krispy Kreme.' She looked up, eyes blazing. 'But I wanted it this way! I didn't want...a big deal the first time, Nile. In case he is bad. But I saw that he was not.'

'And he took you to Central Park on your second date?'

'It was a beautiful day.' Something calculating crossed her face. 'He paid for a taxi.'

'But he pulled all the stops out tonight, didn't he?'

'I don't understand.'

'He took us to an expensive restaurant. Whose idea was it? To invite me? I bet it wasn't his.'

'Oh, but it was, Nile! I had spoken about you so much to him that he said he would very much like to meet you. And so he asked for you to come tonight. He knows that you too are…alone.'

Of course. He thought I was just like her, wounded and pathetic, and that I too would be eternally grateful for an omelette with a bit of parsley in it and a glass of rancid wine. He probably thought that I would swoon with thankfulness at his meagre offerings and go home and tell Ayesha, enviously, that she had found herself a wonderful man and that she must not, under any circumstance, let him go.

'He got more than he bargained for, didn't he?'

'But, Nile, why were you so unkind to him?'

'I know his type, Ayesha.'

'But what type is that, Nile?'

I took a deep breath. 'Listen to me. I am not saying that there is not a man out there who will love you. I am just saying that this is the wrong man. His type feeds on girls like you, who are in unfortunate situations and alone. The more debased the circumstances, the better for him. That's why he likes Asian women, because he thinks you'll be subservient and because western women would scoff at him and his pretensions about being a man of the world, when it's underwire for bras he's really selling—'

'He is not selling. And besides, Nile, it is an honourable job. I ask you, what is wrong with it?'

'There's nothing wrong with it. What's wrong with it is that he is pretending to be something else to give you a false sense that he's a secure man, with a home and family values, and that he will look after you, when all he really wants to do is get you in his cellar and make you his sex slave.'

'Nile!'

'Didn't you notice the way he wouldn't give me a direct answer about his work? Why didn't he tell us in the first place he worked for Lindaco?'

'Perhaps because he thought you would laugh at him. You knew all those important people…'

'He knew I would know him for what he was. All those trips to

300

Manila and Thailand, you can bet he was paying for sex with children or with the teenagers who work in the factories. Men like him take on jobs like that for one reason.'

'I do not believe it!' Ayesha looked stricken and I was glad of it. It was time she faced some realities.

'Did you ask him if he has been married before? He's old enough to have had a few wives.'

'He is thirty-six.'

I told her he looked like fifty if he was a day.

'No, he was born in 1962. And he has never been married.'

'And where does he live?'

'He says he lives near the airport. He says—' she broke off suddenly.

'He says what?'

She stuck her chin out stubbornly. 'That it will be very convenient for us to live there when we are married because we will be doing so much travelling together. I can go with him—'

'Wait a minute! He's asked you to marry him?'

She nodded. 'And I have accepted.'

'When? You've only had three dates.'

'In Central Park. At the carousel.'

'How romantic of him? Did he buy you a toffee apple?'

'Nile, please.'

'But you're already married.'

'No, Dr Mackie says I am not. In her eyes.'

That was clever of her. 'And when is the wedding going to take place?'

'It is not important. I am going to live with him and then we will decide.'

'Ayesha, this is horrible! I bet there's half a dozen dead Filipinos out there stashed in the deep freeze! He probably took them directly from the airport, tortured and raped them, and then hacked them to death with a meat cleaver and stored the pieces in ziplock bags. He probably goes down to the basement every morning and examines each lump of flesh to see how they are deteriorating. He probably gets off on that.'

'You are wrong!'

'He's going to get you out there too and we'll never see you again.'

'Nile, this is enough. Please leave me. You are making me afraid.'

'That's what I'm trying to do, don't you see? Even if Kevin isn't a serial killer, he's still going to hurt you. He's chosen you because you are scarred, because deep down he thinks he's only deserving of scarred women, but when he gets you home and sees those scars every day you'll remind him that you're all he can get, a poor, friendless, scarred woman, and he'll hate you even more than he hates himself, and it will start with language but it will end with fists or knives or guns, and that dear, twisted face of yours will be all bruised and bloody, or cold and waxy. I don't want to visit you in the morgue, Ayesha, I've had enough of that.'

Ayesha was sobbing, but I didn't dare feel sorry for her. If I gave her a moment's comfort she'd suffer a lifetime of hell.

'Where will I go?' she wailed. 'If I don't go with Kevin?'

'You can stay with me,' I told her gently. 'We'll manage.'

'No!' She clenched both fists and banged them against her thighs. 'I do not want your life!'

I was shocked at her intensity. 'What do you mean?' I could feel my voice rising with hers.

'It does not matter,' she said quietly. The colour drained from her face and the whimpers ceased.

'Ayesha, what I mean is, we can go on like we are. We can work for Susan and live here. Even if they turn this place into a hotel, we can rent a room together. Or we can find somewhere else. Maybe Brooklyn. What about Brooklyn? You'd like it out there. I can see us in a room with a fireplace and a couple of cats. Anything is better than living with a drunken wife-beater like Kevin…I bet they don't even have Krispy Kremes out at the airport.'

She looked right through me, like I was air. 'You do not want me to be happy, Nile.'

'Of course I want you to be happy! I don't want you to be a slave.'

'But I am a slave already.'

'No, you're not.'

'I am Susan Mackie's slave.'

'What makes you say that? You're free to come and go. She gives you a salary.'

'But I am beholden to her.'

'Well, you're not beholden to me. You're not my slave. You're my friend.'

'I *am* your slave.' She said this softly but insistently as she stared at the back of her hands, which were permanently mottled from skin grafts.

'How could you say that? I don't demand anything of you, Ayesha.'

'There are many kinds of slavery, Nile.'

We sank into silence. She seemed reluctant to elaborate, but I couldn't let it rest.

'Ayesha, what have I done?'

'Oh, you have been wonderful!' She softened for a moment and smiled at me. Then she looked down again, worrying at her nails. 'But you feel sorry for me.'

I was about to argue, but she interrupted.

'Don't say you are not. I know you are this way. And I am obligated to you, for your sympathy.'

'I am obligated to *you*. You found me the job with Susan Mackie. Surely that cancels it out.'

'But you are unhappy there. And you are sorry for me every day. There is so much sorrow for me in everyone's faces that surely I am the most pathetic person on this earth. I am the lowest of the low. Kevin does not feel sorrow for me—'

'That's because he's a pervert—'

'He is not! He is lonely too. I can give him something.'

'Ayesha, this is all wrong!'

'No, it is not, Nile. You are my friend and you should be happy for me. But you are not. And you are not happy for me to be with Kevin because you are content to see me in this room and on the street and in Dr Mackie's office as I am. You want me to be as I am!'

'That's not true.'

'I was pretty once, Nile, you must remember. My cousin, Vishna, who is like my sister, is not beautiful. She is not ugly, you understand, but she is…you do not notice her when you walk by. And so, I was content to have a plain cousin. When I sat with her at the table, and walked with her through the market, people had eyes only for me. And I was very, very nice to Vishna, you understand, but I saw her as my "poor" cousin.

'When I had my…accident, and I was no longer pretty, Vishna came to visit me with flowers and I could see in her eyes that she was sad for me, but overjoyed for herself too. She came to visit me every day that I was sick and every day I could see, through the fever and the pain, that it was a triumph. I can still see her eyes on me like black diamonds, how do you say? *Gloating*. And that is when I realised that when I was beautiful I must have caused her much sorrow, for my dear Vishna to feel such… *liberation* when I became ugly.

'And so, Nile, every day that I am scarred I am grateful for Var Bhargava and his burning oil. I do not want to be beautiful. I do not want to hurt other women. I do not want them to see pity in my eyes when I think I am looking at them with friendship. To ask a beautiful woman not to look on a plain woman as a queen looks on a peasant is like asking the moon to stop making the tides. Beauty is a terrible thing. It does not give pleasure, only unhappiness. I am content to have you look at me with pity because I am disfigured. It is only right. I have been beautiful and now it is my turn not to be. I have been given a chance many others have not. It is justice.'

You think you're, like, so smart, a voice said in my head. *You think you're better than him. But just watch. She'll go with him. And all you'll have is me.*

can hear the guard's tinny radio playing the single Addam's record company released after Berenger's death. It has not been taken from the recent album, but from a studio recording of *Deviant* made ahead of the stage production. They packaged it and promoted it indecently quickly. I don't know if Addam approved of the haste, I don't know what he feels...There goes that word again.

'Beautiful.'

There's a crack in the word, like a fissure in ice, his voice a wolf howling in the wild.

I am alive and Berenger is dead and still he sings songs for her.

I continued to play nanny/pimp for them, scheduling their loathsome liaisons every week or two. I despised myself for doing it. My motive in betraying Aaron was as pathetic as it was despicable: I wanted to hear Addam's voice, sometimes, on the phone and occasionally, when I was lucky, stand across a crowded room from him. This was all the relationship I could ever hope for with him and still I was prepared to hurt the kindly man who had trusted me and taken me in.

Berenger had, conveniently for them, kept her messy apartment in the old Police Building in NoHo. I wondered more than once whether she knew all along she'd be needing it. Addam was on the road a lot of the time and so was she, which meant their meetings there were infrequent. But it was enough. Enough to give her emerald eyes a malicious gleam and to make me miserable.

It was Addam who finally overstepped the line. Just in case anyone thought fucking his grandfather's wife was not overstepping it.

Berenger had made her fortune from her pout. So, when it was suddenly the fashion for models to smile, she was awash in insecurity.

'I'm not going to smile. I look stupid,' she whined from her position on a big old Victorian sofa under a bank of lights. She was lying on her stomach on a bed of tapestry pillows, her face cupped in her hands and turned towards the camera. The dress she was wearing was something out of Botticelli, sheer and pleated. Her legs were crossed in the air, the toenails polished, the feet bare. It had taken four hours to get her to this point, to get her hair curled and her skin blushed and her foul morning mood to fade in the warm studio air. She had a headache. She felt sick. The coffee was 'off'. The springs of the sofa were digging into her. She was not going to smile.

'But we thought if you projected a little more...*warmth*,' said the account executive from the cosmetics company, standing a little way back, in case a pillow was launched her way, 'it might work...better.' She chose her words carefully, as if she were stepping through a linguistic minefield.

'But last time I didn't smile.'

'Last time we were doing the moody you. This time we're doing the happy you.'

'But why? It's my perfume. I don't want to be happy.'

'Look, love, you don't want to be the only grumpy girl on the block, do you?' This was the photographer, standing by his camera, tapping his fingers impatiently on a tripod leg. 'You don't want to have a little sulky face when Kylie's got a great big beautiful grin.' He said this in baby language.

'I'm not sulky.' Sulking.

'You're doing a pretty good imitation of it, love.' He was getting testy.

Berenger sat up suddenly. 'Erik! Erik!'

Because this was a major campaign, Erik Sklar had dropped in to keep an eye on things. He was over by a window, talking into his cell phone. He turned when Berenger called his name and walked briskly towards her, still talking into the phone.

'Erik, tell them I don't want to smile!'

'Why don't you want to smile?' Erik asked calmly, with the cell phone still at his ear.

'Because I didn't smile last time!'

'Did she smile last time?' Erik turned to the account executive and gave her a withering look.

'No, but that was different—'

'Why?'

'Because we wanted a more sultry look. But consumer research has shown us that smiles work better for this kind of…concept. The consumer wants to see a *friendlier* Berenger.'

'Can you be friendlier, Berenger?' Erik's tone was curt.

'You think I should smile?' A small, querulous voice, like a little girl asking for more sweets.

'If you smile, you move more bottles of that stinking fragrance. I believe that's the argument.'

'But why would I be smiling on this stupid old sofa? It's dumb. Who would I be smiling at?'

'I'm sure you could come up with someone.'

Berenger flashed him an annoyed look. 'It's cheesy. I still don't like it.'

'Berenger, nothing you do is ever cheesy.'

'You're sure?'

'I'm sure.'

'Well, it would be your fault if it was.'

'So humour them.'

She rolled her eyes in a disgusted way and made a few grunts.

'Well…a *small* smile then,' she conceded eventually. 'But I'm not smiling in this outfit. I'd look like the cover of a frigging romance magazine. I want to change. And not into any more crappy Vera Wangs either.' And with that she got off the couch and stomped towards the make-up room.

Thirteen people stood around for the next two hours trying to coax the tiniest lift from the corners of her mouth. Of course, it had occurred to her right from the start that this was a marvellous game and so she played it to the hilt. She'd give a flash of a smile but just as the shutter clicked it would disappear again. She'd smile but she would 'inadvertently' close her eyes. She'd smile but her body would shift to an awkward position. She knew all the tricks.

The time factor didn't trouble me. I had a good book to read. I always remembered to bring a good book.

I had my head in it when Addam appeared. I heard one of the stylist's assistants drop a shoe with a clatter and I looked up from where I was sitting in an old chair in the quietest corner I could find. Several heads turned in the direction of the doorway and then quickly turned away again, feigning nonchalance. It was left to the stylist's assistants to do the tittering. The poor things, I decided, that was their role—to provide the frank adulation that the others dare not show.

Poor things? What am I saying? They were an unpleasant lot, this revolving group of handmaidens in athletic gear, skinny anaemic little things trying to look tough in a world that wasn't fair to anyone who commanded less than $10,000 a day, Courtneys and Tiffanys and Amys and Kellys brought up to think they were pretty and savvy and worthy of the best the material world had to offer, only to find themselves pressing shirts and making coffee and stuffing silicone breast-enhancers down the Wonderbras of sour-faced supermodels who puffed smoke in their faces, dreaming of the day they would rise above all this and ascend to the lofty title of Fashion Director or Market Editor or even

Accessories Associate and take their turn in blowing smoke in the faces of young girls who aspired to be just like them.

These girls—these clothing zipper-uppers, these flat-chest expanders—would have been tolerable, I supposed, if they hadn't given themselves all kinds of airs and graces, as if ironing the cuffs of a shirt that was going to be worn by Berenger was a transcendental experience or being in the same nightclub as some hot young actor and three hundred other strangers was somehow validating. But by dint of my humble status I was always somehow included in their group, in their conversations, as if I really cared whether this season's skirt should be above the ankle or below it. I hated being stuck in a room with this babbling group of public school dropouts whose idea of an intellectual pursuit was deciding which colour polish to put on their nails. Existential Grey? Theosophical Pink? What would Kierkegaard do?

So it was the shirt-ironing stylists' assistants who first registered Addam's appearance in the doorway of the studio. Addam was not there and then he was, in that self-deprecating way of his. Everyone turned to look and then looked quickly away as if Grammy award-winning celebrities dropped in every day. They dropped in so frequently it was *boring*. John Lennon could have come back from the dead and none of them would have offered him so much as a glass of water. They were cool, all of them. The quality they prized above all else.

I watched Addam give a little gesture of hello to no-one in particular. Berenger was having a break from the camera while the hairdresser experimented with another style. She was sitting on a high stool in front of a mirror, a jar of baby food, which was her lunch, in her hand. She noticed Addam almost immediately and stared through her mirror at him, frozen. A little wrinkle of puzzlement, or annoyance, played on her dewy brow. For a moment, I thought she might turn on him, make a scene, shrug him away, although why I did not know. She had never been particularly careful about secrecy. Nor had Addam. It was I who took it seriously, pulled a veil over their meetings like some kind of demented sorceress.

Berenger sat perfectly still as Addam approached. He put his hands on her shoulders and kissed the back of her head. She smiled. A brilliant smile like the warm sun coming up, the kind of smile everyone had been waiting for all day. She put down the baby food. The coolness in the room fell away like the mist from a can of hairspray. People began to chatter again.

The photographer came over to shake Addam's hand. 'Liked your latest album, mate,' he said, loud enough for me to hear from my corner.

'Thanks, *mate*,' said Addam, mocking the photographer's East End accent.

The make-up artist asked him something. He held up both hands and shook his head in a polite rejection. And then he pulled out a stool and sat close to Berenger while the hairdresser rummaged through her hair in search of pins. After a moment, he put his hand on the back of Berenger's stool and put his face into the crook of her neck. Embarrassed, I glanced down at my book again. When I looked up they were kissing.

I do not mean that he was giving her a fraternal peck on the cheek or that she was merely accepting it. Where I come from they call what they were doing snogging. He was leaning across her, into her, with his hands on either side of her head, his fingers raking her hair. Berenger was perfectly still, but she had her head tilted at an angle that telegraphed acceptance. The hairdresser had taken a step back, his hands on his hips, amused. The others gave sidelong glances and little smiles passed between them all. One stylist's assistant had been kneeling on the floor taping a shoe, but now she was just staring, her mouth open.

I didn't know where to look and I didn't know what to do. Was I supposed to defend Aaron's honour and leap between them like a referee at a prize fight? Hardly. I'd attract more attention that way than just letting them go at it for a few seconds...

But it was lasting longer than a few seconds. Addam looked like he was trying to rub out Berenger's face with his mouth and

I didn't much like the fact that one of Berenger's hands had slipped down the back of his jeans. He had on a printed shirt that was unbuttoned at the cuffs and neck, and the tail of it had pulled free from his pants. The robe Berenger wore to cover her lack of underwear was sagging open perilously. They were even making noises.

Disgusting. They were disgusting. And I was disgusted with myself. I'd been acting as their pimp to keep their liaison a secret from Aaron and now the stupid *morons*—there wasn't another word for it—were giving an explicit demonstration of their intimacy in front of the greediest pack of scandal-mongers in the city. The clinch would find its way that very night to the bar at Balthazar, the tables at Bond St, the private room at Moomba, where some roving snoop for *Page Six* would pick it up and turn it into the next morning's hot topic over breakfast. They might as well have been doing it on a stage in Times Square.

I could see that Berenger was actually pulling away a little, if only to catch her breath. But Addam was still insistent, making little jabs at her lips with his tongue. I couldn't stand any more. I got up to go out to the hall but, as I fumbled out of the chair, I inadvertently dropped the book that was resting in my lap. It was a weighty biography of Luchino Visconti and it thudded to the floor. Berenger flinched and Addam looked in my direction. He took his mouth off hers and straightened up. She pushed a damp strand of hair back off her face. She at least had the decency to look a little embarrassed.

Berenger was all smiles for the rest of the shoot. The photographer shrewdly got Addam to stand right in her line of sight. He played the fool, making funny faces to get her to giggle. They were like a couple of fourth graders. I'd never seen her so sweet and co-operative. The neurotic account executive insisted the photographer take hundreds of rolls of the exact same pose. Miraculously, Berenger tolerated it.

I stayed in my corner with my book.

At one point, Addam went past me to go to the kitchen. 'Hello, Nell,' he said.

'Nile.' I glared at my book.

'I remember. Like Egypt,' I could hear the smile in his voice, and he kept going.

On his return, holding a can of beer, he crouched down beside me. 'Mind if I interrupt?'

I shrugged. I was still wild at him.

'You find this boring?'

'Boring?'

'All this standing around. It would drive me crazy. I don't know how the hell she does it. I thought modelling was a joke until I knew Berry. I didn't know what they were complaining about, all those girls. But I'd put my fist through that sheet of paper in about five minutes. I hate having my photo taken.'

I looked up, but not directly at him. I was incapable of looking at him. I stared at his neck instead, at that old leather cord knotted around it. It looked sentimental. I wondered who had given it to him.

'What about all those record covers and magazine articles? I thought someone like you would...' My voice trailed off.

'Love all the attention? Everyone thinks that. Just because my stupid face is all over the place, 'specially when there's an album coming out. They think that I can control it. Well, I cannot. I can *not*. I just learnt to stop protesting. Someone who looks like me turns up to the photo shoots and behaves himself, but it's not me, you know? I'd rather be anonymous.'

'Like today?' I couldn't restrain the cynicism in my voice.

He didn't respond immediately. I could feel him examining me. 'You pissed at me?'

I shook my head.

'You were looking so sweet curled up here with that big book that I forgot for a moment that you worked for my fucking grandfather.'

'That's not it.'

'It is. Look at me.'

I set my mouth.

'Nile.' He touched my chin, tipped it up so that I would have had to close my eyes not to look into his. They were so startlingly blue today in the studio light that I wondered if he got the effect from wearing coloured contact lenses. 'You going to tell him?'

'I haven't so far,' I said defiantly.

He gave me a smile of approval. 'That's right. You haven't. You've left me messages. Now, you wouldn't have been doing that if you disapproved, would you?'

An assistant going past stared at us curiously. I looked nervously over to the set. Berenger was having her make-up reapplied and was facing away.

'I want you to approve, Nile.'

Why the hell did everyone want *me* to approve of them? Aaron wanted me to approve of his marriage, Addam wanted me to approve of his affair. And I didn't approve of any of it. I gathered up some courage, from where I don't know. 'I think you're being a...bastard to Aaron.'

'Do you? Well, I'm a bastard, all right. I can't argue with that.'

'Aaron's a good man.'

'You think so? Good at what?'

'Don't be so bloody...detached!'

'You think I'm detached? That's a laugh.'

'Don't you care that you're hurting him?'

'I'm not hurting him.'

'Just because he didn't like that musical of yours, there's no need—' I stopped mid-sentence. The blue had drained from Addam's eyes. 'Look, I'm sorry. I didn't mean—'

'You really think that?' he said eventually. 'You really think that it's all about *Aaron*? And what he thinks of my work?'

'I—You—'

'I've known Berry since she was sixteen years old. I was

314

twenty-five when I met her. She's always been an immoral little bitch. And I'm a prick. I'm a prize bastard. A self-important asshole. Don't think I haven't had every bad name in the book hurled at me. But if she's such a bitch and I'm such a jerk, why can't we be left alone to make each other unhappy? Why do well-meaning people keep trying to separate us? I've had good, sweet, smart girlfriends in the past, lots of them, and I only make them miserable. Berenger, the bitch, *deserves* me.'

'But she was the one who decided to marry Aaron.'

'Yeah, well, she's fucked in the head too.' He glanced away, his mouth tight.

'I don't get it Addam.' I felt bolder. And I had to know. 'Why do you stick with her? It can't be just because she's…beautiful?' The word stuck in my mouth.

He looked back at me, strangely. 'Of course it's because she's beautiful. You're shocked I said that, aren't you?'

'Well, it sounds a bit…shallow.'

'Nile, I'm a very shallow person.'

'No, you're not. What about all those songs?'

'What about 'em? It doesn't take much depth to flip through old poetry books and sit around with a joint and play a few chords on the acoustic. It's nothing.'

'It's only nothing to you because the talent for it is in your blood.'

'That's a romantic notion if ever I heard one. Where in my blood? My mother's a fucking no-talent groupie and my father peddled drugs.'

'You know where it comes from.'

'Yeah, sure…' He rubbed the back of his neck and looked across at Berenger. She glanced over her shoulder at us and frowned. 'I better go.'

'Addam?'

'Yeah?'

'You're not a bastard. You just act like one.'

'Don't say that.' He looked pained.

'But—'

'Listen, Nile. If you think I'm nice or kind or sweet I'll hurt you. I won't mean to. But it can't be helped…no, don't protest. I've never known a girl who hasn't tried to see the good in me. And who hasn't hated me afterwards. Now you, you have a healthy disgust for me, Nile. I like that. Keep it up. Keep thinking about how I'm fucking around with Berenger. Keep reminding yourself what a prick I've been to Aaron. That way you won't fall for me. But you won't ever really hate me, either. Because you won't care enough.'

I bristled at his nerve. 'What makes you think I'll fall for you?'

'That's the most arrogant thing you've ever heard a guy say, right? But look at me, Nile. Straight into my eyes. You always look away, and I know why. I know what happens to women when they see me. It doesn't matter that I hate how I look, that every time I see a fucking picture of me in a magazine I want to avert my eyes. I don't want to look like that. It doesn't please me. Whenever a girl sees me for the first time, in the flesh, this look crosses her face, I've seen it a million times, it's, like, shock, then she looks away in embarrassment, and when she looks back there's hunger all over her face. Like I'm a fucking Big Mac.'

'But Berenger doesn't?'

'No, she never has. That's because *she's* always been the Big Mac. She doesn't know what hunger is.'

'Addam?'

He was standing now, tucking in his shirt.

'Do I look at you like that?'

He shrugged and smiled. 'Yeah.'

A few weeks later, it became a farce. A full-blown, revolving door, Feydeau kind of farce. And I was the character in the middle with the keys, not knowing which lock they fitted.

Aaron was out with Lilian at the ballet. Berenger had made me accept on her behalf several conflicting dinner dates for that night, but when 8 p.m. came she declared that she was 'bored by all that' and she wanted me to order up a stack of videos for her, including her current favourite, *Spaceballs*. Then she called down to me and said she wanted her driver, Ronny, to take the car down to East Broadway to collect Addam. I told her that wasn't a good idea but she just giggled and asked what the problem was with a young man visiting his poor old grannie.

I did what I was told, of course, but it was I, not Berenger, who sat nervously in a second-floor window waiting for Addam to depart before Aaron returned. By 1 a.m. I was feeling ill. Ronny was still parked in the street waiting to take Addam home and I was sure Aaron would arrive in a taxi any minute. I called up to Berenger's bedroom but there was no answer.

Ronny didn't answer his mobile, so I went downstairs to suggest he wait on West Broadway, so I could get Addam out the back way if necessary. I never knew what Ronny thought of any of this. As he was starting up the limo, Aaron's taxi pulled in behind.

'Is she home yet?' Aaron asked, nervously I thought, as I opened the cab door for him.

'Yes,' I lied. 'Been out to dinner.' I took his arm.

Aaron didn't seem interested beyond this. 'Fine production,' he said as I unlocked the front door.

'That's good.' My mind was galloping like a steeplechaser in the home stretch. The hurdle it had to jump was Addam in Berenger's bedroom. 'Do you want a nightcap?' I asked.

'Don't trouble yourself, Nile.'

'No trouble at all!' I said rather too eagerly, but Aaron seemed too tired to notice. 'Come into the sitting room and I'll get you something.'

'Whisky and warm milk,' he said. 'If you don't mind.'

I deposited Aaron in the second-floor sitting room and took the elevator to the third floor. There was no help for it. I had to knock. Break the door down if necessary. Several thumps on the ashen wood produced no result. I held my breath and turned the chrome handle.

The television screen was flashing blank blue signals. Berenger was cross-legged on the bed staring at it, the remote lying limply in her hand. Addam appeared to be asleep beside her, on his back, one arm flung up over his eyes, wearing a tattoo-print teeshirt and jeans. He still had his boots on, thank God. I ignored Berenger and gathered up Addam's blue fur coat, which was thrown over a chair. I went over and shook him. 'Addam, Aaron's home.'

He blinked a couple of times, smiled, turned on his side and went back to sleep. I didn't wait to make any more polite conversation—I tugged at his legs and pulled them off the bed, and then hoisted him into a sitting position. For a moment there, I sat holding him. He was thin and light, fortunately, and didn't resist. I could feel his ribcage underneath his shirt and smell the smoke in his hair. *God.* I pulled myself together, got him to his feet and half-dragged, half-walked him to the elevator. I thumped on the buttons and it seemed an eternity before the elevator doors closed. I prayed that Aaron wasn't waiting on the second floor.

The doors jerked open on the first floor and I took Addam around to the back, where a service door opened on to a narrow alleyway. He had his arm around my shoulders and was breathing like an infant in the crook of my neck. I almost threw him at Ronny, who was standing by the rear door of the limo. I didn't wait to see them drive off.

I was back on the second floor in no time. 'Your nightcap's coming! Just warming the milk!' I announced brightly to a startled Aaron and, before he could say anything, I dashed back up to the bedroom, taking the stairs this time.

Berenger was still sitting on the bed. I collected the beer bottles and cigarette butts and a dusty little plastic bag I found by the bed in a shopping bag and threw them in the bottom of a closet. I checked the sheets, smoothed down the side of the bed where Addam had been lying and opened a window. I took the remote out of Berenger's hand and turned off the television set. It was only then that she looked at me.

'You idiot!' I said. 'Get into bed. Aaron's home.'

'Where's Addam?' she asked.

'For Christ's sake, he's gone. Aaron almost caught you.'

'We were only watching television.' She sounded half-asleep.

I felt like slapping her. My hand actually itched. 'I'm not going to have him hurt,' I said, straightening the duvet. 'Get out of that dress and get into bed.'

'Why would he be hurt?'

'Because his wife's a whore, that's why.'

'A whore?' The word tumbled around in her head like gum in a gumball machine. That's what my mother was...' she replied, dreamily. 'Chantal says I'm just like her. Funny, isn't it?'

I wasn't listening. 'Just look like you're reading or something,' I said, shoving a Gary Larson comic-book into her hand. 'You've been out to dinner, remember...to Moomba.'

I actually tucked her in. For a minute I thought about checking the covers for semen stains but I stopped myself. Had it come to this?

'I think I'll retire now,' Aaron said, when I rushed back downstairs. 'This milk packs a punch.'

I took him into the elevator and pushed the button for my floor, number three, and Berenger's floor, number four.

'No, no, Nile,' he said, leaning across me and pressing number five. 'Let's let Berenger get her beauty sleep.'

And his smile had a gleam in it, as if he knew everything.

You see, all along it was Berenger's fault. She made me call Addam to arrange their liaisons. She made me go with her backstage at his concerts. She made me put my arms around him to pull him off her bed.

How could I help what happened next?

Six weeks and three days before Berenger died, she and Aaron celebrated his eighty-second birthday. Although, to my mind, 'celebrated' was hardly the word for it.

They went to dinner at Le Bernadin ('boring' she said afterwards) whereupon she gave him a handsome antique clock (chosen by me).

Afterwards, Berenger dumped Aaron at home and changed from her dinner clothes, a tight dress, to her party clothes, a tighter dress. 'C'mon,' she said, shaking me awake. I'd fallen asleep on my bed reading the *New Yorker*. 'We're going to a party.'

'Berenger, I'm too tired,' I groaned.

'No, you're not.' She started poking at me. 'This is going to be a real sexy party. Zillions of cute guys. A person like you should be glad you've even been asked.'

I sat up and pushed Berenger away. 'Should I? Who asked me?'

'I did. So, get up.'

She stood and stalked over to my expansive walk-in closet, which held only a few meagre items. 'God, Nile,' she said, opening the doors. 'What happened to all that great stuff I gave you?'

'I gave it to Housing Works.' I stood wearily.

'What's that?'

'You know, your favourite charity. At least that's what you told them at their fundraiser a couple of weeks ago.'

'I did?' But she wasn't really listening. She'd pulled out a sheer black forties dress I'd found at a flea market years ago and was holding it up for inspection. 'This'll do, I suppose.' She handed it to me. 'But for heaven's sake, Nile, don't wear underwear with it.'

I did wear underwear, but she didn't comment on that when I met her downstairs. She gave me her small beaded handbag, which contained the usual—several $100 bills, a couple of table-spoons of coke, a plastic vial of pills, a packet of Marlboro Lights and a lip gloss—and I followed her into the car. I nodded hello to Ronny and to the beefy security guard in the front seat.

'Where are we going, anyway?' I asked.

'Oh, to someone's house.'

'Whose house?'

'How do I know? It's a big party someone's throwing for someone else, for Thanksgiving or something. Some film producer's kid. But Darien says Matt and Ben are going to be there. Leo, too…Brendan, Brad, Vince, Art, Beck. I mean, *serious* boys.'

'Don't you have enough boys of your own?'

'I'm ignoring that, Nile.'

It had started to rain by the time we pulled up to an east side townhouse. I hadn't paid attention to what street we were on, but it was somewhere between Fifth and Madison, where the windows glowed with hand-blown Christmas lights on mani-cured fir trees. There were a few gawkers and photographers outside but the rain seemed to have dampened their spirits and they all stepped aside meekly as the security guy took us up the stairs and into the house. Several people greeted Berenger at the door, all of them wearing headsets. I left her to them and slipped to the edges of the room. I never liked to be in the centre, where tall people collided and embraced. Fortunately, in rich people's houses, the walls were usually covered with interesting art, which gave me something to do while Berenger flirted and posed.

This house was no exception. There was a Francis Bacon in the foyer and a group of Edward Weston prints positioned up the staircase. I squeezed my way into the parlour. The lights were low but you couldn't miss the Chuck Close self-portrait that filled one wall and the Calder that graced the mantel over the fireplace. I looked vainly around for anyone who looked sophisticated enough to have put a collection like this together—or sophisticated enough to have paid someone else to put this collection together—but everyone in the room seemed to be under thirty and underdressed. The kids had obviously taken over the house while Dad was doing his mogul thing in Hollywood. There was a DJ in a corner downing a beer while he spun some kind of thudding rap and a waiter walking around with hotdogs on a silver tray. The cocktails were the colour of drain cleaner. No wonder I didn't drink.

I went up to the bar and asked for a cranberry juice but the barman looked through me as if I were invisible. The kind of people who passed for celebrities in this town—fashion stylists I recognised, bit-part actors, hairdressers, model agents, nightclub owners—kept jostling me out of the way. One of them sloshed ice on my arm and another ground my toes into the carpet, without apology. In the end, when one of the barmen turned his back for a moment to get some ice, I reached across and grabbed a cocktail glass of something he had been pouring for a couple who were obliviously wrapped around each other, and turned and fled with it.

I stood in an alcove and nursed the drink, which was some kind of bilious pink juice and vodka. I had no intention of sipping it but I needed something to do with my hands. At times like these I had a new respect for cigarettes. Berenger was pressing her willowy body in greeting against an assortment of men and women, some of whom even I recognised from film and magazine pages, flinging her arms around various necks, kissing cheeks and some lips full-on, brushing herself suggestively against the men and dancing hip-to-hip with the girls. The crush around her, which included a gesticulating Darien and a young Scottish actor whose first two films I'd admired, was several people deep.

I left the room and pushed past the groups of people sitting on the stairs until I reached the third floor. There was a kind of den, I supposed they would call it, at the back and I could hear music, but when I pushed the door open five or six people looked up from whatever they were hunched over in the middle of the floor and glared at me. 'Sorry,' I said quickly and left but not before I heard one of them giggle, 'That was the nanny!'

On the fourth floor, a bedroom door was ajar and I was surprised to see a little girl of about seven or eight sitting on a frilly pink bed, her hands clasped in her lap demurely, and wearing a purple feather boa around her neck, a silver strapless top, a red leather miniskirt and high heels.

'Are you all right, sweetie?' I asked.

'Perfectly,' she said through glossy maraschino-coloured lips. 'This is my house.'

'Are your mummy and daddy at home?'

She looked at me scornfully. 'Don't you know anything? They live in Beverly Hills.'

'They do?'

'Yes and my Daddy is making a picture about a giant octypus that eats Manhattan.'

'Well, he better make sure you're not here when it starts to munch on the Upper East Side.'

'It's only make-believe,' she said contemptuously. It was alarming how much she sounded like Berenger.

'Do you want me to take you downstairs? There are lots of people there you might have seen in movies.'

'Oh, I know all of them. I'm only interested in bands, like Hanson. They're not here yet, are they? I think that Zachary is awfully cute. Do you think he's too old for me?'

'I don't know about that. Are you sure you don't want me to take you downstairs? It must be very lonely up here.'

'Oh no it isn't. My brother Noah is right next door with his girlfriend. He's having sex with her. Besides, I am waiting for the right time to make my entrance.'

That seemed the right time to make my exit.

I was unnerved by that child. She reminded me of the little girls who turned up to Berenger's perfume-signings with their mothers, the little girls standing in the front row in packs at Detox concerts, the little girls who thought sex and make-up and Barbie dolls and watching MTV were all the same thing. Maybe they were.

As I turned to go, she called out after me. 'If you don't like your drink, I'll have it. It's got grapefruit juice in it, you know.'

'And vodka,' I told her. 'It's got vodka in it.'

'Oh, that's all right,' she answered. 'You can't taste vodka.'

I went back downstairs again. The third floor had become extremely crowded. I moved through with my now warm and sticky glass in my hand and a fixed smile on my face. I was starting to get desperate for someone to talk to. I was sure people were noticing that I was drifting back and forth in my dreary dress like a widow on her walk. I was getting so desperate I spotted a fashion assistant I'd met a few times and actually contemplated engaging her in conversation.

Why was she here in this star-studded crowd? I thought as I watched her making big eyes at an immaculately dressed boy in a steel grey suit. And then I thought, *She's probably thinking the same thing about me.*

But she wasn't. She wasn't thinking about me at all. Even when I went up to her and gave her a big smile.

She looked me over quickly and went back to talking to the boy. 'But of course I'm not going to be there much longer. They already want me over at *Vogue*. It's only a matter of money, really...'

I was pleased to note that the boy was looking over the top of her side-parted head at a young actor standing in a corner with his tattooed arms broodingly folded.

I found my way back to the parlour floor. The Edward Westons were now hanging crookedly and a cigarette had been butted out on a beautiful small stone, probably a Noguchi, sitting on a lacquered side table. The Francis Bacon was in peril of discolouring from the number of people standing around it flamboyantly exhaling smoke.

I looked around for Berenger to tell her I was leaving. Darien shrugged and pointed to the back of the house. There was a small terrace garden off the kitchen and I stepped out onto it. The rain had stopped and a houseboy was sweeping the puddles off the flagstone. Berenger was sitting on a two-person iron seat in the shadows with the Scottish actor, both of them leaning back, legs stretched out, looking up at the starless sky. He had a beer. They were both smoking.

'I don't see what difference it makes,' Berenger was saying, 'I'm married too.'

I did my very best stage 'ahem'.

Two pairs of eyes turned towards me. I found myself blushing. The actor had mischievous eyes, which seemed to twinkle at me in the moonlight.

If I had expected Berenger to introduce us, I was wrong. 'God, Niley, you could have given me a heart attack! Do you always go creeping around like that?' She threw her cigarette on the ground.

'I'm going home,' I said. It came out sounding petulant.

She wasn't listening. 'I've been looking for you *everywhere*,' she lied. 'Where are my drugs?'

I waved the beaded bag at her.

'Give me,' she demanded, but before she could snatch the bag we were interrupted by Darien, who came out of the kitchen like a matchstick caught up in a gust of air.

'*There* you are! You better come inside, Berenger.' Darien raised her eyebrows and flicked her head in the direction of the house.

'Why? I want to stay out here.'

'*Berenger*,' Darien said sternly.

'Look, I'll come in later, OK? Leave us alone. You too,' she said to me. She smiled at the boy next to her. 'Want some blow?'

'All right,' said Darien. 'Sit out here. I'll tell Addam I couldn't find you.'

'Shit!' said Berenger, standing up suddenly. 'He's in LA.'

'Not anymore,' said Darien.

'Well, why didn't you say?' Berenger complained. She turned to her companion. 'He's a *relation* of mine,' she explained. 'Stay here. I'll be back.'

'I liked the film you made about—' I started to say to the actor, wanting to get the compliment in, and wanting, also, to say something that identified me as human.

But Berenger grabbed my arm and cut me off. 'Niley, don't bother him. He doesn't want to talk to *you*.'

Why didn't I leave right then? Even by my standards I'd had enough humiliation for one night. There was nothing to be gained by following Berenger around with her bag of drugs.

Would things have been different if I had walked out the front door right then, past the tobacco-scarred Noguchi and the smoke-damaged Bacon and the fashion model—one of Berenger's bridesmaids, actually—laid flat-out, snoring, in the middle of the entrance hall?

I dropped back from Darien and Berenger and watched them accost Addam, who was standing with a group of people that included a couple of members of Detox and their wives. Darien went up and planted a showy kiss on Addam's lips. When Berenger kissed him, more modestly, a flash went off. Berenger looked startled until a model who fancied herself as a photographer held up her Elph and admitted to taking the picture. Berenger then posed for another with her arms around Addam's neck.

The noise in the room dropped away. The edges blurred. I watched the way Addam looked at Berenger. He was talking over his shoulder to a guy with lavish dreadlocks but he kept sneaking glances at her, as she hung off his arm. His body language was relaxed, even distant, as he held her slightly away from him. But every time he scanned the side of her face, his eyes went soft and he made a little gesture of gnawing at his bottom lip with his pointed eye teeth. I was standing several feet away and still I saw it, this look of raw longing. I wondered how he could be so unguarded in public. But maybe I was the only one in the room looking for it. The sign that he loved her.

I took my eyes off him for a minute and saw that Darien was glaring at me.

Embarrassed, I looked down at the drink in my hand. Bits of pink grapefruit flesh floated on the surface like tiny nail clippings. What the hell? I thought—remaining sober has never done anything for me. I drank the cocktail down in one gulp. It was warm and bitter. A waiter went by with a tray of drinks and I swapped it for another cocktail, blue this time. It tasted worse, but at least it was cold.

On the third floor there was a bar that was less crowded. I took a flute of champagne. The bubbles made my intestines feel warm and loose. I had another one. I was feeling better, as if I had finally been initiated into a secret club long denied me. The room was soft, warm, fizzing with laughter that included me.

But I needed to find a loo. 'Bathroom?' I asked a few of my new best friends. I was steered to a doorway where a long line formed. Two blobs in front of me were talking about Berenger, I think, but I tuned out. I made it to the stall in time and when I came out a caramel-coloured drag queen in a blonde wig was leaning against the vanity, searching through a tiny gold purse on a chain. She had beautiful legs and a tight body in a bandage dress but, even though her make-up was immaculate and her nails were decorated with silver starbursts, her face was coarse, the nose wide, her pores like pockmarks scouring her skin. I could see all this even though the world was still in soft focus.

'Honey,' she said to me, dropping her gold purse with a sigh. 'You don't happen to have any toot on you, do you?'

'Actually,' I said. 'I do.'

I held out Berenger's little handbag. The drag queen pounced on it and emptied it out in the basin. 'Whoa!' she said, as the $100 bills and the plastic bag of white powder dropped out. 'Have I run into the right genetic female tonight!' She pronounced every syllable: *gen-net-teec*. She put her head out of the bathroom door and yelled, 'Jeneelle! You come in here!'

Then she turned back to me and held out a big hand. 'Shallulah,' she said.

'Nile,' I said.

'Like that dude in Chic?'

I shrugged. I didn't know what she meant.

'Babee!' she said, shaking the bag out onto the black marble vanity. She used her synthetic nails to scrape some of it into approximate lines. She was singing some old disco tune and shaking her muscly backside while she worked. 'C'est Chic...da doo doo da doo...'

The door opened a crack and a person whom I supposed was Jeneelle slipped into the small room, closed the door behind her, clicked the lock and leaned against it. She was smaller than Shallulah and prettier, but her shoulders were disproportionately wide. She was wearing a glitter tube-top and a slashed miniskirt. Not dissimilar, I thought, to what the little girl on the bed upstairs had been wearing.

'What you got?'

Shallulah had already rolled a bill into a straw and was vacuuming up a line. She sniffed, sighed, stood up and stepped aside for Jeneelle. Jeneelle grabbed the hundred-dollar straw greedily. When she bent over I could see the tops of her pantyhose.

'Who she?' she said, suspiciously, when she stood and turned around.

'She the girlfriend with the score. Jeneelle meet Nile.'

328

She pronounced my name Ni-elle.

'Hi,' I said. 'Pleased to make your acquaintance.'

'Bless my soul,' said Jeneelle. 'You sound like Princess Di. Now, honey, move over while I do my lip-line.'

'You?' Shallulah handed me the rolled-up bill.

I shook my head. And then I thought, why not? I held my hair with one hand and leant over the sink. I didn't embarrass myself: the white powder went up my nose and stabbed my frontal lobes, clear and sharp as an ice-pick.

'Good girl. You look like you could do with some pick-me-up. Look here, Jeneelle, Nile could do with some pick-me-up, dontcha think, baby?'

Jeneelle looked at me through the mirror. 'She could do with a face-lift, that's fo sure.'

Shallulah giggled. 'That's not nice.' Then she turned to me. 'Seriously, girl. Look at you. Look at *you*! You a bi-o-logic-al female and you look like *shit*. If I had a va-gin-na I'd be in some penthouse right now, ordering them servants around. I'm a *boy*, baby, and I'm more woman than you.'

Jeneelle turned around and pointed her lip pencil at me. 'You should be ashamed of yo'self, wasting good tushy like that.'

'You should do something about your hair, baby, it's just a *rag*.'

'And who ever seen such a sorry dress.'

'Where your breasts?'

'You call that a *body*? *This* is a body.'

'Ain't no boy gonna look at you unless you do something *fast*.'

'An then it'll be too late 'cos your pussy's gonna be all dry up!'

'And he ain't gonna get it in without a *bucket* of grease!'

'It's bad enough you smell like fish—' Jeneelle snorted. They both started cackling. Shallulah flung her arm around Jeneelle's wide shoulders. Jeneelle pushed down her tube top and cupped two small, hard and perfectly shaped breasts in her hands. Shallulah's hand descended and stroked one of them.

'These are *titties*, honey. What you got?'

Before I could stop her, she reached over and thrust her hand down the front of my dress, popping open the buttons. Her long nails scraped against my breast bone. She found my nipple and pinched it hard. I backed into the stall and tried to push her away. She hung on, cackling. 'They feel real nice, honey!'

Fortunately, she was unsteady on wooden platforms. The second time I pushed, she stumbled, twisting an ankle.

She started screaming. Shallulah was right behind her. 'You pushed my girlfriend!'

She bent over to headbutt me and I grabbed her hair. There was a ripping sound, like velcro, and the wig came off in my hand. A hairless Shallulah yelped and then looked at me warily, her mouth wide, her eyes on the wig. I looked down at it. In that instant I knew what to do.

Someone was thumping on the bathroom door. They'd been thumping for a while.

'Quick, honey, let's get that toot and get outta here,' Jeneelle was saying, but Shallulah wasn't listening to her. Despite the dress, the heels, the cleavage, she was confronting me, arms wide, like a wrestler on the mat. Before she made a move, I turned and flung the wig in the toilet and flushed it. The synthetic blonde hair swirled around like wet spaghetti. Shallulah's heavy jaw dropped.

I made a dash for the bathroom door. Jeneelle was trying to scrape what was left of the cocaine back into the plastic bag. 'Come on, girl!'

I unlatched the door and someone pushed in on me before I could get out. There was a crowd milling outside. As I squeezed through the doorframe, I could hear Jeneelle shriek with laughter, 'Shit, girl, she gone and done that scene from *Valley of the Dolls* to you!'

I ran up the stairs, not down. It was instinctive. I didn't want to end up in the mosh pit downstairs with Berenger and Addam pawing each other and Darien looking at me disapprovingly. I'd already had a seven-year-old girl and a pair of drag queens make me feel like a sexless drudge. I couldn't abide seeing Addam make sad eyes at Berenger again. That was the truth of it. I couldn't abide seeing Addam with her.

I was feeling less than well and the cold air of the roof hit me like an icy slap across the face. It was threatening rain again, but there were a few people up there, scattered in groups, admiring a partial view of Central Park. Topiaried trees in terracotta pots were strung with fairy lights. In the centre sat a small greenhouse lit by flickering candles. On a neighbouring roof an enormous Christmas tree twinkled red and green.

I couldn't make out any faces. I was glad of it. I hoped they wouldn't notice me. All I wanted to do was find a remote corner and cry. Cry for a little while, just enough to get my eyes clear of the tears that were prickling them. That was all. Then I'd sober up and go home.

I gravitated towards the darkest part of the roof, away from where I thought people had gathered. There was a rough structure like a tool shed in one corner and I made for it, but I didn't see that there was a person there standing in the shadows and I ran straight into him.

Him.

'Sorry,' I gasped. 'Sorry.'

He put his hands on my arms. 'Nile?'

I backed away, confused, into the light. His fingers stung where they touched me.

'You all right?'

'You were downstairs,' I said weakly.

'Yeah, well, it got too crowded.' His voice was like strong coffee, rich with a bitter edge. Before I could think of any reply, he stepped closer to me again. He put a hand out gently and touched me on my breastbone. 'You're bleeding,' he said, surprised. 'And your dress is undone.'

I looked down. I was washed in the faint light from the stair-

331

case. All the buttons to my waist were open. I put a hand up to cover myself.

'No,' he said. He took my hand away and started doing up the buttons. The touch of his hands against the thin fabric of my dress made me shiver. 'What happened?'

'I had a run in with a couple of drag queens. One of them scratched me, I think.'

'Why did they do that?'

'I don't know. I gave them all Berenger's drugs.'

I could feel his smile.

'Anyway,' I added, trying to sound light-hearted, 'I flushed one of their wigs down the toilet.'

He laughed then, a big, loud laugh. I watched his throat, the strong neck circled by a cord of leather, the bony shoulders. Then I looked down at his hands. They were working on each button painstakingly, trying to slip the little octagons of jet into the slightly too-small holes. I wondered if he were stoned. I didn't dare look at his face in case I betrayed myself.

'I like you, Nile. You're not full of bullshit like the others,' he said.

You do? I'm not? I wanted to ask him more but I just stood there, limply, while he buttoned up my heart.

'I wish—' he started to say, but I never found out what he wished. Not then.

'There he is!' I recognised Darien's voice before I saw her. She appeared from the direction of the greenhouse with a bottle of champagne and two empty glasses in her hand.

Addam turned his face but he still kept his fingers on my neckline.

'It's OK,' I whispered, 'I don't need them all done up.'

'Fuck her,' he said and gave me what passed in the shadows as a wink.

Darien stalked up to us. 'I've got your drink,' she said to him, ignoring me.

332

'Put it on the wall.' He didn't look at her. He smoothed down the collar of my dress.

'What's she doing here?'

'We're having a conversation.'

'That's not what it looks like to me.'

Addam turned to her and started to roll down his shirt sleeves. Being casual, making that point. 'I don't care what it looks like to you. You wouldn't know what a conversation was. You only have monologues.'

Darien put her hands on her non-existent hips and the champagne glasses clinked. Her hard eyes travelled from Addam to me. 'You little bitch,' she said. 'It's like fucking *All about Eve*.'

'Wait a minute—' Addam stepped forward.

'No, I won't fucking wait. I've been watching this little *cunt* for months. I've been watching her try and take everything Berenger—'

'Are you talking about me?' It was Berenger, with a champagne bottle under her arm and another glass. She looked at the three of us. 'I thought we were having a picnic.'

'I found these two virtually fucking up here in the dark,' Darien told her.

'Don't be stupid. Where's my stash, Nile?'

'Listen to me, Berenger. He had his hands down her dress.'

Berenger looked confused. 'Why would he do that?'

'Because she's been flashing those oversized tits at him for months.'

'I have not!' I cried, mortified. But I covered my chest with an arm anyway.

Addam put his hand on my forearm. 'Leave her alone,' he said coldly.

'You see?' Darien pointed accusingly. 'He's defending her.'

Berenger looked at Addam and then at me. By the slightly dazed expression on her face I could see that my absconding with her bag of mood enhancers hadn't made much difference.

She'd raided someone else's. 'I don't get it. Why would he want to fuck *her*?'

'She's ingratiated herself with him, that's why. Just look at both of them. She's a poor little wannabe who's after everything you've got and he's—'

'What do you mean?' I interrupted.

'Nile, where is my dope?'

'I gave it to a drag queen,' I told her.

'Berenger, wake up,' Darien was ranting. 'She's living in your house and eating your food and wearing your clothes and going to your parties and selling your drugs. But do you think that's fucking enough for her? No way. She's got her eye on the old man and all his money. I've seen her with him. It's all very cosy. But he's not enough. She wants everything you have, your boyfriends…'

I could feel Addam flinch at the plural. 'Darien, fuck off. This is nothing to do with you.'

'Don't you fucking well tell me to fuck off!' Darien suddenly flung the champagne glasses at the wall. They shattered and the sound echoed around the well of buildings. I could hear conversations stop, other people turn to us with interest.

'Calm down,' Addam said. 'What I was doing with Nile is my own business.'

'See?' Darien crowed. 'He admits it!'

Berenger staggered right up to me and pushed me hard on the shoulder. 'All you think about is your fucking self. Who said you could sell my stuff to a drag queen?'

'Berenger, leave her alone.' Addam pulled me behind him.

'I didn't sell it!' I yelled at her, over his shoulder.

'Forget the fucking drugs.' Darien was poking Berenger in the arm now. 'You've got to get rid of her. I've been telling you for months. The bitch is disloyal to you.'

'I'm not disloyal!' I protested. But it was a lie.

Berenger looked from me to Addam. She stepped towards him and put her elbows on his shoulders, folding his head in her

334

hands. 'Let's go home,' she whispered into his neck. But she was looking directly at me, a mean gleam in her eyes. She wasn't that stoned.

To my surprise, Addam disentangled himself from her.

'Hey!' Berenger looked crossly at him.

'I haven't finished talking to Nile,' he said firmly.

'Talking!' Darien snorted.

'It's all right—' I started to say. I just wanted to slip away from them, out of there, back to my bed and never get up again.

'Well, see if I care,' Berenger cut in petulantly. She tossed her hair like she did in one of her shampoo commercials. 'Why don't you take *her* home, then?' She pointed at me. 'I'm sure you can get a lot of talking done at your place.'

Addam looked steadily at her for a second and then turned to me. 'Nile? You want to go?'

'Yes, why don't you?' said Berenger. 'I give you my permission.'

'She doesn't need your permission.' Addam looked at me with fathomless eyes. 'Nile?'

Berenger affected an expression of total nonchalance. Darien was smiling evilly, as if the whole thing were now a huge joke directed at me. Daring me to go with him.

I held my hand out to Addam and he took it. He didn't smile at me and I didn't smile at him. This was serious, for both of us.

'Let's go,' I said.

It started to rain.

Addam led me downstairs by the hand. As we wove through the crowd, I saw the way women looked down at our clasped hands and then looked at me, their faces pinched in envy. It was a new sensation for me and I was giddy with it.

'Stay there while I find a cab,' he said to me in the foyer.

'I'm coming too,' I said, not wanting to let him go.

The rain was coming down in diagonal sheets. A taxi had just dropped a passenger but took off before Addam could hail it. I saw Berenger's car across the road. 'Come on,' I said, suddenly bold. 'Ronny will drive us.'

She wants everything you have, Darien had said.

Six weeks and three days before Berenger died I went home with her boyfriend in her car. This was a very good start.

We didn't speak as the limo slid downtown. I looked out the window at the blurred streetlights, the smudged figures scattering in the rain. I felt like I was in freefall, that if I didn't get a toehold on something real and flinty, in the next few seconds, I'd black out from velocity, from lack of air, from the boiling blood in my ears. It was hot inside the car and so quiet we seemed vacuum-sealed. The world outside was reduced to one wet sound, a muted *whoosh*, and one shimmering veil of raindrops. My stomach felt as if it had risen to my throat and was squeezing all the breath out of me; I clutched at the armrest to anchor myself but my fingers were numb, swollen, as if some rogue artery had atrophied and cut off all the circulation in my extremities. My feet were not there; I licked, but there were no lips.

The neon sign of the Disney Store on Fifth Avenue slipped by, a recognisable thing. I clung to it like a lifeline. There were words; I could read them. Addam was leaning hard against the other door, his head on the window, as if he were hoping to keep the most substantial distance possible between us. I didn't dare look, but I imagined his eyes were closed, his mind tormented by the options of how to get rid of me. He would get out of the car and ask Ronny to take me home. Of course he would. It was all show, for Berenger. I saw how he looked at her. There would be no him and me. Just him. And me, back in the meat locker, in my lonely cot. I could taste bile on the back of my tongue. My eyes, I could feel them, rolled like greased marbles back into my head.

'You all right?' Then there was the distant sound of nylon sliding against leather and a warm, firm hand on the back of my neck, kneading, and I snapped back into the land of the living and cheating on your employer with his grandson.

'You've had too much to drink?' It was a question, whispered.

I made an effort to trawl myself back from the depths. 'No.' I shook my head heavily. I still could not look at him. My eyes were on my own crumpled lap. My dress was bunched up like some hideous growth under my stomach. I must have shifted to pull it straight, because he took his hand from my neck as if he were suddenly stung.

After a while he said, quietly, 'You don't have to.'

I did look at him then. He was staring straight ahead, slumped down in the seat beside me. He didn't look tired or drunk or stoned. There was no irony left in him. His good knee was jiggling, nervously. I realised that he was afraid I would ask to go home. He was afraid!

I took his hand and put it back on my neck.

Don't think the plain girl is going to get to this exquisite moment with the beautiful man and pull away from a blow-by-blow description.

Addam pushed his fingers up from the nape of my neck to the crown, and entwined them in my hair, twisting the roots so that my scalp tingled. His other hand touched my chin and turned it so that I was looking directly into his eyes. The reflection of raindrops shimmered across his skin like sequins. His eyes held no colour, but were all sheen. 'I always liked you, Nile.'

Before I had time to respond, his face was against mine, the spiky hairs at the side of his cheek brushing my eyelashes, making them flutter. I closed my eyes and went down into the leather seat under his pressure, his hands moving from my hair to my shoulders and arms, guiding me. He moved his body so that his hip was pushing into mine and then in one breathtaking sweep he ran a hand up under my dress from the knee to the clavicle and then back down and out, skimming the breast and tugging at the sides of my underpants, lightly.

'It's all there,' I wanted to say, a joke, but by then he was crushing my mouth with his own, a silken thing that tasted of smoke and honey and something acrid like rubber. He sucked on my lips as if they were swollen with nectar and ran his tongue around the perimeter, lapping up the juice. He licked my eyelids and my eyebrows and the soft part under my chin and bit at my earlobe until it almost hurt. His hands were a frenzy in my hair, his chest and hips pinning me down as he lay along me. The buckle on his belt dug into my belly.

I might have swooned with him lying there, covering me with hard kisses and insistent hands, but the little nagging part of me, that detached itself and watched, didn't want to miss anything.

I reached up and clung to the knotted muscles of his biceps, tugged at the long damp hairs under his arms, ran my hands down the slick sides of his polyester shirt. I slid one hand under his belt, feeling for the hollow of his hip-bone. Suddenly he pulled back and thrust a knee between my legs, forcing them apart. He sat back for a moment, surveying me, his knee hard against my pubic bone. I felt a stab of regret that my beige cotton knickers didn't match my serviceable black nylon bra. His eyes were on my breasts and then his fingers were on the tiny jet buttons of the bodice, working quickly to part the thin chiffon. I thought, foolishly, as he was doing this: he has too much respect for clothing to rip it. His palms made smooth circles on my breastbone, contemplating it, and then he snatched my bra straps and pulled them down over my arms. His hands dived into the cups of my bra and forced the whole undergarment down to my waist, trapping my arms by my side. In the same fluid gesture he gripped my breasts and pushed them free of the tangle of nylon, squeezing them together so that my cleavage was a canyon. My breasts were the best part of me, round and high. They swelled and firmed under his touch, the nipples fizzing like firecrackers when he put his mouth on them, one then the other. I think I moaned then and the sound I was making, we were making, travelled like lit gunpowder to the place where I most urgently wanted him to be.

I thought I might die, my heart fluttering in my chest, that there could be no other sensation in this world or the next that could deliver me such pleasure, but then a handful of fingers were inside my knickers, seeking, pressing, twisting and, finally, shoving hard up into the fissure that was opening inside me, while he drooled warm saliva on my nipples and sucked it back up between his teeth.

I tried to reach for his belt buckle, but he looked up and said, 'No.' He extracted his mouth from my breast and his fingers from my cunt and pushed my skirt up over my waist. My breasts felt momentarily abandoned, glistening with cooled saliva. He pulled my underpants down and grabbed my knees, urging them wider. And then he scooped his hands under my buttocks and brought my mound to his face. When his tongue shot out and grazed the budding muscle that was the core of everything, I twitched violently, scalded.

He soothed me with long licks and nuzzled the inside of my thigh and then circled my clit with light flickers, soft as a kitten. I raised my head and pulled his face closer, wanting more of it and harder, but he snaked his tongue down and around, teasing. I was open as a wound, our juices streaming down my thighs, the parts of me that yearned for his mouth bruised and engorged. My breasts felt like volcanos, ready to blow.

The pattern of the rain had slowed and the whooshing was now only intermittent. We were pulled over by the kerb, Ronny faceless, waiting. I wondered for a fleeting instance what Ronny thought, and knew I didn't care. He could be watching, he could be in the back seat with us unzipping his fly even now and it would make no difference. I was ready for Addam and I was ready for all the men in this world, too. There was no judgment, only sensation and longing.

And then, suddenly, there was a finger where there had been a tongue and a tongue where there had been yearning, filling all the spaces, and a thumb, or a nose, there was no way of telling, where all sweetness peaked. And I held on to his ears and I bucked myself at him and the thing I had been wanting ripped through me like a comet, white-hot and searing, and targeted my heart. Everything I had in me—lungs, stomach, intestines, womb—twisted and strained like the ropes holding a ship to port. I was flooded with warm blood, I was rolling on a sea of rapture, I was ravished and sweaty and streaming, but still there was a knot in me.

I touched Addam's shoulders and he came to me. His mouth on mine was sticky and yeasty. I ran my hands down his sinewy thighs, under the fabric, and felt silken hair and rough skin. I could hear myself making sounds, panting, heaving, whimpering sounds, grunting, roaring, growling sounds, encouraging him, urging him on. His breath was shallow and hot against my cheek. I started to fumble with his belt buckle but I felt him stiffen.

'What?' I croaked.

The driver's side door of the car slammed.

'Let's go,' Addam whispered. 'I think he's giving us a hint.' He pulled me up gently by the arms and turned and opened his side door. He climbed out and took my hand. I tugged at my panties to pull them up, and stepped across the river that was the gutter, into the teeming rain. The water pelted my raw skin like flints of ice. The street was deserted. Addam dug his fingers under my elbow and dragged me to his door. The wet dress flapped around my ankles, my shoes filled with water, my hair was plastered against my cheeks. As Addam fiddled with his key, I looked back at the car and saw Ronny looking at me, under an umbrella. My exposed nipples were hard and pink in the freezing rain; I didn't make any attempt to cover them, I didn't care. Ronny put his umbrella down and opened the car door. A moment later his key turned in the ignition.

341

Once inside the hallway, I started for the stairs, but Addam turned me around and backed me into a corner by the front door. A harsh fluorescent light fizzed overhead. I could feel something fuzzy against my legs, an old rolled-up carpet, a pile of rags. He leaned over me with his arms against the wall. This time I didn't close my eyes. He was looking at me intensely. In the second before his mouth captured mine again, I had an eternity to drink in his beautiful face, the way he looked up under his brows with invasive steely eyes, the delicate snarl of his short top lip, the snag-gled bottom teeth, the deep cleft in his chin, the dark stain etched under his eyes. Then the lids of his eyes closed and mine closed too and I could feel his eyelashes against my cheeks and the stubble of his chin against my chin and the soft inside of his lips kneading mine. He smelled of sweet figs and cigarette ends.

We might have been there for days. I felt the front door open and close once or twice, the cold air on my ankles, the muted sounds of bodies shuffling past. But we were joined at the pelvis and lips, two shafts of electricity, galvanised in one place. I had melted into him and he into me. Sweat mingled with rainwater and sizzled on the surface of our one hot skin. And then he pulled back from me and I shivered.

'Come on,' he said and took my elbow, guiding me up the stairs behind him. I stumbled after a few steps, catching my wet hem in my shoe. The linoleum on the stairs must have been tacked loosely in parts because I put my hand down on a nail as I steadied myself. Addam crouched down, a step or two above me, and took my hand between his hands, turning the palm over to investigate the wound. I was bleeding a great river of blood inside and it was all spurting from the tear under my thumb. I didn't look as Addam caught the gush with his tongue. My eyes were on his unbuttoned shirt, his tender nipples, the dank vine of hair climbing to his navel, the big silver 'G' of his belt buckle, his open legs, his straight thighs, the way his pants hung low on his hips, wantonly.

I don't know what came over me. All I knew was that I

couldn't wait for four more flights and seventy more stairs. I shook my hand out of his and started working on his belt buckle. 'G', not for Gucci, but for my greediness for him. He eased back on his haunches, supporting himself with his elbows. He smiled down on my frenzy, heavy-lidded. I kept my eyes on his. At first I was too shy to look at what my hand had found, his penis, the skin stretched so smooth it felt as if it would split, the head slippery with beads of spunk, but my fingers brushed something unexpected and my eyes quickly travelled down the length of him. It was a small gold ring piercing the delicate folds of skin under the silken helmet.

I touched it, tentatively. 'Doesn't it hurt?'

'Only when you tug on it,' he answered, his voice thick and far away.

So I tugged on it, gently, hooking it with my index finger, and then I took it between my teeth and rolled it on the tip of my tongue and coaxed it deep into my mouth so that it tickled the entrance to my throat. I had to stretch my lips to the limit to take him all in and my teeth scraped his shaft. I slid off. 'Sorry.'

He grabbed my skull with both hands and guided me back down. He liked the teeth. I wondered at everything, the juicy veins under my tongue, the taste of tea and salt, the smell of old socks, the soft place between his balls that could make him shudder. I wondered at his admirable self-control.

Was anyone watching us, listening to us? I was too giddy with the sound of his ragged breathing to notice, but he pulled back once and steadied my head as if listening for something. I heard the muffled sound of a door closing, but no footsteps. I could tell the thought of exposure excited him. He began a faster bucking motion and I could barely keep up with him. I pulled my mouth off, gasping, and stuck the point of my tongue in his tip, but he grabbed me under the arms, not wanting that, shifting me so that my breasts dangled over his crotch. The forest of pubic hair was bristly against my skin. He spat in his hand and slapped a great gob of saliva into my cleavage, cupped my breasts around his straining cock and started moving between them rhythmically until the shaft of his penis was raw with the friction.

I could feel him tensing, but I wasn't with him. My knees dug into the sharp step, my back was curved in a tortuous shape. He was squeezing my nipples between thumb and forefinger and it was exquisite and excruciating. The thread that connected the lump in my throat to the tug in my groin was tightening. I had my hand in my knickers seeking it, but my fingers were playing second fiddle.

I took his hands off me and sat up, pulling off my underpants. I moved up him, so that my cunt was wet against his hard belly. He groaned and tried to push me back. I pinned his arms to the step. The veins in his forearms rippled and stiffened. I wasn't strong but I was quick. I grabbed his penis with one hand and lowered myself on to it. There was a moment of resistance and then the unparalleled sensation of swollen nob against swollen cervix. My eyes exploded with sparks. I thrust down on him again with all my strength. I must have been crushing his arms. But he didn't complain.

My brain was scrambled but my cunt took over and squeezed him masterfully. He was on the verge but I wouldn't let him come. I was going to make this last forever: even then, I must have known. I must have known in the secret part of me that harbours all fears. I wanted to suck him up through my vagina to my soul, which was fluttering just above my heart. I ran my breasts over his nipples to please him and then held them out like market fruit for him to taste.

Suddenly, he put his hands on my waist and rotated me off him. I was on my knees, my hands flat on the stairs, my face pressed against the wooden railing. He pushed my skirt up to my waist, pulled my buttocks apart and without hesitation thrust his tongue a inch into my anus. Then two, three fingers, maybe the whole hand, filled my cunt, prodding. It was unbearable, I started panting from fear I would black out, and the worse fear that my bodily functions could not be controlled. I wanted to tell him to stop, but I also wanted him to shove into me harder, go up to the elbow if he could. I no longer craved sweet, tender gestures, but decadence, pain, filth. I wanted him to do things to me that would make me blush in daylight, things that were darkly hinted at in skin magazines sold under the counter. I pressed my face harder against the railing, grinding my cheeks, letting the pain earth me. His tongue was teasing my perineum now. I couldn't hold back any more. I bucked against his force and a reservoir of need burst, seeping warm and viscous down his arm.

But still it wasn't enough, for me or him. He turned me over, pushed me down against the steps roughly. The sharp edges of the treads cut into me at shoulder, back and hip.

His trousers were down, his cock was in his hand. It seemed then a cruel and monstrous thing. I think I whimpered.

But it was all right. He slipped in and covered me with kisses—not the sex part of me this time, but my flushed cheeks, my tearful eyes, the sticky forehead, the sensitive dip between neck and shoulder. I watched him the whole time, devouring me. He was devouring *me*. I felt like a languid pool being skimmed with stones. I stretched and clasped the railing behind, so he could have more of me. When he came, he sighed. We were one long sigh.

He wouldn't let me dress myself. He found my knickers and pulled them up over my knees, licking the juices running down the inside of my thighs as he did. I hadn't known anyone who would do that before but, then, I hadn't known many who wanted to do more than drop their pants and have you do all the work. He untangled my bra and did up one button on the front of my dress. He smoothed my soggy hair flat with his palms.

Then he cupped my chin in his hands and said, earnestly, 'Now you know.'

He made me a cup of coffee in an old saucepan on the burner. I accepted it, to be polite. I sat on a low stool in the front room, nursing it, while Addam rolled a joint.

'Do you want me to go down and get a cab for you?' he asked, eventually.

'I don't want to go,' I said, not knowing how he would respond.

'Good,' he said, blowing smoke through his nose.

Addam had lit about twenty candles in various stages of liquefaction. I looked about the room. There was no decor to speak of, no pictures or posters on the walls, little furniture except a sofa with an Indian blanket thrown over it, a couple of stools and a pink-tiled coffee table, covered with manuscripts and magazines. In one corner, there was an old-fashioned, scarred piano, leaning against it, two electric guitars, and a table covered in computer equipment. There were dozens of ashtrays, though. I picked up one. Cancer Stick, it read.

'Smoke?'

I shook my head.

Addam had taken off his shirt and his boots and thrown his belt on the bed. He lay back into a pile of cushions and took a drag of his smoke. His arms were smeared with dried blood. My hand had stopped bleeding, but it had marked both of us.

'Addam?' I asked.

'Yeah?' He was looking at the ceiling.

'Do you mind if I have a shower? I've got blood all over me.'

'Yes.'

'Yes?'

'I mind. I like my women filthy.' He smiled to himself.

My women? Was I one of his women now? I didn't know whether to be flattered or devastated. Something must have passed over my face because he crawled across the room to me on his knees and lay his arms along my thigh. I put my coffee down.

'Nile?' He leaned over and put the smoke out in the ashtray.

'Yes?'

'Don't think this has anything to do with Berenger.'

'But it has. I wouldn't be here if Berenger—'

346

'How do you know?'

'But we—' I wanted to say, We would never have met.

'I told you I liked you, Nile. And now I like you more.'

He ran his hands under my skirt again. I let him. He pushed himself between my thighs.

'You were wild,' he whispered.

I felt uncomfortable hearing this, I don't know why. 'I'm a plain girl. We try harder,' I said to be flippant.

'That's crap,' he said.

Crap that I was plain or crap that we try harder?

'Not many girls would let me fuck them on the staircase.'

'Oh, did I let you?'

'Ha. The truth be known, not many girls would let me do what I did.'

'I can't imagine any girl denying you anything, Addam.'

'Will you suck my cock?'

I grinned. 'No.'

'See.'

'Addam?'

'Yeah?'

'What sort of things don't the other girls let you do?'

He showed me.

Don't you understand, I didn't care how thick my waist was or how wide my hips, whether I was a size four or a size twelve, or if my teeth were pearly white. Addam didn't even care if my teeth were clean. I walked around naked for him even when I didn't walk around naked for myself. He didn't make me feel beautiful, but he made me like my plainness. My plainness suddenly felt...subversive in his hands.

I was covered in spunk and spittle, in my hair, in my teeth, in my cracks and crevices. It dried on me in places like another skin. Walking around the room, in the moonlight, with the blood and spume crusted on me, I felt like Lady Macbeth, engorged with the wickedness of what I had done.

I couldn't leave him alone, I wouldn't let him rest.

I wound myself around him, I tangled myself in his sheets. He was very obliging. He poured me whisky and blew the smoke from his mouth into mine and whispered me sleepy ditties about lost loves and noble deeds. I liked his songs this way.

We had almost ground ourselves to sleep when Addam's answering machine clicked on. The volume was turned up high, you could tell by the static, but there was no distinguishable sound at first except a sharp crackling. And then a small voice, piercingly clear. 'It's 5 a.m., Addam,' she said. 'It's fucking 5.14 a.m. in fact. Answer your phone.'

'Shit,' said Addam and sat up. He crawled to where the machine was on the floor and crouched over it, feeling for the volume control. But it was too late. He knew who it was and so did I.

'I'm at Ben's place and you'll never guess what we've been doing. If you don't pick up the phone I'm going to tell you all about it, starting with the way—'

Addam picked up the phone, huddled over it. I turned my back to him, pulled the sheet over my head, but I was listening. Oh, I was listening.

'Yes.' He was terse. 'I was asleep…No…Don't be stupid…No-one…'

I knew what she was asking. I was no-one again.

'She went home from the party…That's your problem…I don't care…Because I'm tired. I've got a gig tomorrow…I don't care about him. Do what you like…

'I said no. Go home to your husband…You can stand in the street for all I care…Why would you want to if he was such a good fuck? Haven't you had enough for tonight…Because I'm tired…Maybe. Maybe afterwards, all right…OK. You too.'

I pretended to be asleep, but he knew I wasn't.

He didn't come back to bed. I heard him moving around the room and then all was quiet. I waited for the silence, got dressed quickly and let myself out. He was immovable on the sofa, hunched up, with the empty whisky bottle beside him.

I thought I was safe to have unprotected sex. But I didn't know how unprotected I was.

sat in the taxi in the rain with my head between my knees. As we careered through the backstreets of Chinatown, I felt Addam slipping away from me with every thwack of the rotating tyres on the wet road. I could still smell his scent on me, and feel his guitar-callused fingers on my cheek but I was losing his face, the face that had been mine alone, in a collage of posters and magazine covers of the face that belonged to everyone else. I had been in his bed ten minutes ago and yet, try as I might, I couldn't imagine the sweaty, rumpled sheets against my skin, relive the sensation of stretching my soft body along his sinewy one.

I shouldn't have left. I shouldn't have been so defeated by Berenger's call and his response. Who knows what he was thinking? But I, as always, thought the worst. I fled, where I should have stayed and consolidated. It was force of habit. I was always making exits when I craved entrances. And, oh, how I craved Addam's entrances. Another day might have welded me to him. I should have remembered that a single exchange of bodily fluids never guaranteed anything but a mess between your legs.

I thought about demanding that the taxi driver turn around and take me back. But the five flights of stairs to his room seemed now like a mountain that I would never climb again.

By the time the taxi reached Wooster Street I had sunk into such despair that I must have been sobbing. I wiped snot from my nose as the driver turned to tell me we were there. I could see disgust cross his face. He started yelling at me. 'You stoopid junkie get outta my cab!'

I threw a ten dollar bill at him and stumbled into the gutter.

I could only agree with his assessment.

I went unnoticed to my room and ran a bath. I didn't want to wash Addam off me, but I thought of all those teenagers walking around with hands wrapped in plastic bags where he'd touched them. I had no inclination to turn myself into a shrine. It was 7 a.m. and I bathed quickly, fearing a suspicious Berenger on the prowl. The semen and blood turned to scum on the surface of the water. I couldn't look at my body as it lay beached on the porcelain, islands of stomach and breast and toe floating in the gummy pool. I was as pale and congealed as a bowl of porridge. Was this how I looked to Addam?

I dried myself and dressed in something that would cover me from neck to ankle in case of developing bruises. I brushed my hair and saw my face in the mirror. If I had expected a sudden blossoming of decadent beauty I was disappointed. I saw the same moon face, the same uneven skin tone—blotchier if possible—and the same thin lips. I wanted to ooze carnality from every pore but I just looked clean.

At nine I went down to the office, as if everything were normal. I sat in my chair with my hands on my lap, waiting for Berenger like Marie Antoinette waiting for the guillotine. I was powerless to do anything but wait for my fate. I could leave, but this was the only home I had. Let Berenger fire me, I thought. There's nothing I can do about it. And there would be no point in appealing to Aaron. 'She's jealous because I fucked your grandson' would not go down well.

But Berenger didn't summon me as I expected. She sniffed around me all morning, sending Alison to me twice on ridiculous wild wardrobe chases. She finally buzzed me at midday and I went up in the elevator with the agenda under my arm. If things got bad I could throw it at her.

Oh, but she was sweet at first. 'Hi, Nile. Come in,' she said, sweeping her hand over the bedroom like a hostess on a game show. She looked as well-scrubbed as I was, in white teeshirt and jeans with her wet hair pulled back in a band. There had obviously been need of a lot of soap around there that morning.

I sat in my usual chair. She folded herself on to the bed and pulled her knees up. A girl talk. 'Niley, you're not mad at me about last night, are you?'

'Why should I be?'

'Well, you know. You might have thought that I *really* gave you permission to go with Addam, when of course I was only joking.'

I didn't say anything. What could I say?

'I didn't want you to get hurt, you see. I was mad at Addam. He's so…*furious* sometimes.'

'Infuriating,' I said.

'And, you know, that's cool. He's a very original person. He has *pressures*. But he's a jerk. And so he had to be taught a lesson. But I thought, for a moment, that you…well, that you kind of, like, thought he meant it. That *I* meant it…But you didn't, did you, Niley?'

'I would have been a fool,' I said.

If she picked up the irony in my voice she didn't show it.

'I don't mean to be cruel, Nile, but there's no way Addam would go with you, unless he was *using* you to upset me. And I worried about that all night. About you getting hurt. He might be capable of fucking you, of making the effort if he thought I would be offended. I wouldn't put it past him.'

She sighed and put her head on her knee. 'I don't want to be crude, but Addam fucks a lot of women. He does it practically every night. And why not? He has plenty of opportunity. Now you might think this upsets me, Nile, but it does not. Because when he's fucking them he's thinking of me. So if he *did* fuck you last night, I wouldn't be jealous. In his mind he would be doing it to me. Even if the…details'—she gave a little shudder—'were different.'

She played with a strand of hair. 'That doesn't mean I wouldn't be furious with *you* if you did fuck him. Not because of me, you understand, but because of what Aaron thinks of Addam. Aaron would never forgive you. *Never.* You know that?'

I nodded dumbly, riveted by her performance. I couldn't put my finger on it. Which films had I made her watch recently? *Mildred Pierce?*

'Anyway, it's OK because I checked with Addam and he said Ronny just dropped him off at his place and drove you home. Ronny has confirmed this. So I'm glad for your sake you weren't used and abused. I'm glad for Aaron's sake, too, because the last thing he needs is an assistant mooning over a guy she'll never have again, a guy who fucked her rotten with every intention of dumping her. I've seen girls ruined by Addam. You know that song? Love the one you're with? He loves the one he's with. He puts his tongue in a girl's mouth and she thinks she's special, you know?'

'I know what you mean,' I said flatly.

'I knew you were too sensible, Niley. And I knew he didn't really go for you. He doesn't look at you that way. Anyone can see it. People at the party were laughing...well, I won't go into that.'

'Are we finished?' I asked.

'Have I hurt your feelings? I didn't mean to. I'm sure you're very attractive. I'm sure there's lots of men for you. Look, let me show you something.'

She jumped off the bed and unbuttoned her jeans. I had no idea what she was doing. 'Come closer,' she said, and gave a little giggle.

I put the agenda on the chair and took a couple of steps towards her.

'Closer! You won't see anything!'

I obeyed. I could see it even before she pulled down her G-string. She had very little pubic hair, most of it waxed away. I knew: I made those appointments for her. The ring was golden, the twin of Addam's, gleaming from under the hood of her labia, decorating a clitoris that seemed obscenely large and pink to me in the circumstances. I was horrified.

'Addam gave it to me last week…you remember, when I was out all day and no-one could find me? He's got one exactly like it that he's had for ages. He says they're our secret wedding rings. It hurt like hell, but I only have to slip my finger through it to think of him. Touch it and feel how heavy it is.'

I must have recoiled because she said, 'Oh, I'm sorry, Niley. I know you're embarrassed by this sex stuff. It's dope, though, isn't it?'

'What about Aaron? What does he think?'

'Shit, Nile, you're always worried about Aaron. I told him I did it for him. He likes it. Well, who wouldn't?'

She shuffled over to a mirror and admired her new acquisition from a different point of view. I was hoping she had dismissed me. I went and picked up the agenda and started for the door.

'Oh, Niley, one more thing.' She turned to me as she was buttoning her jeans. 'The good news is I'm not cross with Addam anymore.' She smiled that little wistful smile she usually reserved for people who were paying her lots of money. 'And he wants to see me tonight, after the Tibetan benefit thing, he's begging me to come. You can arrange everything, can't you? Send Ronny around at eleven…no, eleven-thirty. Aaron's going to a stupid concert again. You can make up something about where I am. Oh, and can you tell Addam to get some of that stuff I like? He'll know what you mean.'

I should have seen it coming. But I closed my eyes. The monster always goes away when you close your eyes. Except when the monster's of your own making. Why should one night with Addam change anything? I had brushed the surface of his skin for a few hours, that was all. What made me think I could get underneath it? Berenger already occupied the place that ached. I was the freak show. I had to work to make him happy, while

Berenger only had to lie there.

The prospect of calling him mortified me. I hadn't thought this through, any of it. But how could I? There had been barely time to catch my breath. He said he liked me, but would he like me when I called, all business-like, to procure his services for Berenger? Would he hear the longing in my voice underneath the frost I would have to coat it with? I hadn't had many mornings-after, I didn't know what to do. And this was shaping up to be the morning-after of all time.

The reality was that, although I felt incapable of picking up the phone, there was still a spark of willpower in me, a faint stirring of rebellion. But I was under no illusion about what would happen if I didn't do it. I would have to find another life and it wouldn't include Addam. What would I do without Berenger as an excuse? Beg Trini for backstage passes like all the other groupies? Hang around his doorway waiting for him to come or go? Even Baby, who had been following some fifty-year-old Greek pop star around Europe for the past six months, would be lost to me as a lifeline. I would be yesterday's news. If he had a girl a night as Berenger said, I'd be Saturday 20 November. I'd have to brand it across my skull so that he'd remember me.

If I did call, I would get his answering machine, of course. As far as I could tell he always screened his calls. He left no imprint of his own voice on the tape, there was just a pause and then a piercing tone. It was bad enough, the silence in which you could cough or splutter or say things you couldn't take back, but what if he picked up? I'd be lost. Addam, I'm sending Berenger over to fuck you tonight. Brilliant. Maybe I could fax Trini with the message. Trini, tell Addam that Berenger's coming over to fuck him tonight. But if he didn't pick up it would be worse. I would imagine him sitting there, avoiding me, or rolling around on the mattress with one of those girls-a-night, his tongue grazing her teeth while a mile away I croaked into the phone the arrangements for his next sexual encounter.

Did he have another girl with him now? If he did, she'd be having a bad time of it. He'd spent himself on me...But how did I know that? Maybe there were men who could turn their ardour on and off like streams of piss. And, after our first encounter on the stairs, Addam had smoked a few joints and taken some pills and downed some whisky. Did he need the help of chemicals to get through the night with me?

No. The proud part of me fought back. It wasn't like that. I've always liked you Nile, he said. I was pathetically available, but he didn't have to take me. I could have driven on home with Ronny and never known.

Afterwards, he had said, 'Now you know.' Now you know. What did I know? How he felt for me? What Berenger did with him? What all the fuss was about? But he'd said it modestly, wryly. Now you know I'm nothing. Did I dare to think this connected us, that I understood him and he me? The way he stroked the side of my face...

I was going mad. My brain was trying to make sense of something only my body could explain. To know someone in the biblical sense—that was right. You *knew* and no words could describe it. And you couldn't stop knowing, even when the details had fled to the moon.

Later in the day, the office door was flung open and Berenger stood there, a satchel over her shoulder and a bottle of caffeinated water in her hand. She was on her way out to a fitting. 'What did Addam say?' she asked breathlessly.

'I haven't spoken to him yet.'

'Jesus, Niley—'

'I think there's something wrong with his machine,' I lied. And why not? Everyone else seemed to be doing it.

'Well, it doesn't matter, anyway,' she surprised me by saying. 'Maxwell's going to take me to the benefit. Erik has just been speaking to his people. So I'll see Addam backstage. Cancel whatever I was doing for dinner, will you?'

'You were having dinner with your husband.'

But she wasn't listening. 'Can you imagine what Addam's going to think when I turn up with Maxwell? He'll have a fit. He'll be jealous. Maxwell's cute, isn't he?'

I didn't have a clue who she was talking about.

'In fact, I might not even go home with Addam after all. Let him, like, stew in his own juice for a few days.'

I tried to tune out. 'So I don't need to lie to Aaron, then? You'll be home and all tucked up in bed at a reasonable hour?'

She slurped on the water and looked hard at me. 'I don't like your attitude, Nile. If I didn't know better, I'd think that something happened last night to make you so shitty. And if it did, you wouldn't, like, be here now.'

'I'll bear that in mind—the *next* time,' I said through gritted teeth.

'Good,' she said haughtily, and hoisted her satchel higher on her shoulder. She aimed the water bottle at my wastepaper basket and missed. Then she turned on her frisky heels and started back out the door. But she stopped in mid-stride and turned around to face me again.

'What do you mean by *next* time?'

That night, knowing he would be at the benefit, I called his machine. Speaking to the tape, knowing he was not home, was marginally less traumatic than the prospect of him picking up. This way, I could compose a message that sounded rational, persuasive and affectionate. I couldn't go on with unfinished business between us.

His answering machine clicked on, the silence and then the long shrieking tone. 'Addam...?' I waited a few seconds, to make sure no-one would pick up. 'Addam? Listen, could you phone me? There's something I want to talk to you about...' The tape kept turning over. 'My private line is, well, 5775764 just in case you've lost it. Or you could try my mobile on 9178884555. Could you make it soon? Bye…' I let my voice trail off, not sure what else to say. Then, overwhelmed by a sudden lack of confidence, I added, 'Oh, by the way, it's Nile…you know…Berenger's, um…'

I hung up, cursing myself for sounding so self-effacing. But I could hardly take it back now, short of breaking into his apartment and smashing his machine. Perhaps if I tried again…

'Addam. It's Nile again. I just left you a message. Look, I didn't mean to sound so…vague. It's really important that you call me as soon as you can. I mean, it's not life or death or anything, but…'

Shit. I hung up again. I'd scare him. I was being too dramatic.

'Addam, it's me….*Nile*, again. Call me. 5775764 or 9178884555. No hurry. Thanks…'

For a few days my heart thudded in my throat every time the phone rang, which was about fifty times a day on a modest count. It was never Addam.

Then I got to the point of calculating, well, it's morning so it won't be him on the phone because he'll be sleeping, and it's four in the afternoon so it can't be him because he's rehearsing and, then, it's ten in the evening and he'll be out at some bar and, finally, it's 2 a.m. and he'll be so dog-tired he's gone straight to sleep. There was always a reason Addam never called me. That he seemed to have time to call Berenger didn't factor into it.

Twice Berenger said casually, about as casually as a rattlesnake poised to strike, 'By the way, Addam says hi.'

I kept on trying, day and night, but hung up as soon as the shrieking tone kicked in. And then, one night about a week later, he picked up the phone before the machine clicked on. I got such a shock I almost hung up.

'Yup?' Addam said, sounding distracted. Piano keys were being struck in the background.

'Addam?'

'Yeah.' His voice sounded bored, wary.

'It's Nile.'

'Hey, Nile,' he said, friendlier.

'I've been calling you, Addam.'

'I know.'

'You didn't call back.'

There was a silence. Then he sighed. 'What does she want?'

'She?'

'You know.' He put his hand over the mouthpiece and I could tell he was talking to someone in the background. When he took it off, the piano had stopped tinkling. 'Look, Nile, you don't have to do this.'

'Do what?'

'Tell her to do her own dirty work.'

'But I'm not—'

'Don't you feel uncomfortable about it?'

'Yes. I do.'

'Well, then, don't humiliate yourself like this. Get her to call me herself.'

'But that wasn't why I was calling—'

He didn't seem to hear me. 'Nile, I feel bad about it, all right? Tell her I'll see her here Monday, OK?'

And he hung up.

I stared at the mobile in my hand. What did he feel bad about? Me calling him for Berenger? Or me having sex with him?

I quickly pressed the redial button. The answering machine gave its desultory whine. But I couldn't mouth the words. He was there and he must have known it was me.

yesha still came to collect me every morning for the subway, but she no longer chatted about the stories in her *True Romance* magazines or delivered the latest gossip from the Century 21 grapevine. She had a true romance of her own and she knew I didn't approve of it. The influence of Kevin was reflected in those blue jeans she had started wearing and the hard little gleam in her one good eye.

I'd gone from waiting up for Berenger to waiting up for Ayesha like an anxious mother. Kevin came to take her out three times after our jolly little dinner in SoHo and I'd watch from my window as they left Magdalen House and strolled down 22nd Street. I wondered if he was still playing gentleman or if his sinister intentions were starting show in the clamminess of his hand when it took hers or his hot breath on her neck as he fondled her in the cinema. Each night I expected her to come running to my door breathless and outraged at something obscene Kevin had suggested.

The Friday night following the dinner, Kevin picked Ayesha up in a stretch limo, which made my stomach flip over. Those things had a two-hour minimum. Was he taking her parking to some desolate spot, where he'd pay off the driver to go for a long walk? Perhaps the driver was an accomplice…

'Do you want me to get rid of him? Like, do something spooky so he'll never come back?'

I steadied myself on the windowsill and took a deep breath. She was back, just when I thought I might be free of her. Her heat lifted the hair on the back of my neck. It was bad enough the times she just hovered there, saying nothing, tapping the outlines of her fingernails on the wall or tabletop, impatiently, setting my nerves on edge. But this kind of intrusion was worse— like static on a car radio, she was playing interference with my life. I refused to face her.

'Why are you so interested in getting rid of Kevin?' I asked, keeping my eyes on the street.

'Who says I am? I was only trying to help you. In fact, I think you're being mean to that girl. I don't see what's wrong with her having some fun. If I had known you were a *lesbian*, I would never have hired you. *Ugh.*'

'I'm not a lesbian!'

'Well, you seem to be awfully interested in your friend's private life.'

'She's in danger.'

'Oh, yeah? Of what? Being fucked to death?'

That did it. I turned to her in anger. She was just a smudge against the wall, but she was still capable of saying things that could boil my blood. 'What do you know?'

'I don't know anything, except that you're being, like, a voyeur. Like you were with Addam and me.'

'What do you mean?' I suddenly felt dull.

'Oh, you know. The way you arranged all our meetings—'

'But you made me do it!'

'Yeah, and you loved it. Like you loved going to his concerts and seeing us together. You got off on it, Niley. Admit it.'

'You're wrong. It was horrible the way you betrayed Aaron. You made me feel *sick.*'

'Then why did you hang around? We didn't make you stay. You could have gone off and had a boring life somewhere else. But you didn't, did you? Because every night you dreamt about us. Don't deny it, I could see it in your face in the morning. It was, like, so obvious. Addam and me used to laugh about it.'

I felt my intestines curdle. 'I don't believe you.'

'That's your problem. You should have seen his face when I showed him the stuff you kept in your room. He thought it was pathetic.'

'What do you mean, you showed him my room?'

'Oh, Niley, don't be so ridiculous. We all knew about *that*.'

After My Night With Addam—I had started to capitalise the title of the biggest chapter in the measly book of my life—I began to watch MTV in my SoHo room. I'd hardly ever turned the television on before, but now I searched it mercilessly for images of Addam. I knew that seeing him like this, framed behind glass, untouchable, was making me feverish, mad, but I couldn't stop myself. When I closed my eyes I could no longer imagine him. I needed the screen to know he was real. Detox had a new album, a new single, the hit song from the soundtrack of a Christmas-release disaster movie and tour dates to promote, so there was no shortage of him. There were videos, news items, promotions for music awards and even a clay figure of him in a cartoon death match with the clay figure of a singer from a heavy metal band. (Addam won.)

I taped the videos and played them until Addam was an abstraction, the repetition of an idea of a person who once kissed me.

And I tried to draw him down, like a white witch, by listening to *Aporia*, the Detox CD that Baby had given me for Christmas, until the songs coursed through my veins like my own red blood cells. I ran up to Tower Records and bought the two earlier Detox albums, *Aprosexia* and *Ataraxia* and looked up their meanings in the dictionary, hungry for any message for me. (Ataraxia:

absolute calm and tranquillity. Aprosexia: the inability to concentrate. Well, that was me.)

Then I bought a Discman, pressed the earphones against my skull, turned the volume up until my temples throbbed. I sang along with him, clinging to his swooping melodies like arms encircling a neck. The songs, even when they had titles like 'Julia' or 'Cymbeline', were only for me. The girls in them were all 'pretty' or 'sweet' or 'lovely' but these words were just the shallow rhymes; the undercurrents were all about sex and me.

I began to roam the newsstands and snatch at the music magazines, eager for any mention of Addam, any picture I could fold under my pillow or into my pocket like a talisman. I found postcards of him in the Village, teeshirts on the street in SoHo, a book of concert photos at a stall on Sixth Avenue. An old man on Church sold me a back issue of *Rolling Stone* for fifty cents with Addam on the cover. One night I tried to tear a poster of the band off a wall on Mercer Street but I ended up with only an ear in my hands.

I stashed my relics under my bed during the day, like a naughty schoolgirl, and took them out and spread them over the sheets at night. I thought I was being discreet. I thought no-one knew. I lay back with the Discman turned full blast and fiddled with the television's remote control, and opened my legs to Addam while the screen flickered and filled my head.

But soon the videos and the music and the torn magazine pages and even my own fingers did nothing for me. There was not a picture of Addam in the world that didn't start to look like a smudge of ink on paper. I paced my room, I flicked the remote control continually until I had cramps in my wrist, I lay with the *Rolling Stone* cover over my face, trying to pull him through the pages by force of will. But there was no will strong enough to bring him down.

And then I started to seek him on the internet, becoming as I did gradually aware of the breathtaking extent of the parallel world made up of hundreds of thousands of others similarly exhilarated and tortured by the mere existence of Addam Karsner. There were 300 home pages devoted to Addam and Detox alone.

I entered the world of perverts and gossipmongers and little girls in big cities who posted paeans of love for him on the 'unofficial addam page'. I was irritated by the presumptuousness of his fans, who wrote long letters of love to Addam online. But what disturbed me more was that the things they thought and wrote about Addam started to sound awfully similar to the things I was thinking about him too.

> I was walking down 3rd street with my friend kelly and can you believe it addam comes walking towards us!!!! He's sooooooo beautiful and so im really shy as he walks past but kelly says 'hey' and addam stops and talks to us!!! He's really really flirtatious and asking us where were from and telling us where we should go for a pizza and then he says hes gotta go but its been nice talking and none of us has a pen so I get him to sign my teeshirt with my lip gloss!!! And then I wrote my phone number on his arm and kelly did too, on the other arm of course. kelly says if he calls she is definitely going to fuck him and have his baby even if it means not finishing seventh grade…

After enough hours I couldn't tell where I started and the fans left off.

It didn't help my delicate state of mind that Aaron had decided to do what Fleischer Row had asked and include Addam in his book. We had hired a stenographer by then to transcribe the tapes but it was still my job to read them and discuss alterations with Aaron. I saw him most days for an hour or two except when I was travelling with Berenger. I think he liked my comments on the book, needed my objectivity. But I couldn't be objective about this:

He was a dear little boy and I looked forward to his visits. I hadn't wanted them to move to California but the mother said she had work there. I felt it my obligation to support them. Despite her 'work', the mother never seemed to have a penny. I sent money for his kindergarten and later a series of expensive private schools. There were always music lessons and art classes and class trips to Portugal and Nova Scotia, or wherever they took children those days to teach them to be spoiled brats.

I had no control over the direction of his education, but whenever he came to Manhattan I made sure he accompanied me to classical concerts and stayed up with the grown-ups whenever anyone of cultural value came around which, as you can imagine, was often. Jessye Norman sang him a lullaby one night and Liza Minnelli came once to babysit. So he was exposed to spectacular women at a very early age.

I was in rehearsal for *Rebecca* when Addam's mother announced that she was checking into a rehabilitation clinic in the desert for a few weeks. Would I take Addam? This was in the spring of 1977, I believe. I could hardly leave the little fellow with the Mexican maid, so I had him sent over here and engaged a tutor. I was rarely at home during that period, coming in late after rehearsals, working through the night on alterations, and leaving early in the morning, but my housekeeper, Frances, said the boy seemed happy enough. He was obsessed, apparently, by spiders and went daily on hunts for them in Central Park.

It was Frances who was with him in the park when he fell from the climbing frame, I think they called them then. He fell heavily on his knee, twisted it and popped a cartilage. Frances said he never once screamed although tears ran down his face like someone had turned on a faucet. He was in hospital for three weeks and then there were months of physical therapy. But he never again walked properly on that leg. I believe, however, that teenage females find his limp attractive.

Did you know that he was not named for the biblical Adam or for some foolish English rock star his mother apparently knew, as the fan magazines have it. He was named for Charles Addams, the cartoonist. That explains the A-double D. I think the name suits him rather well...

Poor Addam, his young life spent shuffled between Baby and Aaron. Baby who was mentally absent and Aaron who was physically never there. A little boy who collected spiders and didn't scream. Did he have friends? Teachers who liked him? Schoolboy crushes? When did he first pick up a guitar? Who did he play for? What did he read? There were a thousand things I wanted to know, but Aaron wasn't going to answer any of them.

I didn't think he could: these things about Addam he didn't know either.

Addam's mother encouraged him into this rock business when he was about ten. That's when he came on vacation to New York and asked me to buy him an electric guitar. Of course, I wouldn't do it. He might have been a fine classical pianist if he kept up the lessons. He had the most extraordinary agility in his fingers. But he stopped playing in California and spent the money I sent him on guitar lessons instead. I didn't find out until much later. I was hardly able to supervise his every movement. I might have arranged classical guitar lessons if he had asked. I could have asked Segovia or Bream. But I believe he took up with a session musician in Los Angeles and started hanging around recording studios after school.

He has made quite a success of it and I'm happy for him. It seems as if today success is dependent on how many times the video you make is shown on television. Addam is quite an attractive young man to women, I imagine, and so we see him a good deal on television and posters and magazine covers. It doesn't hurt that he's a fine-looking boy, does it? His music could be anything because no-one really listens to it, they just watch it. These rock videos have ruined the idea of music, they have taken the imagination out of it, they have given us pictures and sounds, not words and ideas. The listener doesn't connect with the emotion in their own way.

And then, finally, Aaron got around to Berenger.

I suppose the whole world knows that Addam was responsible for me meeting my wife. They had been seeing each other on and off for some time. But when he brought her to my apartment for a family dinner they were just good friends, as they say. Berenger had wanted to meet me and I was very flattered that a young girl would be interested in my music. I'm afraid Addam got rather left out. Berenger started to visit me by herself and things went on from there. The tabloids have written a lot of rubbish. Who knows what goes on between two people except those people themselves?

But Addam was very pleased for us. He came to the wedding with his new girlfriend. He has had several more since then! I don't really approve that he is so indiscriminate. He puts too much energy into women and not enough into his craft. It's partly my fault, surrounding him with all those extraordinary women when he was growing up. We Karsner men have always fallen hard for pretty faces.

I felt the blood in my veins drain rapidly away. We Karsner men have always fallen hard for pretty faces. As if it were some kind of…complicity, this hunger in them for beautiful women, something passed down in the genes. Some sickness they were proud of.

Coming from Aaron it seemed even more brutal. Why didn't he say 'interesting minds' instead of 'pretty faces'? Aaron, of all people, should have said 'interesting minds'. I felt abandoned by him.

And then there were the lies. There were lies in what he had written. They puzzled me.

'What's wrong, Nile?' Aaron looked at me sharply.

I shook my head. 'Nothing.'

'You find what I'm saying distasteful?'

'No,' I lied.

'It's damned Fleischer's fault. He wants me to comment on Addam's sex life. But how can I comment on it when I don't know anything about it?'

He raised an eyebrow and studied me with those filmy, pale eyes. I knew then that he suspected something and he expected me to tell. But I had pitched my tent in Addam's camp and I had nothing to say.

You can tell me, Niley, the voice said. *Why won't you tell me?*

watched Ayesha take Kevin's hand one night and resolved, even though Ayesha would hate me for it, to speak to Susan Mackie about Kevin and see what she might be able to do. Surely, I thought, there would be a list of sexual deviants we could check to see if he was on it. I was confident that a woman like Susan would know about a list like this.

I put all this to her when Ayesha had gone out to lunch with her friend Gaina from the Century 21 department store a few blocks away. It was not perhaps the best moment, as Susan had been forced to bring Rufus into the office because the babysitter had unaccountably failed to turn up that morning. Susan looked sweaty and harassed when I entered, which may have been partly due to the fact that Rufus was kneeling on her desk playing frisbee with the stacks of *Psychology Today*. He was a pretty boy with tendrils of copper hair but he had a mean aim for a two-year-old.

Thwack! A magazine hit the wastepaper basket and knocked it over. *Thwack!* A magazine wiped a cup of pencils off the desk. *Thwack!* A manilla folder sheared into my knee and its contents scattered all over the carpet.

'I thought it would be advantageous for him to come in here and see Mommy at work behind a desk,' Susan said before I could speak.

'Good idea,' I said blandly. Another manilla folder shed its

369

contents over the carpet. 'But do you think he should be doing that with the files?'

'What?' She jumped up from her chair, displaying the usual expanse of thigh, snatched Rufus from his trail of destruction and sat him gently on the edge of the desk.

'Now, Rufus,' she told him. 'You haven't seen an office before, not really, so I can't expect you to know what to do. But Susan works here and working is not at all like playing. It's very important work, too, and if we mix things up or throw them on the floor then Susan can't do her work and if she doesn't have any work she can't earn an income and if she doesn't have an income she can't bring Rufus home any more dolls to play with. Do you understand that, Rufus?'

'Na!' shrieked Rufus and slapped Susan across the face with the fist that had a moment previously been in his mouth.

'I know you didn't mean that Rufus,' Susan said calmly, wiping the saliva off her face with the back of hand. To me she said, 'How are you with babysitting, Nile?'

'I have done it before,' I said, noncommittal.

'Do you think you could help out with Rufus when I go up to NYU at two? It might be interesting for him to spend some time in an academic environment, but...' She sighed. 'Stuff it. There's plenty of time for that later. Did you want something, Nile? I have to go in—' she checked her wristwatch. 'Christ! Twenty minutes!'

I told her about Ayesha and Kevin while Rufus occupied himself with an electrical fitting, pulling a lamp cord out of the socket and jamming it back in repeatedly.

Susan collapsed back in her chair with a groan when I finished my story and wiped her damp brow with a silk sleeve.

'I really don't know what I can do, Nile. If I try to speak with her, she won't trust me. She'll see me as a parent, not a friend.'

'But she's beholden to you. Couldn't you just tell her you forbid it?'

'I would never do that, Nile.' Susan looked at me with grave grey eyes. 'It's taking advantage of my position of power. It's not my place.'

'Then whose place is it? Her husband's? You felt it was your place to tell her she was no longer married in the eyes of the law. I wonder how that will go down in New Delhi?'

'Nile, Ayesha is her own person. I doubt from what you say that this Kevin is really some deviant. He's probably just a sad and lonely man with low self-esteem who believes only a scarred woman could love him. We should give him the benefit of the doubt.'

I looked at her curiously. Normally Susan would at this point be on the telephone rallying the troops in support of her endangered charge, but she seemed exhausted, defeated.

Did I have to be the avenging angel of plain women all by myself?

'Look.' Susan's voice sharpened and she made a helpless grimace with her mouth. 'I've been holding off speaking to you and Ayesha about this because I had hoped... Well, I had hoped it wouldn't come to this. But I think it's inevitable.' She took a deep breath. 'I have to close this office. It's costing me an arm and a leg and, well, my funding has dried up. I'm almost finished, you see, and they're redirecting funds to...' She suddenly made an angry chopping motion with her right hand. 'But I'm *not* finished! Not halfway! Every day there's a new cause that demands attention. Look at this—' She jumped up and rustled through a skewed stack of newspaper clippings on her desk. Miraculously, she found what she wanted and handed it to me. It was a photocopy of an article from *The Times*, dated back in October, and headlined 'WOMEN MARKED FOR DEATH, BY THEIR OWN FAMILIES'. I scanned it quickly and handed it back to her.

'Those poor women in Bradford, Pakistani girls who have been educated and raised in England, are hunted down and beaten and murdered when they refuse to go back to Pakistan to take part in an arranged marriage. And not murdered by some stranger, although a whole industry of bounty hunters has grown up to carry out the task, but on the authority of their brothers, their fathers, their *mothers*. Only one man has ever been convicted over the years, a brother-in-law who ran over a twenty-year-old girl in his van…'

I wasn't really listening. There were too many dead girls. And Ayesha would be one soon, especially if she lost her job. Without a job she would go to Kevin, there was no doubt of it. Why couldn't Susan see this? 'When are we finishing?' I asked. 'The office, I mean?'

'I don't know, but soon, I'm afraid. I know you haven't been here long and I am sorry. Let's say two weeks? I'll have to take all this stuff and work from home…alone. I don't know what kind of example it's going to set for Rufus.'

'So Ayesha and I…?'

'Maybe I can talk to some of my colleagues about you.'

'No, thanks. There are plenty of things I could do.' Although I wasn't so sure about that.

'I thought so. I'll give you a reference, of course.'

'But what about Ayesha?'

'There will be someone, I'm sure…'

'Kevin,' I said, mostly to myself. 'That someone will be Kevin.'

The phone suddenly buzzed through to the office, as Ayesha was not there to take it. Susan picked it up. A black look crossed her face.

'Well, you've got a nerve, I have to say. You've planned this for months, you tell me? Now? What am I going to do *tomorrow*, forget about next week. Of course I would have fired you! I need someone who can bond with Rufus long-term, not just for a few weeks and then dump him! Imagine how he's going to feel when I explain to him his caregiver has just up and left for San Francisco? All right, Michael, I'll send it to you if you forward me an address. Goodbye.'

Exasperated, she slammed the phone down. 'Moving to be with his girlfriend, I can't believe it! It's so difficult to get good childcare these days. If only you knew! Since I had those surveillance cameras installed I've had to fire three nannies. One of them actually smacked Rufus on the leg! You could even see the welt on the video!' She looked at me with new interest. 'You don't want a nanny's job, do you?'

'No thanks,' I said and then it dawned on me. 'But—'

Susan had the same thought, but we were momentarily distracted from it by a loud thud and a shriek as Rufus finally managed to work the tip of a paperknife into the electrical outlet.

'But I do not want to be a nanny!' Ayesha was on the verge of tears as we walked from the 23rd Street subway station after work. 'You think because I am from India I can do this work!'

'Not at all…'

'You are a…racist, Nile!' and she stomped off ahead of me. I went to follow her but the strap of my backpack got caught on something and I was jerked backwards.

What it got caught on was Josh Gruen, looking pleased with himself.

'Feisty girl,' he said. He let go of the strap. 'Maybe we can work her into the article as a contrast to all those beautiful women…'

'We?' I asked crossly. 'Since when is this article being written by "we"?'

'I didn't want you to feel left out on account of the fact I haven't called you lately.'

'Left out? I've been overjoyed. How did you find me anyway? Oh, don't bother, I can see it. Your friend Ostrowsky.'

'Look,' he moved in closer and grabbed hold of my arm. 'You got time for a bite? I want to run something by you.' He started walking quickly, dragging me with him.

'More sensational sleuthing for *Confidential* magazine, or whatever it is you write for? How's the Pulitzer going?'

He jerked my arm harder and pulled me around to face him. 'Ow!'

'I've been working on this thing for a month and I'm way past deadline. I'm getting impatient. All I've got is a load of fluff from teenage girls.' He loosened his grip and put his hands in the pockets of his zip-up leather jacket. The bitter wind ruffled his sandy hair. 'I just need you to fill in some gaps. I still haven't got near the old man. They say he's ill. What do you think about that? Feel guilty?'

'Why should I feel guilty?'

'It looks to me like you ran out on him.'

'I don't care what it looks like.'

'And then, of course, there's the famous grandson running off with the famous wife.'

'He wasn't running off with her.'

'Oh, no? You know something about that?'

'Why don't you ask him?'

'Don't think I haven't tried. He's in Europe on tour. But he's a lost cause anyway. I tried to get to him by pitching *Details* a story on his band, but he refuses interviews these days. His PR is sure pissed with him. She says it's a golden opportunity to get some publicity for the album. You know his assistant, Trini? Well, I even took her wretched dog for a walk to get on the good side of her. But she was more interested in what celebs *I* knew.'

'You could have called Baby. You can't shut her up.'

'Oh, believe me, I did. I have hours of tapes which I can't even bear to transcribe. What's with that woman, anyway? All she could talk about was her Greek boyfriend. What a fruitcake.'

'She's a mother.'

'So? What have you got against mothers? Mine is great. She's a gemmologist. Goes out into the desert all alone for weeks.'

'Then you should ask her what she knows. She probably knows more than I do.'

'Come on, Nile. What have you got to lose? Look, I don't want to talk out here on the street…'

'I don't want to, either.' I turned on my heels and started to walk away down Eighth Avenue.

'Well, then,' he shouted at my back, 'I'm not going to tell you what juicy bit of information the cops have been keeping quiet about out of respect for her husband.' I could hear him walking fast to catch up with me. 'And that I, in my sensational sleuthing way, as you put it, have found out.'

'I don't care!' I shouted back at him.

'No, maybe you don't,' he said. 'But try this one on for size. She...'

'What?' I turned around and faced him. He had stopped a few feet from me, a smug look on his face. Fortunately there was no-one else on the bleak street to hear. '*What* did you say?'

'I didn't think you were interested in mothers.'

'That's not what you said!'

'Oh, yes I did. I said the dirty word. Mother. I said, "Berenger was going to be a mother."'

I felt like he'd reached out and slapped me across the face. I put my hand to my cheek, but it didn't do much good. My whole body was smarting. Berenger pregnant? It couldn't be true. I would have known. She wouldn't have kept that juicy piece of news to herself. Unless...But I didn't want to think about 'unless'.

'That's impossible!' I yelled back at him, wanting to believe it was.

'Why, was she secretly a man? I imagine her reproductive organs worked as well as anyone's. Why couldn't she be pregnant? She'd been married for a year.'

'But—'

'But you doubt Aaron's abilty to father a child?'

'No!'

'I find it hard to believe she didn't tell you.'

But she hadn't. She hadn't said a word. Not even when she came in the night to torment me. Why hadn't she told me the thing that would torment me the most?

When I said nothing, he crossed his arms and tilted his head. 'You really didn't know?'

Of course I didn't know! I wanted to scream. If I had

known…'Oh, *shit*,' I groaned, as the realisation of what I'd done overwhelmed me.

'I take it you're not pleased about it.'

'No, it's just…sad.' I struggled to cover my confusion. 'How far…gone was she?' I needed to know.

'Ten weeks, eight weeks the Medical Examiner says.'

I tried to work it out in my head. How long ago was that? 'Maybe she didn't know about it herself,' I offered, limply.

'She knew. I called her doctor. It took some doing, but he confirmed that she had been tested.'

'Dr Gropp?'

'The same.'

Good old Dr Gropp. 'What else did he tell you?'

'Nothing. He was very reticent. Like any other fucking person I try to speak to about Berenger. Why are you all so loyal?'

It wasn't loyalty, I thought, it was self-defence. 'So she was pregnant,' I asked nonchalantly, trying to conceal the fact that my whole body had started to tremble. 'What difference does it make?'

'It doesn't make any difference, I suppose,' he said. 'Except that two people have died, not one.'

What could I say to that? When I didn't answer he said, 'So, do you want to come with me and discuss this? It's cold out here.'

'No, I don't want to discuss it. You've got the angle you want. If you look too hard it might disintegrate in front of your eyes. So I'd go with the popular theory and make that deadline.'

I was afraid I'd said too much. His little eyes bored into me. 'So there *is* another story?'

'No,' I said. 'You've got the story all right.'

You just don't have the truth.

But I didn't have it either.

So now we have to deal with a baby.

The child died with Berenger and it is lost. Maybe, being unformed, it reincarnated into an alley cat, or a subway rodent or a snail working its way along a townhouse fence. In which case, we'll never find it, in this world or that.

Perhaps the baby is fortunate, dying in the womb like that. Berenger would never have made a mother. There would have been nannies around the clock. The baby would have been dragged from smoke-filled restaurant to smoke-filled dressing-room like some prize pumpkin. There would have been no mother's milk and no mother's tenderness, just the baby decorated like a Christmas tree for dinner at Karl's or Lee's and then, having been lavishly cooed-upon in public, dumped back with the nurse in a gilded Paris hotel room while its mother disappeared for days to Amsterdam or Portofino on a whim, with a group of teenagers who thought the Lamaze technique was a new kind of facial.

It is better for a baby with a bad life ahead of her not to be born. I am the living example of that. The best I could make of myself with the hand I was dealt was to become ordinary. I clawed my way to the middle. I aspired to mediocrity. It is a miracle I became so…normal.

I don't speak of my mother because she doesn't exist. She drank herself into a putrid early grave six years ago, when she was forty-five. I say putrid, because even in life she always stank of decay. Pickled decay, how the inside an old mason jar of preserved sheep's bowels or pig's uterus might smell if anyone were bold enough to open it. I haven't seen her grave and I never intend to, although the nursing sister from Vaughan House who sent me a card with directions, in the mistaken belief that it would be a kindness, clearly imagined that the dearly bereaved (me) was going to tramp all over dismal London trying to find the plot of land which was now the 'resting place of your loving mother'.

Ha. Resting place? No matter how heavy and dank that clot of earth that covers her, she won't be resting. I hope she's pacing the halls of hell tearing out her decomposing hair in torment at what she did to me.

I had a brother, too, but I never knew him. That mother of ours went out on a drinking binge and left him alone in the flat and he died of dehydration. He was ninety-three days old. The neighbours said they didn't hear the baby crying, they would have called for help if they had, of course they would. His name was Terence, Terry, an old name for a little baby, and he must have been an old soul because he lay in that grimy flat in silence for six days willing himself to die. He knew what lay ahead of him in life. But he died two years before I was born and couldn't warn me, so I came into the world in stupid, blind, gurgling optimism.

My mother's name was Claire, a ridiculous name. Nothing about her was clear. In my mind she is a fuzzy knot of drool, matted hair and bleary eyes, all sodden endearments ('Come to mummy, sweetie-pie') and sudden bad moods ('Get off me, you little cow!'). It was only me and her, and her drinking companions, there wasn't a father in sight, although I do remember a man in a tweed cap who looked at me with regretful eyes. I might be making him up, it might be all imagination, but I do see him in my mind's eye, holding out a toy rabbit with a plastic face. I can't remember ever actually holding that rabbit and I would have remembered.

I had few toys, the ones my grandparents gave me on my birthday or at Christmas being in my possession for only as long as it took my mother to wake from a festive-season stupor and realise she had something she could trade down the pub for a few drinks. My grandmother, the old racist, gave me a golliwog one year and it was out of my arms and sold before Christmas pud was served. I don't think Father Christmas ever graced me with a visit when I lived with Claire but I always made her something, a pot out of clay, a cotton string of plastic beads, and wrapped it carefully, in the hope that Santa would see that I was a loving little girl and bring me next year what I knew he gave the other children on Bordesley Road.

We lived in many different flats but, as far as I know, all around

Morden. My mother didn't have the finances, or the imagination, to start over anywhere else. And in her cunning, alcoholic way she wanted to stay close to her parents, Malcolm and Jean, because she knew they were always good for a handout when we were really on the skids. All she had to do was present a scrawny, grimy little me to my grandparents and invent some urgent need, such as school books or uniforms, and she'd walk away with enough cash to buy the whole Beverley pub several rounds of drinks. I think my grandparents got smart, eventually, and bought me my clothes and books themselves. But, in the end, that probably brought everything down on their heads. *My* head. When I ceased to be her meal ticket, I might as well have died.

It was a scandal at the time. It made the national newspapers. I can remember the uproar afterwards and my mother in the police station sobbing and a policewoman bringing me a chipped cup of Rose's Lime Cordial and a Marie biscuit. I can remember later being asked questions by a kindly old man and my grandparents nodding solemnly and then taking me home and making a bed for me on an old couch out the back. But I can't remember the incident that set it all off, probably because, to me, there was nothing out of the ordinary about it. It was a Saturday and my mother was inebriated and I was holding her arm to steady her as we left the Beverley. I was cold, as usual, and hungry, as usual, although, as usual, I'd had a packet of crisps for lunch. There were men hanging around on the high street outside, as usual, and my mother was coming on to them, as usual. It might even have been usual for her to try to sell me.

This time she was successful. My mother sold me, for twenty-five pounds, to a passing tradesman. A passing tradesman: it sounds so…*music hall* now, but I suppose at the time it was shocking. 'A passing tradesman' implies someone anonymous and furtive and rough with their hands, surely an unsuitable person to take charge of an eight-year-old girl. And the exchanging of crumpled pound notes suggests he had the worst kind of intentions, although maybe he thought I looked a sturdy and reliable apprentice to help him in his trade. My mother didn't care, she cared more about a flagon of cheap whisky and a carton of Pall Malls, which is what she went and bought with part of the profit from me.

Luckily for me, I suppose, my mother's brain was less than fully functioning—what else would have prompted her to sell me in broad daylight on a crowded footpath with many onlookers who knew us both? As for the passing tradesman, Iain Carter, of no fixed address, I can only guess. According to one newspaper report, which I read years later when I thought I could bear it, his defence was that he had bought me on a dare from some of the blokes at the pub, that he was only taking me for a walk around the block to the sweet shop and had intended to return me to Claire within the half-hour. For a long time, when I read this, I grasped at the delusion that he had taken pity on me until I had woken with a start one night and remembered sitting in his car, down by the British Rail yard, shaking.

I must have been with him only fifteen minutes before the mob descended. It took the lager-drinkers that long to work out what had happened, prompted by the postman, who knew me, didn't recognise the passing tradesman, and had gone looking for my mother.

'Where's my twenty-five quid, then?' the tradesman roared when they took me away from him.

'Nothing' had happened to me. By that they mean that I was not 'interfered with' sexually. But I was interfered with, all right.

I now had a known value, twenty-five pounds, and even that was not a bargain for the purchaser. Iain Carter, the passing, itinerant electrician, ended up in jail for abducting me. My mother landed in the welfare courts, sober enough to plead to keep me, but I was taken from her and placed in the care of my dull, resentful grandparents, who had been planning a once-in-a-lifetime trip to the Canaries and could see that it now would be postponed until I was old enough to leave home.

They were decent in their habits but unknowledgeable about the needs of an eight-year-old child. Given what a mess they'd made of my mother this was not really surprising, looking back now, but at the time I was grateful to be fed breakfast, lunch and dinner and for those meals, no matter how overstewed and clotted with heavy sauces, to consist of at least some of the essential daily vitamins. I knew I was a strain on their patience and their finances, as they kept on reminding me of it, so I tried to be good and quiet, appearing only for meals and the mandatory weekend ritual of driving somewhere, anywhere— to a wholesale market where they bought tinned food in bulk, a visit to a rheumy old friend in a stuffy, overheated living room across town or a trek across some Godforsaken windswept field to hunt for dirty-tasting mushrooms to stew and pile on toast for tea.

I stayed in my room and read and did my homework rather than watch television with them at night. I didn't bring friends home. I was a lodger, not a daughter. But it suited me. I didn't want to make a fuss, lest they decide to get rid of me. I thought that's what adults did, throw children out like old clothes when they grew tired of them. I have had no reason since to change my opinion.

By selling me and dumping me with Malcolm and Jean, my mother cursed me with a life of middling respectability. I would have been happier with Claire, cold and hungry and cowering in the corner of some pub, than with those two sanctimonious old drears. At least, later in life, my travels with Claire would have made an interesting story, an excuse for me to hold court at parties with amusing tales. I might have become…eccentric. I could have lived with eccentric.

I found out, later on and purely by accident, what turned my mother to drink. A second cousin, from Glasgow, whom I barely knew, ran into me in the bookstore on Crown Lane and over tea, rather gloatingly I thought, revealed the family secret. There had been another baby, a first baby, before Terry and me. Claire had got pregnant at fourteen and delivered a healthy full-term baby at home. She wanted to keep the infant, but Malcolm and Jean forced her to adopt it out. A deep and protracted depression followed, which I imagined was dismissed by Jean, unironically, as 'the baby blues'.

I can see Claire lying in bed, tangled in her sheets, staring at the ceiling, a stolen bottle of Malcolm's single malt cradled in her arms. I suppose I should have felt sorry for her, hearing this story told by a smug suburbanite whose only interest in telling it to me was to make her own boring life seem superior. But all I could think of at the time and all I think of now is this: if she loved that baby so much, why didn't she love me?

watched to make sure Josh went in the opposite direction up Eighth Avenue and then I started running. I didn't care that the street was busy at that time and people stopped to stare. I lifted my coat and skirts and sprinted for home.

One of my neighbours, Keesha, accosted me by the elevators. She told me she was getting together a posse to go and see the mayor, to implore him to intervene and make a last ditch effort to save Magdalen House. I told her, a bit more sharply than I should have, I admit, that the only way the petition was going to work was to have someone glamorous on our side for the photo opportunity, like a young and beautiful star of independent movies or the vivacious wife of a major Republican party donor. Or a deeply sensitive, crippled rock star.

In my room, I flung off my boots and coat and sat on the bed. I was still panting, but I steadied myself. Concentrate.

'Berenger?' I asked the wall.

The cover photograph of her from last July's *Cosmopolitan* would have stared at me if I hadn't scratched out the eyes.

'Berenger?'

She danced on the pages of *Harper's & Queen* in a corset with the stake I had drawn piercing her heart. I closed my eyes. 'Berenger,' I whispered inside my brain. 'Come here.'

Had she finally become so bored with me she had moved on? Or had she just been ink and paper all along? I could feel the edge of the curtain behind me lifting in the breeze. The window wasn't open. 'Berenger,' I said, more urgently. 'You have to come back now. I have to know about the baby.'

And then the breeze suddenly fell out. I felt Berenger trickle away like tears down a cheek. The room became dead calm. And I heard a little voice echo, 'The baby…'

Ayesha didn't come and collect me for the train the next morning. Was she still angry with me for suggesting she work as Rufus's nanny? Or was it a deeper shame, at her weakness in allowing Kevin—that sadist—to dominate her life. I could imagine him pawing her in the back of taxis and crushing her underneath him on his creaking bed. I knew her flaming red face reminded him of Nam and napalm and village maidens pegged to the ground with their legs skewered wide, while he stood over them with his ant-sized dick between his index fingers. Ayesha had been bred for contempt. She thought she needed a man. Why should she listen to me?

As I stepped on to the C train I thought I saw Ayesha down the platform. If she didn't want to sit with me, that was all right, I thought, and squeezed myself into a seat between an expansive woman in white nurse's shoes and a man reading a computer magazine who wore a trenchcoat exactly like Kevin's. As I looked around the car I saw that there were more Kevins than usual on the train that day, strap-hanging with shabby briefcases wedged between their feet, or sitting, feet spread wide, with open copies of the *Wall Street Journal* between their legs, their beady eyes glued to some international report about the increasing number of clitoridectomies in Somalia or the exploitation of bar girls in Manila.

'If ah had a gun right now, ah'd kill all dem white people,' muttered a jittery teenager pushing his way through the car. I wished he would, the Kevins first. Then put me out of my misery. Please.

But it was not going to be so simple. There were Kevins in the subway car, head down in their newspapers, avoiding my angry stare. There were Ayeshas on the platform, ignoring me. There was a Berenger, smiling smugly at me from the back cover of a magazine held between the claws of a girl with diamante-studded nail tips. And there was an Addam, on the sweatshirt of a messenger steadying his bike by the door, an old image of him, faded but not gone, like the Shroud of Turin.

I didn't see Ayesha get off at Park Place. And neither she nor Susan Mackie were in the office when I arrived. I got the key off Rasheed at the front desk and let myself in. On the machine there was a message from Susan for Ayesha explaining that she was at the hospital with Rufus. He had some kind of fever. She didn't expect to be in the office that day.

There was also a message from a Christine Tanner at the University of Bradford regarding Susan's 'proposal for a fellow-ship in the Department of Applied Social Studies'. They had, apparently, 'looked upon it favourably' and 'wished to discuss details and logistics' at her earliest convenience.

So, Susan Mackie was going to Bradford to write a paper, a dissertation, a book, on the British-born Pakistani girls who were persecuted because they refused arranged marriages. She was following the money. She had spent too many years on her burning brides and they had gone out of style.

Well, I'd been to Bradford once, and I wished her luck.

I closed the office at midday and walked down to Century 21, thinking that perhaps Ayesha might be there, hiding out with her friends in the European designer department, giggling in the storeroom about sex and boyfriends and new hairstyles.

I was *hoping* that she would be there, gossiping in corners with Gaina and Beryl, her two friends, because if she was not with them then there was only one other place she could be.

The department store was crowded with tourists speaking in different tongues and accents—Russian Mafia wives in beaver coats, miniskirted French students toting bored-looking boyfriends, packs of Australian girls in flared jeans calculating the exchange rate on Helmut Lang skirts, whole families from the north of England in parkas stocking up on sheets and towels—and I had to fight my way to the escalator through a cluster of Koreans filling a shopping cart with Calvin Klein underwear. Ayesha loved that place, spent part of every day here, even if it was only fifteen minutes at lunchtime.

'I did not know there were so many clothes in the world, Nile. But who would wear them all?' she asked me once.

As far as I knew the only thing Ayesha had ever bought at Century 21 was a small electric-blue fake-fur handbag which delighted her so much she carried it over her wrist everywhere she went and opened and closed it constantly, smiling joyfully at the lime-green silk lining like a kid playing with a jack-in-the-box. I knew that Gaina sometimes gave her clothes from the ten-dollar rack but I'd never seen her wear any of them. The last thing she showed me was a ruined pearl-encrusted bodysuit with broken snaps at the crotch. Maybe she has worn it for Kevin, I thought, and shuddered.

I had only met Gaina once or twice and so it took me a while to find her among the scrum of women rifling through the racks for discounted clothing. When I did spot her, she was standing patiently with an armful of jackets alongside a well-groomed woman who had unselfconsciously stripped down to an expensive bra and panties in front of a column mirror and was expertly placing one stiletto-heeled foot into the unzipped opening of a white miniskirt.

Gaina said that she was having her lunchbreak in half an hour and that she expected Ayesha to meet her in the cemetery as usual. When I told her Ayesha hadn't shown at work she didn't seem all that surprised but I was unable to interrogate her further because the woman in the white miniskirt was asking her if she had it in size four. Size four! This city was full of mutant women.

The churchyard was bleak and the branches rattled. There was only one other person in there, an old man in a check coat eating a sandwich out of a paper bag. There was absolutely no sign of Gaina or Ayesha in the whole hour I sat and shivered there. Maybe I've scared them away, I thought. Perhaps I was the scary thing in this scenario.

I let myself back into the office and sat at Ayesha's desk. I resented the idea of doing any work as I had, effectively, been dismissed. I decided that I wouldn't come in again. I'd find some other kind of job. There was a flyer for some Democratic assembly woman on top of one of the neat stacks Ayesha had made on the desk. Maybe I would work in politics. It couldn't be more hypocritical than this.

Ayesha was exceptionally tidy. There was even a bud vase on her desk with a slightly wilting rose in it. Another gift from Kevin? My eye strayed to the yellow legal pad she kept beside the phone to jot down callers' names. Underneath a number of precisely written notations was the sketch of a big heart with KEVIN in the centre of it and what looked like a phone number carefully etched below.

I ripped the page from the notepad and put it in my pocket. Then I closed up the office and tossed the key at Rasheed as I went by downstairs.

If I couldn't find Ayesha, at least I knew where to find him.

My neighbour Nola was checking her mail in the lobby when I got back to Magdalen House. She had just returned from her weekly blast of chemotherapy at Bellevue and was looking very waxy and damp. I offered to take her up to her room and she held onto my arm with little claws, like a frightened squirrel.

Nola lived on my floor, so I deposited her at her door, opened it for her and saw her in safely and then went down the hall to

Ayesha's room to knock on the door. There was no answer.

As I was standing there I gradually became aware of a strange odour permeating the hallway, like the smell of burning leaves. For a moment I thought it must be the animal-rights activist Bernadette smoking a joint in her room but as I followed the faint haze down the corridor I realised that it was coming from under the door of my own room. Fire? I fumbled for my keys. There was a slight resistance as I pushed the door in. I was greeted by a heavy veil of putrid smoke that made me choke.

Domenica was standing in the middle of the room waving what looked like a burning bunch of dried weeds. She had her eyes closed tight and she was chanting something unintelligible in a low growl. She was dressed in white cheesecloth with a string of dried red chillies around her neck. There were tiny iron bells around her wrist which clattered as her hands undulated. As the smoke started to clear into the corridor I began to see that she had laid out an Indian blanket at her feet and on it were arranged chunks of crystal and some ceramic bowls of what looked like dirt. There was a tambourine on the rug and a small drum, football-sized and covered in a stretched animal hide. There were thick candles spluttering away on the dresser, on top of the television set and the bookcase. For a minute I was reminded of Addam's room, the melting candles, the haze of marijuana, Addam kneeling between my legs…

I heard myself groan but it sounded like it was coming from Domenica. Her brown eyes flew open and she stopped muttering.

'What are you doing?' I cried out, stepping forward and almost tripping over some kind of long stick which was wedged against the door. 'You'll set the place on fire!'

Domenica looked up to the ceiling and pointed to the sprinkler. It had been covered with white masking tape.

'What is that stuff?' I reached for the smoking sticks in her hand.

'Is sage,' Domenica said, pulling her hand back so I couldn't take the herbs off her. 'Is for smudging away evil spirits.'

'What evil spirits?' I asked, as if I didn't know. 'There are no evil spirits here! Stop it!'

'I ask for protection for ju. Is necessary. I clean jor room in a different way!' She looked extremely pleased with herself.

'Domenica, stop it!' I didn't want her to scare away Berenger. Not now, when I had to find out about the baby. 'Give me that stuff!'

'No way!' She made a big circle in the air with the smoke.

'Domenica, the nuns are going to have a fit,' I cried, desperately trying to think of something that would make her stop, short of wrestling those 180 pounds of solid Panamanian flesh to the floor.

She snorted. 'Nuns, huh! What can they do for ju?'

'It's black magic.'

'Is good magic. See—' She bent down and picked up a strange object from the blanket. It looked like a rattle made out of bones. 'Llama toes,' she explained importantly. 'Very good for chanting.' She put it down carefully and picked up a chunk of grey slate. 'This from Andes mountains. Very good for fertility.'

'Domenica—'

'And this,' she said, picking up a smooth hunk of pink quartz, 'is good for the little baby...'

'Domenica, stop it!' I shouted, frustrated. 'Leave the spirits alone!'

'What the—?' Bernadette had appeared in the doorway, aghast, her waist-length hair wrapped in a towel.

'Domenica's getting rid of the evil spirits,' I yelled over the sound of clacking llama toes. 'Help me make her stop it.'

Domenica kept chanting and waving the smoking sage.

'Look, Domenica.' Bernadette was casting her eyes about the room nervously. 'The fucking sprinklers are going to go off in the hallway if you don't put that thing out. The last thing we need round here is the fire brigade. I've got dope plants on my windowsill!'

'Give it to me, Domenica,' I said.

She folded her arms stubbornly. 'Spirit still here.'

'I don't care!' I said.

'Is very evil,' Domenica warned.

'I'll be the judge of that,' I said and finally managed to snatch the sage. I headed for the bathroom, choking on the fumes.

As I plunged the smudge stick in the basin and turned on the cold water tap I heard Bernadette shriek. 'Hey! That's cowhide on that drum! How *could* you, Domenica!'

The smoke eventually dissipated. I cursed Domenica for her metaphysical meddling. I didn't want to scare my personal evil spirit away. I needed her back to answer a few questions. The fire brigade did arrive, three screaming trucks of them, and when we were assembled downstairs, and a head count was done, it seemed as if one spirit Domenica had managed to smudge away was Ayesha.

She was not at Krispy Kreme or anywhere in the vicinity.

I wandered the neighbourhood, but to no avail. It was cold and dark and I paused many times to peer underneath scarves and wraps, expecting to see Ayesha's miserable face reflected back at me. But the spectres of Chelsea were of a different kind from the ones I sought. They huddled over subway grates in musty rags, stared from inside the windows at Twin Donut, sickly and drawn, and shuffled along the sidewalks, thin as twigs, ravaged by alcohol, disease or their own personal demons.

I stopped at the Garden of Eden, suddenly craving potato salad. As I passed through the checkout I ran into, of all people, Alison Bow, the housekeeper from Wooster Street, weighing persimmons in her hand to test their goodness. My mind conjured up the image of one perfect section of clementine and one sliver of pink ginger on a white plate—Alison's idea of dessert.

There was no hope for a hasty retreat. I knew my smile of greeting was coy, maybe even guilty. I was sure she thought I was some kind of coward for deserting them. I braced myself for some frosty Zen chastisement. I wished that I didn't have a super size tub of oily potato salad in my hand.

'Oh, hello, Nile,' she said casually and picked up another piece of fruit.

'What are you doing up here?' I blathered. It *was* odd, she usually did all her shopping in SoHo or some pan-Asian emporium in Chinatown.

'I live on 24th Street now,' she said, frowning at the fruit.

'You do? Since when?'

She looked at me as if I'd just dropped in from Jupiter. 'Only for two weeks. I'm working for Ruda Baker,' she said, as if I should have known it.

I didn't even know who Ruda Baker was, but I didn't dare admit it. 'Oh, really?' I tried to sound impressed. 'How is Aaron managing without you?' I admitted I shoved my tongue firmly in the side of my cheek.

'He went back to Central Park. I didn't go with him. That kitchen—very bad feng shui. I refused to work there.' She shook her long black braid.

I remembered feng shui. It was another of Berenger's excuses. She probably got the idea from Alison. For a while there, whenever she wanted to just up and leave where she was, whether it was a restaurant or a location or even, once, in the middle of a flight, she'd complain that the feng shui was all wrong, that she couldn't work or sit or snort coke in a room that wasn't spiritually balanced. I did a lot of furniture moving in that phase.

'So is Frances back with him?' I asked, thinking that Aaron would have been glad to be rid of Alison and her meagre macrobiotics, in favour of Frances's corned beef hash.

'No. I think she went to live with her son in Killingworth. I believe there is a cleaner, twice a week. That theatre woman—Lilian—I've heard she is there working with him on the book.'

How cosy for Lilian.

She sniffed a pineapple and looked at me over the top of it.

'You know, Nile, you should let go. You chose to leave. It was your decision.'

'I was in shock.'

'But perhaps Aaron needed you then and you walked out. Now it's no longer your business. I'm very disappointed in this pineapple. It lacks...nose.'

'Alison, tell me,' I took a deep breath. 'How is he? Is he still...devastated?'

Her lips curled into a hint of a smile. 'You know better than that.'

'What do you mean?'

'It's time you faced it, Nile. You've got to unload some of that psychic baggage.'

She turned away from me and started filling a plastic bag with fresh dates. I watched her blankly.

'Alison—'

She turned and handed me the bag of dates. 'There,' she said. 'You should take these. They have some excellent essential nutrients for pregnant women.'

I clutched the bag. And then she walked off. This was Alison's way of ending a conversation.

It was very efficient.

burst out laughing when I found out for sure.

I remember that Dr Gropp looked at me curiously at the time. Now I knew why. He'd been treating Berenger for the same condition. He must have thought it ran in the family.

It did.

My laughter had an hysterical edge to it, of course. A baby was incomprehensible. It was the size of a fava bean in my womb but it might as well have been King Kong. Dr Gropp had not said, 'You are going to have a baby.' He had informed me I was pregnant. There was a difference. A baby was a thing that churned and kicked in your belly or gurgled and squirmed in your arms. What I had inside me was a passive little zygote, a hard little pod swimming in a sea of hormones, a gallstone, a tiny pouch of acid in my blood. I didn't feel anything for it at first. It had nothing to do with its own conception.

'Is there a father...around?' Dr Gropp asked in his most delicate manner.

'Yes,' I answered and then decorated it with a lie. 'He's got a clerical job at NYU.'

Dr Gropp nodded, satisfied that I had found the perfect boyfriend for me, dull and worthy.

'And he will be pleased with this...development?'

'Oh, he'll be thrilled.'

Dr Gropp tapped his fingers together. 'Good. Then we will

have to set up a number of tests. Hilda will make the appointments for you.'

'What kind of tests?'

'Routine blood tests. A sonagram. Amniocentesis when you're at twelve weeks. We estimate you're at six weeks now. Early days.'

'Dr Gropp?'

'Yes?'

'How long will it take to show?'

He considered my question. 'Well, you're a good-sized girl. I don't think you need worry about that until sixteen, eighteen weeks.'

'Oh, I'm not worried.' I tried to sound blithe.

He looked down at my card. 'You still live at this address on Wooster Street?'

'Yes.'

'Remind me—you're what connection to Mrs Karsner exactly?'

'I'm her personal assistant.'

'I see. How interesting.'

Thinking back, I realise now that he expected me to say something about Berenger's pregnancy. Some polite comment about how much fun it would be to be planning babies together. But, of course, I couldn't do that. I didn't know about Berenger's baby.

Fool that I was, I smiled to myself all the way back downtown from Dr Gropp's office.

I didn't feel the sap rising or the womb teeming or any of the rushes of vitality that are supposed to accompany conception. I wasn't overcome with the sudden urge to pinch babies on the cheek or wallpaper the bedroom with pink bunny rabbits. I had no desire to gobble chocolate peanut-butter cups by the hundreds or knit woollen booties. I wasn't sick or sore or prone to weepiness. The only quickening in me was the stirring of my heart and brain, not my loins. The pregnancy might have been a fiction, except that the urine had turned the paper blue.

But it was real and the tough little bud in me was Addam's son, Aaron's great-granddaughter. I was family now.

That's what made me smile.

I'd forgotten what kind of family they were.

They took sweet little Elisabeth Westbrook from me that terrible day when I watched her father fall to his death from the sundeck in South Wimbledon. It still hurts to think of how the mother blamed me. She went quite hysterical, even though she was the one who went off all day with her briefcase to the city and never returned until Lizzie was fast asleep at night. She was the one who left her accountant husband home all day to his own devices, which always included an afternoon bottle or two of chardonnay and a frustrated attempt to get me in a corner somewhere and put his hand down my knickers.

It wasn't fair, I was a good nanny. I cared for Elisabeth as if she were my own. I bathed her and mashed her vegetables and nursed her through the croup. I made sure she never knew that her mother didn't care. She was only five months old and for three months she had got all her love from me. When her mother took her from me the baby cried and cried. I loved her more than her mother did and she loved me too.

I did not let my hatred for John Westbrook interfere with my concern for his child: I held Lizzie tight, and watched as he skidded down the shingled roof, landed on his spine and broke his neck. There was never any chance that Elisabeth was going to fall too, even as he reached out to grab something to stop his descent. He would have snatched her from my arms and taken her with him if I had not pushed him away. I told the mother that. I told the police that. I told them I was a good nanny. But still they took her away.

But they weren't going to take this baby away. I was the mother this time. I could do what I wanted with my child—

neglect it, throw boiling water on it, smother it in its sleep, sell it for twenty-five quid. But of course I wouldn't do any of things. I would love it. I loved it already.

There was never any doubt in my mind that I would tell Addam. I didn't expect that he would be overjoyed at first but I was sure he'd come round to accepting the idea. Once the child had been born, he couldn't help but feel the same way about it as I did. And even if the baby and me didn't live with him—it might be bad for his career to have a live-in girlfriend—we would go with him on tour and I'd hand him the baby whenever he came offstage and he'd jiggle it up and down in his arms and croon to it and put his arm round me and all those little girl fans would watch us jealously in the wings and shed tears over our happiness and go home after the concert and compose missives of heartache on the internet.

The baby would be beautiful. He, for it would be a boy, would have Addam's pale eyes and dark brows and pointy little ears and lean physique, he would have to be lean, and he would have the fingers with the pearly spoon-shaped nails and the black curly hair that grew out in all directions and the lips that were the colour of old silk nightgowns. If he had anything from me, it might be the pale, fine skin, but nothing else. I hoped he would have nothing else.

He started to take shape in my mind, this little pixie who was a kernel of Addam...and Aaron. He would be musical, of course, extremely gifted, more disciplined than Addam, his great-grandfather's boy, a concert pianist or a conductor perhaps. He'd play at Carnegie Hall when he was twenty-one and I'd be there in the front row in my black chiffon dress, the one I'd worn when we'd conceived him, and Addam would be beside me, proudly holding my hand, ageing but still handsome in his black Armani suit. And Aaron might be in the picture too, very old, over one hundred years old like his colleague Irving Berlin, sitting in a wheelchair with a rug over his lap, his eyes closed and his head nodding in time to the music, a nurse with an oxygen bottle on wheels standing by. I would be generous and have Baby there too, but she would have not aged well, a ruin of a person with a ghastly face and shredded hair, her once-shapely ankles puffy with oedema under a zebra-skin miniskirt. And Berenger? She would not be in the scenario at all, long faded from everyone's memory, reduced to the foolish mistake we, the family, had made twenty years before, put in a box and filed under 'Life Experience' and only rarely dragged out and puzzled over.

We, the family. I was Addam to the power of two.

Of course, if the baby were a girl...But she couldn't be a girl. I wouldn't know what to do with a girl. A boy like Addam I could love, but a girl like him? A beautiful teenager with long black hair and pale skin and crystal eyes? Experience had taught me I could not love a girl like that.

When I got back from Dr Gropp, I went straight to my room, kicked off my old boots and lay on the bed, my own version of the soliloquy from *Carousel* running through my head.

I was going to call Addam, I wasn't going to hesitate, but my hand could barely lift itself to reach for the mobile by the bed. I was suddenly overwhelmed with a crippling exhaustion, as if the hormones that had been ricocheting around in my arteries for a few weeks had now taken their toll. Perhaps I should have a little sleep first...

I remember Alison knocking on my door and coming in with some laundry at one point. She returned with a cup of something hot that tasted like licorice when I sipped it and left it by my bed. Perhaps that was when she worked it out. The baby. I don't know how. The thing was barely fluttering in me.

I slept all afternoon, the heavy dreamless sleep of a mind shutting down. When I woke up night had come. I must have slept for half a dozen hours.

It was after six and I could hear Berenger, who had returned from a day shopping with Darien, thumping around in her room above mine. In fact, a series of thuds over my head was what tugged me from oblivion. I could hear the creak of footsteps on parquetry and the bump of large objects banging against the walls and floor.

I sat up, turned on the lights, went to the bathroom and splashed my face with cold water. I stared at the dozens of unopened packages of beauty products Berenger was always tossing in my direction, products that would never strengthen my jawline or widen my eyes or get rid of the stubborn turn-down of my mouth. Above me, in Berenger's bathroom, something crashed to the floor and shattered.

But she might as well have been trashing a hotel room thou-sands of miles away, in Las Vegas or Kowloon, for all the impact her penthousal fit of pique was having on me. If she'd had a bad day it was no longer my problem. I had already put myself in Addam's life and left hers behind.

I scrawled a ragged line of red lipstick around my mouth. I suppose I wanted to look sexy when I phoned Addam. That's how deranged I must have been.

He didn't pick up the first time. Or the second and third. Each time, I allowed the static-laden tape to unwind for sixty seconds or more without leaving the imprint of my voice. I kept pressing the redial button on the phone, six, seven, eight times. I was at ten or eleven redials when I heard the unmistakable click of the receiver being picked up.

I didn't say anything. Neither did he.

Eventually he broke the silence. 'Berry?' His tone, to my naive ears, sounded cautious, suspicious. I hung up.

He was home.

I stood outside the Mobil garage on East Broadway, looking up at Addam's window across the road, as I now know Berenger had done a few hours before. I had taken trouble with what I wore although I was already regretting the choice of one of Berenger's unworn cast-offs, a stretch Versus dress that was too short, too tight and the wrong colour for me, for anyone, a sick apple green. I pulled my navy wool coat tighter around me in the evening chill. It was one of those clear nights when New York's dingiest streets sparkle and even old men slumped in doorways guzzling cheap whisky take on a debonair aspect. One of those clear nights that makes your brain ache with the romance of massive bridges and cheap neon against inky star-blighted skies.

The lights were on in Addam's loft. Below that, on the fourth floor, a Chinese woman leaned against a forest of fabric rolls smoking a cigarette near an open window. On the next floor down dozens of spider plants made a spiky curtain of green and white against prying eyes. I could see straight into the second-floor loft—a television flashing cold blue light against a wall of neatly arranged, black-framed photographs, the type you get at Pottery Barn. On the first floor, at ground level, the Kum-Cho Jewellery Corp had pulled down its metal shutters for the night. Bohemia had long since fled Chinatown, leaving behind sweat-shop workers, financial district yuppies and millionaire rock stars.

I wondered, as I stood there on the pavement, which of them had pushed past Addam and me at the bottom of the stairs that night. I looked back up at the smoking woman and thought, Was it you, on the night shift, bustling by with your arm full of pattern pieces? And then, above her, I could see something move. I stepped back into shadow. Addam appeared in his window and folded his elbows against the pane, leaning into them. He was looking down but away from me, his forehead pressing against his arms. I couldn't tell what his body meant by this gesture—it was either the most nonchalant pose I'd ever seen or the most forlorn. He was like a long black question mark in the night.

I moved quickly to his front door and found it slightly ajar, the lock broken. I wondered how he could live somewhere so exposed, without a doorman or security officer to keep the fans and the weirdos at bay. But there were no fans, no weirdos that I could see. Perhaps anonymity was the best protection. He could walk the streets and not many would notice him—because he was walking the streets. Bodyguards, limos drew attention: who would notice a young man in cargo pants and teeshirt, pushing a bicycle? Maybe the Chinese teenagers who hung around the games arcades knew where he lived but they respected his desire to live quietly among them.

The buzzer for Addam's floor read FUCK OFF in faded biro. I ignored that and stepped through the street door. A pile of rubbish, maybe the same pile of rubbish, cluttered the space at the bottom of the stairs.

I took the stairs carefully, trying not to trip on my long woollen coat. I wondered: is this the step where I stumbled on my skirt? Is this the step where he crouched when I unbuckled his belt? Is this the banister railing I grasped when he had his tongue in me? Going up those stairs was like the twelve stations of the cross.

When I reached the fifth floor I sat down on the top step and waited. What I was waiting for I had no idea, except that I needed balance. A balance between the me who was outside in the street and the me who fucked uninhibitedly on the stairs and the me who was about to wrap her arms around Addam and tell him the secret that would bond him to me forever.

I'd only been sitting for a moment when the floorboards behind me started to creak. I turned around, startled, expecting a stranger to be lurking. But there was no-one. And then I realised that the creaking sound was coming from inside Addam's door and that a lock was clicking and a handle turning.

Before I could think about getting up, Addam was in the hallway. With him was a scrawny girl with blonde hair in a rust suede coat and high-heeled boots. They didn't notice me at first. She was digging gloves out of her backpack. He was thanking her for something. He went to kiss her on the cheek and then saw me cringing against the banister. He pulled back from the girl and she turned to look at me in surprise. Then she turned back to him with a smirk and a raised blue eyebrow, as if to say, Is this what you have to put up with? She had a red jewel in the caste-mark between her brows.

'See you,' he said to her, not smiling, and she gave a tinkling laugh and skipped by me down the staircase.

I stood up. I didn't say, Hi Addam or I was just in the neighbourhood and thought I'd drop by, or any of the greetings he might expect. Instead, I said, and I could hear my voice sounding querulous, 'Who was that?'

'What?' he asked, looking confused. 'Oh, her. That's Agnetha.'

'Agnetha?' I asked. 'You mean the blonde one from ABBA?'

But I did recognise her then. She was one of those female singer-songwriters I'd seen when I'd been combing MTV for sightings of Detox. She had a new video out. In it she rode a horse through a forest of birch trees and went in and out of focus a lot. In real life she looked…harder, older. Or maybe that's just what I hoped.

Addam put his hands in the pockets of his black jeans but his shoulders were tense. 'We're writing a song together,' he said.

'Oh, fantastic!' I overreacted because I was relieved. 'What's it about?'

'Nile, why are you here?' He didn't look angry, which was good. He looked weary, which was maybe not so good. And he wasn't looking directly into my eyes but at a point somewhere under my chin. That wasn't good at all.

'Can I come in?' I bit my bottom lip.

'I've got to get some stuff done.'

'Addam, I really need to speak to you.'

He sighed. 'OK.' It was then I noticed he didn't look just weary, he looked ravaged. His eyes were unknowable under heavy lids.

He stood aside for me while I stepped through the door. His place was brightly lit and I could see scuff marks on the walls. I turned around to look at Addam and he had scuff marks on his face too, deep shadows bruising the sides of his nose.

I followed him up to the front of the loft. His computer was turned on, the screensaver a pulsing neon atom. There was sheet music on the keyboard and the piano lid was up. I glanced at the bed on the floor and it was a mess. I glanced away.

A bottle of Jack Daniels sat on the window ledge. Addam picked it up and held it out to me. I shook my head. He took a swig and put it back down. I wanted to go over to him and stroke the shadows on his face but it didn't seem a good idea. He seemed jittery. I sat on the edge of the sofa instead. I was still in my long coat but I was shivering. I was determined to hang in, though. It was one of those milestones in life, telling your boyfriend you were having his baby.

He turned away from me and looked out the window.

'Addam—'

'Look, Nile, it's not a good time, OK?' He kept his eyes on the street.

'But you don't know why I'm here.'

'Berenger sent you.' It was a statement, flat and hopeless.

'Of course not. Why do you always think someone sent me? I'm not anything to do with Berenger. Or Aaron. I just work for them.'

He turned around and looked at me with guarded eyes. 'You haven't seen her tonight, then?'

'No, I haven't. She's been out shopping with Darien all day. Do we have to talk about her?'

'No,' he said. 'We don't.'

I watched him for a moment standing there, hugging himself as if he were afraid that if he let go he would shed bits of himself all over the floor. He was looking down at his boots and I was looking up at him and thinking, those poor teenagers on the internet and in the fifth row of his concerts, those kids who have to be satisfied with his face on a TV screen or cut from an issue of *Spin*, they're never going to know how...*delicate* he looks close up, how fine his edges are, how he smells like herbs, figs, earth, tobacco, how he lives in this strange, shabby place, sleeps on the floor and lights candles scented with mandarin for his lovers, a skinny boy all in black with dark shadows under his eyes, standing before me, trembling, like a wraith…

The F train thundered over the Manhattan Bridge and shook the whole block. Or maybe it was me shaking. There was something wrong with Addam, not just surprise at seeing me and a certain tension, awkwardness, about the situation. This I expected. I expected strain. Me, turning up like this, in a long buttoned-up coat, with something important to say. But I didn't expect him to look frayed, shattered. He was still looking at his boots, his mouth set, as if he were trying to untangle the laces with his eyes.

Drugs, I thought. It's drugs. He and that Agnetha with the jewel between her brows shooting up on the bed. But wouldn't he be comatose, not jittery and agitated? I really didn't know what Addam did, whether he used needles or noses, except that I sometimes had to put Berenger under a cold shower after she'd been with him. He'd been drinking, but he wasn't drunk. Drunk I knew. I'd been raised by drunks.

I was missing a crucial piece of information but I couldn't tell what it was. God, when I think now of what I didn't know and what I said…

'Addam?'

He looked at me. And gave a twisted smile. 'You think I'm a total fuck-up, don't you?'

I was astonished. 'No! Why would I?'

'I don't deal with things very well.'

'That's ridiculous—'

'Nile, you know I don't.'

I felt myself flush red. No, crimson.

'I did a bad thing to you.'

'No, you didn't—'

'You know I did.'

He was rubbing his shoulders with his hands like he was cold.

I, on the other hand, was self-immolating, the hair on my head and arms crackling like a brush fire. 'Can I take my coat off?'

He nodded. While I stood and unbuttoned, he went and turned off the bright lamp near the piano. He came back and took my coat. Our hands brushed. I was embarrassed by my tight apple-green dress. It looked calculated to be sexy. Which it was. Not sexy, calculated.

He put my coat neatly on the mattress and then came back to the middle of the room, crouched down by the coffee table, and shook a cigarette out of a packet of Camels. 'I'm not supposed to smoke in front of the kids,' he said, concentrating on striking a match, 'but these people send me crates of the stuff anyway.' He was making an effort, I could tell, to keep his voice even.

I didn't want to sit again. I knew my stupid skirt would ride right up my thighs. My legs couldn't compete with Berenger's— or Agnetha's for that matter.

He stood. 'Don't look at me like that,' he said mournfully.

'Like what?' I asked, but I knew: like a kid in a pet-shop window. The way he didn't like girls to look at him.

'Addam, you didn't do anything to me. I understand. It was a bad situation…with Berenger.'

'I thought we weren't going to talk about her.'

'We're not. We've got other things to talk about.'

He took a drag on his cigarette and the smoke obscured his eyes. 'Don't you want to sit?'

No I don't, I thought, I want to lie on top of you. 'Not here,' I told him and my eyes drifted to the bed.

'Nile, it's not a good idea.'

'I only want to sit,' I lied.

'OK.' It came out as a sigh but I read it as a sigh of capitulation. He wanted to be on the bed with me. I still think that. It's just that everything else made it impossible…

He watched me curl up on the mattress and pull my skirt to my knees and then sat on the opposite corner, an ashtray between us. 'All right,' he said. 'We need to talk. What is it, Nile?'

He sounded like he knew what it was. He had stubbed out the cigarette and was chewing on a thumbnail.

But I couldn't talk. Something bad hung between us. I thought I knew what it was. 'I'm not going to work for Berenger anymore,' I announced. It was as much an announcement to me as to him. 'So you don't need to worry.'

'Jesus! Do you have to keep bringing her into it!' He thudded the bed with a fist and flipped the ashtray over. I was horrified at the sudden violence of his action.

'I'm sorry.' I crawled across the bed and tried to sweep up the ashes.

'Stop acting like a fucking servant!' Then he dropped his head in his hands.

I knelt there, not knowing what to say.

'I'm sorry,' he said eventually. He put his hands down on his knees and gave me a rueful sideways look.

I crawled over to him. 'It's my fault,' I said. 'I'm always doing that.'

I couldn't not touch him. It was beyond my control. I sat beside him and put my hands through his limp right arm. He didn't shrug me off. We sat there for a while. I leant the side of my face against his shoulder and started stroking his forearm from fingers to elbow. He didn't stop me. I turned and put my right hand against his left cheek and softly rubbed the palm against the stubble on his jaw. He didn't stop me. I twisted my whole body so that I was leaning into him. He didn't stop me. I hitched up my skirt and swung my leg over his hard thighs and pressed my buttocks into them and took his face between my hands and he didn't stop me. And then I kissed him full on the mouth, inhaled his smell and taste, felt his lips quiver under mine. He didn't stop me.

'I love you,' I said.

Then he stopped me. He grabbed my arms hard and moved from underneath me. He kept holding my arms to keep me out of kissing distance. I struggled. Of course I struggled. I was like

405

a baby that had been pulled off the breast before she had finished drinking.

'What?' I asked, confused.

'Nile,' he said, looking me straight in the eyes. 'We can't do this.'

'Of course we can,' I said mindlessly, and lunged at him again.

'Nile,' he said. 'No.'

His face was so close to mine I could hardly breathe. I'd kissed the television screen and the cover of *Rolling Stone* but I'd forgotten how soft and rough, peach skin and pumice stone, the real thing was.

'No,' he said again.

When I looked I saw pity in his eyes. God. How many times had I seen that look before, from others? I wiped my hand across my mouth. 'I thought you guys fucked anything that moved,' I said, bitterly.

'Look...don't.' He let go of my arms.

I pulled my skirt down and glared at him. His eyes were wet. The anger and frustration fell away from me, like I was an apple being peeled. 'It will be all right when the baby comes,' I said gently.

'That's nothing to do with me,' he said coldly.

And then he looked at me suspiciously. 'When did you find out?'

'Today,' I said. 'This morning.'

'How nice for both of you,' he said, getting off the bed. 'Or should I say *all* of you?'

What did he mean, both, all? Why was he acting like this? Was it shock?

'Addam,' I said, struggling to my feet to keep up with him. 'You'll love it when it comes. I'm sure you will.'

He groaned and ran a hand over his face. 'Nile, I'm sorry. I'm sorry I've done this to you. I always screw up. It's like I can't help myself. But I don't want to know about the baby. I don't *ever* want to know about the baby. OK?'

He turned his back on me and went over to the piano, opened an old cigar box and took out a bag of dope.

'Do you always act like this?' I tried to keep the tremor out of my voice.

'Like what?'

'So cool. When a woman tells you she's going to have your baby.'

'It's never happened before.'

'I don't believe that.' I was angry…anguished. I wanted to lash out.

He licked a cigarette paper and looked at me over it, eyebrows raised. But I could see his hand was shaking. 'You shouldn't believe everything she says. She's as jealous as a banshee. Which is a joke, considering everything.'

I stopped listening. I couldn't keep up the tough talk. I started to cry. Pathetic. Pathetic. But maybe pathetic would work on him. I was that desperate.

He came over to me and put his arm around me. 'It's all right. Don't you think I feel like crying too?'

'Addam, what am I going to do?' I really didn't know.

'Just get the hell out of there, like you said you were going to. They're *sick*, both of them.'

'But Aaron needs me.'

'The only person he fucking well needs is himself.'

'Why do you hate him so much? He's your family. Everyone says you blame him for Kurt—'

'Listen to me, Nile, as you're so infatuated with that genius of a grandfather of mine, I'm going to tell you something that only about three people know. My own fucking mother doesn't even know, that's how much attention she paid to me as a kid.'

'What?' I asked. 'What is it?'

'See this knee of mine?' He tapped his bad leg angrily. 'The one that meant I couldn't play Little League like all the other kids? Which then meant my star-fucking mother started sending me to guitar lessons and pushing me into acting school so that

I could become a quote rock star unquote like all the guys she liked to bring home when I was a kid? Well, do you know how I got it? Baby went into rehab and sent me to stay with Aaron. The old bastard couldn't be bothered with me at night when Frances went home—I used to sleepwalk, have nightmares, who wouldn't with a family like mine—so he would lock me in the fucking bathroom all night, every night for two months. I was seven years old and I slept in a bath, just with a little plastic mattress. And one night I wanted to get out of there so bad. I thought a monster was after me, a really bad nightmare. I climbed up on the old porcelain sink and actually managed to get myself on to the ledge of the open window above it. It was a small window about eight feet off the ground. Too small for me as it turned out. I couldn't get through it and I fell backwards. I hit my leg on the sink and crashed onto the tiled floor and smashed my whole kneecap. I was concussed for a while and then I woke up and cried. But Aaron didn't come. He never came when I cried. Frances found me in the morning. I was in physical therapy for months. I couldn't go to school. I couldn't be a normal kid.'

'Aaron says in his book that you hurt it in a fall at the playground.'

'The bastard. And you know what, after that, whenever I'd call him to tell him about some small success I'd had, like signing with Columbia or watching my first song hit the top ten, Aaron would always have to go one better. "That's nice," he'd say, "but I've got such and such a musical running simultaneously in nine world cities or I've been nominated for two Tony Awards or this producer or that producer has just given me a million bucks to do my play." His fucking theatre was always superior.'

'I'm sorry, Addam. That's horrible.'

'Yeah. And you know the worst thing? I told that stupid bitch Berenger all about him and she still went and married him.'

'Addam—'

'So you see, Nile, he's not worth the loyalty. You're smarter than Berenger. You should leave.'

'But where would I go?'

'If you need money, come to me. I mean it. I've got plenty of it around here somewhere.'

'Then I can visit you?'

'Nile, I'm not in love with you.'

'I know,' I nodded. But it wasn't true. How did he know he wasn't in love with me? He wanted me to get away from Aaron, like he wanted Berenger to. That showed some feeling for me. And when the baby came...

'Then you understand?'

I nodded again. I was playing the game.

He stood in front of me again and then kissed me on the cheek. 'I always did like you, Nile.'

When he stepped back from me I felt the rift, like a cold burst of air from an open doorway. I watched him go back to rolling his joint.

He lit it and the smoke rose around his head. In old movies, the smoking scenes were always the ones charged with the most sexuality. Addam was a movie, standing there all in black, his curly hair cropped around his head like a cherub in a Renaissance painting, his concentration on stage directions that didn't include me. I could go over and kiss him now but it wouldn't make any difference. He'd gone back behind that screen, to the world of pretty girls on white horses and oil stains that turn into beautiful phantoms.

And I was in the fifth row of the auditorium, waving.

pulled my coat around me against the cold night air and staggered out of Addam's building onto East Broadway. I turned and looked up at his window, but he was no longer standing in it.

He didn't want to know about our baby. That's all I could think about as I struggled through the dark Chinatown streets, heading for SoHo but not really caring if I ever made it. *I don't ever want to know about the baby,* he said. I was crying so hard I could barely see where I was going. As I stumbled from intersection to intersection, I skidded on rotting vegetables, slammed into wooden crates of refuse, crashed into passing bodies wrapped in heavy coats and scarves. Cars honked angrily as I lurched across their paths, unseeing. Someone grabbed my arm to help me across the street, but I shook them off. I could hear voices calling after me, indignantly, and the sound of sirens passing and fading in the night. But I didn't slow down. I needed the momentum. I didn't care where I was going but I didn't want to stop. If I faltered, the burden of what Addam had said to me would have driven me into the ground. And, no matter what I felt about myself or Addam or the desperate circumstances I found myself in, I could not hurt the baby. I wanted to keep the baby. I wanted to be a good mother.

I wiped my face on my sleeve before I turned the key in the lock at 89 Wooster. The last person I wanted to see was Berenger, but there she was, in the kitchen with Darien, their heads close together, whispering. I crept past the doorway and she didn't look up, thank goodness, but I wondered why Darien was there at that hour when Berenger was supposed to have spent the whole day with her. Whatever the crisis was—a new model who had snatched a contract off one of them, a booker who had swapped agencies—I didn't want to hear about it.

I could tell Alison had been bustling around in my room while I was out because there was clean linen on the bed. The copy of *Details* with Addam on the cover had been placed on the bedside table, its corners perfectly in line with the edges of the carpentry. She had obviously been digging around under my bed: had she just wanted to make the room look 'homey' or was there a message for me?

I stared at Addam's face and a fierce anger suddenly pushed aside my despair. Stuff them all, I thought. They can't exclude me. I have more right to Addam now than anyone else on earth.

I knelt by the bed and dragged out the rest of my collection and put it prominently on the bookshelf. I took out my cut-out pictures of Addam from a drawer and found a few drawing pins and stuck them into the wall beside my bed. Then I unfolded the Detox poster that had been a bonus-with-purchase with the *Aprosexia* CD I found at Tower and taped it to the bathroom door. That would give Alison something to think about in the morning.

My burst of energy disappeared as quickly as it came. I sat on the bed, exhausted, and started to pull off my boots when there was a knock at my door. I braced myself, ready for Berenger and Darien to descend on me for a chemically enhanced girl talk, or for Alison to slip in on some pretext, like having to change the toilet roll, so she could remind me this was her territory as much as mine.

But it was Aaron. He was standing at the door in grey flannel trousers, a blue shirt, and a yellow alpaca cardigan. He looked dapper, as if he had dressed for company, but prickles of beard grizzled his chin and made him appear grey and drawn. 'Nile, would I trouble you if I stepped in for a moment?' he asked. He was clutching a book under his right arm.

I blinked.

'Oh, but I am troubling you,' he said.

'No, no,' I said quickly and held the door open for him. He had never, in the whole time I had been living there, come to my room.

He took a few steps in and then stopped. 'I'm not disturbing anything, am I?'

'No, not at all,' I said weakly. 'I hadn't gone to bed yet.'

'Good,' he nodded. 'Good.'

'Do you want…a seat or something?'

'No, no, I'll just be a moment.'

I stared at him, appalled. I didn't know what to say. He was not the same Aaron. The man who had taken me in, paid me handsomely and shown me great kindnesses was not the man standing before me now, the man who had lain in bed and heard seven-year-old Addam crying in the bathroom from the pain of his smashed knee and had not gone to help him. In my confusion about Addam's reaction to our baby, I hadn't thought about Aaron. But now it was as if I had spirited up an ogre from a child's nightmare and he was looming over me, demanding I make sense of his appearance. He was my child's great-grandfather but my lover's foe. I wasn't strong enough to confront the contradictions yet.

'Oh, I brought you this book.' He handed me the weighty volume. It was a new biography of Truman Capote. 'Lilian gave it to me. I believe it's very good.'

'Thanks,' I said wanly and took it over to the bookshelf. Addam stared up at me from the covers of *Spin* and *Rolling Stone*. I quickly looked back to Aaron to see if he had noticed that my room was a shrine to his grandson, but he was staring into space. 'I trust everything went well at the doctor's today, Nile?' he said from across the room.

I must have looked startled. I hadn't told him I was going.

'Berenger mentioned something about it. You're not sick?'

'No…just a routine check-up.'

'Good. I might have to steal you back for a few weeks. To get this damn book finished. Fleischer wants to rush a fall publication date. He's worried that his investment is going to die on him, I suppose.'

'Don't be ridiculous,' I said, automatically. 'You'll live to see…' What? His great-grandchildren? I couldn't finish the sentence.

Aaron was looking at me, amused at the lie. 'You don't need to flatter an old man. The way I feel this week, I'll be damn lucky to make that publication date. Fortunately, we've made him pay out so much money in advance he's going to have to publish whether I'm around or not.' He gave a little chuckle. 'Anyway, I've already spoken to Berenger about having you here while she's in Morocco. Is that all right, Nile? I know I'm a crusty old customer but I thought you might rather like a…break.'

'Yes…I would.'

'That's settled then. The agency can handle all her trivia. I've got a meeting with Fleischer tomorrow at some damned new restaurant in a parking lot. Can you imagine it? I wondered if you wouldn't mind getting the new chapters in some kind of order in the morning so that I can take them with me.'

'Yes…I'll do it first thing.'

'Don't know why I bother to show it to him, though,' he grumbled. 'He doesn't read, you know. He gets other people to read for him.'

I stood there and I watched Aaron's eyes drift around the room. They were old eyes, rheumy eyes, but there was nothing wrong with their long vision. I watched, helpless, as he scanned the pictures of Addam I had pinned over my bed ten minutes before. 'I see my grandson has won another heart,' he said dryly.

'No, not at all. I…' But what could I say?

'I've done a terrible disservice to you, Nile.' Aaron's eyes were profound with some emotion. Sorrow? Anger? He was the second Karsner to say this to me in a day. *I did a bad thing to you,*

413

Addam had said. But it hadn't been bad. When the baby came it would be good.

'I don't understand—' I started to say.

Aaron didn't stay around for the explanation. 'I'll see you in the morning, then.' He was at the door and closing it behind him before I could recover.

I dashed to the door and stepped into the hall. 'Aaron?' I called after him.

He turned around and looked right through me.

'It's not what you think.'

But, of course, it was.

The next morning, I upheld the routine. I felt it important that I upheld the routine. I rose at seven, I showered quickly, I went down to the kitchen, made a pot of tea, brought it to my desk and turned on my laptop.

I woke up knowing what I had to do. It had come to me as I lay on the bed dreading the day. I had to make Addam love me more and I thought of a way to do it. I would make him an offering. I would get the poison about Addam out of Aaron's book. It was within my control. Aaron didn't even to have to know I was doing it. All I needed to do was alter his manuscript.

I scrolled through the chapters of Aaron's book and deleted any mention of Addam. I riffled through the files and found the hard copies of the manuscript, pulled out the pages about Addam, and put them in an envelope in the bottom drawer. I then went to the box of back-up floppy disks and wiped those same pages off them. I had obliterated all Aaron's lies before 9 a.m.

And then I thought: why not put the truth back in? I scrolled back through the files on the computer, pulled up the chapter where I'd deleted Aaron's version of Addam's accident and started typing.

'I'm afraid I am to blame for Addam's terrible injury…'

I wrote it as Addam told me, but in the familiar cadences of Aaron's language. It was easy. It came out in one long stream-of-consciousness and I had to go back and put the punctuation in. I typed furiously: it only took about half an hour. I copied it back onto disk, printed out three hard copies and slid them into the manuscripts.

And then I decided to print out another. I put it in an envelope, and marked it to Addam at his address. When the messenger came, he looked at the envelope and said, 'So that's where he lives, huh?'

I felt a moment of irrational jealousy. This messenger would be seeing him sooner than I would. But the jealousy faded as soon as it came. Addam would call me when he got the envelope. He would know it was from me. He'd be grateful for what I had done and he'd love me a little more.

I never once in my recklessness realised that all Aaron had to do when he discovered my deception was change the text back. It would take him some time, but he could do it. And he would fire me first. But I was too disturbed to think of consequences. I could have pleaded insanity on that fact alone.

At 10.30, Darien Apps' assistant, Louisianna, called to run through the acceptances for the Manson party that night. I'd completely forgotten about it, forgotten even to check the answering machine that morning which, when I got round to it, was full of one day and two nights' worth of people calling to try and cajole invitations.

A party promoter was handling most of it, the nightclub was providing the expenses, but it was it Darien and Berenger's job to pull in most of the celebrity guests. Berenger couldn't see why Charles Manson couldn't come even when I explained to her he was serving a life sentence in California State Prison. But Shirley Manson's people had promised that she'd turn up and Marilyn Manson's people had told us his plane from LA would land in time but whether he would attend they couldn't say. I had found it difficult to summon up any enthusiasm for an event where hundreds of drunk, stoned and chainsmoking teenagers would be crushed into a basement for several hours without food or air when we were doing the invitations two weeks before, but now I cared even less. I doubted Addam would be there. I hoped he wouldn't be there. I didn't ever want to be in the same room with him and Berenger again. And now Louisianna was reminding me that I'd promised to go over and supervise the set up. I had even less inclination for it than I'd had the day before, but I didn't have the energy to resist. Just get through the day, I told myself.

'Who are you, like, going as?' Louisianna asked me, breath-lessly. This was the girl who used to be Darien's manicurist, picked up Darien's mobile to answer it one day when the Living Skeleton's acrylic wraps were drying, and landed herself a job.

'Going as?' I had no idea what she was talking about.

'It's a costume party. You're supposed to wear costumes—and stuff.'

I groaned. 'I forgot.'

'Darien's going as Charles Manson, we've got the wig and the beard and knives and everything.'

'I don't know that Charles Manson actually did any killing, Louisianna.' I knew my serial killers.

'He didn't?'

'No, he just manipulated. And Darien's a bit tall for Charles Manson, isn't she?'

'She is?'

Thus having sent Louisianna into a tailspin, I hung up. I wasn't going to have to put up with this much longer. This…idiocy. These stupid people who only thought about what they were going to wear and who they were going to stand next to at a bar. Berenger was going to Marrakech the next day. Tomorrow morning, after I'd seen her off with her trunk of minuscule bikinis, I'd tell Aaron I was leaving. He would think I had defected to Addam's side. And it was true, my future was

416

with Addam. Even if he didn't know that yet. I could find some-where to live, have the baby…I didn't even feel sorry about it. And with luck I'd never have to see Berenger again, except on bus shelters.

I have to think about this day very hard. Berenger's last day on earth, as it turned out. Her last day of flesh and blood and bones you couldn't see through.

The fact was, Detective Ostrowsky, I hardly saw her at all during the day. I had booked her into a spa in SoHo, for a few hours of being pummelled, steamed, squeezed, exfoliated, moisturised, bronzed and blasted with oxygen. She liked to go there to meet all her friends, models and editors and movie actors, who between treatments hung out in the waiting room in robes, sipping spearmint tea and flipping casually through the piles of maga-zines in search of their own faces. I'd gone with her once or twice, to answer her cell phone while she was being scrubbed down with raw pineapple skins, and she'd once booked me in for my own series of treatments, but I'd felt uncomfortable and embarrassed lying on a table wrapped in wet herbal sheets while a beautician plucked at my eyebrows with a pair of tweezers. I couldn't see what was relaxing or sensual about all this poking and pillaging of blackheads and why one would want to pay hundreds of dollars for the privilege. But that was my puritan upbringing coming out. Waste not, want not, said Nana Jean. Although I suppose you could argue they were recycling the pineapple.

By the time Berenger had returned from the spa, I was at the nightclub with my hands in red paint, scrawling HELTER SKELTER on a wall. When I'd arrived at the club, which was housed in an airless bunker under Lafayette Street, there were no decorations to supervise. It was 6 p.m. and nothing had been started, although I was told by the pair of stoned East Villager types who greeted me—black jeans, scraggly hair, multiple piercings—that this was not unusual.

'Man, no-one's gonna come 'til midnight. What's your problem?' one of them drawled, scratching his crotch.

But when I explained the theme of the party they seemed disproportionately enthusiastic, splashing red paint everywhere and stopping occasionally to admire their handiwork with slow headshaking and murmurs of 'Oh, man!' I didn't want to think what the clean-up would cost.

I don't know how I did it. I just tuned out. We got through it all in a couple of hours. By then the promoters had arrived and the barman was experimenting with various blood-red cocktails. I washed the water-based paint off my hands in the bathroom and turned my cell phone back on. It rang immediately.

'You've been turned off all day!' A slight exaggeration.

'I've been over here at this bloody nightclub doing the decorations for *your* party. I'm coming home in a minute.'

'Well, there's no need to get snappy with me.' Her voice wavered at the end.

'What's wrong now?' I sighed.

'I look fucking horrible, that's what's wrong!' she howled. 'I've come out in sort of blotches all over my skin and the witch who was supposed to do my make-up just called in to say her apartment got burgled and she's waiting for the cops and can't come over. I can't believe she can be so selfish! So I'm stranded here looking like I've got diaper rash on my face and there's no-one to fix it!'

'I'm sure we can rustle up someone,' I said with perfect calm. I wouldn't have to do this much more. 'Who's coming to the party? What about Susan?'

'But I don't know her number!' Berenger wailed. 'You've got them all!'

'How many times have I told you that everything's in that organiser by your bed? I've shown you how to use it a million times. And what about the speed dial on your phone? There are at least three make-up people on that.'

'I'm too upset. Can't you come now?'

'I'm coming,' I said and hung up.

It took me about twenty minutes to finish at the club and get back to SoHo, but in that time Berenger's face miraculously cleared of all blemishes except for a blotch in the middle of her forehead where a blackhead had been too vigorously squeezed. By that time, she'd thought up a dozen other complaints, not the least of which was how she hated her Sharon Tate costume and wasn't going to wear it. Somehow I managed to change her mind. I think it was my lack of real interest that finally did it.

'Well, I don't think it matters what you wear,' I said after she'd rejected several possibilities. 'They all look the same to me. Wear the black dress. No-one will care.'

'What do mean no-one will care?' she frowned.

Ten minutes later she was standing there in the pale blue beaded mini again, with the pillow fastened underneath it and the long blonde wig smoothed down over her own hair.

'You need blood,' I said. I went to her bathroom and found a dark red lipstick, then I set about ruining a dress that might have cost over $2000 if Berenger had paid for it.

I have to admit, I enjoyed it.

When I finished, Berenger posed in front of the mirror for a while in that curious way she had of drawing herself into herself, as if the performance were just for her. By the little mouths she made, I think, under the hair and the lipstick stain, she was pleased with the effect.

Suddenly, she stopped what she was doing and whirled around to face me. 'Niley, do you think this is bad karma?' she asked, biting her lip.

I didn't know that underneath the wound we had made with lipstick there was a tiny heart beating, a real life that Berenger must have started to feel surging within her. I realise now she must have had an inkling that she was tempting the Furies by mocking pregnancy in this way. But I missed the symbolism of it altogether, although the non-existent child I had helped create and rip from its feathery womb should have made me reflect on my own delicate condition. I so much wanted this infernal night to end that I'd shut out all thoughts of anything other than getting Berenger dressed and to the club so that I would then be free to come home again and sleep off the few hours until the glorious moment when she flew off to North Africa. I wanted to get rid of her, very badly. I was concentrating on that. Get her to the party, get her home, get her on that plane.

'Well, do you think so?' she was demanding.

'Think what?'

'That this is bad karma?'

'Bad karma?' I asked, surprised. 'No, not unless you're pregnant.' Did I really say that? Or is fantasy stepping in where memory has failed?

I remember, I'm sure of it, that whatever it was I said she looked shocked, that the colour drained from her face, and that she took a step backwards and sat heavily on the bed.

She might have said something to me about the pregnancy, but the make-up artist arrived at precisely that moment, and brought with her the tumult of the outside world. In less than the blinking of an eyelash, Berenger had turned her attention wholly on Susan, and the tools and potions that could turn a nineteen-year-old with a blemish on her forehead into an icon of sixties popular culture.

If only she'd said something about the pregnancy.

I closed the door on their animated discussion of which exact shade of beige would be right for the lips and went to my room. I changed out of my paint-splattered clothes and into the first thing I found hanging in my wardrobe. Then I sat on my bed and played my Detox videos over and over, fretting that Addam hadn't called to thank me for my gift to him. Tomorrow, when Berenger's gone, I thought…the buzzing of my mobile woke me from a deep sleep.

'Where have you been?'

'What do you mean?' I asked sleepily, flopping my hand to the bedside table to activate the light on my digital clock. It read 11.37. 'I've been here waiting for you.'

'Well, I've been ready for *ages*,' she lied. 'I want to go now.'

'OK. OK.' I said and got off the bed.

Downstairs, Berenger took one look at my black dress and said, 'What serial killer are you?'

'I'm just myself,' I said.

'You were supposed to come as a murderer!' she grumbled.

But I had.

It was midnight in a part of Manhattan where few families lived, but the crowd around the entrance to the bunker included several little girls of about ten years old who were collecting autographs. They squealed with delight when they saw Berenger and fluttered their books at her but she strode past them without a glance. Chalk up another one to bad karma, I think now.

I was feeling bloody-minded so, in the first half-hour or so, I kept on passing Berenger cocktails and glasses of champagne, deliberately mixing them, wanting her to be sick. She'd down a glass and wave her hand around and I'd take it and replace it with another. I didn't think at the time that she noticed what she was drinking, she was so busy dancing and air-kissing. I knew from experience she had the constitution of a tank, so I wasn't surprised that after about seven drinks she was still steady on her pretty feet. When she disappeared to the bathroom for fifteen minutes and came back looking as bright and fresh as if she'd just woken from twenty-four hours sleep, I gave up.

I retired to a corner of the room and nursed one of the barman's blood-red cocktails. I had no intention of drinking after my last fiasco. Besides, there was the baby to think about. A group of tall people stood in front of me and pushed me further into the recess, but I was glad to have the camouflage: if Addam turned up now, I'd have to flee.

From what I could see peering into the darkness, the guests

had taken great liberties with the party's theme. There was a mermaid and a robot and someone dressed like a giant slug. Half the people hadn't bothered…or perhaps they were going for authenticity, wearing the plaid shirts and jeans that John Wayne Gacy and Jeffrey Dahmer might have worn committing their crimes. Americans certainly produced lacklustre specimens, I thought, looking around the room at all the plaid shirts and fake machetes. In Britain we had characters worthy of the name 'serial killer': Sweeney Todd, Jack the Ripper, Bernard Crippen and Myra Hindley. I was thinking about this when the performance artist we'd hired to play Charles Manson sidled up to me and tried to stare me out.

'Why don't you piss off?' I said in my sweetest voice, but to no avail. He kept hovering around me, trying to spook me.

I wondered how long I would have to wait before Berenger wouldn't notice that I'd gone. She was across the room draping herself around various celebrities having her photograph taken, clutching another glass of champagne in one hand and a cigarette in the other. I noticed that the pillow under her dress had been discarded. Darien came up to her, in beard and long hair and striped pyjamas which were supposed to echo prison garb, and Berenger wound herself around her, feigning lust. Then she went to her knees and faked an enthusiastic blow-job. I turned away.

But I shouldn't have turned away. I realise now, after everything, that Berenger was acting strangely. It wasn't the drinking and the smoking and the outrageous flirting. There was nothing unusual about that. It was the determination with which she did it, as if she'd set her mind on showing the world how carefree she was, like a crazed flapper dancing like there was no tomorrow. I was no longer keeping track of her drinks or the number of times she disappeared to the bathroom for long stretches but I should have. It was my job. I was so involved with my own misery it didn't occur to me she might be troubled too. Worse than that, I had added to her psychic fragility by making her wear that disturbing costume and then goaded her by passing her all those drinks. She had snatched them off me and downed each glass in one, like she was seeking oblivion. I thought at the time she was just being greedy, that the intemperance was all her own. But the drug pusher always has to justify her actions.

I did turn away, in search of somewhere more private. People were gathered in dense clusters and everyone was so tall that simply going to the other side of the room felt like making an attempt on Everest. Eventually, I found a wall and traced it round to a model-free zone underneath one of the artistic efforts of my punk painters. I studied their handiwork: they could apparently spell DEATH TO PIGS but not COK SUCKER.

I looked at my watch. We'd only been there about forty-five minutes. I could probably stretch it out another half an hour and then leave. By then, Berenger finally would be drunk and wouldn't miss me.

It was definitely 2 a.m. when I left, Detective. I remember it now, 2.06 a.m., in fact. That's ten minutes after I went looking for Berenger to tell her I'd had enough.

I found her in a dark alcove by the bathrooms, down on her knees in front of Darien again, her mouth pressed against Darien's pyjama fronts. Except it wasn't Darien. It was the Manson impersonator.

I was so disgusted with her I walked away without saying anything. I went up to a photographer taking snaps at the bar and tapped him on the shoulder. He turned and I pointed towards the bathrooms. 'You'll find what you're looking for down there,' I said.

The two pregnant women at 89 Wooster Street both slept the sleep of death that night. But only one of us woke up in the morning.

was the one who cleaned up all the evidence of drugs. Who else would it have been? I was always the one who ran behind them with a dustpan and brush.

I fished the wad of gum out of Berenger's foul mouth and then I shook her hard. When she didn't respond I looked around the room wildly and found the hatpin on the bedside table. I picked it up and clasped her hand and forced the sharp point under a nail. When she didn't flinch, I tried it again. I must have tried it more than once, but I can't remember. All I remember is sitting on the edge of the bed, holding her hand, my eyes wandering all around the room, looking for some clue to what had happened.

There had been white powder all over the bedside table and some of it had formed a tiny drift on the edge of a drawer. There was a plastic ziplock bag on the floor and, near that, Berenger's antique Chinese necklace, hung with silver charms which, on closer inspection, included implements for drug consumption—a tiny knife, a filigree vial and a silver tube with nostril-sized openings. I reached down to pick the necklace up and my hand touched an empty pack of Camels beside it. I picked up the packet and held it in my hand. And then I panicked.

I managed to scrape some of the powder into the bag and used bathroom tissues to take care of the rest. I flushed the tissues down the toilet. I folded up the bag of powder and tucked it into the front of my knickers so that it sat flat and then squashed the pack of Camels and slipped it in there too. Then I wiped off the traces of powder from the necklace and fastened it around my neck.

It was stupid, of course. It looked worse that someone had cleaned up. It suggested guilt. It suggested that someone had been there when Berenger died and then systematically destroyed their connection to her.

I thought that that someone was Addam. Like the police, I imagined, stupidly, that all drugs led to him. I thought he must have been waiting for her when she came home from the party. I told myself he wouldn't have known that she'd been drinking and drugging all night, that he shared what he had with her innocently enough, like he'd done many times before. That he had kissed her sleeping brow and closed the door on her, gently, not knowing that she would never wake again.

I sat there on the bed with Berenger's lifeless body and thought of how Addam had rejected our unborn baby two nights before. And how, the very night afterwards, he had been carousing with Berenger again in her bed. Did we matter so little to him, the baby and me? But I didn't shed a tear. This wasn't the time to cry. I knew I wouldn't be alone for long, that someone would find us. I was focused on one thing only: I had to protect the father of my baby. So I hid his drugs.

When I left Wooster Street for Magdalen House I thought, I'll lie low, away from all of them. I'll nurture this baby. I will make a decent interval between Berenger's death and the birth of our child. I will disconnect myself from Aaron, the person who gives Addam the most pain. When the baby is born it will be born to me, Nile Kirk, not to the former personal assistant of Aaron Karsner and his wife. Addam will forget that I was ever the flunkey who ran Berenger's evil little errands. I will be the mother of his child. When he looks into the clear blue eyes of the tiny soul that is the mirror of him, Addam won't help but love it, and me.

Ayesha was still missing on Thursday morning.

I had spent the night crouched on the end of my bed, playing over and over again in my head the scene of Addam in Berenger's room, leaning over her, his black curly hair, his faceless face. No matter how hard I tried, I couldn't see his face.

All I could see was Berenger's little baby, floating in its sac of blood-streaked fluid, drifting away into the sky in an embryonic balloon, getting smaller and smaller until it was no bigger than a speck.

I saw clearly that it was a girl. A little girl who would have soon been wearing miniskirts and feather boas and smoking Marlboro Lights. A little girl who, in that ever-decreasing moment between babyhood and womanhood, would play with Barbies, pop bubblegum, guzzle vodka with her cranberry juice, devour *True Romance* magazines, be wooed with Krispy Kremes and dried roses, bestow efficient blow-jobs on teenage boys, run away from home with the family savings account and end up dead in a basement near the airport with a dozen Filipino mail-order brides...

I knocked on Ayesha's door for the twentieth time that afternoon. Bernadette stuck her head into the corridor.

'Hey, Nile, quit it will you? She's obviously not there. You're frightening the rabbits.'

'Do you know where she is, then?'

'How would I know? Probably out canoodling with that new boyfriend of hers. I saw them the other night.'

'You did? When?'

'I don't know. Wednesday?'

'But she's been gone two nights.'

'Lucky her.'

Bernadette slammed her door, which must have made the rabbits she had rescued from a pharmaceutical lab over in Paterson jump out of their furry little skins without the assistance of a vivisectionist.

I couldn't sit in my room another night and think of Ayesha

with Kevin. Think of the things he might be doing to her. I suppose I should have called the police, but I'd had enough of them. But they hadn't had enough of me, as it turned out.

It's not difficult to find out someone's address when you have their name and telephone number. Directory assistance was very obliging. I waited nervously until I thought Kevin would be home from work and then hailed a taxi that had pulled up to deposit someone at Magdalen House.

The driver pulled into a side road that runs parallel to the airport freeway. It was dark and the streets weren't well marked and we took a few false turns, which made the cabbie wild because he had already boasted of his encyclopaedic knowledge of the New York suburbs.

Eventually, we found the right address. I asked the driver to go past it and stop on the next corner. It was cold, but I didn't want to arrive with headlights blaring. I really didn't have a plan. All I thought of was how relieved Ayesha would be to see me. I paid the driver and he gunned his Ford and sped off. I wouldn't have wanted to have hung around there either. It was too quiet. The street was wide and lined by shabby wooden houses and small front yards that spilled right into the gutter. In summer there were probably leaves on the trees and children playing with the inflatable swimming pools and plastic tricycles discarded on the lawns, but now, after several months of winter, it all looked forlorn.

Kevin's house was exactly as I imagined, anonymous and barren. It was pale yellow in the street light and the paint was starting to bubble and peel, like festering cream. Kevin was obviously not a handyman. The lawn on the front yard was bald and there was a row of ugly bushes planted beside the crumbling steps and underneath the aluminium windows. A plastic supermarket bag was caught on one of them. There was a hole the size of a fist in the wire door. Maybe a fist made it, judging by the look of the neighbourhood.

The house looked dark, except for a dim porch light. I lingered outside the house next door, wondering what to do, until a light went on and someone opened the wire screen to peer at me. There wouldn't be many strollers on a night like this. I looked at my watch, pretending I was waiting for someone, and the wire door closed. Then, decided, I marched straight up to Kevin's porch and put my finger on the doorbell, mentally preparing a speech. But no-one answered. I kept my finger on the bell—more of a buzz really—until it was evident no-one was coming. But that didn't mean there wasn't anyone inside.

Fallen twigs on the lawn snapped under my feet as I went round the side of the house to investigate other windows. A dog rattled a chain in another yard but fortunately didn't bark. The lights all appeared to be off. It crossed my mind I should have brought a torch, a flashlight, but I didn't expect to be lurking around the house peeping in windows.

What I was actually looking for was a cellar of some kind, a place where Kevin might practise his deviant acts. A quiet place where no-one could hear the sounds of young women screaming.

My toe kicked something wooden and I bent down to examine it in the hope it was a trapdoor of some kind, but it was just an old box of rotten leaves which left mulch on my gloves. I brushed them off. Then I noticed a vent in the timber cladding, close to the ground. I was thinking about how to get closer to it without getting muddy when a car door slammed on the street. A moment later I saw Kevin briskly crossing the lawn. Alone. I shrank back in the bushes like a stalker in a horror movie. Well, this was a horror movie. And it would be more horrible if I didn't get Ayesha out of there.

Kevin seemed to be carrying groceries in one arm but I couldn't really make much out in the dark. After a few steps he went out of view. I heard the front door close softly and after a minute a light came on in the window over my head. I ducked down. There was the sound of running water and cutlery being rattled. Was he making Ayesha's last meal? Or was he making a meal of *her*?

I decided not to wait too long. I needed an element of surprise. He probably had an arsenal of weapons stashed in the hall cupboard which he took out and lovingly polished every night. Besides, it was freezing out in the yard. I'd worn gloves, but not a hat, and my ears felt like ice chips.

I scampered around the perimeter of the yard until I reached the front steps. I took a deep breath and pressed the doorbell again. This time, I heard footsteps and then some shuffling. Kevin opened the door on a chain and then peeped out. The door closed and then he opened it wide. He was wearing a dark grey sweatsuit with some kind of coat of arms on it. There was a silver oven mitt in the shape of a fish on one hand.

'Yes?' He peered at me, sheltering his eyes from the porch lamp.

'Hello, Kevin,' I said brightly, not to arouse suspicion. 'It's me, Nile.'

'Nile?' he rolled the word on his tongue.

'Ayesha's friend.'

'Oh, yeah,' he said, sounding relieved. He probably thought I was some social worker come to check up on a runaway teenage girl. Or boy.

'Can I come in?'

'Why?' he asked, looking bewildered. 'You got lost in the neighbourhood or something?'

'It's about Ayesha.'

He wiped his mitt-less hand vigorously on his hip. Then it dawned on him. 'Nothing has happened to her, has it?'

'I thought you might be able to answer that. Is she here?'

'Why would she be here?'

'Why wouldn't she be here? She isn't anywhere else.'

'Oh, I get it.'

'You do?'

'You're looking for her and you think she might be here?'

'Well, is she?'

'No way. Ayesha's a young lady. It wouldn't be decent to have her here at night.'

'Can I come in?'

'Look…I'm busy.'

'It's cold out here.'

'Then I'll call the car service. They come real fast.'

'Kevin, I have just driven all the way from Manhattan in a cab. It set me back thirty-three dollars. I'm not going back there until you talk to me…If you don't invite me in I'll scream.'

'All right, all right,' he said, unlocking the wire door. 'But only for a minute. I've just put dinner on.'

And he had. He led me down a hallway to a scrupulously tidy kitchen with pine stools around a bench. Over the sink, brown tiles alternated with ones depicting scenes of peasants baking bread or scything hay. There was a bright orange electric kettle on the bench and a single mustard-coloured plastic mug standing next to it with a teabag dangling from the rim. Something was sizzling in the oven. A hastily discarded Weight Watchers lasagne box was lying on the bench next to a stack of neatly ironed and folded kitchen towels. A strange thing for a big man to be eating. Was it for him or the prisoner in the cellar?

Kevin pulled out a stool and motioned for me to sit on it. 'I don't know why you're here, Nile. I have no idea where Ayesha is.' He bent over and poked at the meal in the oven with a fork. There was a giant mole on his white skin where the sweatshirt and sweatpants separated.

'Aren't you worried about her?'

He stood up and wiped his forehead with a towelling cloth. 'You say she's missing?'

'She hasn't been home for two days. You don't know anything about that?'

'Why would I?' But I thought he said this nervously, fidgeting with the towel.

'Well, I thought she might have mentioned something to you about where she was going.'

'Look, I don't know why you think that, Nile. She's got a right to do what she likes.' He cast a furtive glance over my shoulder at the doorway. I turned, but there was no-one there.

'She's been gone two days.'

'Two days? You're sure she hasn't gone…shopping?'

'Not Ayesha. Ayesha only goes to Century 21 and they haven't seen her.'

'I see,' Kevin pulled out a stool for himself. 'What about the woman she works for? Does she know?'

'I haven't actually asked her. But she's been at the hospital. Her son's very sick.'

'I'm sorry to hear that. But I don't see how I can help.'

'Kevin, you don't sound very concerned for someone whose fiancee has just disappeared into thin air.'

I suppose I did say this a bit loudly. Kevin's eyes darted about nervously. 'Can you keep your voice down?'

'Why?'

'The neighbours…' He wasn't very convincing. He'd worked up a sweat, too, and I was sure it wasn't just from the oven.

'Who else is here, Kevin?' I got up from my stool. 'Tell me that. Who else is here?'

'No-one.'

I walked over to the kitchen door. 'Why don't I believe you?' I looked into the hallway. There was a reproduction mahogany side table with a dried flower arrangement on it. Above it hung a painting of junks against a sunset on Hong Kong harbour. Through the hallway was a room with a door slightly ajar. I could make out the arm of a sofa and a pile of magazines on a coffee table.

'Look…young lady. I don't know what you think you're doing—' Kevin was saying as I moved quickly in the direction of the room across the hall.

I flung the door to the room wide open before he could stop me. But I was disappointed: apart from an ancient tabby cat which hissed at me when I disturbed its sleep, there was no-one there. Everything was extremely neat. There was no sign of a struggle, no scattered cushions, no spilled glasses, no tell-tale high-heel shoe peeping out from beneath the skirt of the sofa. But the magazine on the side table was *Good Housekeeping*. Perhaps he bought women's magazines to keep his prisoners occupied. I wondered where he kept his pornography.

Kevin was right behind me. 'You've no business barging in here,' he said indignantly and grabbed my arm. His forearm was a strong as a girder on a bridge, but he let go when I pulled away.

'Where's your cellar…basement?' I demanded.

'Why do you want my basement?' He had his arms folded across his chest, defiantly. He looked like a genie in a cartoon.

'Not to look at your wine collection that's for sure,' I told him. And then I followed his eyes to a small yellow door at the end of the room.

'I want you to leave,' he said, calmly.

'Through that door?' I pointed to the other side of the room and bolted for it. I flipped up the catch before he could stop me. I was confronted by a staircase that fell away in the dark.

I started down it. 'Ayesha!'

The light overhead snapped on and I could hear Kevin following me. 'I don't know what you think you're doing,' he called after me, 'There's nothing down there.'

I reached the bottom of the stairs and pushed the door in. The room was black, but the light from the staircase pooled in the entrance and I could see a switch. I flicked it up and two fluorescent lights in the ceiling stuttered to life.

'Ayesha?' I called, but I could see she wasn't there.

I walked into the room. It was a gym. A rowing machine, a treadmill, free weights. Golf clubs in a corner, trophies on a wall, a few bottles of wine on a wooden rack beside the door. Next to the rowing machine there was a copy of *Sports Illustrated*. On one wall, a rifle hooked into a rack. There were no doors leading anywhere, that I could see.

I turned to Kevin. 'Where is she?'

'I've been trying to tell you. She's not here.'

'But there's someone else in this house. I can feel it.'

He looked sheepish. 'Yeah, my mother.'

'Your *mother*?'

'She's upstairs in the bedroom. She's asleep. I hope.'

'Well, why didn't you say?'

'You didn't ask.' He made a sour face.

'But what about all the secrecy?'

'I haven't told mother about Ayesha yet.'

I suddenly saw. And I saw even more. 'You want Ayesha to marry you so you've got someone to look after your mother!'

'Now look, you've got it all wrong. I proposed to Ayesha because she is a very lovely woman. Who do you think you are, making accusations like that?'

But I didn't believe him. 'I was right! You *did* target her. You saw her on television and you thought, "Poor thing, she'll do anything for a roof over her head. She'll even marry me and clean my mother's bedpan." '

'I think it would be very offensive to her if you suggested that. In the first place my mother—'

'You proposed to Ayesha after two dates! You hardly knew her!'

'Anyone could see straightaway that Ayesha has a beautiful soul.'

'That's rubbish, Kevin. She does have a beautiful soul but a man like you couldn't possibly see it.'

I'd struck a nerve. Literally. There was a large vein running across one eye and it started twitching. 'I think you better leave. Right now. Or I'll—'

'Or you'll what?' I suppose challenging him wasn't the smartest thing to do in the circumstances. I was in a basement of a quiet house in a suburb where the neighbours were clearly oblivious to each other's recreational pursuits. If Kevin did have a penchant for chainsawing Filipino mail-order brides into little morsels, he couldn't have picked a more suitable neighbourhood for wielding a noisy instrument. Even the backyard dogs couldn't work up much interest in an intruder like me.

But I had to admit that the murder and mutilation part of my Kevin scenario was looking very shaky. If there had been any kind of disembowelment and dismemberment in this room, then Kevin had to be an extremely fastidious cleaner to get it back to the innocuous shape it was in now. From the look of the rest of the house I thought this highly unlikely. And the mother would have to have heard the screams and pleadings—unless Kevin had her permanently drugged to the eyeballs. Which was always a possibility. Creeps were capable of anything. There had been no sound from above, not even the creaking of a floorboard or the coughing of phlegm into a handkerchief, the usual invalid sounds.

Kevin was grimacing at me, his teeth clenched and his neck muscles as rigid as struts holding up a wall. He looked like he was in the middle of a particularly rigorous thrust and jerk. His eyebrows had lifted right to his hairline. It was probably a very good time for me to leave.

But I stood my ground. Maybe Ayesha wasn't down there, but it was possible she was upstairs, that Kevin had been lying about his mother, that it was Ayesha up in the bedroom, her ankles and wrists tied to the four posts of the bed. The rape part of the Kevin scenario was still possible. Rape didn't make much mess, especially if you were in control of it from the start. I thought of that deserted shopping arcade and wiping myself down with my cardigan.

In his sloppy sweats, Kevin looked stronger than I'd thought. He had one of those beefy military bodies, tight sinews, muscles disciplined to flex away fat. He could overwhelm Ayesha in an instant. If she needed overwhelming. In fact, he could easily overwhelm me...

He stepped forward and grasped my wrist in his hand. It felt strong as a monkey wrench. I tried to twist away but he held on. 'Let me escort you out,' he said, coldly.

'I can go myself,' I said, trying to plot how I could break away from him and up to the bedroom.

'I don't think so,' he responded, and pulled me behind him up the stairs.

'Ow!' I protested, wriggling and rotating my trapped hand to no avail.

When we got to the top of the stairs, I tried another tactic. 'Look, Kevin,' I said, digging my heels in, so that he would have had to drag me, and trying to sound as reasonable as possible. 'I realise I've made a mistake.'

He stopped but kept hold of my wrist. 'You sure have.'

'I know Ayesha isn't here—'

But he didn't seem to be listening to me. He was looking right through me. '"A man like you," you said. A man like me. But what is a man like me, Nile? Do you know? Have you ever met a man like me? I lie awake at night thinking who a man like me could be. All you girls, we're not good enough for you, men like me. But still you can't say what is wrong with us. We're decent. We're healthy. We're not in the poor house—'

'Look, Kevin, I understand—' I was getting frightened now. His veins were dancing a rumba on his forehead. I could smell the pheromones being released on the surface of his skin.

'Do you?' he almost roared it, and I jumped. 'I don't think so.' He gripped my wrist tighter. I thought he was going to crack it. 'Snobs like you are the worst.'

'Snobs?' I gulped.

'Yeah, snobs, with your toffy accents and your uppity ways. You think you're better than me because you know some guy in a tuxedo who can show you to a table ahead of a lot of other schmucks at the bar. That's better? As far as I can see all you do is lie in that hole of a place on 22nd Street and get fat. You haven't fought in a war or watched your father die of asbestos poisoning or held down any kind of a job that involved sweat and devotion—'

'You don't know anything about me—'

435

'Shut up! I know everything about you. I've met you before, in any damned Manhattan bar you could name. You're the one who won't talk to me when I sidle up next to you for a chat, just for a chat, because I'm not wearing the right kind of a suit or I'm not driving the right kind of a car or I don't have the right kind of mobile phone stuck to my,' he hesitated at the curse, 'my *fucking* ear. I feel invisible with girls like you.'

He let go of my wrist but grasped my shoulders and pushed me against the door jamb. The stairs fell away treacherously behind me. 'Kevin, I'm not like that.' I was trembling.

'I don't want to hear any more from you.' He shook me. 'You've done enough. You've made a woman who could make me very happy...doubt me. That is unforgivable. I know in the fullness of time I could make her happy too.' He relaxed his grasp and I managed to duck under his hands and move away a little.

'OK, I admit at first I was attracted to Ayesha because of her...injury,' he said, almost wistfully. 'I knew I would have a chance with a girl like that. The rest of you won't look at a guy with an income under a hundred grand. The first three questions a New York woman asks you are, What do you do? Where do you live? How much do you earn? And not necessarily in that order. But Ayesha didn't care about any of that. She didn't demand anything—restaurants, flowers, gifts. Those stupid donuts were all she ever wanted! She charmed the socks off me right from the start.' He smiled at a private joke.

'Look, Kevin, I was only trying to protect Ayesha. I'm her friend.'

He narrowed his eyes and took a step towards me. I edged away along the wall a few inches. 'Protect her? You couldn't bear for her to have a man who would provide for her when you didn't, that's the truth of it, isn't it? I could see what kind of friend you were from the start. I tried to tell her, this girl isn't so great for you, Ayesha. She's nothing, a nobody, and she's hanging around you because your sad life makes her feel good. She wouldn't listen to me, she defended you. Nile isn't like that. Nile is kind. Ayesha has too sweet a nature to see any evil in the world. But I've got tabs on you—'

'This is all ridiculous!'

He reached out before I could stop him and cupped my chin in his big hand. I jerked my head, but it wasn't any good. He pulled me away from the wall, so that I was facing him where he stood at the top of the stairs. 'Look at you, Miss Plain Jane, barging in here all mud-splattered and thinking you're going to save Ayesha—from what? From a man who might love her and want to look after her? That would be a fate worse than death to you, wouldn't it?'

I tried to lunge at him, but he stepped back. He dropped his hand from my chin to my upper arm. His fingers gouged my flesh. 'This is how you expect me to act, isn't it? You think because I don't wear nancy-boy clothes I'm some kind of animal. I can see how your spinsterish mind works, getting into a lather about Ayesha being out here with me, what we're doing together…'

But I wasn't listening to him. My arm was hurting but the pain was only a circle around my thoughts.

I had almost felt sympathetic with him, back there. Back when he said, I feel invisible with girls like you.

But then he blew it. 'Look at you, Miss Plain Jane, barging in here all mud-splattered…'

I will not be called Plain Jane. It is not my name.

ran from the house into the dark street, the wet bottom of my coat flapping at my ankles. Behind me, a light went on somewhere in Kevin's house, illuminating the mangy bushes outside. I turned into the side road and ran parallel to the freeway. There was no hope of any taxis there. I slowed down and caught my breath. At the end of one of the cross streets I saw a fluorescent sign, probably a convenience store. I headed in that direction. But before I got there, a taxi pulled up and deposited an old man at a house that still had its Christmas lights blazing. As he hobbled up a path arched with angels blowing trumpets, I nabbed the cab.

I sat low in the back seat and let the reflection of the outside world wash over me. I took off my gloves and threw them out the window. The outsides of them felt sticky to the touch.

The driver was heavy-footed and we alternately sped and screeched to a halt all the way to Manhattan. Even in the dark I could make out the hundreds of thousands of tombstones that covered the hills of Queens—somewhere out there, Harry Houdini was buried. Houdini had always promised his many fans that he'd come back from the dead. But dozens of seances conducted over ten years by his wife, Bess, failed to bring even a shimmer of him. The greatest illusionist of all time could not manage the greatest illusion of all. Berenger had easily outclassed him. I wondered if he were up in heaven, his nose pressed against the window of life, trying to get back in.

I went to my room and fell on my bed. I must have gone to sleep like that, in my coat, flat on my back.

I didn't wake up until the cold morning light cast a blue hue on the room and there was an insistent tapping on the door. I struggled up off the bed and realised I still had my coat on. The steam heat had come back on hours ago and I was as clammy as if I'd spent the night in the tropics. I struggled out of the coat and threw it on a chair.

I must have still been half-asleep when I opened the door. 'Berenger?' I asked, hopefully.

It was Ayesha, standing there in her jeans with her fuzzy handbag over one arm.

If I was shocked to see her, she was registering equal shock at my appearance. 'Nile! What happened to you? What happened to your feet?'

I looked down and my cream wool tights were soaked dark red in patches. 'Oh, Christ,' I said and closed the door on her.

Ayesha started thumping harder on the door. 'Nile!'

I pulled off my boots and rolled down my tights. I screwed them into a bundle and threw them into the waste basket under the bathroom sink. As I bent to stand up again I caught my reflection in the mirror. My cheeks were vivid spots of pink, my hair the kind of rats' nest that only vigorous back-combing can achieve. I looked like I'd spent the last twenty-four hours in the crawl space under a building, with the rest of the vermin.

I tried to flatten my hair and splashed my face with water. Ayesha's thumps were probably attracting attention from the other tenants. I went to the door, opened it narrowly and pulled her into the room.

'Nile?' she asked me, alarmed.

'Where have you been?' I yelled at her, as a parent might a child who has been out past curfew. I had that same paradoxical mix of anger and relief at seeing her alive again. 'Visiting cousin Revi at his restaurant. Why?'

439

'What do you mean, why? You weren't at work Wednesday. Where were you last night? I've gone half mad worrying about you!'

Ayesha looked at me with innocent eyes. 'Oh, Nile, I am sorry. But I told you last week. I told you that cousin Revi offered me a job at his restaurant. Not in the kitchen this time. But behind the counter, taking orders. You don't remember? I went yesterday to see…if I could do this job. And I think I can. I think it's not so hard. The hours are long, but I can sleep at the back. And when I am married I can stop. So it is agreed. I start one week from next Monday…Nile, are you ill?'

Did Ayesha tell me this? About cousin Revi's 5th Street restaurant? I truly couldn't remember.

'And what happened to your clothes? You had red on your legs. And I can see…splodges of it on the bottom of your skirt. Did someone hurt you, Nile?'

She stepped towards me with a hand outstretched gingerly. I backed away automatically.

'What is it? Has something terrible happened?' She looked frightened.

'No, nothing terrible,' I lied. 'Everything is perfect.'

I made an attempt to smile. It must have been a good attempt because Ayesha beamed back at me. 'Oh, I am so glad you feel that way! I knew you would be pleased. And I know you will soon come to…what is the expression?…hit it? with Kevin. It is only a matter of time.'

After Ayesha left, I folded up my skirt and took my tights out of the bin and put them in a plastic bag. I thought that perhaps I should get rid of them. I wasn't experienced at this. I shoved the bag under my bed. And then I took it out again. Should I find a garbage can on the street and dispose of it? I looked out the window at the bleak street. There was hardly anybody about in this weather, even though it was a Friday afternoon. I squeezed the offending articles into my shoulder bag and shut the bedroom door quietly behind me.

I walked for hours, through Hell's Kitchen and the theatre district, then down past Murray Hill and the East Village to the seaport and back up through SoHo and Greenwich Village to Chelsea. In the end I threw the incriminating plastic bag into a dumpster only a block from Magdalen House. When I finally dragged myself back to the hostel, it was after seven. Ayesha was sitting in the solitary chair in the lobby, in a dress I'd never seen before, her hands folded in her floral lap, waiting for Kevin.

I took my suitcase from the top of the wardrobe and opened it on the bed. It was plain to me I couldn't stay there any longer. I had made myself vulnerable. Everything I had done I had done to protect someone I loved. Addam. Ayesha. My baby. But no-one would believe me. Like they didn't believe me about little Lizzie Westbrook. They took her off me and they'd take Ayesha and Addam too. I had to get out of there. I'd find another room in another house. Under the Manhattan Bridge, perhaps, so I could be close to him.

Idly, I turned on the television set while I packed. Of all the channels on my dysfunctional little set, Channel 7 was the worst. The picture shimmered and fragmented like a polygraph when the subject is not telling the truth. So, when I first turned to get some underwear out of a drawer and saw Aaron's face on the tiny set, I didn't recognise him, distracted as I was by his kinetic eyebrows that vibrated all over the screen. But the word 'Berenger' made me stop my packing and peer intently at the image: four Barbara Walters holding a conversation with a quadruplicate guest.

I dropped what I was doing and sat back on my heels in front of the set. It was Aaron, all right. When the eyebrows calmed down, I could make out the high forehead, the strong nose, the chin still stubbornly delineated from the folds of skin draping his throat. Framed by the screen, he looked more like a Marcel Duchamp painting than a person. But there was one thing I could tell despite the sputtering dialogue and the splintering shapes: Aaron was not grieving.

Of course he looked suitably mournful. He was sitting low on a leather couch with his knees crossed and his hands clasped in his lap. He was dressed, fastidiously, in a grey formal suit with a white shirt and a wide, light-coloured satin tie. There was something in his breast pocket, perhaps a flower or the points of a handkerchief, and its multiple images fluttered across the television screen like a dove in flight.

Six weeks ago, when I last closed the door on him, he seemed so deeply anguished I was sure his heart could not bear the strain. But now, there was a sparkle about him he couldn't quite repress. And he looked a long way from death like he had been miraculously cured of a wasting disease.

Barbara's voice crackled and I couldn't make out what she was saying at first. I crawled closer to the set, right in front of it, my eyes only a few inches away, and touched the screen with my hands, scrutinising every wavy line for a gesture that might reveal something true about Aaron. And then, the elements took pity on me. Whatever weather pattern had played havoc with my television reception suddenly receded. The sound flared and then levelled out.

The interviewer looked at Aaron with big moist eyes. Her brimming, sympathetic smile was almost a grimace. 'Shall we talk about Berenger?'

Aaron nodded sombrely.

'What do you miss most about her?'

'Oh, her unpredictability!' He made an attempt at a smile. 'She was such a bright little thing. I lived a very monastic life, you know, just me and my piano, and I was getting stuck in my ways. Berenger turned everything upside down, of course, but that kept me on my toes.'

'We've read so much about her in the magazines, but I find it very hard to get a sense of what she was really like. Some words come to mind. Spoiled? Was she spoiled?'

'Naturally…the kind of profession she was in, it was difficult not to be. She was very beautiful, you know, and beautiful women, in my experience, are always spoiled.'

'Here's another word: intelligent. Was she intelligent?'

'She had her own kind of intelligence. I would say, more than intelligent, she was…clever.'

'Affectionate?'

'Well, certainly.'

'But you were apart a good deal?'

'We had a very modern marriage.'

'A happy one?'

'You know, Barbara, I don't exactly believe in happiness. It is mostly elusive.'

'You *don't*? With the life you've had? All the successes and awards? Surely you've been happy some of the time?'

'Oh, yes, I have been happy. But what I meant to say was this—you shouldn't look for happiness. You'll only be disappointed. It can never live up to expectations. As to my marriage with Berenger, I don't want you to think we were in any way *un*happy. We adored each other. It's simply that we didn't have stars in our eyes.'

'What I wanted to ask was, what did you give her and what did she give you? It must have been a very extraordinary relationship.'

'It was…extraordinary. But it was so short. I like to think I gave her a sense of permanence in her life, something…*rooted*. She needed that, you know. With all those flighty fashion people around her.'

'And what did she give you?'

'Oh, much, much more love than I deserved.'

'How do you feel when you read all the speculation that she married you on the rebound from your grandson, Addam Karsner? Does it hurt you?'

'I'm too old to get hurt, and I've never particularly cared what other people think.'

'It's no secret that you and Addam aren't close.'

'We have our differences. Mostly artistic.'

'In an interview in *Spin* magazine in 1996 he said he never felt he really knew you—that you were remote during his childhood.'

'Most grandparents are remote, I think. All I can remember of my grandfather was that he was very stern. I think that's fairly usual. Addam was raised by his mother on the west coast. They rarely came east.'

'Do you ever wonder what happened to your son, Kurt? He disappeared in 1970, didn't he?'

'Kurt had his own agenda.'

'Would you be surprised if he turned up on your doorstep tomorrow?'

'I long ago accepted that he was dead in a ditch somewhere. End of story.'

'Can you talk about Berenger's death?'

'If we have to.'

'The police say there was a fairly potent cocktail of drugs in her blood. Did you know about her drug taking?'

'She didn't take any illegal substances in my presence.'

'But surely there are signs…'

'Often the people closest to you are the last to know.'

'There has been a persistent rumour that Addam was with her that night.'

'Which he himself has denied.'

'But he was booked on a flight with her to Marrakech the next day.'

'Of course he was. I suggested it.'

'You did?'

'I couldn't go with her because of the deadline on my book and I thought she should have some…family with her.'

'Aaron, I don't want to broach another unhappy subject, but

I believe Berenger was pregnant. You've kept this quiet until now. Was there a reason?'

Aaron bowed his head. 'She told me two weeks before she died. It was early days. We were planning to tell everyone after three months, in case...' His voice cracked.

'I'm so sorry.'

'Yes, to lose one beautiful child is a tragedy, to lose two is...unspeakable.'

They went to a commercial break. I placed my cheek against the warm screen, on which a shiny black car was speeding along some circuitous European road.

My mind was doing loops with the car.

Aaron had asked Addam to look after Berenger? It hardly seemed possible. Why would he do that when he and Addam were barely talking? And if there was such an innocent explanation why had Addam denied it, as Ostrowsky said? Had Addam felt guilty about something?

I thought about the night when I'd kept Aaron downstairs while I pulled Addam out of Berenger's bed. Had Aaron really no idea at all about Addam's relationship with Berenger, after all those months? I had been a diligent double-agent, but he had other spies. Alison, for instance. She knew about my pregnancy...

That damn car was still speeding around those mountainous hairpin bends. I felt woozy and closed my eyes. Did Aaron know about my baby, too? He knew about the doctor's visit. He might have put it all together. He would have felt betrayed by me, and yet he didn't say a word. I thought about that. I had found out one day and Berenger had died the next. There hadn't been time for anything.

But he sent Addam away with her, knowing she was having his baby. His baby. The ambiguity suddenly struck me. I felt every organ inside me twist into a knot. *Which* 'his'? Addam's or Aaron's? What if Aaron suspected the baby was Addam's? What if the baby *was* Addam's? It was possible. In fact, I started to realise, with growing dismay, it was probable. I'd had one night with him and look what had happened to me. Berenger's chances would have been magnified by a dozen. At least. Why hadn't I thought of it before? Because, I sadly concluded, I had felt the rush of being the only pregnant woman on earth. And Berenger was a child. How could she have a baby?

And Addam didn't want a baby. I know it. *'I don't want to know about the baby,'* he had said. *'I don't ever want to know about the baby.'*

But he had said *the* baby. Not *a* baby. I turned so that the back of my head rested against the television screen. I sat with my legs crumpled underneath me, trying to remember. Addam had not wanted the baby. *I had nothing to do with it,* he had said. But he'd had everything to do with our baby. Was it possible he was talking about Berenger's? Had she gone to him and told him first?

I had to concentrate.

I thought now of how skittish Berenger was the morning that I had gone to see Dr Gropp. She had seemed distracted when I explained I had my 'annual check-up' with the gynaecologist. 'What would he have to check *you* for?' she had asked listlessly. It was plain she had other things on her mind and I was glad of it. She had made some excuse about 'hanging out' with Darien all afternoon and I was too nervous about my own appointment to wonder why she changed outfits about a dozen times that morning when she was just going to sit around Darien's apartment gossiping and drinking her latest craze, caffeinated water. When she left the house it wasn't in her usual dark denim jeans, tight sweater and trainers, but in a light floral dress that was totally inappropriate for the weather. She'd applied pink lipstick as shiny as vinyl as if she were going on a date. I suppose I might have wondered about that if I hadn't been so keen to shut the door on her.

I'd come back from the doctor and fallen asleep. Berenger must have gone to Addam then and told him about the baby. Before I could get to him and tell him about ours. Of the evil things she'd done deliberately to hurt me, this accidental little twist damaged me the most.

I became aware of Barbara Walters' rasping tones in the background. I threw my arms over my head to block my ears.

'Oh, Berenger,' I moaned. 'Why didn't you tell me?'

But she didn't answer.

I'd heard her throwing things around in her room when I'd woken at six that night. I thought it was just the usual tantrum. But what if Addam had told her he didn't want the baby? What if he didn't believe it was his? *It's nothing to do with me*, he had said to me. He might have believed that the baby was Aaron's or Christophe's or any of the shadows he suspected she played with. Or possibly he did believe her but wanted her to get rid of it. They must have wrangled over it for hours. Perhaps she threw an ashtray at him at one point. He might have shaken her until she screamed. Certainly the little bruises his fingers could have made were there on her arms when she died.

Whatever happened between them, Addam didn't want that baby. And then I came along, ecstatic, uncomprehending, and thought it was my baby he didn't want.

I rubbed my eyes. Addam had misunderstood me! He thought I'd been talking about Berenger. Which meant he didn't know I was pregnant. He *still* didn't know I was pregnant. He hadn't rejected my baby at all. If I could reach him, explain to him…but he was in Europe.

I struggled to my feet. As I did, I saw Aaron's face on the television screen, looking directly at me. I put a hand on the screen. Aaron would know. If Berenger had given up on me, I would ask Aaron. He would know whose baby it was. And at least I knew where *he* was.

once again stood on Central Park West and looked up to the balcony of Aaron's eleventh-floor terrace in the San Remo. It was easy to think of Berenger as the petulant Rapunzel who once lived here and let down her hair to every passing prince. I'd had a sleepless night, anxious to confront Aaron, but terrified of him. He would despise me now. Not only had I deserted him but he would have realised by now what I'd done to his manuscript. He would know that I was in Addam's camp, if those posters in my room hadn't already told him. *I've done a terrible disservice to you, Nile.* But hadn't it been me who had done the disservice to him? I'd reacted angrily to his cruelty to Addam and forgotten all his kindnesses to me. And yet, something in me was not repentant. Aaron was not telling the truth and I needed to know why.

Somewhere in me I found the courage to enter the lobby. The doorman on duty was delighted. 'Miss Nile!' he said in his Italian-accented Brooklyn drawl. 'Long time no see!'

'Too long,' I told him. 'But I'm back.'

'Tell you the truth, I'm worried about Mr Karsner. He don't come out much.'

'I'm here to fix that,' I said, and dangled the set of door keys I'd kept since we moved.

He beamed at me and called the elevator.

When I put the keys in the door I expected resistance. If Aaron had become a recluse he had probably fastened the security chain and maybe even moved some furniture across the door. But the key turned as smoothly as it ever did and the door glided open over the thick hallway carpet.

The hallway looked the same, with its scattering of small Persian rugs, the framed theatre programs along the walls, the vase of fresh oriental lilies on the ebony-inlaid deco side table. What did I expect? A layer of dust an inch thick? Crumbling flower arrangements? Cobwebs strung from chandelier to chair? Aaron appearing in his bridal gown, gibbering?

It was about ten in the morning and I could hear Chopin coming from the direction of the sitting room. If Aaron was still working on the book, he was probably having a break to read the newspaper. I could smell coffee grounds and toast. There was the clinking of spoon against porcelain and the faint murmur of voices. This momentarily startled me. I hadn't expected voices. But maybe Frances was back after all. That would explain the immaculate hall and the domestic sounds and smells from the kitchen. I was suddenly overwhelmed with a dizzy kind of happiness, that things were precisely as they were before Berenger, before she entered our lives and shattered our peace.

I turned right into the sitting room and through that I could see clearly into the dining area, where Aaron was indeed seated, with the newspaper folded on his lap. He was in his tartan robe, the one with the black velvet collar, and he was holding a cup to his lips. I expected to see Frances come from the direction of the kitchen with a tray, but I was stunned to see that it was Lilian who entered the room, with the coffee pot, to top up Aaron's cup.

It was not so much the shock of Lilian being there at that hour—I don't think I'd ever seen her before dark—but the fact that she looked so *cosy* there with him, pouring his coffee and adjusting the pillow at his back so that he could sit more comfortably.

I was going to turn on my heels, but Lilian looked up then. She was startled, but not embarrassed. She made no attempt to stop pouring the coffee until she was finished. She kept her eyes on me and put down the coffee pot. 'We have a visitor, Aaron,' she said evenly.

Aaron followed her gaze to me. He jumped up from his chair, dropping the newspaper at his feet and using the back of the chair to steady himself. 'Good God, Nile! What are you doing here?'

Not so easy a question to answer: why was I there? 'I...I saw you on Barbara Walters last night.'

Lilian stood up straight and frowned at me. 'You've got a nerve coming here. You might have called first, and we would have told you not to bother. I don't understand why didn't they let us know downstairs that you were coming up.'

I waved the keys at her.

'Aaron?' Lilian looked at him. I imagine she thought she was the only one with a set of keys to the place.

'Nile always had her own keys.'

'Well, I think she should hand them back. After the way she brutalised your work and then walked out on you.'

'And left him to *you*,' I pointed out. She could at least be grateful.

'Why don't you sit down?' Aaron suggested and gestured to a chair beside him at the table.

'Thank you, Aaron,' I said, pointedly avoiding Lilian's antagonistic gaze. If Lilian hadn't been there in that frowzy velour jogging outfit it might have been just like old times, Aaron running through the plans for the day with me while he finished his breakfast.

'Did you bring the manuscript with you?' Lilian said sharply before I could even sit. 'You had a nerve, you know. It set us back quite a bit.'

'Now, Lilian,' said Aaron.

'Well, I don't know who she thinks she is, rewriting your life like that. The child has a problem with reality.'

'I do not,' I protested. 'You're the person who spends most of your life stuck in a theatre with grown adults playing make-believe.'

'Nile, enough. We wondered where you went until that police-woman told us.'

'It wasn't very far, Aaron,' I said.

'You're lucky we didn't set the police on you,' Lilian sniffed. 'We chose not to press charges.'

'Come on, Lilian,' Aaron said. 'Nile has come to see us now. She must have something to say.'

Lilian raised a mangy eyebrow. 'I'm all ears.'

'This is between Aaron and me,' I said.

'Go on, Lilian,' Aaron said. 'I'm sure what Nile has to say will only take a minute.'

She looked like she was going to protest but Aaron gave her a look that said, 'Don't you dare.'

'If you're sure,' she said ungraciously. 'I have some things to do in your office then.'

'Good,' I said to myself, except I knew she could hear.

About Aaron, I wasn't so certain. He was sitting again, looking at me expectantly. I noticed a vein twitching over his left eye. And he was tugging at his right ear.

'Since when did Lilian start working with you?' I asked when she was out of earshot.

'She's been a very great help, Nile.' Before I could say anything, he added, 'You did leave, you know.'

'I panicked.'

'We were all panicked, Nile. At my age, to have death in the house…I was devastated, as you know.' He held my gaze in his, alert to where the conversation might be going.

'You didn't take long to recover.'

'When you've got as little time left as I have, you try not to spend too much of it deeply depressed.'

'I would imagine that it wouldn't be difficult to be depressed, though, with Lilian jabbering in your ear all day.'

Aaron coloured. 'Why are you here, Nile?'

'I want to know what happened.'

'You know what happened.'

'With Berenger? No I don't. With Addam? No I don't. In the beginning I felt sorry for you, the way Berenger behaved. But now I'm not so sure.'

'I wouldn't feel sorry if I were you.'

'Why did you ask Addam to go with her? On that trip? You threw them together.'

'Is that all that's troubling you, Nile?'

'No, it's not all. But it's a start.'

'I didn't ask him to go with her.' He smiled at me.

'You told Barbara Walters—'

'Of course I told her that. Wouldn't you have? We were on national television. It was an irrefutable fact that Addam was booked on that plane. I didn't want to look like a cuckolded husband.'

'But you were. You were a cuckolded husband.'

'Yes, and I was grateful that you kept me informed of it.'

'I didn't say anything because I didn't want to hurt your feelings.'

'Then you would have been making a terrible mistake.'

'You don't care?'

'Of course I care, damn it! I don't like to be made out to be an old fool.'

'But that's all you care about? You wouldn't have cared if they were having an affair as long as they kept it secret?'

He didn't say anything.

'But you loved her.' I didn't know whether this was a statement or a question.

He didn't say anything.

'But you were devastated when she died.'

'It was a sordid death. Berenger could have been more considerate of my feelings. I'm an old man. I don't like to be reminded of such things.'

'But Aaron—she couldn't help it. It was an accident.'

'There was nothing accidental with Berenger. She fooled me into marrying her and took away a year of my life. And now

452

where are we? Still with the police sniffing around and the wretched newspapers drumming up scandals. Imagine what it's like to read speculation on page one about your ability to have sexual intercourse.'

'But you must have expected that when you married her?'

'I admit I was infatuated.'

'With her beauty.'

'Was it beauty? It was a…weakness on my behalf, I admit. Not since I'd met that empty-headed first wife of mine, Ada, had a young girl thrown herself at me like that. Oh, there were flirtatious actresses, always actresses, but they were more sophisticated than Berenger. And my two other wives had been so…formidable. She really was naive, you know, despite all that time spent in Europe. I found it touching. I thought she would be an elixir. A tonic for an ailing old man. She turned out to be…poison.'

'You told Barbara Walters—'

'Can you blame me for anything I told Barbara Walters? It has become my story now, not Berenger's. I have taken possession of it. She's not around to dispute it, is she? How do you think it would have played if I had admitted what a mistake I had made, that Berenger was whiny, manipulative, moronic—*nothing*? That was the worst of it. She was negligible. *Un peu de chose.* A trifle.'

I was horrified at the venom in his voice. 'Aaron, what are you saying? That you *hated* her? But—'

'But? You think because she was pretty and young I should be grateful for her?'

'I thought you were absolutely…besotted with her.'

'Like an old fool, you mean? I'm sure you weren't alone.'

'I never thought you were a fool.'

'You're not telling the truth, Nile. I was a fool. But she was more of a fool. Oh, maybe we could have coexisted happily if she had been content to be decorative. But she never shut up. God knows what she was talking about half the time, with all those "likes" and "cools" and—what was it?—oh, yes, "dopes". It was this is "dope" and that is "dope". I didn't know what in hell she was saying. I would ask her a question and she would say "whatever". *Whatever?* I remember one evening, after we'd been to a revival of *Mother Courage*, Armand Colon, the director of the production, which was very good by the way, sat in Sardi's bar with Berenger and very patiently explained to her about the McCarthy witch-hunts and Bertolt's testimony and, even though, of course, the rest of us knew the story intimately, had lived through those dark ages, Armand was telling it with such conviction and intensity we were all enthralled. But what was Berenger's comment? "Cool." And she said it with such...blankness, it sounded like a brush-off. Poor Armand, who had been enchanted with her at first, was devastated. She played her wretched computer game for the rest of the night. I never took her to the theatre again.'

'Surely you'd seen her enough before you married her to know what she was like? She used to visit you here. You must have had time alone.'

'Clearly not enough, my dear Nile. I thought because she liked me to play her my songs she had some...taste. It was vanity on my behalf. And I admit during our time together I was the one who did most of the talking. She seemed so interested. Perhaps she was, but she tired of me.'

'She did have the attention span of a tadpole.'

'But how did I miss that? In retrospect there were enough signs. Remember that first night with Addam? How abominable they were? I thought then, my grandson and his girlfriend are trash. Their culture is trash, their manners are trash, their future is trash. I only had to read a few pages of that terrible thing Addam had written, the thing he dared to think was good enough for the stage, to know the whole thing was meaningless. It was a self-indulgent dirge without any redemption. There was no elegance there. It wasn't even frivolous in an entertaining way. It was merely inane. It had no wit.'

'But Aaron, you're putting too much faith in wit.'

'I owe everything I have to it.'

'What I mean is, maybe Addam's trying to find something else. Maybe all the wit's been used up.'

'He has corrupted you, hasn't he?'

'What do you mean?'

'I saw it that night when I came into your room. Those posters on your wall. Like a silly teenager. He'd somehow insinuated himself into your...heart, was it, Nile?...your heart, just to get to me. And then I saw what you'd done with my manuscript, that stupid, exaggerated story he had told you, and everything became clear. He approached you somehow, didn't he? Maybe through Berenger? And he paid attention to you? Courted you, perhaps?'

'That wasn't it at all—'

'Oh, don't worry, Nile. I'm accusing myself...of neglecting you. I should never have let Berenger have you. Even a sensible girl like you is going to get carried away in that world. All those trips to Europe, the money thrown around, the celebrity circuit. I know it well. It's natural that you're going to lose a sense of yourself, the things that make you a good girl...intelligence, integrity, loyalty. I should have picked it up earlier and guided you. Instead, I let you get romantic notions about a young man who only hurt you.'

'Addam hasn't hurt me.'

'I think he has. Perhaps you can't see it right now. But you're carrying a lot of anger around. Some of it you are directing at me. And rightly so. I didn't protect you enough.'

'I didn't need protecting.'

'Don't be so defensive, Nile. You know, it hurt me more that you had a...what do you call it?...a *crush* on Addam than it did that my wife was carrying on with him.'

I could feel myself turning beet red. 'You make me feel like a schoolgirl. It wasn't a crush. It was mutual. Addam likes me.'

'I'm sure he does! And why not? You have some remarkable qualities. That's why, I admit, I felt let down by you. I'd given up on Berenger long before.'

'You did know they were having an affair all along.'

'Know? I suspected. It wasn't difficult to work out. Give me some credit. People said things…out of kindness, I'm sure. And, of course, I am aware Addam came to the house once or twice. He didn't come to visit me and he didn't come to visit you, did he?'

'Aaron, why do you say you felt let down by me? Because of Addam? Why weren't you happy for me? He's your grandson. We could…could have been a family.'

'Forgive me, Nile, I didn't realise how bad it was.'

The pitying look on his face made me angry. 'Why do you hate Addam so much? You've hated him since he was a child.'

'That's not true. I wouldn't listen to his fantasies if I were you. The only reason he limps is he has such a big chip on his shoulder.'

'But he was a little boy and you rejected him.'

'I did no such thing. His mother took him away. I sent them money.'

'But she wasn't any kind of mother. You must have known that. Why didn't you get custody when she went into rehab? Then he might have become the concert pianist you so badly wanted. You didn't give him a chance. And now you blame him…for something he didn't do.'

'I admit that certain things about his upbringing were not his fault. And in retrospect I might have tried harder to care for him. But do you know what, Nile? I didn't hate him. He hated *me*. Those eyes of his, they were always full of…well, at first they were full of fear and then they were full of *disgust*. Can you imagine an eight-year-old boy looking at his grandparent with disgust? That woman poisoned him. She made up some goddamn story about me driving Kurt away and the boy believed it. He blamed me for not having a father.'

'But didn't you try and talk to him? Explain that no-one knows what happened to Kurt? That it might have been an accident or—'

'I know what happened to Kurt, Nile.' He folded his hands on the table primly.

'You do? But in your book—'

'By now I thought you might have worked out not to trust the book.'

'But, Aaron, why haven't you said? Why have you kept it a secret?'

'I didn't keep it a secret. I sat Addam down when he was eight years old—after the accident—and told him. I wanted him to stop hating me. But it only made things worse.'

'How?'

'I loved Kurt, Nile. When his mother died he was all I had. But my third wife, Margaret, never took to him. I don't blame her, really, he was a small child when she came on the scene. I think she tried to love him, she was a very capable woman, but she put all her energy into my work. And really he was a trial! A very bright boy, never stopped talking, running around… he was strong-willed, impetuous, always getting into scrapes. And shrewd! He knew how to aggravate her. She talked me into putting him into boarding school, a very good one—his education was excellent. He was exceptional at mathematics. His teachers said it came from me, that skill in music and math often were linked. I was enormously proud of him. You can't imagine it! Things seemed to go well for a while, for a long while. There were no complaints from school, he was an exemplary student…'

He closed his eyes a moment and went on. 'Then something happened. I do not know to this day what it was. But one term, when he was about sixteen, he came home from school and he was sullen, resentful. Resentful of what? I couldn't understand it. This morose creature bore no resemblance to my energetic, enthusiastic son. Margaret tried talking to him, we sent him to a psychiatrist, we paid for a holiday in Europe. I suspected for a while it was a girl. That was the simple explanation, wasn't it? So I tried not to be too hard on him. But perhaps I should have been. He started to steal, you see, small things at school at first, escalating to objects and money from my friends' homes, I'm ashamed to say. I always replaced them. And then he devised an elaborate scheme for...well, one could only call it embezzlement. It was quite brilliant and quite complicated. But he was immature and he got the psychology of his victim wrong. The victim wouldn't let it go at me compensating him for what Kurt had...done. There were police involved. But it's easy for a man like me to pull strings. So there were no real consequences, except a fine and a rap on the knuckles. But it was all over the newspapers. And you know what, Nile? He was pleased about that. He cut out every single article and stuck them to his wall.'

'Was it drugs? Is that what happened? I've heard—'

'The drugs didn't happen until later. I don't think. But he never *took* drugs himself, Nile, not seriously.'

'But he sold them?'

'Oh, yes, it was his big scheme. Financed by me, I'm sorry to say. I thought I was investing in some invention of his, some new technology, a kind of tape, cassette, I don't know. I didn't pay too much attention. I was glad he was using his brain at last.'

'What about Baby?'

'He met her much later. By then, I knew what he was doing, with the drugs. He'd moved out of home when he was eighteen. I wouldn't see him from one year to the next. He preferred some Lower East Side dump to what we had up here.'

I thought of Addam then in his modest loft.

'He was often away. I believe he toured with some of the bands he supplied. I can't say what his state of mind was. I can only think that he was totally unstable by then. Although I don't know unstable is the word for it. Warped, perhaps.'

'You didn't try to help him?'

'Haven't I made that clear, Nile? I couldn't help him. What I had—money, influence—was the opposite of what he wanted. I had to back away...'

'There was the matter of your reputation, too.'

'I can see you think I was only thinking of myself, my work. But you have to understand, Kurt made a very definite choice. In many ways he was stronger than I was. I am an artist and he was a...calculator. He made a choice to kill himself and there was nothing I could do about it.'

I was shocked. 'Kill himself? Is that what he did?'

Aaron nodded. He breathed out deeply. 'He came to me one night, out of the blue. I was actually having a soiree at home, after *Promises Promises*. He took me aside and told me he was having a baby with some woman and that he was going to kill himself. He was going to kill himself because of the baby. Of course I got very upset and told him he couldn't ruin a beautiful life just because some slut hadn't taken the proper precautions. And he said it was his fault, that he had wanted a baby, that it was the most dangerous—that's what he said, *dangerous*—thing he could think of to do in life, having a baby, but now he had changed his mind. I naturally suggested an abortion, it was the rational thing to do in the circumstances, but he said he couldn't kill his child, even if he didn't want it. It sounds now like he was quite mad, Nile, quite mad, but in fact he sounded completely sane. This is what I did and this is why I did it and this is why I think I was wrong and this is what I'm going to do about it.

'And I couldn't deny him anything...even this. He'd thought it all through. He told me that I had to buy the woman health insurance because she was estranged from her family—it was a well-known west coast family, I'd actually heard of her father when Kurt mentioned his name—and I had to be responsible for the child, even if it didn't look like a Karsner. He was very insistent that the baby was his. But you know, all this protesting—I didn't think he was sure. And so I said I would, to humour him, because I didn't really believe he would go through with it. "Don't worry," he said, as he was leaving, "it won't make the newspapers." I thought he meant the birth, but of course he meant the death. I never saw him again. He went away somewhere remote and did it. Probably the mountains, a gun through the mouth, that would have been Kurt, grizzly bears devouring the evidence. He would have made sure they never found his body...to torture me.'

'And you told Addam this story?'

'An edited version.'

'But you told Addam that Kurt killed himself because of him? Because he was going to be born?'

'I didn't want Addam to think it was because of me.'

'And you didn't expect Addam to hate you for telling him?'

'I wanted him to hate Kurt, not me.'

'Aaron, I can see it now. Addam has spent his whole life thinking he killed his father. Because you told him so. And he didn't. He didn't kill him. How could he have? But he's lived with that idea all his life. You've made a beautiful, sweet and talented boy think he's some kind of criminal. You've twisted more than his knee. I'd hate you for that too.'

'I can see you're just like Berenger.' His eyes were hard as marbles. You could almost hear them scratching around in the dry sockets as he examined me.

'How?'

'He has cast a spell on you.'

aron was grasping the arms of his chair, his look defiant. My eyes stung with tears. 'Don't you realise what you've done? He's Kurt's child. If you loved Kurt so much, why did you damage his child? He's your own flesh and blood.'

'A watered-down blood.'

I was so disturbed by Aaron's detachment, I couldn't help asking, 'What if Addam had a child? Would you hate it too?'

'But Addam was going to have a child.'

'You mean Berenger's child,' I said, to make sure.

'Of course, who else?' He raised one eyebrow and that instant I knew he knew.

'You knew it was Addam's?'

He nodded.

'What were you going to do?'

'I don't know.' He shrugged his shoulders.

'When did she tell you?'

'Just before…she died.' He looked uncomfortable now. He tried to adjust the pillow at his back, but gave up, folded his hands in his lap. 'She came back to my room…after the party, I think it was. Certainly she was wearing a ridiculous costume. Fake blood everywhere.'

'What time was that?'

'She woke me up. It was about…4 a.m.?'

'You didn't tell the cops that.'

'They would have asked questions.'

'Not about a wife visiting her husband in the middle of the night.'

'There was what you might call a heated discussion. I wasn't certain whether you heard it or not. But Alison happened to. I didn't want to put her in the position of having to lie to the police.'

'You think Alison would have lied?'

'Oh, yes. Alison had an open mind. If it wasn't for her I wouldn't have known anything about what was going on in my own house.' Including my pregnancy, I thought.

'What was the heated discussion about?'

'Nile, you're starting to sound like the police yourself. I don't have to continue with this.'

'Oh, yes you do, Aaron. Did you talk about the baby?'

'She said it couldn't wait any longer. Of course, she tried at first to tell me the baby was mine. But I wasn't so much of a fool to think I could get her pregnant on two measly ejaculations a year.' He looked at me sadly. 'There you have it.'

'What did she say?'

'She was very upset. I'd never seen her so upset, in fact. She argued that it was perfectly possible the child was mine. How dare I think it was someone else's? I repeated that I thought it unlikely. I'm afraid I did say some rather harsh words to her.'

'Did she tell you Addam was the father?'

'Not at first. She demanded to know whether I would be a "father" to the child. She said Addam had told her I hated children. I said of course that wasn't true. And she said, How is it then that your son despised you? She didn't say it quite like that, but you get the gist. I was very angry with her, but I was angrier with Addam. What right did he have to talk such filth?'

'It was the truth for Addam,' I said, but he behaved as if he didn't hear me.

'And so I told her that I had no intention of claiming as my own her bastard. It was very melodramatic. If we were in the

462

theatre we would have been laughed off stage. And she said that if that was how I felt, if I didn't want *my own* child, then she'd run away with Addam the very next day. He was booked on the flight to Morocco with her. She said he didn't care if the baby wasn't his. He'd go with her if I let her down. He'd give the baby the name Karsner. And if it was a boy they would call it Kurt.' He stopped and wiped his brow with a faded hand. 'Imagine the nerve of them! Calling it Kurt!'

I flushed with guilt at my own fantasies about that name.

'So I told her to go with him. I gave her permission. That's why I said I had suggested it. It was almost true.'

'In a melodrama, you would have strangled her right there and then.'

'No, I would have told her never to darken my doorstep again. Which is virtually what I did.'

'She didn't, did she?'

'What?'

'Darken your doorstep again.'

He shifted in his chair. 'You're very judgmental, Nile. I didn't drive her to suicide.'

'It wasn't suicide, Aaron.'

'I hold on to that. It makes me feel better, that she did not take her own life deliberately. But I'm still not…certain.'

'Why would she kill herself if she was going off with Addam? If she wanted that baby.'

'I suppose you knew about it too. Like everything else.' He sounded dejected.

'I didn't know about it Aaron, I swear. Not then. Did she seem drunk or stoned?'

'Yes, in fact. She wasn't very coherent.'

'They say she'd ingested heroin. I didn't think she did that kind of thing.'

'But you don't know a lot about drugs do you, Nile?' He was looking at me in a strange way. 'You're not very observant?'

'I suppose not. But a lot of girls did smack. Berenger always said she wasn't interested. I think, underneath it all, she was…wary.'

'Perhaps she wanted a bigger rush. Maybe Addam introduced her to it. It runs in the family, you know.'

It runs in the family. Something about that nagged me. Hadn't Addam said that? 'The police blame Addam,' I said.

'Well there you have it.'

'But if she was with you she couldn't have been with him. Unless he was waiting in her room for her.'

Aaron's expression troubled me. His eyes were blank, but something very much like a smile was playing at the corner of his mouth.

'You were pleased the police went after Addam, weren't you?' I said.

'I thought he was responsible. I still do.'

'No you don't.' I was suddenly very sure.

'I don't know what you're saying, Nile.'

Some of it fell into place. 'She didn't pretend it was your baby at all. She told you it was Addam's right from the start. And you had been thinking of getting rid of her, divorcing her, but this meant you couldn't. It would be too shameful, her leaving you for Addam…But it doesn't make sense. Why didn't you start the proceedings before? You knew…*suspected* she'd been carrying on with Addam—and God knows who else.'

He gave me a pained look. 'Lilian,' he said.

'*Lilian?*'

'Lilian didn't want me to. She didn't think I could bear the scandal. But of course I could. I can bear this, can't I? It's a much worse scandal.'

'But why are you so influenced by Lilian? You put up with Berenger because Lilian said so?'

'I have been in love with Lilian for a very long time.'

'With *Lilian?*' I was appalled.

'I'm disappointed in you, Nile. Despite everything you say you're just like the rest. You can't imagine I'd prefer a middle-aged woman to a young girl. I remind you that Lilian is twenty years younger than I am. She's just a girl to me. The miracle is that she's fond of me too.'

There wasn't a word on earth for how I felt. Lilian!

'Come on, Nile. I'm surprised you didn't see it.'

'But if you've been in love with her for...years, why didn't you marry her?'

'Because Lilian is not free to marry. She's married to someone else.'

'She *is*? But she went out to things with you all the time.'

'Is that so unusual? Her husband is not interested in the theatre. My wife was not interested in the theatre either.'

'And she approved of you marrying Berenger?'

'She was...hurt. I can see that now. But she encouraged me— and stood by me. She's very loyal. She is also remarkably clever. She knew Berenger was no threat to our relationship. And she wasn't. As you can see.'

'You were carrying on all along with Lilian? While you were married to Berenger?'

'I wouldn't call it carrying on. But, yes.'

'But you hardly ever went out.'

'You're very naive, Nile. Berenger gave me a lot of leeway. She was always out. Or away. And so were you.'

'I don't believe it. It's like Charles and Camilla all over again.'

'We took some amusement from that, in fact.' His smile was thin.

I hated him then. 'Amusement? Aaron, a teenager has died. And a baby. Your grandson is being harassed by the police.'

'But this is nothing to do with Lilian and me.'

'Of course it is! You talk about protecting me from Addam, but if you had protected Berenger—'

'From what? From her own stupidity?'

'Maybe she guessed about you and Lilian.'

'Come now, Nile. She was too self-absorbed. She never saw Lilian as a threat.'

I thought back to the night when her Gameboy went haywire

and she'd called for Addam. She'd gone to her room in a huff over Aaron taking Lilian to the theatre. Had it just been the drugs that sent her over the edge? Or had she known about Aaron and Lilian all along?

'I don't understand. If you wanted to get rid of her to be with Lilian why didn't you just let her go with Addam?'

'But I did. I think I explained that to you. It was only the baby that...caused a problem. She could go with whoever she liked provided she was discreet. And I knew you'd make sure she was discreet, Nile. Because you didn't want my feelings to be hurt. Why do you think I let her take you in the first place?'

They're sick, Addam had said. They're all sick. Aaron had used me as Berenger's minder, nothing more. But I'd failed him. 'No, Aaron. Let's go back to what you said at the start. Maybe you didn't care what faceless male models she fooled around with, but the fact that Berenger went back to Addam drove you crazy. He was the one person you couldn't abide with her.' And she knew that, which was why she sought him out?

'It always has to come back to Addam in your mind, doesn't it, Nile?'

'I was just going to say that about you.'

He sighed. 'Let me show you something.' He slowly arose from his chair and went over to a side table, on which were stacked several framed pictures. I'd seen them before. Aaron with Frank Sinatra. Aaron with JFK. Aaron with Martha Graham. Aaron and Margaret with Jerome Robbins. He selected one of them and brought it back to the table. It was a photograph I recognised, of Aaron and Lilian, in a pearl-inlaid frame. His arm laid loosely over her shoulder had a new significance now. He came back to the dining table and sat down. I thought he was going to go into some new speech in defence of his relationship with her, but instead he turned the frame over and unfastened the back. From inside he slipped out a smaller photograph and showed it to me.

It was a black and white photograph of a young man standing

466

on a wharf in a long tweed coat. Even from a distance you could see the huge eyes under dark brows.

'It's Addam,' I said.

'Look again.'

Aaron's eyes held a sharp gleam. I examined the photograph again. It couldn't be Addam, I realised. There were people on the wharf in old-fashioned clothes.

'Kurt?' I asked, momentarily touched that Aaron would keep a picture of his lost son tucked in a frame.

'Use your eyes!'

But it couldn't be Kurt. There was a ship in the background, grey and immobile, a warship. A woman in front of it wore a coat with a huge fur collar and a hat with a veil. All of the men, except the subject of the picture, wore hats. I looked up at Aaron, amazed.

'You're shocked, aren't you? You look at this liver-spotted thing, the flabby jowls, the fallen eyes, the floppy lips and you can't imagine that once I had the same effect on young women then as Addam does now.'

'But Aaron, I've never seen any pictures of you as a young man. As a baby, a little boy, yes. But you as an adult? I've only seen you with grey hair.'

'When Madeleine died my head went prematurely white. That's when I stopped being sexy and became *distinguished*.'

'Do you have more of these?'

'Of course. I couldn't bear to destroy them. Some kind of tribal superstition. But I can't bear to look at them, either. You're too young to know what it's like to spend your time avoiding mirrors. To imagine yourself in your head as handsome and then catch a glimpse of yourself as…something else.'

But I did know all about it. 'Aaron, you can't hate Addam because he reminds you of yourself—'

'I don't hate Addam, why do you keep persisting with that? But when I see in Addam's eyes how much he hates me, it's not Addam hating me, it's me hating myself. It's self-loathing. And

467

I can tell you, Nile, there is no worse feeling in the world.'

'Is there any way you and Addam can be friends?'

'I don't think so.'

He looked remorseful. It was an opening.

'Aaron, what if Addam did have a child?'

'What do you mean?' He looked at me sharply.

'What if there was another baby, one that Addam loved and wanted to keep? Would you want to be a grandfather to it, like you never could be with Addam?'

He sighed. 'I don't expect Addam would let me near it.'

'But what if the mother wasn't like Baby? What if *she* wanted you to know it? To spend time with it and love it?'

'I'm too old for babies, Nile.' I knew he was being evasive.

'But why?'

'I'd become…attached. It's not good at the end of your life to become attached to anything. I told Berenger that. I told her that even if the baby were mine I wouldn't want it to be born.'

'But you said before that you regretted that it died.'

'And I did. I'm not inhuman. I hate to think I'm responsible for any death.'

I studied him carefully. There was something mocking in his eyes.

'You did something to her.'

'I only meant that I was responsible for being too harsh on her. I'm sorry that I allowed her to leave me in that state of mind.'

'No you're not.'

'What?'

'You're not at all sorry. You didn't want her. You didn't want the baby. You didn't want Addam to go away with her. You did something. I can feel it. You did something to kill her.'

'Nile, you're being quite silly about this. There's nothing I could have done to make her overdose. It's not possible. You know that. As for anything I said, I've already told you I was harsh and I regret it. But I didn't stand over her and intra-venously feed her alcohol and Rohypnols and cocaine.'

'I know that. But—' I stopped myself.

'It runs in the family, you know,' Aaron had said. It runs in the family. But what was it I knew? I thought of Kurt, whom I didn't know, whose photograph I'd never even seen, but whose doctor's bag of pharmaceuticals hung over everyone's consciousness like a heavy black pall. I thought of Addam and his whisky bottle, his casual way with pills and powders, the less-than-one-gram of pot the police found in his room. I thought of Baby, always stoned or drunk or both and the chainsmoking, coke-snorting Berenger, terrified of her Gameboy. And I looked at Aaron, who didn't smoke and hardly drank, whose only peccadillo was those occasional snorts of snuff…

Aaron saw what passed across my face and smiled. 'It took you long enough to work it out, Nile.'

'But you—'

'You mean you never saw me comatose? In a smack-induced stupor?'

'No I didn't.'

'Of course you did. If I had been Addam's age you might have been suspicious. But I'm an old man and you thought I was just nodding off, having my "nap". Naturally I let you think it.'

'But why did you keep it a secret from me?'

'Because I thought you wouldn't approve. And I was correct, judging by the way you are looking at me now.'

'How long have you…'

'Been a junkie? Let's not beat around the bush. Forever. I've been doing this stuff forever.'

'Since Madeleine's death?'

'Well before that, Nile. Don't be such a romantic. That over-active imagination of yours has already got you into trouble with Addam. I didn't develop a heroin habit because I had a tragic life. I've had a remarkable life. And I want to continue to have one. To a great extent it's the junk that's keeping me alive. Although junk is hardly the word for it.'

'Keep you alive? But how? I thought it would kill you.'

'I'm very controlled in my use of it. And I can afford the best. You don't think I buy it off the street, do you? Some men take their heart pills...I take mine. Back during the war, when there was a shortage, I had friends in high places get it for me. It wouldn't set a very good example for America's favourite composer to die from ingesting poison mixed with his morning hit of heroin, would it?'

'Was Kurt your source?'

'His product was far too unreliable. Of course, the fact that I told him this didn't endear me to him.'

'And Addam knew?'

'He did.'

'Did he ever say anything to you about it?'

'He got the wrong impression that I'd turned Kurt on to drugs. That I'd somehow influenced him. That was another thing between us.'

'But Berenger must have known, too.'

'Only at the end. She was like you. She thought drugs were the province of the young.'

'That unusually pure heroin the police discovered in her system...that wouldn't have had anything to do with you?'

'It appears she raided my dresser as she was leaving my room. She must have done it when I wasn't looking. I only discovered the fact in the morning. Naturally, I didn't tell the police.'

'I don't believe you, Aaron.'

'It doesn't make any difference if you do or not, does it? Who but me and Berenger really know? And one of us is dead.'

'Dead from drugs that were too potent for her body. Your drugs.' And helped along, I thought, by all that alcohol I encouraged her to pour down her throat.

'It wasn't a drug that killed her. It was stupidity.'

'I don't know how you did it, but you convinced her to take your stuff, knowing it was dangerously...is strong the word? Maybe you swapped it for her coke.'

'You're starting to irritate me, Nile. All these boring assumptions. You always demand an answer that makes sense.'

'But this is the answer that makes sense.'

'No, it isn't. Go and do your homework. Have you seen the police reports? I took a particular interest in them, as you can imagine. She had a cocktail of chemicals in her body, all right. But not enough to kill her. They've analysed every cell in her body and there's nothing there that conclusively points to why she died. Snorting smack is never going to kill anyone. She suffocated in her pillow, that was the cause of death. The Medical Examiner himself called it a 'crib death'. As if she were a baby…'

'She was a baby.'

'And so, don't you see, whether she stole or was offered my little stash is irrelevant.' His eyes were now shining brightly, as if he had finally convinced himself of this notion. 'I've always thought that you were too ordinary for this family, Nile.'

'What do you mean?'

'You keep insisting on judging us by your…*mundane* standards. I have been famous for sixty years. Addam has been famous all his adult life. Berenger, too, to a certain extent. And not just famous…adored. We don't think like you do. We don't need to be nice to get people to co-operate with us, to like us. People automatically like us. Whatever we do. All this…grovelling you do is alien to us. It's impossible for us to be humble.'

I thought then of Addam's latest album, *Aporia*. It meant 'false modesty'. And what he said to me once, *Whenever a girl sees me for the first time, in the flesh, this look crosses her face, I've seen it a million times, a kind of shock, then she looks away in embarrassment, and when she looks back there's hunger all over her face…Like I'm a fucking Big Mac.* Was Addam, at the core, driven by the same vanity as Aaron?

'I can see you are offended. Don't be. Do you know where all this celebrity puts a person? Halfway between heaven and hell. Mortals with the mandate of gods. I can do virtually what I like on this earth, Nile. But what is the guarantee in the next world? Or in the next life, if you believe the spiritualists? Will I have to come back and learn the humility I forgot in this life? I am not looking forward to it, believe me.'

But I didn't believe him. Aaron wasn't afraid of death, at least not for the reasons he said. He sat there, perfectly still, knowing there was nothing more I could say to him. He thought he had made his point, had put me in my place. Had convinced me of the ineffable superiority of his mind. But I never had doubted that he was superior. That any of them were superior, even Berenger, whose mind was twisted in ways that were out of my league. I only had one song in me but the Karsners had whole operas.

I got up from my chair.

'Nile, you mustn't leave before we discuss your...severance. I want to make things right for you. I don't like to think that you're living in reduced circumstances, especially now that...well, anyway. Will you wait while I get my cheque book?'

This is the part where I say, I don't want your dirty money. This is the part where I turn on my heels and walk away from him forever. Leave him there in his dressing-gown, corrupt and unrepentant.

'I think fifty thousand will do it, don't you?'

That's not Aaron, that's me. A modest amount for a rich man, really. But I have another mouth to feed. And there's no guarantee there will ever be a father around. Of any generation.

ut I didn't ever get the chance to deposit the cheque. I suppose it's still in the pocket of my coat, which the police have taken from me.

All the way downtown on the C train I kept my hand in my pocket, clasped around the piece of paper. Aaron had written it without hesitation and with some relief. In accepting it, my claim on him had ended. Or so he thought.

I took the money because I thought I would need it. It was simple economics. I didn't care if Aaron thought me a cheap little opportunist. He would understand why I took it soon enough, when my belly curved out like a crescent moon. If he didn't know already.

I wondered briefly if he considered it to be hush money.

But what was there to hush? Aaron didn't physically force Berenger to overdose, if you could call what happened to her an overdose. She suffocated in her pillow, they said. It was a kind of crib death suffered by babies who had reached the age of nineteen.

When Aaron handed me the cheque he said, 'I hope this will help with whatever you do in your life.'

Thanks, Aaron, having your great-grandchild is what I'm going to do with it first.

Why didn't I say that? I was sure he knew. But I was happy to keep up the charade. After what he'd done to Addam I didn't want him near our son.

I sat in the carriage and plotted my steps. I was going to use the money to find an apartment to rent in Brooklyn Heights with a parlour floor and an English garden in the back and wait for the birth of the child. Ayesha would come with me. When my belly got big enough I would walk across the Manhattan Bridge to Addam's place and explain everything. He had misunderstood the first time. But there would be no misunderstanding now. There was only one baby. And it still might be called Kurt.

A Haitian nanny clasped a sleeping white baby to her breast on the seat opposite me in the railway car. The train jerked and screeched but the baby slept on. I thought about my older brother, Terry, dead at ninety-three days, and the soul of Berenger's baby floating around in the space between this world and that, crying for its dead mother.

There were two dead babies but there wouldn't be a third. I wasn't sure I was going to be any kind of a mother but I had to be better at it than Claire and Berenger. And Baby, for that matter. An ordinary mother was all any of us ever wanted. Addam, too, he wanted an ordinary mother and an ordinary life. Things he could never have.

But I was the ordinary one, that was my advantage over all of them...

The train slammed to a halt at 23rd Street. As I got off, I smiled at the black nanny with her white baby, thinking, there are many things that pass for ordinary in New York.

I walked back a block and bought Ayesha a dozen Krispy Kremes, hot off the conveyor belt, exactly how she preferred them. A bitter wind blew at my back and made me scurry along the street. I was more concerned with pushing my hair away from my eyes and mouth than the sight of a squad car parked up on the gutter outside Magdalen House.

I nudged my way through the glass doors and for a moment I thought that another rally was going on in the lobby to save our little hostel from the forces of gentrification in the neighbourhood. Keesha was there, in a huddle with Nola and Mary Ann. Sister Pansy was with them, looking unhappy, her hands thrust in her jeans pockets. My eyes scanned the lobby, missing the sense of it. I saw a dark-blue uniform and I thought that there must have been some sort of struggle between the protesting residents and the management, or the press, or some passer-by…But there was Ayesha, in the middle, her face in her hands, with Sister Impatiens beside her and an unfamiliar man with his hand on her arm.

'Ayesha, what's wrong?' I asked and stumbled towards her. All faces turned to me and I saw that the man with her was my old friend Grace Ostrowsky, in a bomber jacket, her ashen hair cut in the shape of a bicycle helmet. 'I…I brought you these donuts,' I started to say. I stood there stupidly, holding out the box.

No-one moved at first, as if they were waiting for something. Finally, Ostrowsky took a few steps towards me, the uniform following. She took the box of donuts out of my hand like I was a small child and handed it to him.

'What's going on?' I couldn't see what a crying Ayesha had to do with Ostrowsky.

'People keep dying around you, don't they, Nile?' Ostrowsky said to me.

'What do you mean?' I was confused. 'Berenger died of crib death.'

'That's an odd way to put it.' Ostrowsky gave me a wry look.

'Nile, tell them you didn't do it!' Ayesha had come forward, wringing her hands.

I looked between Ayesha and Ostrowsky. Ayesha's face was flaming red. I didn't understand why she'd be so upset about Berenger. And Ostrowsky confused me. She shouldn't have been there. She belonged in my Berenger box, along with Darien and Erik and a couple of dozen fashion assistants with sweaters tied around their shoulders.

'Please, Nile!' Ayesha implored.

'Look, I didn't kill Berenger—' I started to say.

Ostrowsky had a hand on her gun holster. 'I believe you know Kevin Kendricks.'

'Who?' The name wasn't registering.

'Miss Bhargava's fiance.'

I looked at Ayesha. Tears were streaming down her cheeks. 'Oh, him,' I said.

'He's...dead, Nile and they think you did it!' Ayesha tugged at my arm.

Ostrowsky tugged at her and sent her back into the open arms of Sister Impatiens, who was scowling at me. 'You don't look very surprised.'

'Of course I'm not surprised. Whatever happened to him he had it coming.'

It probably wasn't the smartest thing to say. I could hear Ayesha gasp.

'Well, if that's the case, we'd like to take you downtown to help with our inquiries,' Ostrowsky said. 'This is Officer Malo, by the way, from the Tenth Precinct.' Officer Malo, a mass of knotted muscles in a uniform a size too small, nodded. He was still holding the box of donuts in front of him.

'Me? What have I got to do with Kevin dying?'

'They think you hit him, Nile,' Ayesha sobbed.

'It's not true,' I said, mustering up a gesture of outraged innocence, but inside I felt dull. I'd been to this place before. This place where they accuse and you deny.

'We can establish all this down at the precinct. If you'll come with us,' Ostrowsky said.

'Do I have any choice?'

'No.'

The room fell away. All I could focus on was a bit of dry skin lifting off Ostrowsky's lower chapped lip. There was a hand on me and a shock of cold air and I was looking at the cracks in the pavement and then the scuffed black floor of the squad car. The car door slammed and Ostrowsky slid in beside me.

'Sorry if I was a bit rough,' she said and helped me back up on the seat. 'I wanted to make sure we didn't run into any press.'

'Press?' I asked weakly. I had been here before all right and not just with Berenger.

GIRL SOLD FOR £25

DEADLY BOOKWORM

KILLER NANNY

'You know,' Ostrowsky said, as Officer Malo steered the car into Ninth Avenue, 'it was me who connected you.'

Outside, on Ninth Avenue, gay couples were walking hand in hand. It was an ordinary day in Chelsea. 'Connect me?' I shrugged, as if I was…disconnected.

'Yeah. It's possible we might never have linked you to him. Two precincts, entirely different cases, nothing in the computer that would have rung alarm bells out in Queens. But, as luck would have it, the cabby who dropped you at Kendricks' place was a regular Citizen Joe. He heard the APB we put out on Kendricks' address, remembered his mystery passenger and resolved to report her to the cops as soon as he put down his next fare. Well, guess where that happened to be? The Odeon. And guess which precinct is closest to the Odeon, a few blocks away in fact? And guess which detective was busting her ass doing some paperwork by the front desk because her own desk was being used for an impromptu ladder by some maintenance guy fixing a light in the ceiling? And guess whose little ears pricked up when he told us the passenger came out of a certain notorious 22nd Street boarding house? I know whose team the big guy in the sky was on today. And it wasn't yours.'

'You've connected the wrong person.'

'I don't think so.'

'I didn't kill Kevin.' And I didn't. He killed himself. He goaded me into it. By his behaviour towards Ayesha, the things he said to me. It was probably his karma for being a murderer in another life and I was just the agent of it…but now I was starting to sound like Berenger.

Ostrowsky recited my rights. Then she ignored me. She crossed her arms on the back of the driver's seat and gossiped with Malo all the way to Beach Street. Beach Street! The grey precinct building loomed like a giant cinder block over a scrappy

477

park intercut with the exit to the Holland Tunnel. Perhaps once there had been a beach by the river at the end of the street, but it had long been eroded by lack of interest. I read once that this had been the cesspool of old New York and I could well believe it now.

They searched my room at Magdalen House, found my passport, showed it to me and then took it away.

They were interested in Jane Ann, they said. But the photo of her looked nothing like me. It was taken in the days when she'd tried to be pretty, I'd explained. Bleached blonde hair, black-rimmed eyes, clumpy lashes, tweezered brows. They examined it again and said all right, we can see the resemblance. But I couldn't.

There were fingerprints on record in Britain for Jane Ann but none in America for Nile. What did they expect? That I was a mass murderer who left sticky whorls and swirls at the scene of every crime? So they took a complete set. I protested at first: can't you see I'm just an ordinary girl living an ordinary life? I didn't do anything. One of them quipped, it's the ordinary ones you've got to watch, and winked. But they took great pains to be polite and explained that they were just trying to eliminate me from the scene of the crime. 'How do you eliminate me?' I asked them. But there was no answer, just a lot of shifty glances.

I told them I wanted to make a phone call. That's what you do, isn't it? And they said, 'Why don't you wait until Detective Ostrowsky comes back? She might only need to talk to you for ten minutes to clear this up, and then you'll be home.'

'Where has Grace gone?' I asked and they looked startled that I knew her first name. She's in the next room, they said. Clearing up another thing.

I sat for two hours in that airless room. A female officer brought me magazines but it seemed as if they were all about Berenger or Addam or people they knew. *People. Us. Parade.*

Newsweek. It made me long for a copy of *Popular Mechanics.* I tossed them all aside and stared at the walls. They were green. It was a green room. But it wasn't the kind of green room I'd been used to, full of smoke and booze and music, boys with slim hips and girls with jewels on their brows...

When Ostrowsky came in she wasn't alone. 'You know Detective Breen.'

I looked at him standing there in a crumpled brown suit. 'Oh, yes, Detective Breen, the proud father,' I said.

Ostrowsky looked at Breen, who glared at me. 'You're not going to help your case by being hostile,' she said.

'What case? I thought I was here to clear some things up. I didn't think there was a case.'

Ostrowsky looked exasperated. A third person entered the room. He was dark and sleek in a grey suit.

'This is Detective Castro from Queens.' He nodded at me and stood in a corner, his arms folded.

Simultaneously Ostrowsky and Breen scraped two chairs away from the scarred wooden table and sat down. 'There's a case all right,' Ostrowsky began. 'In fact, there may be several cases.'

She spoke into her tape recorder. 'You've been read your rights and you understand them?' she asked me, for the purposes of the tape.

'If that little speech you gave me in the back of the squad car was my rights, then yes,' I replied.

'The answer is yes,' Ostrowsky said to the tape.

'Is your name Jane Ann Kirk as stated on your passport?'

'Yes, Grace, but you can call me Nile.'

She ignored that. 'And you were born in...let's see...Modern, England.'

'It's Mor-den.'

'And you currently reside at Magdalen House, 462 West 22nd Street, New York, NY.'

'And you are employed by Dr Susan Mackie of 169 Dean Street, Brooklyn?'

'No.'

'No?'

'I resigned.'

'I see. And you were formerly employed by Berenger Karsner of 89 Wooster Street, New York?'

'Yes. No. Well, strictly by her husband,' I was getting impatient. 'Look Detective—'

'And from June 1991 until May 1994 you were employed as a sales clerk by Dalton's bookstore of 45 Crown Lane, Morden?'

'Yes, but what's that got to do with anything?'

'And after that, from July 1994 to November 1994, by a Mr and Mrs Westbrook at Pall House, Highsmith Road, South Wimbledon? You were nanny to their baby daughter Elisabeth?'

Now I knew where she was going. 'But that wasn't my fault.'

'We're not saying it was your fault.'

'He slid off the roof. He was fooling around, he had a few too many to drink, and it had been raining earlier. I couldn't help it that there was no-one else up there to see...except poor little Elisabeth. He was prancing on the sundeck like the stupid oaf that he was and he slipped. I couldn't do anything, I was holding the baby. The coroner said it was an accident.'

'Jay Stockdale had an accident too, didn't he?'

'Jay?'

'He worked with you at the bookstore. Fell off a ladder. You were the only one who saw it.'

'Well, it was after lunch. He'd been down to the pub. Even the police could smell the booze on his breath.'

'It's funny, though,' she smiled. 'Kevin Kendricks fell, too, down a flight of stairs. After he'd hit himself on the back of the head with a bottle of Montecillo. He hadn't been drinking but it was still the booze that did him in. Don't you find that interesting?'

'Not one bit.'

'I take it you didn't like him much,' Breen said.

'I'm sure half the factory workers of Asia didn't like him either. He wasn't very likeable.'

'Why's that? He looks like a model citizen to us. Helped out at the Police Athletic Club over there, by the way.'

'Yes, well you might think he was Mr Fabulous, until you went digging in his cellar and came up with the bodies.'

'What bodies?' Ostrowsky was suddenly alert.

'All the Asian women he's bumped off. At least, I used to think he'd bumped them off…'

'What gave you that idea?'

'The way he exploited Ayesha. She was very badly deformed and he pretended to love her so that he could…I don't know. I suppose it wasn't to murder her. He has a mother, you see, who lives with him and there's no-one but him to look after her and Ayesha…'

'You think he was marrying her just to have a nursemaid for his mother?'

'Yes. The creep.'

'But in fact, Nile, the mother doesn't live there at all. She was just visiting. She lives with Kevin's sister in Schenectady.'

'She does? Then why did he say—'

They were both looking at me hard. 'What did he say, Nile?'

I didn't answer.

'You might as well tell us,' Ostrowsky said, pushing her chair back from the table and feigning nonchalance. 'Mrs Kendricks saw a young woman answering your description leave the house last night by the front door at around 7.15 p.m. That was a few moments *after* she'd been startled by a crash downstairs.'

'How could she see out the window? She was in bed incapacitated. Kevin said that.'

'So you admit being there?'

'I didn't do anything. I was only there to talk about Ayesha. Why do you believe a woman who is bedridden and probably quite mad?'

'I don't know where you got the idea that Mrs Kendricks is bedridden. She's a yoga teacher at a spiritual retreat upstate. She had a flu and was confined to bed. It was when she smelled the

Weight Watchers' dinner burning that she came downstairs…and found Kevin crumpled at the bottom of the stairs. Where you left him.'

'I told you I didn't.'

'Why don't you just go through the events of last night for us, step by step, and we'll be the judges of that,' said Breen.

So I told them, leaving out my crawling around in the mud outside and certain things Kevin said to me. They kept at me for hours, Castro too, needling me, but I knew they couldn't have any evidence. I'd admitted I'd been there. And my reasons were entirely plausible. I'd said I didn't like him and I didn't want him to marry my friend. But does this make me a killer? My fingerprints weren't on the bottle—how could they be? I hadn't taken off my gloves. Not that the police would know that. And the rest of their 'evidence' was thin: who was to say that the crash the old bag heard was not Kevin rearranging his barbells after I left? Who was to say a burglar didn't enter the house in the thirty or so minutes before she came downstairs to investigate?

I suppose I should have stayed alert to the questions, but I tuned out. They were just going over the same ground, the same ground they went over in London and Wimbledon…and elsewhere. I thought of Jay backing me into the store-room corner and the coconut smell of his dreadlocks, the rancid weed on his breath, the hard hands with the paper cuts all over them as they held my throat. I thought of John Westbrook with his soft accountant's hands in my bra, flicking my nipples and drooling in my face, wanting to suckle them like a baby, while Elisabeth gurgled in my arms. I remembered all the men that thought I'd be grateful for their drunken advances. Filthy students at the pub, the signet ring on that hand, Iain Carter in his car, short twenty-five quid but with a trembling eight-year-old virgin as his prize…

I tuned back in. Ostrowsky was talking about Berenger now. 'We know you did something to push her over the edge,' Ostrowsky said. 'No-one noticed you leave the party. In fact, no-one noticed you there at all. You could have followed her directly home and had your argument with her in her bedroom. We know someone cleaned up after her, removed most of the traces of drugs. You were the one who "found" her. There is the question of the mutilation of the fingertips. The forensic psychologist says that it was done with extreme anger. That kind of rage usually displays murderous intent.'

'I thought the case was closed. That it was an accident.'

'Some accidents can be helped along.'

'But why would I have wanted to kill her? We've been over all this before.'

'Because you had become obsessed with Addam Karsner, whom we have established was Berenger Karsner's lover. Over the past weeks we have put together several statements from people associated with you who observed your behaviour towards him.'

'And what was my behaviour towards him?'

'Deranged is the word they used.'

'Yes, well, "they" always use words like that, don't they? Which "they" are we talking about?' My tongue was sharp but inside I was thinking, how many people had noticed? I thought I had kept my secret—our secret—to myself. Berenger said everyone knew about my room, my stash of magazines and videos.

'It's time you stopped being delusional, Nile,' Ostrowsky's eyes gleamed. I suppose she thought she was in for the kill now. 'You were driven by jealousy. You were jealous of Berenger's beauty, you wanted her wealth, you wanted her husband, you wanted her boyfriend and when you couldn't have them…'

I couldn't help it. I laughed and it came out with the force of a sneeze. Ostrowsky sounded so dramatic. She'd been talking to Darien, it was obvious. Darien whose idea of great literature was the novelisation of the 'Ally McBeal' television series.

Breen was looking uncomfortable. He probably thought Ostrowsky was overdoing it. Castro just looked bored. Berenger's case had nothing to do with him. He was there to nab me for a crime in his model neighbourhood.

'I think you should go back and do another course in pop

psychology, Grace,' I said. 'You people always think jealousy is the motive.'

'Is that right? Can you give us another motive, then?'

'I'm not going to answer any more questions about Berenger. Can I go now?'

'But it's interesting, isn't it, how people who are inconvenient to you keep dying?'

But I didn't say any more. I stared at the scarred table in front of me, stubbornly. I hated the way they always jumped to conclusions. Jealousy. Envy. Greed. That was always the motive. If the roles had been reversed and it was Berenger who found me dead on my bed, would they have immediately concluded that a crime had been committed because she was jealous of me? It was the face that did it, the solid chin, the lack of cheekbones, the small and colourless eyes, the turned-down mouth. I had envy written all over me. I may as well have been painted green.

But they were wrong. It wasn't Berenger's life I wanted. I already had the part of it I wanted, and it had been inside me for fourteen weeks.

Castro came and sat on the edge of the table and went over my visit to Kevin again and again. Breen interjected a few limp questions while Ostrowsky sat back in her chair, sulking.

They were stalling. All this talk about Berenger, it was just a ruse to keep me there until they'd had a match with the splashes of red wine on the hem of my coat and contents of Kevin's wine bottle. Which they did.

The policewoman who took me to the cell showed me the 'facilities' and then checked her clipboard. 'Is it Jane Ann or just plain Jane?' she asked me chirpily.

It's not a good idea to punch a police officer in the face. They hit back.

idney van Doren, the lawyer Aaron sent me, had a black beard with a little triangle of silver in it under the lip. He listened to my story patiently, all of it, a modified Addam-less version of the story of course, and then he went away. The next morning he passed me on to a pack of criminal lawyers, two of them young women, who showed me the newspapers and discussed 'tactics' for my appearance before the grand jury—there are 'tactics' apparently—and reported on which booker from which television show had already called to secure my exclusive appearance.

I am not American, I said, I don't want to see my round face on a square screen. It is not the sole object of my life. I know the difference between fame and infamy. I've seen enough of both of them. I am a person not a personality.

The partners have since tried to jolly me up, telling me that they are optimistic I will not have to 'do time' even if they get me on a technicality. The technicality being me bashing Kevin's head in with a bottle of red wine. But it was the fall down the stairs that killed him, the Medical Examiner has decided. So what I did with the bottle of wine is irrelevant to the prosecution's case. At least, that is the cumulative opinion of my many lawyers. They admit the wine-bottle wielding is tricky because it puts me at the scene of the crime (or 'accident' as they prefer to call it) but as I have already admitted to being there it's a non-essential piece of information. They may even get it thrown out of court because of something with the paperwork.

So what is my story? Why did I bash Kevin's head in?

Well, your honour, he made a pass at me. He tussled with me at the top of the stairs. And fell. I did not push him. He lunged at me and fell. (Like all the others—but the prosecution cannot bring those up in court.)

I was appalled, of course (best British accent), and went down the stairs to see if I could help. I thought he grabbed my ankles but, as I now know he was dead as soon as he hit the bottom, I must have mistaken my skirt getting caught on his hand for his grasp. I was frightened that he'd overpower me, so I reached for the nearest thing…which was a wine bottle. I hit him twice to make sure.

I didn't mean to kill him, your honour. I was at his house only because I was concerned that he was not being true and loyal to my friend, Ayesha, to whom he had proposed. I was horrified and humiliated that he made a pass at me. Which only goes to prove I was right about him, doesn't it?

My lawyers coached me well. I almost believe it. So do they. If 90 per cent of what you say is true, no-one will notice the dubious ten.

There was one partner, however, who hung back. It was a woman, of course, about fifteen years older than I am, with a dehydrated face like a character peeled off a painting by Munch. Dressed in a black shift with a sweater tied around her shoulders, like all the ghosts. She didn't like me, that was plain to see. She said very little, just tapped her gold pen on the side of her face and stared.

She said, in front of me, as if I were a piece of furniture with a wooden soul, I don't think any judge or jury is going to go for it, they're not going to believe a man would make a pass at her. They're going to think she made a pass at him and he rejected her and so she killed him in a fit of pique. She has no remorse. And a sharp tongue that the jury is not going to like. What we must do is glamorise her a little. Not too much, we don't want her to look cheap. A haircut, a hint of blonde, natural skin, pink lipgloss, maybe she could lose fifteen pounds. If she looks a little *sweeter*, a little less capable of overwhelming a strong man like Kevin Kendricks, we might get away with it.

Please, your honour, I am not guilty. I roll that around on my tongue. Please, your honour, I am guilty. That sounds better. I was always guilty of something.

Of not getting the bucket quick enough, so that the liquid contents of Claire's stomach splashed all over the bedspread or the kitchen table or the bathroom floor. Of just sitting there in Iain's car, not trying to fight or run away, until they came and got me. Of not having an inheritance, so that Jean and Malcolm had to scrimp and save to be able to pay for my keep. Of not having the charm or looks to make an early marriage and get myself off their hands. Of being ungrateful when drunken animals drooled all over me, their hands down my bra and in my knickers, kneading. Of not keeping Berenger alive. Of breaking Ayesha's heart. And now, of not being repentant about the baby.

The correctional officer called Nancy comes to tell me I have a visitor. Another visitor. I run the teeth of a metal comb through my hair, for all the good that is going to do me. This visitor has to be more interesting than the measly bunch who've come already:

Sister Forsythia who has brought some of my things from Magdalen House and tells me that the archbishop has intervened on the tenants' behalf and arranged for the residents who have been there longer than three years—Keesha, Mary Ann, Nola and Bernadette—to continue to rent their rooms at the same rate. She then tries, unsuccessfully, to engage me in a conversation about God and redemption. The only thing I know about redemption, I tell her, are those little coupons you find in the drycleaners that you redeem for half-price tickets to Broadway shows. She doesn't stay long.

Susan Mackie has come, bringing with her a bawling, feverish Rufus, still apparently not entirely over whatever put him in hospital a few days before. She is more distressed about my predicament than I am, being of the school that believes Kevin has done something to me and I am repressing it. She looks at me with a kind of admiration now and asks me if I would agree to meet a professor friend of hers who is working on a book about Women Who Kill. I tell her I am innocent and she says, patting me on the shoulder encouragingly, of course you are. Rufus toddles up to a guard and tries to take his gun, which sends Susan into hysterics. She has brought him because she thought it might be good for him to see the inside of a remand centre, but now she's not so sure.

Bernadette has been elected to come and give me a message from Ayesha. Ayesha forgives me, she says. But she has agreed to be a witness for the prosecution. They are going to solve her visa problems so she can stay and testify. It's funny how good things come from bad, says Bernadette, trying to be positive for Ayesha. But she's jittery being in such close proximity to the cops—she mentions in a whisper that she's got a record for unlawful behaviour at her animal rights protests and a cannabis possession arrest—and leaves after a few minutes.

Josh Gruen has been here, too, but I have refused to see him, along with all the other members of the press. To them, I am just DEAD SUPERMODEL P.A. who has been ARRESTED FOR SEX CRIME. TWENTY-EIGHT-YEAR-OLD HAS HISTORY OF SUSPICIOUS DEATHS, bleated one tabloid, taking liberties with the truth.

I suppose SUPERMODEL P.A. is better than KILLER NANNY or DEADLY BOOKWORM, but it makes me feel like a jar of mulchy baby food that needs a label. The only tabloid that used my name—WHY DID NILE DO IT? SOBS MUTILATED FIANCEE—probably didn't sell many copies, despite the valiant attempt to link Ayesha's disfigurement to Kevin's death. The next morning I had been reduced to BERENGER P.A.'S JEALOUS RAGE and in smaller print, a few pages later, AILING LEGEND SAYS P.A. IS INNOCENT: A 'LOVELY GIRL'.

P.A., at least, is better than P. J.—PLAIN JANE. I have been waiting for that.

He is standing with his hands in his jeans pockets, the knit cap pulled right down over his brows, but people still recognise him.

'Hey Addam!' a pretty milk-chocolate coloured girl in hand-cuffs calls out to him as two guards lead her back to her cell. There are about twenty people in the room, clustered in small groups, lawyers, sobbing relatives and grim-faced detainees, and all of them look up at this, momentarily forgetting their anxieties, even the lawyers. In a detention centre, as in the outside world, the close proximity of a celebrity brings an irrational flood of joy.

I see him before he sees me. He looks exceedingly uncomfort-able, tense, hunched-up, the dark bruises of insomnia—what I hope is insomnia—making deep channels down his face. He is very pale, very thin, ethereal, almost not a physical presence at all. I can feel the others looking at me and so can Addam. He follows the communal gaze to where I'm standing. Even from this distance I see that his eyes have become Berenger's eyes, glassy and flat, deflecting the world.

I have been waiting for this moment for weeks, for Addam to come back from Europe and claim me. I imagined opening my door at the hostel one day and finding him there, bathed in the yellow light of the hallway. I imagined living my whole life with him on that mattress on the floor, in tour buses, in dingy roadside motels, in the green rooms of concert halls. But I can see from the darkness on his face that we are not going anywhere.

He scrapes back a chair and we sit across a table from each other. I am trembling, but it might be him, his leg vibrating under the table. I keep my eyes on my folded hands. My lawyers have made me remove the remnants of my black nailpolish and my naked nails are stained yellow, ugly as cigarette butts. I curl them into my palms.

'Nile?' His voice is less than a whisper.

I dare to look at his mouth. His bottom lip is bruised, like he has been making a meal of it with those sharp, snaggled upper teeth.

'When did you get back?' My words are tiny.

'Yesterday…I'm sorry. I came here as soon as I knew.'

'Who told you?'

'About a dozen reporters.'

'You should have stayed away.' It comes out sounding…hard. 'You shouldn't get involved.'

'But I am involved.'

I raise my eyes to his at that. He is still looking down at the scarred table. 'Addam, please don't have this conversation with me now. I'm going to be out of here soon. Maybe tomorrow. They're appealing for bail.'

'I'm going out to LA tomorrow. We play the whole fucking west coast.'

'I could meet you out there.'

He swallows hard and the cord of leather around his throat jumps. And then he lifts his eyes. The pleasure of again being the focus of his gaze sweeps over me. Even if that gaze is as cool and slow-moving as a glacier. 'Nile…did you really kill that guy?'

'It was an accident.'

'They're saying there are others.'

'It's not true…' My protest sounds weak even to my own ears.

'I'm sorry.'

I look at him in surprise. 'Why are *you* sorry?'

'I thought you understood.'

'What are you talking about?'

'About you and me.'

I suppose hearts don't really sink. It's probably more technical than that, something to do with ventricles and arteries. But my heart sinks, nevertheless. 'What didn't I understand about you and me?' I have more courage in me than I thought.

He rubs the side of his face with a hand, and I realise, miserably, that it is a gesture of frustration. 'I didn't mean to hurt you.'

There's a guard standing next to us, listening in. Addam slides his eyes in her direction. She turns her head away, but she's still listening.

'I wanted to go home with you that night. I thought... afterwards...this is a sophisticated girl, she knows about Berry and me, she can enjoy the moment. And you seemed to. You didn't give me a hard time, we all continued as we were. And then you turn up one night, on my stairs'—he closes his eyes— 'and you're in some kind of frenzy. Like a fucking groupie, Nile. And you make me feel bad about you, when I'm already trying to cope with the concept of Berry's baby...and the next night she goes and snorts so much scag her brains bleed through her nose. And there you are, cleaning up the mess, wiping Aaron's brow, making arrangements for a funeral. I thought you'd done something to her...because of me.' He is staring at my scrunched-up fists like they're a murder weapon.

'But you don't think so now?' My voice is steady, it's my mind that is shaking.

'No.'

'Why not? I'm in jail, aren't I? That should just about put the cap on it for everyone. What is it that they're calling me? Deadly P.A.? Something like that? I'm a killer, Addam.'

'I don't know about your friend's boyfriend, but I know you didn't have anything to do with Berry.'

I am alarmed by the certainty in his voice. 'You know because you were there,' I said dully. Despite what Aaron had told me, maybe Addam had been waiting for her.

'You think that too?' His eyes flash.

'You weren't?'

He shakes his head. 'I wish I had been.'

'Well, then why are you so certain I wasn't? For all you know, I goaded her all night, stuffed pills and booze down her throat, and took her over the edge with some intentionally potent smack

I'd procured from some handy South American drug connection I just happened to have. That's what the cops think. Fortunately for me they can't prove it.'

Addam drums his fingers on the table. 'You'll think I'm an idiot…If you don't already.'

'What is it?' My voice is sharper than I mean it to be.

He wraps his arms about himself as if he expects me to hit him. 'Berenger told me.'

Oh, God. 'Addam—'

'Listen to me.' He hugs himself tighter. 'I know it sounds crazy, but I've been having these dreams…for a few weeks. I call them dreams, but…'

'Go on.'

He studies me for a minute, then nods. 'OK. Ever since Berry died, I've felt she hasn't really gone away. I know what you're thinking—everyone says that. The living cling to the idea of the dead. I've been reading books…for therapy. She was just a voice in the beginning. I thought I was going mad. Talking to myself. There really weren't any words, just breath, like air brushing my skin. But I knew it was her. I *knew* it, Nile. I've had friends OD, die of AIDS, die in car crashes, but none of them have felt the need to communicate with me from the grave. I'm not one of those people who believe in…a spirit world. Ever since I was a little kid I've tried to *break through* to Kurt. If he was up there, he'd answer me, right? Every single day of my life I've talked to him—*at* him, because he doesn't ever answer. And if Kurt doesn't answer, when I've sent him so many messages, when sometimes I thought my heart would shatter with the strain of it, then there's no-one up there at all. When we're dead, we're worm meat.'

I can feel the guard leaning closer. I throw her a dirty look.

'But last night…I was fucked from the flight. I'd taken some rohies because I couldn't sleep. I admit I wasn't exactly clear-headed. But I don't dream when I'm doing that stuff, so I know she wasn't some kind of…fantasy. She was there, sitting on the end of my bed, like I'm talking to you. Except she was missing an arm.'

492

He gives me a rueful smile. 'Stupid, isn't it?'

'You *saw* her?' If Addam saw her too, then I wasn't mad.

'I'm going crazy, aren't I?'

'Listen, Addam. What was she wearing…in the dream?'

'What?'

'What was she wearing? It's important.'

'A short dress. It sparkled.'

'With a stain on the front?'

'I don't know…I guess. It's what she died in, isn't it?'

'Did she say how she died?'

'She said I did it. She said she killed herself over me.'

He sounds so dejected I want to put my arms around him. But I can't. He would have been a puff of smoke in my embrace.

'She *did*?'

'Because I wouldn't accept Aaron's baby.'

'*Aaron's* baby?' I say dully.

'I thought you knew about that.' He looks at me quizzically. I suppose my face has just drained of colour.

'I didn't know about it. Not then. Are you sure it was Aaron's baby?'

'Yes, I'm sure.' He frowns. 'Why wouldn't I be? That's what she told me the day she found out.'

'She told you that?'

'Nile, what is this?'

'I thought it was your baby.'

'It was not.' His mouth tightens, he shifts in his seat. 'Jesus, can we smoke in here?'

'But, Addam, you were running away with her to Morocco.'

'You know better than that. You know what she was like. She concocted some stupid fantasy, made the booking herself. I don't know why. I didn't even know about it until the cops brought it up. The assholes.'

'Aaron thought you were running away with her.'

'Yeah, well, that's the only good thing that came out of it.'

I am shocked by the cruelty in his voice. But I am hardly in a position to defend Aaron. 'Addam,' I ask gently, 'what else did Berenger say?'

'She said she killed herself because I wouldn't be a father to the baby. That she didn't really mean to…she wanted to make me suffer a little. She thought that…you'd come in and find her before it was too late. You always checked on her. She called you her nanny.'

'Addam, what makes you think Berenger was telling the truth? People don't just die and become good. She lied all her life. She's still lying now. She still wants to hurt you.'

'But she's right. I did kill her. Don't look startled. I wasn't there at her death. But I interfered with her. I wanted her back from Aaron and I fucked with her mind. If I had scrounged together all the smack in the East Village and injected it in her veins I couldn't have made her more dead.'

'But you loved her.'

'Did I? I think maybe I hated her. That's the worst thing, Nile. I hated her in the end. And I let her see that. I should have known what she'd do. She was a kid. She thought she could fuck with death. That she'd never die. I've seen it before. It's my fault for not stopping her. I don't feel like a person anymore, I feel like a running sore.'

'Oh, Addam, you can't blame yourself! She had a husband.'

'I knew you'd say that. Everyone says that, to comfort me. But it's no fucking comfort at all. I should have protected her from him. He's evil.'

'Addam, why are you here? You said you don't love me.' I paused, waiting for him to protest, but he said nothing. 'I'm scandalous. I'm a murderess.'

'I told you I don't believe that. I know it's a misunderstanding. Somehow Berenger's death got the police suspicious about you…it's all my fault again. If I hadn't introduced Aaron to Berenger…'

But it was my fault, of course. I'd been the one who'd raised the spectre of Berenger first. 'Go home, Addam.'

'There's something else, Nile.'

'No,' I say. Not wanting to hear.

'Berenger told me something else. And I need to know if it is true.'

I wrap my hands across my stomach, automatically.

'She said, "Nile is having your baby and you have to look after her." It's true, isn't it? I've been going over it in my head. That night you came to tell me something—that's what you were going to tell me. And I was so full of anger at what Berry told me, I didn't listen to you.'

'It was a dream, Addam.'

'I can see it's true, Nile. You don't have to hide it.'

'If I was having a baby what makes you think it's yours? That's very arrogant of you.'

'I won't abandon you.'

'Like Kurt?' I ask sharply, wanting to hurt him.

'Not like Kurt,' he says sadly.

Here I am with Addam, pregnant with his baby, and he is telling me he won't abandon me. That there will be a life for me, the one I imagined not so long ago, where I am perpetually back-stage, waiting in the wings for him with the baby in my arms.

But I am not an angel sent from heaven to help Addam make amends for Kurt and Aaron. I am not a salve for the Karsner wound. I am a murderer and, despite my lawyer's upbeat mood and Aaron's money, I know I am not going to get away with it. Not this time.

'Addam, I'm about to spend a very long time in prison.'

'I'll look after it. I promise.'

But Addam can't see the future like I can. I can see it unfold like the hope in his face. Little Kurt will be born in a prison hospital and his father, meaning well, will take him away. It will be the best thing for the baby, everyone will agree. He will have the best that money can buy. Toys, a musical education and a doting father, always on the road.

But he will never have a mother, just a series of nannies who will never love him as his mother does. And I will love him, fiercely, more than I loved Elisabeth Westbrook and my little brother Terry rolled together. I couldn't give him over to strangers, brood in my cell while some other woman wiped the baby food from his face and sang him to sleep at night. He would grow up and what would I be to him? I'd be the stranger. And he'd hate me for abandoning him. I couldn't allow him to think his mother didn't fight for him tooth and nail. Like our mothers didn't.

I couldn't be responsible for another wounded child without a mother's love. I couldn't let Addam have him. Even if that meant me not having Addam.

'Addam?' I hold myself tighter, to keep the sorrow from spilling over.

He looks at me with brimming eyes, still so clear they project my lumpen form back at me. 'Nile, it will work, I promise you.'

But it won't. Addam should know that more than anyone.

I summon up every last remnant of rationality in me. My voice is gentle, but firm, the voice I use on children. 'You mustn't listen to whispers in the night,' I say. 'Berenger was a dream. I'm sorry she misled you. But there isn't any baby. There never was. It was a phantom pregnancy.'

I close my mind to the terrible disappointment in his face.

When I get back to my cell, she is wafting back and forth below the ceiling, a spectral form of pacing, I suppose.

'Where have you been?' I demand as soon as the guard has gone. 'I've been bloody well looking everywhere for you. What the hell are you doing here now?'

She has finally appeared, now that I want to be alone. There's nothing she can tell me anymore. Except, perhaps: why? And even that I don't care to know. All I want to do is dig myself a grave in that hard prison-cell mattress and cover myself with the blanket as if it were a clod of earth.

She doesn't answer my question. 'Why did you do that?' she asks.

'Do what?'

'You denied you were having our baby!'

I look up at her. She's a conventional ghost now, a trailing nimbus cloud with eyes and lips. '*Our* baby?'

'I made everything right between you and Addam and now you've gone and spoiled it.'

'Well, thank you very much, but I didn't need your help.'

She churns back and forth above my head, agitated. 'You don't understand! It was my good deed! The thing I was doing to seek forgiveness for my stupid life! I tried for *weeks* to make him see me. To be able to go to him. And when I finally get through, you ruin it! We would have been happy, the three of us...the *four* of us.'

'What do you mean *four* of us?' A familiar dread starts its long crawl down my spine.

'You, me, Addam and our baby, of course. We could have been a family.'

'Not "our" baby, Berenger. My baby.'

'Oh, Niley,' she sighs and shakes her filmy head. 'Haven't you worked it out yet? That baby in your body is *mine*. Mine and Addam's. I died and the baby's soul had to go somewhere. And where it went was in *you*.'

I feel myself falling, blacking out. To have Berenger in my cell is one thing, but her child in my womb is another altogether.

I come to and Berenger's face is so close to mine I can see the red-hot pinpoint of hysteria in her white eyes. 'I want our baby!' she demands.

I struggle to think. 'But your baby wasn't Addam's in the first place. You told Addam it was Aaron's baby.'

She bares her broken teeth. 'Well, Addam was being weird. I said, "I'm going to have a baby, Addam," and he went completely white and looked right into me and said, "I'm not ready to be a father." And I was so angry with him that I said, "Well, for your information it's not your baby, anyway. It's Aaron's." And then he went apeshit. He started yelling at me and throwing stuff. CDs, ashtrays, things that could hurt me. So I left. I ran down those stairs…'

'But don't you see what you did? He believed you. Aaron was your husband after all.'

'I thought he'd know it wasn't Aaron's. He'd work it out. I mean, I always say things that aren't true. I thought he'd come after me. Like he always did.'

'But he didn't? And so you went to Aaron and told him it was his? Oh, Berenger, that wasn't very smart.'

'I did it because I thought Aaron would be pleased, that he would…like me more because of the baby. He always treated me like such a fool. He used to say, "Oh shut up and just look beautiful." I thought if I had a baby, I could look, like, grown up. I mean, even Madonna, she looked more *dignified* when she had that little girl. And that ridiculous Lilian…it was something she couldn't do.'

'You knew about Lilian?'

'The whole world knew! I felt like an idiot when he told me.'

'Aaron told you? When?'

'A few months after we were married…I can't remember exactly. I was complaining about him always going out with Lilian and he said, "Lilian is my mistress and you have to accept it." Just like that. I mean, Niley, he was an old man, it was not like there was so much of him to go around.'

'What did Aaron do when you told him about the baby?'

'He yelled at me and called me a *moron*.' She says this as if such a thing were unimaginable. 'He said he didn't want to have a baby with me. Because he knew where I came from.'

'What do you mean he knew where you came from?'

'He meant my parents…'

'But you don't know who your real parents are.'

'I know who my mother is.' She says this in a small, shamed voice.

'You never told me.'

'I didn't want you to laugh at me.'

'I'm not going to laugh at you.'

'Chantal couldn't wait until I was old enough to tell me. I was, like, twelve when I found out. She said my mother was sixteen years old when she had me. She gave birth to me at the senior prom…in a toilet stall…and dropped me in the bucket where they put all the tampons and stuff. I only got found because she had blood running down her leg. She'd gone back and danced…with her boyfriend. Like nothing had happened. I suppose he was my father. Chantal said he didn't know about me. She said my mother didn't really, either. They sent her away to a mental asylum.'

'How does Chantal know all this? I didn't think that adoptive parents were told anything.'

'Chantal knows. She knows the family. But she won't tell me who they are.'

'You could have found out, if you had wanted to.'

'I know that. I asked Aaron to help, once. Remember that film about the guy who goes all over America looking for his parents and his mother turns out to be Lily Tomlin? I thought Aaron might know where to look. But that was the dumbest thing I ever did. From that point on he thought I was *trash*. And I was trash. My mother had thrown me out…like bathroom tissue.' She shimmers in front of me, a filigree of sorrow and regret.

'But it sounds like she didn't know what she was doing, Berenger. That she was…disturbed. I'm sure she didn't mean it. If she had realised she'd had a baby, she would have loved it.'

'Do you think so? Do you think she might have been looking for me all this time?'

I don't know anything about mothers, except that they had it in them to find you if they really wanted to. 'Yes,' I lie.

She gives a crooked smile, the lips like fraying ropes. 'So Aaron rejected his own baby?'

'No, because then I told him it was Addam's. And it *was* Addam's.'

'Berenger, do you realise what you did? You told Addam you were having Aaron's baby and you told Aaron you were having Addam's.'

Her mouth turns down again. 'I wanted to hurt them.'

'You hurt yourself the most. And you haven't learnt anything. Last night you told Addam you killed yourself over him. You say you were trying to do good. Imagine how bad he feels now.'

'But I didn't tell him that, Nile! He *fantasised* that part. It was his guilt taking over. I could barely make him see me…and I was only there a moment. The effort almost killed me.'

'It killed your baby.'

'Well, that's where you're wrong.'

'Berenger, it's my baby. Mine and Addam's. It has its own soul. I'm sorry about yours, really I am—'

'What do you care, anyway?' There's a catch in her voice, if it is a voice. 'You never liked babies.'

'What makes you think that?'

'You never cuddled Trish's baby backstage. You walked away. It was so cute, too. Like a doll.'

I remember the models with their babies, children with infants. There was a whole rush of them that year, like the latest craze in toys for Christmas. 'I had enough babies of my own.'

'Then give me this one.'

'Berenger, you've done your good deed. You've repented.'

'I'm not leaving my baby! I'm not doing what my mother did to me. I don't want to be a child anymore. I want to have a baby and be grown up.'

I feel her sadness like droplets of mist on my skin.

'All I ever wanted to be was, like, be grown up. But none of you would let me. You all ran after me like I was some kind of...*toddler*. I thought if I married Aaron you'd all take me seriously. *He'd* take me seriously. But he didn't even make me feel like a woman...just a brat who could be seen but not heard. At least Addam understood, he'd been treated the same way all his life.'

'But Berenger,' I try to say this gently, 'children have babies all the time. Look at your mother. It doesn't mean you automatically grow up the minute you become pregnant. Not telling the truth about the father wasn't the most mature thing you could have done. And taking all those drugs...'

'But I didn't mean to! I didn't mean to take all those drugs! Aaron made me do it. He killed the baby. Except it isn't dead.'

'Berenger, look at you, you're in no fit state to look after a baby. You don't even have any arms.'

'And you think you are? You're a murderer. You're going to spend the rest of your life in jail. Is that a life for a poor little baby? You've got to let Addam and me have the baby. I'm going to haunt you until you do.'

With a chill I realise that it's not me Berenger is haunting, but my baby. If I gave the baby to Addam, she would follow it.

501

I would be rid of her. But the baby would be spooked all its life, by Berenger...and by the idea of a mother who gave it away. I look at her hovering there. Her eyes, her brows, her petulant mouth, all clear, sharp and in focus. But the rest of her is fading away, a finger here, an elbow there, the shape of a waist, the curve of a shoulder. She has texture, like clouds reflected on cellophane. But there is no ribcage, no intestines, no uterus. I can see right through her.

She had been unformed in life, so how could I expect her to be formed in death?

As if she were reading my mind, she says, sadly, 'I'm always going to be a child now, aren't I?'

But they would never have let her grow up, even if she had lived to be seventy. They had already started taking out the wrinkles and the bags under her eyes and she wasn't even out of her teens. They would have made her go on this way until she was twenty-five, thirty, thirty-five, forty. And then, when they let her loose on the world with a softening jawline and deepening lines, she'd be too old to grow up. The perfect computer-generated face would continue to be Berenger, like the robots that replaced the Stepford Wives, but where would she be? In the same kind of limbo she was now. Nothing more than a psychic imprint on the air.

Limbo. That's all this world offered girls like Berenger—and girls not like Berenger. I thought of the little girls with their autograph books waiting in the street for Berenger. I thought of that little girl in the feather boa on the uptown bed. I thought of the girl in cut-off shorts outside Addam's place, snarling, 'Now the bitch is dead he's mine.' Little girls pumped full of hormones, like battery chickens, and then dumped on the world to fend for themselves with women's bodies but children's minds. Seen but never ever heard.

I can feel Berenger slurping up my thoughts like she used to suck Krug through a straw. She is, faintly, smiling.

And for a blessed moment I think she is, finally, going to leave me. To go over to that other place, whatever it might be. She starts to glow, like a sunset dropping behind the clouds. She's all-embracing. Warm, like she's reached a kind of enlightenment.

Wishful thinking.

'Nile?'

I snap back to earth with a crack. I'm the one who has let my astral spirit wander. Berenger is picking an invisible piece of fluff off her cloud-patterned dress.

'What?'

'What do you think of Drew?'

'*Drew*?'

'For the baby. Like, it works if it's a boy or a girl.'

'Drew,' I say, weakly.

She looks at me, expecting approval.

You can't say this baby is in danger of not being loved.

'Drew,' I repeat, slowly, feeling the pull of the word on my lips. 'I like it.'

She smiles radiantly. She's putting her good face on.

You can't ever argue with a ghost.